REVISITING
NARNIA

REVISITING NARNIA

Fantasy, Myth and Religion
in C. S. Lewis' Chronicles

EDITED BY
Shanna Caughey

BENBELLA BOOKS, INC.
Dallas, Texas

"*The Silver Chair* and the Silver Screen" © 2005 Charlie W. Starr

"On the Origins of Evil" © 2005 Lawrence Watt-Evans

"Elusive Prey" © 2005 Natasha Giardina

"God in the Details" © 2005 Naomi Wood

"Coming of Age in Narnia" © 2005 Sam McBride

"The Chronicles of Narnia: For Adults Only?" © 2005 Martha C. Sammons

"Believing Narnia" © 2005 James Como

"The Correct Order for Reading The Chronicles of Narnia?" © 2005 Peter J. Schakel

"The Chronicles of Narnia: Where to Start" © 2005 Wesley A. Kort

"Narnia and Middle-earth" © 2005 Joseph Pearce

"Aslan Is On the Move" © 2005 Russell W. Dalton

"The Beginning of the Real Story" © 2005 James V. Schall, S. J.

"Heathen Eye for the Christian Guy" © 2005 Jacqueline Carey

"Would the Modern-Day C. S. Lewis Be a PETA Protester?" © 2005 Ingrid Newkirk

"Greek Delight" © 2005 Nick Mamatas

"Why I Love Narnia" © 2005 Sarah Zettel

"Daughters of Lilith" © 2005 Cathy McSporran

"The Last of the Bibliophiles" © 2005 Peg Aloi

"C. S. Lewis and the Problem of Religion in Science Fiction and Fantasy" © 2005 Vox Day

"Redeeming Postmodernism" © 2005 Louis A. Markos

"*The Horse and His Boy:* The Theology of Bree" © 2005 David E. Bumbaugh

"A Reconstructed Image" © 2005 Mary Frances Zambreno

"A Knight in the Mud" © 2005 Marie-Catherine Caillava

"'Most Right and Proper, I'm Sure...'" © 2005 Sally D. Stabb, Ph.D.

"Narnia in the Modern World" © 2005 Colin Duriez

Additional Materials © 2005 Shanna Caughey/ BenBella Books, Inc.

BenBella Books, Inc.
6440 N. Central Expressway, Suite 617
Dallas, TX 75206
www.benbellabooks.com
Send feedback to feedback@benbellabooks.com

Printed in the United States of America
10 9 8 7 6 5 4 3 2 1

Library of Congress Cataloging-in-Publication Data

Revisiting Narnia : fantasy, myth, and religion in C. S. Lewis' chronicles / edited By Shanna Caughey.
    p. cm.
  ISBN 1-932100-63-6
  1. Lewis, C. S. (Clive Staples), 1898-1963. Chronicles of Narnia. 2. Children's stories, English—History and criticism. 3. Christian fiction, English—History and criticism. 4. Fantasy fiction, English—History and criticism. 5. Narnia (Imaginary place) 6. Myth in literature. I. Caughey, Shanna.

PR6023.E926C53646 2005
823'.912--dc22

2005017899

Cover art and design by Todd Michael Bushman
Text design and composition by John Reinhardt Book Design

Distributed by Independent Publishers Group. To order call (800) 888-4741. www.ipgbook.com

For special sales contact Laura Watkins at laura@benbellabooks.com

For ∂-n

Acknowledgments

I'd like to thank Meghan Kuckelman and Chris Curotolo for the thorough research they did in the early stages of acquisitions, Rebecca Greene for the heroic proofreading effort and Leah Wilson for bringing her organizational expertise to the Smart Pop line. Most of all, Glenn Yeffeth has my deep gratitude for creating this opportunity.

Contents

Introduction

PERSONAL ANECDOTE seldom has a place in an editor's introduction.

I'm supposed to be some academic-minded compiler of incredible content, the acquirer of articulate and thoughtful contributors. My hand should guide the content, the flow— my voice should not set the tone for the anthology.

But the impetus to contribute some thought, some small bit of story is ineluctable. Narnia is too important to me.

When I read The Chronicles as a child I missed something *important*: Aslan lets the Tash-serving Calormene into new Narnia. Despite all the talk of Aslan not being a tame lion, he seems to be quite gentler than his allegorical counterpart when it comes to allowing people into heaven—at least according to the theology of salvation in my fundamentalist upbringing.

A couple of years ago I reread the series and was stunned to discover this twist of plot in *The Last Battle*. Say what you want about Lewis' portrayal of women or the simplicity of his narrative structure (and many do in this anthology)—I respect him immensely for this daring move. This is but one example of how complex and controversial Narnia actually is; beyond the deceptively simplistic story lies a wealth of theological and social insight.

The essays herein tap into this tension. Want discourse that goes beyond the Stable Door? *Revisiting Narnia* will bring the Lion back to life.

So, what distinguishes this book from the others that come out this fall?

Well, it's probably the sheer diversity of the contributors.

Or the fact that they all have a deep love for the series.

We've got agnostic fantasists, Lewis scholars, devout Christians, pagans—you name it. All in this one volume. Each essay grabs onto one aspect of the series, gives it a good tug and delivers a detailed exploration.

Read this book. If you don't already love Lewis' Chronicles, you will.

—SHANNA CAUGHEY, *July 2005*

CHARLIE W. STARR

The Silver Chair and the Silver Screen: C. S. Lewis on Myth, Fairy Tale and Film

I N PLATO'S "THE ALLEGORY OF THE CAVE," people sit in a cavern chained against a wall; a fire behind them lights the chamber. Puppet figures and objects are passed before the fire, and their shadows are cast where the viewers can see them. The people chained to the floor look at the performance of the shadow puppets and think it's real life. Plato's cave is the classical version of the Matrix: people trapped in a world of illusion they believe is completely real. And some of them actually like it.

I myself, just the other day, subjected my entire family to such an experience. There we were, glued to our seats (admittedly they reclined and had cup holders) while the fire of a high-luminance projector shot pictures of people and objects which weren't really there onto a great white wall before us. And we paid good money (fifty bucks with popcorn and drinks) to sit there, watching sights and listening to sounds that didn't exist—total illusion, complete lies. Plato would say we needed to break the chains of illusion and turn and walk out of the cave into the light of the sun. That's where the real world is. That's where the illusion of the Matrix falls from our eyes. But what if Plato was wrong?

What if movies are a window, a doorway like Narnia's magical wardrobe into a world far more real than the illusion first suggests? What if Plato's real world of sunshine and truth were to be found on the cave wall all along, or, at least, what if it's there now, in that wondrous, magical place of shadow and light we call the Cineplex?

C. S. Lewis was not a big movie fan. He once wrote to his friend Arthur Greeves, "You will be surprised to hear that I have been at the cinema again! Don't be alarmed, it will not become a habit" (2004, 120). But he said some positive things about movies as well the few times he talked about them. And what he said connects film to art forms and ideas he did spend a lot of time talking about: myth, truth and fairy tales. Through Lewis' vision I want to argue something that may very well belong in a fantasy book. I want to explore the possibility that fairy tales are true, that myth is history and that movies may be more real than the reality we see around us.

How Everything Meant More

Lewis understood that there was a magical window capable of showing us things that are as far from illusion as are people from the shadows they cast. His description of the window appears in the final book of The Chronicles of Narnia, *The Last Battle*. At the end of the series, the old Narnia has passed away, and the human heroes from the stories have come into the heavenly realm known as Aslan's country. They begin to notice something strange. This new country looks like their old Narnia. Hills, mountains, valleys—places in the old Narnia look like places here. And yet they're different. Lucy, the youngest of the four Pevensie children who enter Narnia in *The Lion, the Witch and the Wardrobe*, says of the hills and mountains, "They have more colors on them and they look further away than I remembered and they're more...more...oh, I don't know...." And Digory, who saw the creation of Narnia in *The Magician's Nephew*, answers, "More like the real thing...." (1956, 210). The heroes of Narnia have entered Lewis' version of Plato's most real world. Digory explains that the old Narnia was not the real one and so will pass away. It was only a copy of the real Narnia which never had a beginning and will never see an end. And so of course they are different from each other, "as different as a real thing is from a shadow or as waking life is from a dream.... It's all in Plato, all in Plato...." (211–12).

Lewis' next challenge is to describe the difference between the two Narnias. Here is where he describes the magic window to another world:

> You may have been in a room in which there was a window that looked out on a lovely bay of the sea or a green valley that wound away among mountains. And in the wall of that room opposite to the window there may have been a looking-glass. And as you turned away from the window you suddenly caught sight of that sea or that valley, all over again, in the looking-glass. And the sea in the mirror, or the valley in the mirror, were in one sense just the same as the real ones: yet at the same time they were somehow different—deeper, more wonderful, more like places in a story: in a story you have never heard but very much want to know. The difference between the old Narnia and the new Narnia was like that. The new one was a deeper country: every rock and flower and blade of grass looked as if it meant more. (212–13)

Theology speaks of heaven, fairy tales of a magical world and philosophy of a higher Platonic reality outside the cave, a reality more real and truer than the one we see around us. Lewis suggests we get a glimpse of it through a window framed in a looking-glass (the one Alice falls through and Neo gets consumed by, and the one that mirrors images back to us when we go to the movies).

Have you ever seen an advertising brochure made for your workplace or hometown? Every time you look at the pictures, you recognize the location but somehow it doesn't look the same. That happens whenever a place is put into a frame. Whether still photo or motion picture, places look different, even better than they do otherwise, once they're inside a frame. Lewis' heavenly Narnia looks like our own world would in a quick glimpse in a mirror: "deeper, more wonderful, more like places in a story" (213). Or a movie. In film, a picture of the world is cast onto a frame and mirrored back to our eyes, and everything in the picture is deeper, more wonderful and looks "more real...as if it meant more."

Reality and meaning—there's an interesting pairing. Like Plato, Lewis believed in a higher reality more real than the one we see around us. Lewis referred to our existence as "Shadowlands" (228) and said real life hasn't yet begun for any of us. Echoes, again, of *The Matrix*. Think of the difference between a balloon filled with air and one filled with water. The one is fuller; there's more to it, even though the sizes are the same. And somehow, says Lewis, that fuller, heavenly, more real reality—somehow it *means* more. To which I then want to ask, "What in the world (or whatever reality you want to focus on) does that mean?"

"What does it mean?" is a question we ask all the time, often about the symbols and images we encounter in books, songs and movies. But have you ever asked, "What does *meaning* mean?" Usually when we ask for the meaning of a word, a line in a song or a symbolic image, we want an explanation in words. In *The Empire Strikes Back*, Luke journeys down into his own cave of knowledge and confronts Darth Vader. He cuts Vader's head clean off only to find his own face looking back at him. When my daughter first saw that scene she asked me what it meant. I told her, "It means Luke's worst enemy is himself. He has to fight his own fear and doubt before he can face the real Darth Vader. What happened in the cave was a dream or vision." I explained the meaning in words.

But movies mean more than the words in them. Their magic is in the meanings they communicate beyond words. Their truth is in their images and experiential quality. In an obscure essay called "Bluspels and Flalansferes," Lewis helps us begin a search for the meaning of *meaning*, the truth of fairy tales and the magic that can be found in movies:

> [I]t must not be supposed that I am in any sense putting forward the imagination as the organ of truth. We are not talking of truth, but of meaning: meaning which is the antecedent condition both of truth and falsehood, whose antithesis is not error but nonsense. I am a rationalist. For me, reason is the natural organ of truth; but imagination is the organ of meaning. (1939, 157)

This paragraph, unfortunately, is more of an addendum to "Bluspels," and so there is no complete context for understanding exactly what Lewis means when he says imagination is the "organ of meaning" and meaning is the "antecedent" to truth. But hold on to two ideas at this point:

1. Lewis believed that imagining was as important as reasoning. We don't normally associate imagination with a practical search for knowledge, but Lewis did.
2. Lewis connected meaning to imagination and truth to reason.

Understanding Lewis' definition of meaning and how it shows the value of fairy tales and film requires looking at two more concepts important to Lewis. One is a problem we face in knowing; the other is Lewis' theory of myth.

Thinking Versus Experiencing

In an essay called "Myth Became Fact," Lewis talks about the problem of thinking versus experiencing. He says experience allows us to know things concretely, in a way that is intense, intuitive and immediate on the one hand but critically vague on the other. Thinking (more specifically, reasoning) allows careful contemplation that is clear, but abstract—distancing us from the reality we long to know. How can reality be known with the clarity of thought but without the space of abstraction, of separation? And how can reality be experienced intensely but with a knowing that is complete? Humor shows the dilemma: we can laugh at a joke or think about why it's funny. We can't do both at the same time. Why is this a problem? Lewis' own example is of pain. He thinks to himself, "If only my tooth would stop hurting, I could write another chapter for my book about pain. But when do we really know pain except when experiencing it in all its intensity?"

> Human intellect is incurably abstract. . . . Yet the only realities we experience are concrete—this pain, this pleasure, this dog, this man. While we are loving the man, bearing the pain, enjoying the pleasure, we are not intellectually apprehending Pleasure, Pain or Personality. When we begin to do so, on the other hand, the concrete realities sink to the level of mere instances or examples. . . . (1970, 65)

Our dilemma as knowers is that we can "taste" while not knowing or "know" while not tasting. We can have the kind of knowledge that comes from being in an experience, or we can have the kind that comes from being outside it. The one excludes the other so we can't have both at the same time. When we think, we're "cut off from what we think about," and the better our reasoning, the more cut off we are, the more abstract our thinking becomes. Conversely, the deeper we go into an experience of reality itself, the less we can think. You don't study humor when you're laughing, pain when you're suffering, or pleasure when you're making love (65).

The problem with being unable to know by reasoning and experiencing at the same time is clearest in regard to ethics. In the arena of public policy, we often hear pundits and politicians speak of "putting a face on" a particular problem. It's easy to talk about war, poverty, hunger or injustice in the abstract and come up with what appear to be reasonable policies until a face is put on the problem—until we ourselves see the dead, the poor, the starving, the persecuted. When we *experience* our political and moral dilemmas, our compassion is far more awake than when we reduce them to abstract numbers and theoretical people. Lewis decried certain trends in the educational system of his day for teaching that emotional responses to imaginative texts and beauty in poetry and nature were purely subjective and revealed no truth. Without emotional and imaginative elements in the teaching of morality, he argued, no philosophical arguments for virtue, however clear, would produce virtuous people. Instead the educators of Lewis' time were in danger of fostering "Men without Chests," people who either live by their animal appetites or cold, compassionless reason (or an inconsistent combination of both) (1947, 34).

Lewis gives an example of a boy educated by the trends of the day in his Narnia novel *The Voyage of the Dawn Treader*. It begins, "There was a boy called Eustace Clarence Scrubb, and he almost deserved it" (1952, 1). Eustace is the worst kind of child Lewis could imagine: one raised by "modern" parents. Eustace hates fairy tales, preferring books of information containing "pictures of grain elevators or of fat foreign children doing exercises in model schools" (2). Eustace is pretentious, petty, spiteful and selfish. He is cruel to animals (even talking ones), steals water on a sea voyage when low supplies demand strict rations, acts a coward while hiding behind the self-righteousness of claiming to be a pacifist and complains when the only girl on the voyage gets the only private cabin. Eustace's problem is that he hasn't read any imaginative books like fairy tales or adventure stories and so hasn't received proper moral instruction. He doesn't even recognize a dragon when he sees one because "he had read none of the right books" (89). Upon approaching a dragon's cave, Eustace is confused by what he finds there. Says Lewis: "Most of us know what we should expect to find in a dragon's lair, but, as I said before, Eustace had read only the wrong books. They had a lot to say about exports and imports and governments and drains, but they were weak on dragons" (92). Later in the novel, Eustace's cousin

Edmund is able to solve a mystery because he is the "only one of the party who had read several detective stories" (131). In other words, his imagination has been trained through the experience of fiction so that, in his thinking, he is capable of seeing what others cannot.

What Eustace most needs is to experience reality so that he can know with his heart and not just his head; however, because he is too far gone into the abstract, theoretical shadow world of facts, figures and practical applications, he needs more than just a dose of reality. He needs a higher reality, a world of the fantastic far more real than his own. He gets Narnia. And he gets *to* Narnia through a motion picture. Okay, to be honest it's a moving picture. A painting of a ship on a wall comes to life—the still picture begins to move—and Eustace is pulled through the frame into Narnia, where, having learned before only in the abstract, about lifeless things, he can now learn by concrete experience of the really real. It takes becoming a dragon himself, and then being "undragoned" by Aslan, but Eustace does finally learn what his cold, analytical heart had been missing.

Concrete Thought

Lewis theorized that, in heaven, the dilemma of knowing by thinking versus knowing by experiencing will not be a problem. In his novel *The Great Divorce* a ghostly man who has a passion for inquiry (though not for actually finding any truth) is visiting the outskirts of heaven. There he meets an old friend who has moved beyond the ghostly stage to full presence, full being in heaven. The glorified man is there to invite the ghost to go further in. But the ghost refuses unless certain guarantees are met, especially "an atmosphere of free inquiry." The glorified man tells his friend he will find no such thing; he will find final answers. The ghost responds that there is "something stifling about the idea of finality" to which the other replies, "You think that, because hitherto you have experienced truth only with the abstract intellect. I will bring you where you can taste it like honey and be embraced by it as by a bridegroom" (1946b, 43). Thus, in Lewis' vision, what can only be an abstract idea on earth is concrete reality in heaven. In "Myth Became Fact," Lewis distinguishes between reality and truth: "truth is always about something, but reality is that about which truth is" (1970, 66). Reality is what is; truth is a proposition (a statement or thought in words) about reality. In his vision of heaven, however, Lewis sees the distinction disappearing. The space between the reality around us and what we know of it is gone. Abstraction disappears. Experiencing and thinking simply become knowing. Imagine a place where ideas are alive, where Love and Beauty are solid and Truth is a Person. Knowing like that would be knowing completely. Of course this doesn't help us here in the Shadowlands, does it?

In "Myth Became Fact," Lewis suggests that myth is a partial solution in our world to the problem of experiencing versus knowing. I think film is too. Let's go back to the question of meaning. Lewis believed that meaning can be abstract language statements like my explanation of Luke's internal struggle in *The Empire Strikes Back*. But it can also be concrete and can precede language. Look at "Myth Became Fact" again: Lewis is struggling to understand "the fading, vanishing of tasted reality as we try to grasp it with the discursive reason" (66). It's such a difficult concept to grasp that he suggests another approach: think about the myth of Orpheus and Eurydice. Orpheus was allowed to lead Eurydice by the hand, but the moment he tried to turn around and see her, she disappeared. If we focus on the myth, the abstract concept of thinking versus experiencing is suddenly "imaginable" (experience is Orpheus holding Eurydice's hand; thinking is her disappearing when he turns around to get a clear look at her; the myth, apart from this explanation, is an image of the idea). We may respond that we've never seen that meaning in that myth, to which Lewis replies, "Of course not. You are not looking for an abstract 'meaning' at all." If we were looking for abstract meanings in the myth, it would stop being a myth to us and become nothing more than an allegory. Lewis says that, in receiving the myth as a myth,

> You were not knowing, but tasting; but what you were tasting turns out to be a universal principle. The moment we state this principle, we are admittedly back in the world of abstraction. It is only while receiving the myth as a story that you experience the principle concretely. (66)

In other words, when we take a meaning out of a myth, we turn it into an abstract statement, an idea. When we leave the meaning in the myth and do not try to turn it into language statements, the meaning remains a concrete experience. Through myth, ideas can be experienced as concrete thought. Lewis gave a hint that this occurs in the imagination, a mode of thinking that shares qualities of both reason and experience.

Imagine a teacher drawing a line on a chalkboard representing a spectrum. At one end of the line he writes the word "Abstract," and on the other end the word "Concrete." The instructor applies these kinds of knowing to the definition of a man. Thus, at the abstract end of the spectrum is written a dictionary definition of a man, followed by a more imaginative poetical expression of a man, a photograph (that is, an image) of a man, and, at the concrete end of the spectrum, the instructor himself standing beneath the line:

ABSTRACT			CONCRETE
A man (male gender of the species) is a bipedal primate capable of speech.	"What a piece of work is a man, how noble in reason, how infinite in faculties...." (*Hamlet* 2.2.292–93)	Photograph of a man	The instructor himself

Nowhere in this spectrum do we yet see *concrete thought*. Even the photograph perceived in the imagination is still an abstraction of the real man, despite its close approximation to the concrete reality. But let's turn for a moment to Lewis' good friend J. R. R. Tolkien[1] and ask where in this spectrum we should fit his hobbits? Admittedly hobbits are like people, a version of the human, but in Tolkien's myth they are *not* people, and so they are not abstractions of anything. Hobbits are concrete realities; they are *real* imaginary objects, that is, concrete objects of thought. When our minds turn to hobbits, we both think about and experience them at the same time in the imagination. And this happens when we encounter myth and the best of film.

A good movie example of concrete thought, where thinking is experientially immediate yet has the clarity of discursive reason, occurs at the end of M. Night Shyamalan's *The Sixth Sense*. The protagonist, a child

---

[1] Tolkien authored the Lord of the Rings trilogy. He was one of Lewis' closest friends for over thirty years and was an instrumental influence in converting Lewis to Christianity. Additionally, without Lewis' encouragement, Tolkien might have never finished the Rings books.

psychiatrist played by Bruce Willis, has helped a small boy who literally sees the dead to deal with his special gift. But when he tries to restore his own troubled relationship with his wife, he experiences a brilliantly edited climax. At the moment the hero realizes he is dead, the audience is presented with a montage of fleeting images from throughout the film that causes us to remake its meaning in an instant. New knowledge arises not with the clarity of thinking but the speed and intensity of direct experience. Those who have seen the film can likely describe their first viewing like I have: "When I first saw *The Sixth Sense*, I thought I was watching one kind of movie; when I got to this key point of revelation in the film, I reconstructed it in an instant—it happened so fast that I could not immediately put it in words, but I knew and knew it completely." This is an experience of concrete thought. In myth and film, meaning is often communicated to the imagination with the clarity of reason and the intensity of experience but without abstract language. You might respond, "But language is used in the climactic *Sixth Sense* scene." Yes, but in it the language does not have the same effect. It is more like sounds than words; the concepts recalled come back to us in an instant, in the same way solid objects come into view.

Now we can make sense of Lewis' "Bluspels and Flalansferes" essay. When we receive myth as story, we are experiencing a principle concretely. Only when we put the experience into words does the principle become abstract. But if we can know a principle either concretely or by abstraction, then meaning can be either concrete or abstract. This agrees with the statement in "Bluspels" that meaning is the necessary antecedent to truth (1939, 157). Some meanings are abstract propositions—word statements like my explanation of the scene from *The Empire Strikes Back*. Word statements that correspond to reality are statements of truth. But there are other kinds of meanings which can only be grasped in the experiential imagination. Such meanings, the kind we get in myth and film, for example, come prior to abstraction and apart from language. From them we do not get truths about reality but tastes of reality itself.

Think of some of your favorite songs, the ones that blew you away the first time you heard them. They move you. They connect to you. They evoke feelings and thoughts you can't quite describe. Then recall how a month or two (or six) later you actually bothered to pay attention to the lyrics, and you finally figured out what they were saying. "Oh, that's what the song's about!" In one sense you knew all along what the song was about. You understood meanings in it that couldn't be put into words—meanings in the music itself, or in the way a certain phrase touched your heart or connected with a memory. The analysis of the lyrics was your reasoning self becoming aware of abstract, propositional meanings that your experiential self had not encountered. To use Lewis' terminology, you first tasted the song, then you came to know it.

Fairy tales are like that; they're like the songs we hear that break our hearts with joy, the sunsets that make us cry happy tears, the mountains and canyons that fill us with wonder. One of Lewis' greatest complaints about modernity was its rejection of wonder. Freud taught us to believe that our romantic longings were overactive libidos, that our love of the beautiful was only sexual desire, that our demand for our lives to have meaning and purpose was merely aggression, the fight to survive, and that our longing for heaven was mere wish fulfillment to compensate for our fear of death.

Originals and Copies

Lewis questioned the logic of saying that a higher thing naturally had to come from a lesser thing, that our loftiest thoughts and desires were mere products of biological processes. Could it not be the other way around? Rather than love being a product of a procreation instinct, couldn't sex be an expression in the physical plane of a love that permeates the universe, descending from spiritual reality above? Rather than humanity projecting its own personality on the universe in the search for purpose and meaning, couldn't it be that personality and the desire for purpose and meaning exist in us because there is a Person behind the universe who created it with purpose? Rather than our belief in heaven being a product of our fear of death, couldn't it be that our fear of death arises out of our having been meant to live forever all along? "By what rule do you tell the copy from the original?" Lewis asked this question in his first work of fiction, *The Pilgrim's Regress* (1981, 52). And he asks it with fairy-tale clarity in his fourth Narnia book, *The Silver Chair*.

A much improved Eustace returns to Narnia in the novel where, joined by his schoolmate Jill Pole and a Narnian Marsh-wiggle named Puddleglum, he must search for the lost Prince Rilian. In caverns far below the sunlit world, they discover both the prince and a witch-queen's plot to conquer Narnia. Upon attempting escape, the four companions are confronted by the witch in her dark underworld. The situation, and the conversation that follows, suggest a parallel to Plato's cave—a dark hole filled with lies which must be escaped. True. But this is not a cave of shadows and light; it is one that denies dreams and desires. It is one that looks at the so-called facts and demands a "realistic" (heavy on the quotation marks) view of life.

When Prince Rilian makes known their intentions to return to the overworld of Narnia, the witch casts a spell to confuse their thinking. Then she begins to question them. First she wonders what Narnia is. She doubts its existence, claiming that Rilian is mentally ill. But Puddleglum says Narnia does exist and that he has lived there all his life. The queen responds skeptically: "Tell me, I pray you, where that country is?" (1953, 182). "Up there," says Puddleglum, fighting against the witch's spell. "I—I don't exactly know where." The witch laughs a patronizingly sweet laugh and asks if there is a country among the mortar and stones of her roof. Puddleglum replies that Narnia is to be found in "Overworld." The queen pushes her attack: "And what, or where, pray is this... how do you call it... *Overworld*?" But she is then forced to change her tactics slightly when Eustace reminds her that she herself met him, Jill and Puddleglum in Overworld. She doesn't remember meeting them and says, "But we often meet our friends in strange places when we dream. And unless all dreamed alike, you must not ask them to remember it" (183). Rilian denies her accusation that Eustace has only been dreaming, reminding her that he is the son of the Narnian King. "'And shalt be, dear friend,' said the Witch in a soothing voice, as if she was humoring a child, 'shalt be king of many imagined lands in thy fancies.'"

The witch-queen's greatest lie here is not in denying that she met them in Overworld. It is in making the imaginative knowing of myth, fairy tale and heart's desire out to be mere dream and play. If our dreams and play are mere fun and fancy, then our deepest wishes and desires for life can just as easily be reduced to nothing, to an illusion or projection of our own psyches. This Freudian reduction of all human behavior to mere animal impulse is the witch's next method of attack.

Rilian, Puddleglum and the children almost fall under the spell and start believing there is no world but that of the witch. But then Puddleglum remembers having seen the sun, and for a moment the spell is broken. The queen, however, begins the reductionist argument. Rilian explains that the sun is like the lamp hanging in that underground chamber. Just as the lamp hangs from the ceiling and lights the whole room, so the sun, larger and brighter, hangs in the sky and lights the whole world. "But what does it hang from?" wonders the queen. A perfectly reasonable question which, of course, can't be answered because, while the description is an analogy, the witch makes it literal. And since they can't define the sun clearly, but only by comparing it to the lamp, the sun must be merely a dream, a copy of the lamp. "The lamp is the real thing; the *sun* is but a tale, a children's story" (186–87).

Here the witch attacks not only knowledge of the heart but another quality of imagination as well: analogic. Call it comparative, associative, metaphorical or analogical thinking, it is a kind we most associate with the arts, and it was considered an equally important mode of human knowing until the literalism of the scientific age elevated cold, calculating fact as the most valuable form of knowledge. But how can love be explained *but* by analogy? Would you say to your lover, "I am having a strong and positive emotional response to your presence?" Or rather, "My heart beats at the sight of you?" And would you express grief as "a set of psychological complexes and biochemical reactions" or as "a broken heart?" Some things can neither be said nor understood in any way *but* by analogy.

Once again, then, the spell seems sure to succeed till Jill remembers the existence of the great lion, Aslan. But then the witch retorts that, just as the sun is an overblown image of the lamp, so Aslan is an overblown image of a cat: wish fulfillment, "make-believe" and "foolish dreams" (188–89). In the end it is only Puddleglum's heroism and conviction that his deepest desires are truer than the world he sees around him (the humdrum facts of lamps and cats) that saves the heroes from the witch's spell. He says,

> Suppose we *have* only dreamed, or made up, all those things—trees and grass and sun and moon and stars and Aslan himself. Suppose we have. Then all I can say is that, in that case, the made-up things seem a good deal more important than the real ones. Suppose this black pit of a kingdom of yours *is* the only world. Well, it strikes me as a pretty poor one.... We're just babies making up a game, if you're right. But four babies playing a game can make a play-world which licks your real world hollow. That's why I'm going to stand by the play-world. (190–91)

How can you tell a copy from an original? Lewis' answer is the answer of all fairy tales: look to the desires of your heart. Nature abhors a vacuum; it would never evolve in us a desire that could not be fulfilled. Hunger is not proof that a man will eat, but it is proof that food exists somewhere in the world. If there were no food, people would not need it to survive (1980, 8). In the deepest desire of our hearts, we long for heaven, for our lives to matter, for beauty, for love and for life to have purpose and meaning. We long for life to be like magical fantasy and our most favorite movies. We desire these things because the desire can be fulfilled. Why do we long for fairy-tale lives where we are the princes and princesses of the realm? Lewis would say it's because we are already children of the King.

Myth and Film

For Lewis, meaning is connection, the perception of a relationship. Some connections are auditory, some visual, some intuitive, some bound by language, some clear, some vague, some conscious, some semiconscious or even unconscious, some propositional and philosophical, some imaginative and heartfelt. What's most important for us to understand is that we can't think of meaning as solely an explanation in words. When we break out of that thinking, we begin to see the value of myth and film: in them we enter worlds where meanings become infinite.

Myth is the most ancient of languages, film the most modern. Each is a language without language—a mode of *languaging* in form. Myth is a communication which is not in the words used to communicate it but in the form of the myth itself. Lewis explained this in his introduction to *George MacDonald: An Anthology*:

> We all agree that the story of Balder is a great myth, a thing of inexhaustible value. But of whose version—whose words—are we thinking of when we say this? For my own part, the answer is that I am not thinking of anyone's words. No poet, as far as I know or can remember, had told this story supremely well. I am not thinking of any particular version of it. If the story is anywhere embodied in words, that is almost an accident. What really delights and nourishes me is a particular pattern of events, which would equally delight and nourish if it had reached me by some medium which involved no words at all—say by a mime, or a *film*.[2] (1946a, 26–27)

---

[2] Emphasis added.

Myth communicates meaning apart from language. And the same thing can be said for film.

Lewis and Tolkien shared views on the significance of myth and fairy tale. In an essay entitled "On Fairy-Stories," which was written as a contribution to a book edited by Lewis, Tolkien argues that language owes its origins and development to myth more than the other way around (1968, 50). M. Night Shyamalan offers a similar view in his film *Unbreakable*, in which language is seen as originating in pictures. Says the Samuel Jackson character: "I believe comics are a last link to an ancient way of passing on history. The Egyptians drew on walls. Countries all over the world still pass on knowledge through pictorial forms. I believe comics are a form of history that someone, somewhere, felt or experienced."

Though we may be skeptical about comic books revealing the hidden nature of the universe, the movie makes a point that is verified by Lewis' close friend Owen Barfield, whose book *Poetic Diction* influenced the thinking of both Lewis and Tolkien on myth and fairy tale.

In *Unbreakable*, Shyamalan presented a theory of myth, of a concrete picture language that precedes modern language forms. The image form, surviving in the collective human unconscious, intrudes itself into contemporary culture through comic art. What it reveals is an archetypal pattern of the hero, the "monomyth" that myth theorist Joseph Campbell writes about in his *The Hero with a Thousand Faces*. *Unbreakable* shows us a quality of communicating which Barfield reveals in *Poetic Diction*: a careful study of linguistic history led Barfield to conclude that a strong distinction between sign and signified (between the word "cow" and an actual cow, for example), and between literal and figurative thinking, is new to human thought. For people before the modern era (even up through the medieval period), to name a thing was to invoke it; speech had physical consequences in the world; words were what they signified; metaphorical meanings were possible because their connective representation was in some way literal (1973, 45–92). Film resonates with Barfield's view of earliest language. What it says is what it is, and what it shows is what it means. In the past, words were more like pictures, in fact more like physical actions.

Barfield suggests, for example, the metaphor, "I have no stomach for that." This phrase is used to express our dislike for a thing. It is figurative...mostly. When I say, "I have no stomach for modern art," I'm not saying I get nauseous when I look at an abstract painting. However, if I say "I have no stomach for horror films," I am not only expressing my dislike for them, I am also saying that the blood, gore and suspense in them *do* make me nauseous. Here is an example of a phrase that is both literal and figurative at the same time. Barfield claims humanity used to both think and use language this way constantly. Speech and action were much closer to each other than in our own day.

Well, just as myth is a form of languaging and an expression of concrete thought, so film too is a mode of languaging which communicates to us like a physical action, as a concrete experience, and it is able to do so either without language or by converting language into experiential form. An example of film communicating as form without word can be seen in the early Tim Burton movie *Edward Scissorhands*. In the middle of the movie, we see a long shot of the street on which Edward's adoptive family lives. Husbands simultaneously walk out to their cars from the various homes to begin the morning commute. They get in the cars at the same time, pull out of their driveways at the same time and drive off after a bit of hesitation and jockeying for road space. There are no words, only pleasant, *Leave It to Beaver*-esque music. But here's what's really strange: the houses and the cars are all painted pastel colors. From a greater distance the street might look like an Easter basket. The colors are all solid, no two-tones: whole houses and cars painted pink, or blue, or yellow or green pastel. Actions, sights and sounds—all of them deliberate, intended (movies are too difficult to make without most everything in them being intended—someone had to paint those houses). And without language, meaning is communicated in this scene. We certainly can, in this instance, put the meaning into words: "Suburbia is a world of conformity and façade." But the point is that we get the meaning without having to put it into words.

What film most shares with myth, and what makes it such a valuable art form, is its ability to communicate multiple meanings on multiple levels at the same time. Barfield calls myth "the true child of Meaning" for its ability to make so many simultaneous connections (1973, 201). He illustrates:

We find poet after poet expressing in metaphor and simile the analogy between death and sleep and winter, and again between birth and waking and summer, and these, once more, are constantly made the types of a spiritual experience—of the death in the individual soul....And in the beautiful myth of Demeter and Persephone we find precisely such a meaning. In the myth of Demeter the ideas of waking and sleeping, of summer and winter, of life and death, of mortality and immortality are all lost in one pervasive meaning. (91)

Different ideas find singular unity in myth. The connections are not logical but analogical, associative, visible in the imagination. They are varied and multiple, and so Barfield claims that myth is the true child of meaning; that is, in myth there is multiplicity of meaning. We catch here a hint of Lewis' new Narnia where everything *means* more. "Mythology," Barfield continues, "is the ghost of concrete meaning. Connections between discrete phenomena, connections which are now apprehended as metaphor, were once perceived as immediate realities" (92). Lewis echoes Barfield, calling myth "a story out of which ever varying meanings will grow for different readers and in different ages" (1993, 458).

In film, multiplicity of meaning occurs through technique. In any single shot of a movie, the following elements, each with its own meanings, will be present:

1. Images: people and their actions, objects (sets, props and costumes), designated colors, lighting, titles and the deliberately constructed composition of all these visual elements within the frame.
2. Sounds: dialogue, narration, background/setting noise and music.
3. Literary Elements: plot, symbol, imagery, metaphor, climax, character, setting, point of view, allegory, allusion—most of the elements of meaning we associate with literature are to be found in the best of films.
4. Editing: Movies will be edited in ways unique to film which contribute additional visual, auditory and literary meanings. Editing is done for the presentation of a variety of visual points of view, for emotional and experiential pace, for narrative structure, for the juxtaposition of images with images and images with sounds.

All of these meanings, then, operate at once in film, often with a simultaneity and thickness of meaning greater than anything that even myth experienced through literature can manage.

Though Lewis himself was a lover of books, the theory of myth he shared with Barfield and Tolkien works too well with film to deny its application to film. When Lewis wrote Arthur Greeves about going to the cinema, he went on to say it was to see *King Kong* because of its mythic qualities—it reminded him of his reading of Rider Haggard's mythic adventures (2004, 120). Years later he indicated having enjoyed those parts of the movie which took place on the island, though he deplored the last half set in New York (910). He liked the film when it was its most mythic.

Conclusion

C. S. Lewis' theories on myth and knowing have sent me into the cave of cinema, where I freely admit to having come to some *edgy* conclusions about myth, film and fairy tales. I'm saying that fairy tales are true—That is, they teach us truths, especially about right and wrong and the truth to be found in our deepest longings. I'm saying that myth mimics the thinking of heaven and the thinking of humanity in our primordial past; as such, it is truer than history in that history can only tell us what happened while myth tells us what is always happening beneath and above human events. Finally, I'm saying that film, as well as or even better than written myth and fairy tales, is capable of returning us to the thinking of heaven and ancient earth, a process of concrete knowing more complete than any we've known since the Enlightenment elevated the head above the heart.

George Lucas has noted several times that myth is psychological archaeology, and he built his Star Wars films around those archetypal patterns of human perception. He is convinced that the success of *Star Wars* is due to the apprehension of the deeper reality people have perceived from the roots of time through this holistic mode of thinking called myth. We are returning to that ancient mode of thought through a modern technological magic, a mode of thought that glimpses heaven through a silver screen.

Postscript: The Upcoming Narnia Films

Whenever novels are adapted into film, the books' lovers often worry about whether the adaptations will be faithful to the original stories. This was a major concern for the Lord of the Rings films (and the debate there continues). Though not a great fan of film, had he lived in our time to see its greater flowering, Lewis might have become one, since, even in his day of limited special effects, he still saw film's mythic qualities. We can only guess as to whether or not he would like the upcoming adaptations of his Narnia books. But even we can't judge them till we see them; then the debate can begin.

Lewis aficionados would likely be skeptical about Lewis' ever liking film adaptations of his books, and even more skeptical of my applying his theories on myth to movies. They would argue that books were simply too important to Lewis. He was a true bibliophile, no doubt. But he was at least as much a lover of myth and the joy[3] it evoked, and he acknowledged receiving that joy through pictures, music, opera,[4] books—many of them mythic—and he at least acknowledged the possibility that mythic experience might come through film. Lewis experienced joy in the imagination through concrete thought. He did not experience it through books alone, and die-hard Lewis fans know this. Even the Narnia novels did not begin as books. They began as pictures in Lewis' head (1966, 42). Lovers of Lewis and books in general need not fear the rise of the image. Books will not fade away in the postmodern age and neither will the need for rich verbal language. Not our culture's return to imagistic thinking, nor graphics-heavy electronic media, will kill written words. Even the controllers of images in our culture will only be so if they can command words as well.

At the same time, what lovers of Lewis' books must realize is that movies are not books and should not be judged with the exact same critical tools. Movies must be judged by their application of the elements of film which are centered more in images and sounds than in words. And so any critique of film adaptation must take into account not only the original books, but both the limitations and unique advantages of film. How best to do that is an issue for another essay.

As a true Lewis fanatic (with just enough Gen-X mentality in me to see the value of film), I look forward to the Narnia movies, though I can't judge their quality until I see them. If they are done well, I will gain new knowledge from them, experience new joys. They will not be

---

[3] Lewis' theory of Joy was central to his thinking about literature, myth and theology, and his experience of joy was central to his conversion. His most complete explanation of joy can be found in his autobiography, *Surprised by Joy*.

[4] Lewis was a great fan of Wagner's *Ring Cycle*; he loved Norse mythology and any artistic form that expressed it.

everything the books could give me. But they will give me things that the books could not.

Charlie W. Starr teaches English, humanities and film at Kentucky Christian University in eastern Kentucky, where he specializes in "all things C. S. Lewis" and also makes movies with his students and family. He writes articles, teaches Sunday school and has published three books. Charlie describes his wife Becky as a full-of-life, full-blooded Cajun, who can cook like one, too. They have two children: Bryan, who wants to be the next Steven Spielberg, and Alli, who wants to be the next Jacques Cousteau.

References

Barfield, Owen. 1973. *Poetic Diction: A Study in Meaning*. Middletown: Wesleyan Univ. Press.

Campbell, Joseph. 1973. *The Hero with a Thousand Faces*. Princeton: Princeton Univ. Press.

Edward Scissorhands. 1990. Dir. Tim Burton. Twentieth Century Fox.

Lewis, C. S. 1939. "Bluspels and Flalansferes: A Semantic Nightmare." *Rehabilitations and Other Essays*. Oxford: Oxford Univ. Press.

———. ed. 1946a. *George MacDonald: An Anthology*. London: Fount Paperbacks.

———. 1946b. *The Great Divorce*. New York: Collier.

———. 1947. *The Abolition of Man: Or Reflections on Education with Special Reference to the Teaching of English in the Upper Forms of Schools*. New York: Collier.

———. 1950. *The Lion, the Witch and the Wardrobe*. New York: HarperCollins.

———. 1952. *The Voyage of the Dawn Treader*. New York: HarperCollins.

———. 1953. *The Silver Chair*. New York: HarperCollins.

———. 1955a. *Surprised by Joy: The Shape of My Early Life*. San Diego: Harvest/HBJ.

———. 1955b. *The Magician's Nephew*. New York: HarperCollins.

———. 1956. *The Last Battle*. New York: HarperCollins.

———. 1966. "It All Began with a Picture." *Of Other Worlds: Essays and Stories*. Ed. Walter Hooper. New York: Harvest/HBJ.

———. 1970. "Myth Became Fact." *God in the Dock: Essays on Theology and Ethics*. Ed. Walter Hooper. Grand Rapids, MI: Wm. B. Eerdmans.

———. 1980. "The Weight of Glory." *The Weight of Glory and Other Addresses*. Ed. Walter Hooper. New York: Macmillan.

———. 1981. *The Pilgrim's Regress: An Allegorical Apology for Christianity, Reason and Romanticism*. Grand Rapids, MI: Wm. B. Eerdmans.

———. 1993. *Letters of C. S. Lewis*. Ed. W. H. Lewis. Rev. ed. Ed. Walter Hooper. San Diego: Harvest/HBJ.

———. 2004. *The Collected Letters of C. S. Lewis, Vol. 2: Books, Broadcasts and the War, 1931–1949*. Ed. Walter Hooper. San Francisco: HarperCollins.

Star Wars: The Empire Strikes Back. 1980. Dir. Irvin Kershner. Twentieth Century Fox.

The Lord of the Rings. 2003. Dir. Peter Jackson. New Line Cinema.

The Matrix. 1999. Dir. The Wachowski Brothers. Warner Brothers.

The Sixth Sense. 1999. Dir. M. Night Shyamalan. Hollywood Pictures/Spyglass Entertainment.

Tolkien, J. R. R. 1965. The Lord of the Rings. New York: Ballantine.

Tolkien, J. R. R. 1968. "On Fairy-Stories." *Essays presented to Charles Williams*. Ed. C. S. Lewis. Grand Rapids, MI: Wm. B. Eerdmans.

Unbreakable. 2000. Dir. M. Night Shyamalan. Touchstone Pictures.

Dates listed are for editions from which the author quoted; they are not necessarily original publication dates.

On the Origins of Evil

"The Lion growled so that the earth shook (but his wrath was not against me) and said, It is false. Not because he and I are one, but because we are opposites, I take to me the services which thou hast done to him, for I and he are of such different kinds that no service which is vile can be done to me, and none which is not vile can be done to him. Therefore if any man swear by Tash and keep his oath for the oath's sake, it is by me that he has truly sworn, though he know it not, and it is I who reward him. And if any man do a cruelty in my name, then, though he says the name Aslan, it is Tash whom he serves and by Tash his deed is accepted."

—The Last Battle, CHAPTER XV

IN NARNIA'S FINAL DAYS, a Talking Ape named Shift and a Calormene nobleman called Rishda Tarkaan declared that Aslan, the Lion of Narnia, and Tash, the vulture-headed god of the Calormenes, were two aspects of the same being and convinced many Narnian creatures of this.

Aslan himself explicitly denies it, as quoted above. Aslan was the true creator of Narnia, and Tash was the god of all that is vile, and the two are opposites, not parts of a larger whole.

But that leads to an inevitable question: *where did Tash come from*?

There can be no doubt that Tash does really exist; he appears on-stage in *The Last Battle* and eventually carries Rishda Tarkaan off to a hideous, if unspecified, fate. He comes to the land of Narnia because Rishda Tarkaan inadvertently summoned him. But how did he come to be in the *world* of Narnia, a world Aslan created?

Lewis never explains that.

In fact, Lewis tells us very little about Tash. He is never mentioned in five of the seven books in the series. In the fifth, *The Horse and His Boy*, Tash is referred to repeatedly as the chief god in the Calormene pantheon, but we are given no reason to believe he actually exists at all; other Calormene deities, such as Zardeenah and Azaroth, are spoken of, often literally in the same breath as is Tash, and we never *do* see any sign that they have a basis in reality. There are no tales about visits from Tash, no mention of his appearance anywhere. Aslan does tie the punishment of the despicable Prince Rabadash to the temple of Tash in the Calormene capital of Tashbaan, but that is clearly *Aslan's* doing, and not evidence of Tash's existence.

But then, in the final volume, Tash follows his worshipers into Narnia, where he can be seen and his presence felt by most (though not all) of the characters. The rest of the Calormene pantheon does not accompany him; in fact, they're never mentioned at all, even by the Calormenes.

How does *that* work?

Was Tash present all along and simply not concerned with the doings of mortals, or at least not the ones we read about, while the other Calormene gods were mere myth? That would seem to fit the evidence well enough—were it not for the sixth Narnia book, *The Magician's Nephew*.

In that story, we get to see the creation of Narnia's world. Aslan, the great Lion, son of the Emperor-over-the-Sea, sings Narnia into existence—a genesis interestingly similar to the one Lewis' friend and compatriot, J. R. R. Tolkien, gave his own Middle-earth in the tales collected in *The Silmarillion*. In this beginning was not just the word, but the melody, as well.

One major difference, however, is that Narnia's creation is witnessed by four people and a horse from our own world, as well as a wicked witch from the dead world of Charn. Aslan's reaction to the witch's presence is to note that an evil has been brought into this new world, not yet five hours old.

The implication would certainly seem to *me* to be that there was no evil in it before that—and therefore no Tash.

Then where does Tash come in? How does he fit the story?

In some ways, the history of Narnia parallels the biblical account of the history of our own world. *The Lion, the Witch and the Wardrobe*, while ostensibly a fairy-tale adventure, retells in its way the Passion of Christ—The great Lion, Aslan, son of the Emperor-over-the-Sea, gives up his life that others might be saved and then returns from death.

The next four books really *are* mostly just fairy-tale adventures, though Aslan is always there, putting things right in the end. Then in *The Magician's Nephew*, Lewis goes back to show us Narnia's Genesis, complete with a walled garden and forbidden fruit and Jadis of Charn playing the role of the Serpent—but Digory, unlike Adam and Eve, resists temptation and does not eat the apple, so that Narnia's history is happier than our own. The presence of the White Witch ensures that it's not *all* happy, by any means, but it's better.

And the final volume, *The Last Battle*, is Narnia's Apocalypse, with Shift the Ape as the Antichrist, Stable Hill as Armageddon and Tash as Satan, the dragon. Lewis even *calls* it *The Last Battle*; how can it be about anything but Armageddon?

It's not a retelling or recasting of the whole of Revelation, of course; even had he wanted to, Lewis probably couldn't have worked the whore of Babylon into the story, nor are there angels opening seven seals. Besides, Lewis said in his other writings that he did not mean the Narnia stories as allegory; they aren't biblical history in a clever disguise, but the history of another world where God is present in the form of the lion Aslan, rather than the man Jesus.

But all created realms must have a beginning and an end, and Narnia's were clearly meant to be similar, but not identical, to God's plans for our own world. There is a final battle, and there is a beast—poor Puzzle the Donkey—and his false prophet, Shift the Ape, who rule over Narnia just as the Antichrist in chapter 13 of Revelation 13 shall rule all the world except the saved.

Revelation 13:15 can be seen as a passable description of Shift's hold over the Narnians: "And he had power to give life unto the image of the beast, that the image of the beast should both speak, and cause that as many as would not worship the image of the beast should be killed." Shift's ability to present his false Aslan is what compels the Narnians to obey him, and the Calormenes kill those who resist.

Tash, then, is pretty obviously equivalent to Satan the deceiver, the dragon whose servants make war on the righteous. Chapter 20 tells us Satan will be cast into the bottomless pit when judgment is at hand, and so Aslan sends Tash away.

So that's the role Tash plays, but the problem remains: where did Tash *come* from? He wasn't there at the creation of Narnia; in *The Magician's Nephew* the role of Satan the corruptor and tempter is filled by the White Witch, not by a vulture-headed god. And the White Witch was killed, quite thoroughly, in *The Lion, the Witch and the Wardrobe*. Narnia should have been free of evil.

But we know it wasn't.

In our world, in the Christian view, Satan was present from the start; it was Satan who took the form of a serpent and tempted Eve. In Narnia, the only tempter seen was the White Witch; Tash was not there.

Lewis carefully explains how the White Witch arrived in Narnia. In *Prince Caspian* he makes a point of explaining that the Telmarine invaders who ruled Narnia were descended from a band of pirates from our world. Narnia was created without evil, and without a human race—but a married couple from our world provided the human inhabitants of Narnia and Archenland, and the White Witch brought in evil. The pirates of Telmar later added more of both.

But where did *Tash* come in?

For that matter, where did the Calormenes who worshiped Tash come from? And the Emerald Witch who ensorcelled Prince Rilian in *The Silver Chair*? They're never explained, either. The Calormenes are first mentioned (spelled with a K instead of a C) in *The Voyage of the Dawn Treader*, and not described beyond the fact that they buy slaves; we get much more about them in *The Horse and His Boy*, but no explanation of how they came to be running a great empire to the south of Narnia. And the Emerald Witch is assumed by Prince Rilian to be of the same kind as the White Witch—but since we learn in *The Magician's Nephew* that Jadis was the last survivor of the world of Charn, we know that can't be correct. There must be another explanation.

The easiest explanation for the Emerald Witch and the Calormenes is simply that there were openings to other worlds now and then—perhaps our own, in the case of the Calormenes, perhaps others we know nothing about. There is no proof that the Calormenes were, as Lewis called us, sons of Adam and daughters of Eve—when Aslan speaks to the Calormene Aravis in *The Horse and His Boy*, he never calls her "daughter of Eve," though almost all the girls from our world are addressed as such at some point.

Lewis never tells us whether this explanation is the correct one or not—but then, why should he? It's not part of the stories he tells us. Aslan says in *The Horse and His Boy*, "I tell no one any story but his own," and it seems likely that Lewis, too, preferred to stick to one story at a time.

So while we're never told, it's perfectly reasonable to say that the Emerald Witch and the Calormenes wandered in from other worlds, just by happenstance, and stayed, either because they liked the world they found themselves in, or because they couldn't find the way back.

Tash, though—could *he* be there by simple chance? He's no mere enchanter, nor a man of any sort. He is plainly, if not actually, a god, something more (or less) than mortal. Surely, divinities of any sort do not accidentally walk through transmundane portals.

Aslan says Tash is his opposite; how thoroughly does he mean that? Aslan created Narnia—and Aslan destroyed it, in the end, so it's not an issue of creation versus destruction. Nor are they equal—Aslan is clearly superior in that when he orders Tash to be gone, Tash is gone. It appears that the two are opposites in purely moral terms; Aslan, the incarnation of all that is good, and Tash, the embodiment of evil.

But perhaps there's something more. The one time we hear Tash speak, he says, "Thou hast called me into Narnia, Rishda Tarkaan. Here I am. What hast thou to say?"

When people call on Aslan, he often doesn't answer; he is not a *tame* lion. He may summon others, as he several times summons English children to aid Narnia, but he is not himself subject to summons.

Tash, however, *is* summoned by Rishda Tarkaan, even though the Tarkaan himself did not believe in Tash's existence. I would hardly go so far as to say he's a *tame* monster, but might it be that this is another way in which he is Aslan's opposite? Perhaps he does not guide men; rather, he is guided *by* them.

He is in Narnia because the Calormenes summoned him thither. He is in Narnia's world, in Calormen, because the Calormenes unknowingly summoned him. Just as Digory brought the first evil into an innocent world, in the form of Jadis of Charn, later known as the White Witch, so did the people of Calormen, through their ferocity and cruelty, bring in Tash. It might even be that some Telmarine magician inadvertently brought the Emerald Witch to Narnia's northern frontier, that *all* the evils visited upon that land were brought by men.

It's a theory that fits the facts, but Lewis does not *tell* us, so it remains only a theory.

It's a theory, however, that fits not just what we're told about Narnian history, but also suits Lewis' theology. In his other writings about Christianity he sets forth very plainly the idea that all good comes from God, and all evil from mankind's refusal to accept God. In the world of Narnia, Aslan is the Son of God, for the Emperor-over-the-Sea can be nothing and no one other than God the Father.

Aslan created Narnia, but right from the start there were those who refused to acknowledge him—Digory's Uncle Andrew did not allow himself to understand Aslan's words, and convinced himself that the song of creation itself was just a lion's roaring. Jadis, the White Witch, knew perfectly well who and what Aslan was, but refused to concede his authority, and tried to claim the world he had created as her own. Both rejected the joy Aslan offered in favor of their own preexisting selfishness.

And that, to Lewis, was the essence of evil—selfishness, the inability to put anyone else's needs or wants above one's own. Nor did he see this as a small thing, easily escaped. In his short fantasy *The Great Divorce* he describes damned souls allowed to visit heaven and given a chance to stay if they can, just for a moment, really think of someone other than themselves—and most of them can't do it. Selfish evil, even very petty evil, can be seductive, addictive, something that traps a soul and separates it from divine grace—though not necessarily forever. In *The Lion, the Witch and the Wardrobe*, Edmund's selfish lust for Turkish Delight turns him against his own siblings and makes him a traitor to Narnia, but in the end he is rescued and restored to Aslan's company. In *The Great Divorce*, while most of the ghosts fail and return to hell, with divine aid, a few do free themselves and enter heaven.

In many ways *The Great Divorce* is a direct ancestor of *The Last Bat-*

tle—the descriptions of heaven in *The Great Divorce* are very similar to the descriptions of Aslan's country, the true Narnia, in the final chapters of *The Last Battle*, and many of the issues confronted by the ghosts in *Divorce* are reiterated among the Talking Animals and other Narnian creatures in how they react to the false Aslan. In particular, the Dwarfs in *The Last Battle* and their refusal to see the salvation Aslan offers them are very much like the ghosts who refuse to accept the reality of heaven in *Divorce*, and quickly board the bus that will take them back to hell— or who decide not to take the bus out of hell in the first place.

So, if *The Great Divorce* is considered a look at Lewis' views of heaven, and what determines whether a soul is damned or not, and *The Last Battle* is a presentation of how those theories apply to Narnia, is there anything in *The Great Divorce* that might provide an explanation for the presence of a real Tash? Is there a Satan who rules over Lewis' dismal, rainy hell, dragging the souls of the damned down into its dreary grey streets?

No. There isn't. This is, in fact, pretty much the only point of theological disagreement between the two stories. Hell, in *The Great Divorce*, is an anarchy created by its inhabitants; no one rules, there are no demons, no devils, but only unhappy people making each other miserable. The only character who could possibly be construed as a lord of the damned is the bus driver, and it's quite clear that he's a power for good, rather than evil—either one of the blessed, or an angel, giving the damned another chance at salvation.

But that's not to say there are no demonic creatures in *The Great Divorce*; on the contrary, there are several. There's an evil little lizard who whispers in a ghost's ear, representing his addiction to lust, and a sort of marionette that takes over one poor dead soul, representing the victim persona he puts on.

And all of these were *created* by the people they torment.

Perhaps, then, the Calormenes *created* Tash. Their centuries of rejecting Aslan and calling him a demon, their selfish and brutal society built on slavery, eventually made their evil manifest as an actual Tash. Uncle Andrew was able to transform the speech of the beasts, including the Lion himself, to mere growling and roaring; the Dwarfs could see and feel the interior of the stable rather than the realm that truly lay beyond the door. Why, then, could not the Calormenes create their own deity?

This would be yet another way in which Tash would be Aslan's opposite; Aslan created the world's inhabitants, and the world's inhabitants created Tash.

And naturally, as the world's creator, Aslan would still be infinitely more powerful than this monstrous godling.

And this theory would also explain why Aslan called Rishda Tarkaan "lawful prey" for Tash—because it was Rishda Tarkaan and his kind who had summoned Tash into existence in the first place, through their own evil. Thus it was Rishda Tarkaan's own evil that truly carried him off to a hideous and unknown fate, and that's exactly how Lewis says, in almost all his writing, that reality works. Each of the damned creates his own hell.

And Tash is the hell the Calormenes have created for themselves, thereby providing the Satan needed to oppose God in the last battle.

Lawrence Watt-Evans is the author of some three dozen novels and over a hundred short stories, mostly in the fields of fantasy, science fiction and horror. He won the Hugo Award for short story in 1988 for "Why I Left Harry's All-Night Hamburgers," served as president of the Horror Writers Association from 1994 to 1996 and treasurer of SFWA from 2003 to 2004 and lives in Maryland. He has two kids in college and shares his home with Chanel, the obligatory writer's cat.

References

Lewis, C. S. 1946. *The Great Divorce*. New York: Macmillan.
————. 1994. The Chronicles of Narnia Boxed Set. New York: HarperTrophy.
The King James Bible, Quarto Edition. 1853. Oxford: Oxford Univ. Press.

NATASHA GIARDINA

Elusive Prey: Searching for Traces of Narnia in the Jungles of the Psyche

I T HAPPENED AT A DINNER PARTY RECENTLY. The conversation, having exhausted sex, religion and politics, moved inevitably to children's books (doesn't it always!). There we sat, fortified by slightly too much chardonnay, reminiscing about children's fiction we'd read—the best, the worst, the ones that changed our lives. And then someone asked the fateful question: "Do you remember when you first read *Narnia*?" Immediately there was a torrent of excitement. Like September 11 or the first Moon landing, everyone remembered their first amazing experience of Narnia.

Everyone but me.

For some reason, although I was sure I had read at least one of the Narnia stories, I couldn't really recall anything about reading them. Me—the party's resident expert on children's literature! I felt like an outcast, a freak, like someone who had been at the greatest party of the century and spent the entire time in the kitchen, doing the washing up. Of course, I was too embarrassed to blow my cover and say anything then and there, but later I did a little frantic mental interrogation. I googled my brain on the search terms: "Me AND childhood AND books." A huge number of results emerged: sites devoted to various stories, favorite authors, influences, memories. A constellation of sites on *Gone with the Wind*—the favorite book of my thirteenth year; a veritable galaxy— all hyperlinked—on Roald Dahl's fiction. But where was Narnia?

Finally I saw it. One lone reference tucked in between Choose Your Own Adventure and the *Jacaranda Junior School Atlas*. It said simply: "Natasha read *The Lion, the Witch and the Wardrobe* at age ten." Was that all, I wondered? This was arguably one of the top ten children's books of the twentieth century; it was both popular and controversial, but I hadn't found it at all memorable. Maybe I'd made a search error, or perhaps some of my mental hard drive had become corrupted. I double checked, but I wasn't wearing my underpants on my head, so the latter explanation seemed unlikely.

I had to find out the answer to this mystery: why did Narnia have so little effect on me that I could barely remember it? I now knew the answer wouldn't be found by a simple mental google; instead I would have to trek through the deepest, darkest jungles of my psyche to find out why Narnia was missing, where it had gone and if any trace of it was left. Like a rare wild animal, Narnia was an elusive prey; I would need every ounce of my skill, knowledge and cunning to track it.

So in order to prepare for my safari, I reviewed what I'd learned about Narnia as an adult. One of the most enduring contentious issues about Narnia has been the extent to which child readers are influenced by the various religious and secular messages Narnia presents. C. S. Lewis himself was quite open about what he wanted the Narnia chronicles to achieve. Discussing his motivations for writing *The Lion, the Witch and the Wardrobe*, Lewis revealed that as a young person, he found that the imposed obligation to feel certain emotions toward God and Christ, together with the stultifying sense of reverence inherent in Christian teachings, made the Christian message unappealing and difficult for him to understand. Consequently, as an adult, he wanted to bring that message and experience of Christianity to child readers in its "real potency," devoid of any negative or dull associations. By writing the Christian message into a fairy tale, Lewis knew that what he was doing was deceptive: he hoped that the essence of Christianity would "steal past [the] watchful dragons" of readers' resistances to religion (1966, 36–37).

This aspect of the stories has caused no end of controversy between Christians and non-Christians alike. Some groups have encouraged parents to read the Narnia stories with their children specifically to teach them about Christianity, while other, secular interest groups have had concerns about inculcating religious sentiments in children in this politically correct and possibly post-religious age. Many who read the stories as children say they never noticed the religious elements and understood the stories as plain fantasies, but some, as adults, have felt betrayed by Lewis' subterfuge.

But Narnia is much more than a vehicle for Lewis' lessons of Christianity: it also reveals his understanding of childhood and his desire to make a special connection to his child readers. In his portrayal of childhood, Lewis kept mainly to the standard of his era. Sheila Egoff notes that in the 1950s, childhood came to be seen as "an existence in tandem with adulthood": a time for the young person to learn the qualities necessary for maturity and so "writers portrayed behaviour that society hoped for from its children" (1981, 9, 11). The Pevensie children accurately reflect that standard: they are, with the initial exception of Edmund, happy, curious and wholesome. The older children are obviously preparing for their future adult roles: Susan is motherly, while Peter is a born leader, and taken together, the four of them appear like a microcosm of the idealized 1950s family.

Lewis may have crafted his child characters represent a cultural ideal, but he understood some things about real kids too. For instance, he was aware of the "difficult relations" that sometimes exist between children and their parents and teachers, but felt that as an author he was able to sidestep that and connect with children as a "freeman and equal" (1966, 34). Yet evidently he was torn between two contradictory positions: he wanted to side with children, but he had difficulty stepping outside his adult subjectivities. Both his juvenile fiction and his essays reveal that he took his own position of power and intellectual superiority for granted. Lewis assumed he knew what was best for children of his era and that these children would accept his guidance.

Armed with this background knowledge, I set off on this trek into my psychological wilderness and ponder my route. Given that Lewis was writing to a 1950s British understanding of childhood, my first stop must logically be Australia in the late 1980s, backdrop to my own childhood. How well would Narnia translate over a nearly forty-year and ten-thousand-mile gap?

As the jungle closes in around me, one thing I'm quite sure of is that while Lewis may have had some idea of what British childhood in the 1950s was all about, he couldn't anticipate a late-1980s childhood of the sort I'd experienced. Children by then were a very different species, probably because we were growing up in a very different world. In Western countries like Australia, the AIDS epidemic was changing the social and political landscape. But what does AIDS have to do with Narnia? Not much directly, but I certainly found it hard to connect to, let alone sustain, the kind of innocent curiousness of the Pevensie children in a time when the intricacies of intravenous drug use, straight and gay sexual practices and the transmission and mortality rates of AIDS were being discussed throughout the media. A White Witch who turned people into stone didn't seem quite so scary in an age when many people thought you could die if you touched a homosexual.

Around the same time, scientists began to talk about another growing concern: the greenhouse effect. It seemed that even if we managed to emerge unscathed from AIDS, our energy-hungry, pollution-producing lifestyle was seriously screwing up the environment. Animals were becoming extinct, oceans were rising, and the hole in the ozone layer meant that even sunshine was dangerous. In my young mind's eye, the earth was not a Narnia-like natural Eden, but rather a smoky and polluted ball in space, where the last vestiges of the natural world were rapidly disappearing under a tide of overpopulation and rampant overdevelopment. I don't know how much issues like AIDS and global warming affected others, but they certainly loomed large in my childlike understanding of the world. I felt a great world-weariness, even at the tender age of ten, as I contemplated an inevitable future of disease and decay. Of course, it wasn't *that* bad—it never is!—but things just seemed bigger when I was smaller.

Pop culture separated me from Narnia even further. I understood the Simpson family better than the Pevensie family, which is perhaps unsurprising, given that when *The Simpsons* first went to air, Bart and I were the same age. Like Bart, I was sarcastic and cynical, I watched far too much violence on TV, and I didn't respect adult authority figures. I played hide-and-seek on computer games more often than in real life, which was better anyway because hide-and-seek on a computer game included carrying serious firepower to destroy your enemies in gouts of blood when you finally did find them. I was part of that first generation of kids to have computers in the classroom, and I think that to a large extent I took the science-fictional nature of modern life for granted—magic was just science we didn't understand yet.

My late-eighties childhood provides a big clue to the disappearance of Narnia from my memories: in truth, I had few ways of making a connection to that idealized 1950s era. Neil Postman has identified access to information as the key to the divide between adulthood and childhood (1983). By this definition, childhood in the 1980s was less distinct than it had been in the 1950s, because children like me had access to a greater range and quantity of information, much of which was adult-oriented. Perhaps, between the influences of AIDS, global warming and pop culture, the real world simply intruded too far to allow me to believe in the simple mysteries of Narnia's fantasy.

From this vantage point, I can see a little way into the jungle. Having stirred up the old psyche, some long-forgotten memories are hesitantly emerging into the light. I can now remember a few things about reading *The Lion, the Witch and the Wardrobe* at age ten. For instance, I can remember just how irritated I was by Peter, Susan and Lucy, who were far too gormless and saccharine for my liking. I took particular offence at Lucy. I could tell the story was setting me up to like Lucy and to want to be like Lucy: brave, curious and valiant, sweet-tempered, feminine and polite. I knew just as clearly that Lucy was everything I did not want to be and could not afford to be. She had no street cred; she was, in the parlance of my times, "a dweeb," "a dork" and "a complete drip." And her girlishness? Well, that was a problem too. While femininity may have been a virtue in the 1950s, when I was growing up it was no longer valuable: girls my age were being told that they were just as good as boys and could do anything boys could do. Our toys were as likely to be Tonka trucks and Legos as Barbie dolls and Cabbage Patch Kids, so we felt it was important for us not to be too girly—and certainly not as girly as Lucy.

My adult self understands this situation better. Lewis uses Lucy as a focalizing character and the opening chapters of *The Lion, the Witch and the Wardrobe* are arranged precisely to bring readers into the story by enabling them to identify with Lucy. Throughout the story, Lucy functions as a model for the sort of behavior Lewis thought appropriate for children, and Pat Pinsent suggests that through her close relationship with Aslan, Lucy helps readers understand Aslan as an implied Christ figure (2002, 11). Lucy also has a symbolic role in the story: she represents a feminine ideal, one that has its roots in religion through the Virgin Mary as well as in medieval concepts of chivalry through the Lady of Courtly Love (Pinsent 2002; Filmer 1993). Lucy's nature is thus heavily invested with adult values and ideologies, which, given the strong, cynical, anti-adult sentiments of my peer group, I was not predisposed to accept. In a social environment where "teacher's pet" was the worst insult there was, a child cleaving so closely to adult notions of good behavior was a traitor to everything we kids stood for.

If I didn't warm to Lucy despite all the text's prodding, I certainly wasn't going to warm to the adults in the story. Apart from that wicked witch, all the grown-ups in *The Lion, the Witch and the Wardrobe* were so certain that they knew just what was best for kids and it was merely sensible for kids to follow their advice. "Eeeuw Spew!" as I probably would have shouted at the time. I had cut my teeth on Roald Dahl's fiction and I knew darned well that the only cool adult was a flaky, eccentric adult like Willy Wonka from *Charlie and the Chocolate Factory* or Grandmama from *The Witches*: all other adults were bone-crunchingly disgusting and deserved horrible, nasty ends. Grown-ups? Can't trust 'em!

But the Pevensies operate within a great circle of patriarchal protection, guided primarily by the narrator, the Professor, Mr. Beaver and Aslan. At various points in the story, these adults function in ways that show Lewis trying to connect to kids on their own level, but not always with great success. The narrator, for instance, tries to show his kid credentials by scathingly referring to "the grown-ups" who prevent him from telling readers about the really scary creatures in the Witch's army (1980, 138), but his adult sensibilities are revealed much earlier in the story, when he goes on *ad nauseum* about leaving wardrobe doors open (honestly, what kid would care about this?). At ten, I didn't get why these adults were trying to tell me what to do and be my friend at the same time, and I certainly didn't understand that Lewis was constructing these characters to represent him in the context of the story. But I did know I was being manipulated in some way, and I didn't like it, and I wasn't going to have a bar of it. "Eeeuw Spew" indeed!

By this point, I can see why Narnia didn't have much effect on me; why it disappeared almost without a trace. And yet, at the very moment when I'm about to pronounce this prey extinct, I hear a rustling in the bushes. We're in a deep part of the jungle now: the trees are thickly intertwined and very little light gets through from the outside. Yet it's here, inexplicably, that aspects of Narnia have thrived, hidden in the deepest recesses of my mind, but definitely coloring my outlook on life. They're not the bits I expected: I shrugged off Lewis' moral code, his notions of the feminine ideal and his attempts to be on my side. No, what stayed with me were not Narnia's lessons for my consciousness, but those for my senses and emotions.

The Lion, the Witch and the Wardrobe is strongly focused on the joys and delights to be found in nature. The passages where Lewis describes aspects of nature, like the birth of spring, the dawn after Aslan's death, the landscape around Cair Paravel and even the Narnian winter are arguably the story's most poetic sections. For me, *The Lion, the Witch and the Wardrobe* didn't just describe nature; it redefined it. For instance, I grew up in a sultry, tropical area of Australia. I had never seen snow or experienced cold weather in my life, but *The Lion, the Witch and the Wardrobe* created an image of winter that actually outweighed my lived experience. I loved the idea that the beaver's dam could be frozen instantly into "a glittering wall of icicles, as if the side of the dam had been covered all over with flowers and wreaths and festoons of the purest sugar" (67). It was a far cry from the ice I knew, which came in two types: cubes and freezer frost. Neither of these varieties looked anything like "festoons of the purest sugar," especially when you could see the bread crumbs and other freezer gunk embedded in them, but I was undeterred. Winter suddenly meant snow and ice, and I was determined from that moment on that I was going travel the world until I found this ultimate wintry ideal.

Narnia didn't just gift me with an enduring love of nature; it also gave me an understanding of something far more subtle and difficult to describe: it taught me what spiritual ecstasy felt like. I will be quite open in saying that this aspect *never* registered while I was reading the story, but in an art history course I took at university, I did some research on baroque art depicting moments of divinity. The images were a little over the top, with saints collapsing theatrically and much eye-rolling. But at some point I had a weird sense of déjà vu: I knew exactly what experiencing the divine was all about—*I had felt this already*. It was just like something that happened to me in Narnia.

How exactly did Lewis manage to give a kid like me an experience of the spiritual sublime? Surely it has to rank up there with things that can't be adequately explained in words, yet Lewis managed it brilliantly. The secret is once again in the imagery. It begins when Mr. Beaver mentions Aslan for the first time: all the children have a strong reaction to the sound of the name, even though they don't know who Aslan is. The narrator likens the feeling to the experience of having a dream that inspires awe, terror or joy. The wording of this section is vital to its success. The narrator not only describes the unknown in terms that child readers might find familiar, he speaks to the readers directly in order to prompt an emotional response: "Perhaps it has sometimes happened to you in a dream that someone says something to you which you don't understand but in the dream it feels as if it had some enormous meaning" (65). The text then describes the children's reactions, which further classify this unknown feeling in ways readers will understand. Peter feels "brave and adventurous," Susan hears music and smells something delicious, Lucy gets the classic "beginning of the holidays" feeling, while Edmund—whom we know is a bad egg—feels "mysterious horror" (65). (Oops! Don't react this way, kids—it might mean you're enthralled by the forces of evil!)

Once the text establishes a relationship between "Aslan" and the "weird but really amazing feeling," it reinforces this over and over again. Aslan is the source of "the strange feeling—like the first signs of spring, like good news," (74) he "isn't safe. But he's good," (75) and he is "good and terrible at the same time" (117). Aslan's physicality is equally potent: when the children finally meet him, "they just caught a glimpse of the golden mane and the great, royal, solemn, overwhelming eyes; and then they found they couldn't look at him and went all trembly" (117). Aslan, Lucy finds, has "terrible paws...if he didn't know how to velvet them!" (118); this comment cleverly contrasts the emotion of terror with the comforting sensation of velvet. Each emotional and sensual episode builds on the one before, and they come to a climax when Aslan's body disappears from the Stone Table. Here, the act of resurrection is itself an emotional catalyst because it is beyond logical interpretation, and it's no wonder that Susan and Lucy are "almost as much frightened as they were glad" (147).

All of these episodes illustrate Lewis' conscious purpose in the Narnia chronicles: they work to steal past the watchful dragons and prompt a religious experience in readers *without mentioning religion*. Each episode focuses on certain defined emotions—wonderment, awe, terror and joy—which are often associated with spiritual ecstasy, and by connecting them with Aslan, the text is also mapping a firsthand religious experience of the Son of God in our world: Jesus. It worked on me: though I was never particularly religious, the experience of the spiritual sublime in Narnia has stayed with me ever since.

Perhaps I should have ended up a little bit more saintly because of this experience—after all, it's not every day one has a significant religious moment. But Narnia was also responsible for teaching me a very different lesson. It was a lesson that possibly didn't have quite the effect Lewis may have imagined, but it has shaped my entire approach to life. I can see it here, right down in the deepest, fetid, swampy hole of my psyche. Look away, please—it's hideous! Narnia taught me all about sin, which, as I learned in *The Lion, the Witch and the Wardrobe*, comes in "a round box, tied with green silk ribbon" (37). If you don't know what I'm talking about, you've *definitely* never been to Narnia.

As *The Lion, the Witch and the Wardrobe* teaches, sin occurs when you know something is bad and you do it anyway. Who could for a moment imagine that the cruel-voiced woman with the weird white skin and overly red mouth could be anything other than evil? For Edmund and other children of the 1950s, the White Witch's appearance and manner may have been their only clues to her evil nature, but as a child of the 1980s, I had no excuse: I lived in the era of Stranger Danger campaigns, and I was programmed to run a mile if a strange grown-up offered me sweets and a ride in a car.

The confectionery itself was another dead giveaway: while Lucy ate wholesome and prosaic foods for her first meal in Narnia, the sugary stuff tempting Edmund was a mysterious and unnatural concoction, product of the decadent and ungodly Orient. Its appeal lay precisely in its dark, guilty, sensual pleasures, its rich, exotic and emphatically un-British flavors and its improbable, magical origin. The underlying religious message was clearly that sin is dangerous because it is so tempting and seems so sweet. The text is constructed specifically to make readers feel that temptation, otherwise Edmund would have been enthralled by the taste of magical spinach. I wasn't just tempted—like Edmund, I was transfixed by that Turkish Delight, "sweet and light to the very centre" (37). And as the text shows, once you give in to temptation, you're on an express train to hell. Edmund couldn't stop eating the stuff and betrayed his siblings to the Witch in the hope of another taste. I knew just how he felt. Lucy could keep her sardines and hot buttered toast;

I wanted to gorge myself on this devil's dessert for all eternity, even if I had to sell my own grandmother down the river to do so.

Although the text manipulates readers to feel Edmund's temptation, it actively prevents them from enjoying the experience by showing that sin results in guilt and punishment. It implies that Lucy and other "good" children could and would resist that Turkish Delight; only the morally weak would give in. I knew it—I was as bad as Edmund. Both of us were marked like Cain for our sins. On him, you could see it in the eyes (80); on me it was dental cavities, zits and an odd sticky residue from where I'd stuffed oodles of those gooey pink morsels into my gaping maw. But somewhere along the line, Edmund and I parted ways. Edmund's sins were redeemed by Aslan, he got over his Turkish Delight addiction and he went on to become a great king. The lesson of the story is that sinners must atone for their sins and seek forgiveness, but for some reason, I didn't get that part. Perhaps Lewis crafted his demon-food too skillfully, because once I had experienced those guilty pleasures, I never could go back to hot buttered toast. I must be a hard-core sinner, because even now, I wouldn't take redemption if it was offered.

With my psychological safari over, I reemerge into the outside world. Narnia did leave an impact on me after all, although it took a while to trace its spoor across my psyche. It may not have made me less cynical, or more saintly, but I can probably thank Narnia for the nature art on my walls, my enthusiasm for international travel and my occasional moments of previously inexplicable transcendental longing. It's been quite a trip, and as I fish the last lingering psychological creepy-crawlies out of my socks, I find I'm pretty wrung out by the whole experience. Luckily, I can think of just the thing to make me feel good, even if it makes me feel very, *very* bad. . . .

Natasha Giardina lectures in children's literature and young adult litera-ture at the Queensland University of Technology, Brisbane (Australia). She also specializes in youth and popular culture, communication theory, fantasy literature and science fiction. She holds a Bachelor of Arts with first class honors and a Graduate Certificate of Education from James Cook University and is currently completing a Doctorate of Philosophy in twentieth-century children's fantasy literature. In 2002, Natasha received the James Cook University Gluyas Prize for most outstanding postgradu-ate candidate in English literature.

References

Bowman, Mary R. 2003. "A Darker Ignorance: C. S. Lewis and the Nature of the Fall." *Mythlore* 91: 62–78.

Egoff, Sheila. 1981. *Thursday's Child: Trends and Patterns in Contemporary Children's Literature.* Chicago: American Library Association.

Filmer, Kath. 1993. *The Fiction of C. S. Lewis: Mask and Mirror.* New York: St. Martin's Press.

Lewis, C. S. 1966. *Of Other Worlds: Essays and Stories.* Ed. Walter Hooper. New York: Harcourt, Brace & World.

———. 1980. *The Lion, the Witch and the Wardrobe.* London: Lions.

Pinsent, Pat. 2002. "Narnia: An Affirmative Vision." *Papers: Explorations Into Children's Literature* 12, no. 1: 10–19.

Postman, Neil. 1983. *The Disappearance of Childhood.* London: W. H. Allen.

Rudd, David. 2002. "Myth-Making—or Just Taking the Myth? The Dangers of Myth Becoming Fact in Lewis's Narnia Series." *Papers: Explorations Into Children's Literature* 12, no. 1: 30–39.

NAOMI WOOD

God in the Details:
Narrative Voice and Belief
in The Chronicles of Narnia

S A CHILD GROWING UP in a devout Evangelical Christian family, I knew that imagination must be carefully constrained by distinguishing between revealed truth and the merely make-believe. Though gifts appeared in stockings every Christmas morning, we did not believe in Santa Claus because Santa was not real; though we could not see them and tangible evidence for their existence was more scant than evidence for Santa, God and Christ were real. Of the many books I read, none played a larger part in my imaginative life than those by C. S. Lewis. With them, I could be confident that no unauthorized doctrine need be feared—no suspicious tendencies toward Roman Catholicism, pantheism, occultism, atheism or any of the myriad belief systems deemed untrue. And in those books my imagination sought relief from the scarier aspects of the Bible—the seemingly random way some were blessed no matter what they did (King David, for example) and others were cursed no matter what their intentions were (what *was* so wrong about Cain's offering "the fruit of the ground" instead of a blood sacrifice?), the fear that I might inadvertently have committed the unforgivable sin. By contrast, the Narnian chronicles offered, to use Tolkien's famous phrase, "escape, consolation and recovery" (1947). Lewis is known for the force and accessibility of his narrative style; the narrator of The Chronicles of Narnia is a fine example: he draws readers in and then establishes parameters for spiritual fulfill-ment and moral agency through the imagination. What is the result of such a strategy?

The Chronicles of Narnia inspire belief because of the distinctive narrative voice, a seductive voice that makes the marvelous seem rea-sonable, almost (but not detrimentally) mundane. Peter J. Schakel en-capsulates the narrator's appeal:

> He establishes the appealing tone of the stories and creates an inti-mate, personal bond with the reader. He conveys a reassuring feel-ing that events are under control, that ultimately, for the followers of Aslan, everything will turn out in a satisfactory way. And he creates a moral center for the stories, a sense of decency, honor, respect, com-mon sense and intelligence. (2002, 88)

However, even though the narrator reassures, The Chronicles con-clude in an apocalyptic melee. In *The Last Battle*, the narrator relin-quishes his story after having killed off his entire cast, destroyed his lovingly created world and transferred the action to a new location:

> "And for us this is the end of all the stories, and we can most truly say that they all lived happily ever after. But for them it was only the be-ginning of the real story.... [N]ow at last they were beginning Chap-ter One of the Great Story which no one on earth has read: which goes on forever: in which every chapter is better than the one before" (2000a, 210–11).

Employing standard fairy-tale closure, the tale requires us to detach from any imaginative fulfillment experienced in Narnia to gesture to stories that cannot be told and will never be read by anyone alive. The shift may be intentional on Lewis' part to drive readers back to this world and the religion he sanctioned here. On the other hand, it also opens the possibility of exploring other prospects for imaginative spiri-tuality beyond the "merely Christian," to reference his famous apologia, *Mere Christianity*.

"It's All in Plato"

The Narnian chronicles employ a pervasive Platonism that emphasizes the secondary nature of representation—and of nature itself as a representation—while at the same time insisting upon a necessary correlation between works of the imagination, of material reality and of Reality Beyond (or Within).[1] In *The Last Battle* the Lord Digory, an old professor, explains that the Narnia the characters have hitherto known was only "a shadow or a copy of the real Narnia which has always been here and always will be here: just as in our own world, England and all, is only a shadow or copy of something in Aslan's real world.... It's all in Plato, all in Plato" (2000a, 195). Even the "shadow" Narnia is better than the cavern (an allusion to Plato's cave allegory) that the malevolent Lady of the Green Kirtle insists is the only reality in *The Silver Chair*. Puddleglum insists,

> Suppose we *have* only dreamed, or made up, all those things—trees and grass and sun and moon and stars and Aslan himself. Suppose we have. Then all I can say is that, in that case, the made-up things seem a good deal more important than the real ones. (2000e, 182)

Of course, the reader knows that Puddleglum has *not* made up Narnia and Aslan and has actually seen them, so that his faith in them is justified, even if the applications to Christianity in our own world might seem a bit more tenuous. As Eleanor Cameron perceptively notes of Puddleglum's credo, "It is a surprising statement, in a way, coming from Lewis, for it reminds us of the existentialist saying that he will live with as much dignity as possible, according to moral principles which he himself must create, in a universe of the Absurd which is not aware of his existence" (1969, 43). And, indeed, this is one of the ironies of the entire Narnian cycle—that this alternate world inspires desires for connection between human and beast, between beast and tree and between the mundane and the marvelous that cannot be satisfied, however much some may wish it.

---

[1] Lewis belongs to a long tradition of imaginative writers who put their own stamp on reality, authoring new worlds with powerful words, as does God in the book of Genesis. J. R. R. Tolkien contends that fantasy develop his own version of reality; moreover, as a Christian and an idealist, Lewis insisted that his desire must derive from some reality, if not here, then elsewhere.

The Lion, the Narrative "I" and the Reader

The Chronicles' narrator describes an intimate relationship not only between the reader and the author, but also between humans and the divine. This relationship is conveyed through two registers: one a combination of the avuncular and the professorial, associated with the main narrator of the books; the other hortatory and ecstatic, associated with the Lion, Aslan, the King of Beasts and the "God" of that world. These different registers appeal to different sorts of desire: the one to the reader who wishes to be taught, the second to the reader who wishes to be engulfed. Lewis' flawed and less-than-omniscient narrator may be an inadvertent result of hasty writing and incomplete editing, but the work also enacts the difference between the narrator and The Narrator, secondary creator and primary creator, analogous to Plato's distinction between the copy and the real thing, the imitation and the Form.

Although the narrator of the Narnian chronicles does not participate in the events of the story, he does break in with personal comments, reminiscences and reminders of his presence. Of the seven books, five begin with an announcement that this is a story: the first two, in fact, begin almost with the same sentence: "Once there were four children whose names were Peter, Susan, Edmund and Lucy...," emphasizing that these are *stories* and also that they connect with the fairy-tale tradition ("once there were"). Drawing his reader in by encouraging connections between the experiences he's described in Narnia with the reader's presumably similar experiences, the narrator establishes common ground by involving the reader in memories or, more interestingly, by *creating* memories. In *The Lion, the Witch and the Wardrobe*, for example, the narrator asks

> Have you ever had a gallop on a horse? Think of that; and then take away the heavy noise of the hoofs and the jingle of the bits and imagine instead the almost noiseless padding of the great paws. Then imagine instead of the black or gray or chestnut back of the horse the soft roughness of golden fur, and the mane flying back in the wind. And then imagine you are going about twice as fast as the fastest racehorse. But this is a mount that doesn't need to be guided and never grows tired.... (2000b, 165)

Here the description constructs two imaginative experiences instead of one (for those who have never ridden either a horse or a lion): thus, the description first relates the sounds and tactile experience of riding a horse and then subtracts from that to describe the sounds and experience of riding a lion. In keeping with an overarching allegorical sensibility which searches for likenesses between unlike things, here the narrator begins with what is like, simile-fashion, and then contrasts with what is unlike, emphasizing the pleasurable difference between our world of riding horses and Narnia where lions are ridden. By emphasizing materials, sound and touch, the narrator makes this imagined world real in a way that less sensory description would not accomplish; we are invited first to imagine a terrestrial experience we know might occur and then, by subtraction, led to the more unbelievable experience of riding a sentient and willing lion.

In addition to creating and then amending memories and personal connections, the narrator also acts as tutor or expert teaching the reader the (un)natural history of this world, evoking the mock-pedantic tone of the titles Lucy sees on Mr. Tumnus' shelf in her first, memorable, visit to Narnia (*Nymphs and their Ways* or *Men, Monks and Gamekeepers: A Study in Popular Legend*). He first evokes the mundane and familiar and then connects it with the marvelous. In the first chapters of *The Lion, the Witch and the Wardrobe*, the narrator tirelessly points out that it is a very stupid thing to shut oneself in a wardrobe (while omitting an even more important safety tip about not going to have tea with strangers!), rather in the spirit of the cautionary tales Lewis Carroll parodies in *Alice in Wonderland*. The prosaic quality of the warning lends credibility to the wondrous events that follow, reminiscent as it is of the sort of thing uncles might say to nieces and nephews, offering explanations that invoke common sense and allow for the marvelous without the shrillness and urgency of parental admonition.

Other examples of the narrator's tutorial function abound. When Mr. Beaver calls the children and Mrs. Beaver out of their hiding place to witness that Father Christmas has at last made it past the White Witch's defenses to bring Christmas to Narnia by shouting "It's all right! It isn't *Her*!" the narrator comments: "This was bad grammar of course, but that is how beavers talk when they are excited; I mean, in Narnia—in our world they usually don't talk at all" (2000b, 106). The focus on grammar detracts from disbelief that beavers talk; then he reminds us that in Narnia, if not here, they do. The reason "you so seldom find more than one dragon in the same country" is that they fight and eat one another (2000f, 94). Even the miraculous returning of the stone statues to life is described through the mundane simile of starting a fire with newspaper (2000b, 167).

One of the most appealing traits of the narrator is his enthusiasm for matters of eating and drinking; the frequent feasts and meals described in The Chronicles again combine the marvelous and the mundane in unforgettable mixtures. Meals of tea or breakfast include buttered toast or skillets of bacon, eggs and mushrooms, but the chefs are fauns and dwarfs and the dwellings correspondingly miniature and cozy. No puritan, this narrator describes with relish the flavor and effects of beer and wine, showing Bacchus and Silenus joining a romp with Aslan in *Prince Caspian*. Even the meals of trees are described with pungent appreciation for the probable tastes of loam versus Somerset's pink soil (the first "looks almost exactly like chocolate," the second is "lighter and sweeter") (2000d, 212).

The narrator evinces a marked passion for natural beauty, a conservatism not usually associated with the religious right today: the desire to preserve trees, landscapes and other natural features and to do away with human interventions into the landscape. In *Prince Caspian*, such signs of human progress as bridges are summarily destroyed when Aslan returns to liberate the country. One of the most horrifying episodes in *The Last Battle* is the felling of the trees by the Calormenes using talking horses as slaves. The reader sees the trees as independent and beautiful beings, and their desecration is the equivalent of rape and murder, the scars left on the landscape signifying gross violation of *people*, if not humans.

In addition to constructing his own obviously masculine persona, this avuncular, professorial narrator constructs an implied reader by frequently referring to the reader as "you"; this reader is assumed to share certain priorities, experiences and values, or, perhaps more insidiously, is willing to learn the implicit and explicit values the narrator attempts to teach: not just openness to wonder, but also disgust and distaste for progressive politics or certain kinds of social engineering. On many different occasions the reader is invited to dismiss certain characters simply because of their physical qualities—the "prim dumpy little girls with fat legs" or the boys who look like pigs in *Prince Caspian* who don't "deserve" the Lion's liberation. In *The Voyage of the Dawn Treader*, Eustace is criticized for enjoying informational books (the "wrong sort" of book) and a scientific mindset; his parents are criticized for the sin of being "up-to-date" vegetarians and teetotalers. In the Narnian chronicles we learn to classify people according to their type or species: there are two "sorts" of giants: respectable, though dim, ones with old families, and the "other sort," bad ones who allied themselves with the White Witch (2000b, 174); "Black Dwarfs" are more hostile to humans than "Red Dwarfs." The dark, turbaned people of the South, the Calormenes, are "wise, wealthy, courteous, cruel and ancient" (2000f, 62) and embody every Orientalist stereotype. To be the "right sort," to belong to the wondrous country that is Narnia, readers may infer that they must accept all these classifications as natural and correct, with all their connotations of British elitism and racism.[2]

If Lewis' narrator draws the reader in with appeals to adventure and appetite, his representation of Aslan suggests other things about the project of imagining worlds, for good or evil. After he had already written the series, Lewis commented that one of his unspoken purposes was to reinject readers' sense of the divine with new romance, new magic: the fairy-tale form allowed him to "steal past a certain inhibition which had paralyzed much of my own religion in childhood. Why did one find it so hard to feel as one was told one ought to feel about God or about the sufferings of Christ? I thought the chief reason was that one was told one ought to." Figuring Christ as a lion allowed Lewis to "steal past those watchful dragons" guarding against the "ought to" of Sunday-school dogma (1982, 73).

We are only gradually introduced to the Lion, Aslan, who is the King of Beasts and, therefore, King of the Narnian country of Beasts. We first learn about him through characters' responses to him: even the sound of his name makes Peter feel "brave and adventurous," causes Susan to

---

[2] Such indoctrination was not unconscious: Lewis described the power that iconic fictions have to convey not only a sense of character and action but also a sense of social history. Praising Mr. Badger from *The Wind in the Willows*, Lewis writes, "Consider Mr. Badger in *The Wind in the Willows*—that extraordinary amalgam of high rank, coarse manners, gruffness, shyness and goodness. The child who has once met Mr. Badger has ever afterwards, in its bones, a knowledge of humanity and of English social history, which it could not get in any other way" (1982, 62). Of course, this naturalizing of privilege and virtue as somehow inherent in species, family or class is precisely what Lewis' critics object to in The Chronicles of Narnia. Like Grahame, Lewis promotes ideologically conservative behaviors, attitudes and values in his imaginative play, understanding that this could give readers "a knowledge of humanity and of English social history," through inculcating prejudice and bigotry.

experience the pleasure of "some delicious smell or . . . delightful strain of music," and Lucy to feel as you do when "it is the beginning of the holidays or the beginning of summer," while Edmund the traitor feels "a sensation of mysterious horror" (2000b, 68). Tiresome Eustace, enchanted in the form of a dragon, is afraid when he meets Aslan: "You may think that, being a dragon, I could have knocked any lion out easily enough. But it wasn't that kind of fear. I wasn't afraid of it eating me, I was just afraid of *it*—if you can understand" (2000f, 106–7). And indeed, Aslan is frequently introduced by means of his effect upon characters in the book. We learn indirectly about Aslan's goodness, solemnity, ferocity and so forth, along with the imbibed message that any hostile reaction to Aslan is an indictment of the moral status of the one who responds. Though everyone who encounters Aslan experiences a degree of fear, the worthy love him, while the unworthy can hear only the roar of a lion (as Uncle Andrew does in *The Magician's Nephew*) or feel only hatred (as does Jadis/the White Witch).

An important difference between Lewis' childhood's Sunday school, stained-glass Jesus and Aslan is Aslan's physicality: repeatedly his vibrant golden color, rich mane and "velvet" paws are mentioned; Lucy and Susan actually plunge their hands into and stroke his mane on several occasions. Aslan's embodiment permits a relationship with the divine that combines delight in the wildness and power of an iconic predator with the pleasure of playing with and stroking pets. The narrator vibrantly describes many scenes of play and celebration, romping and feasting so that there is no doubt that a relationship with Aslan is about celebrating the body as much as the spirit. Aslan can even joke, albeit aggressively: when he first encounters the disbelieving Trumpkin, he tosses the unhappy, humiliated and terrified dwarf in the air like a kitten before making "friends" with him (2000d, 154).

As the series progresses, Aslan is increasingly associated with, and credited with writing, an ineffable script. The boundaries between story, vision and truth begin to dissolve, pointing to a reality beyond the real. In the first book, *The Lion, the Witch and the Wardrobe*, Aslan stresses that he must follow the "rules" as they are written, even at the cost of his own life (the "Deep Magic" that created the world is Aslan's Father's— "the Emperor-beyond-the-Sea"—and Aslan seems not to know if his self-sacrifice will gain his goal). Rules are reiterated in *The Voyage of the Dawn Treader* less portentously: Aslan is made visible by Lucy's spell because he "follows his own rules." Toward the end of the series in *The Magician's Nephew*, however, Aslan has become the creator of Narnia, the one who sings the world into being, and the one who determines the way the world's story will end. From sharing uncertainty and fear with Lucy and Susan in *The Lion, the Witch and the Wardrobe*, Aslan in later books displays a superior knowledge of the grand narratives of the world (albeit acknowledging that they depend upon mortals—humans, talking animals and so forth—making the right choices). Almost every book features a test of faith and challenge to act irrationally or blindly simply because Aslan has said so: Lucy must wake her elders to follow an Aslan only she can see, Jill must follow signs whose meanings make no obvious sense, Digory must retrieve an apple of life without eating it or taking one for his desperately ill mother. These tests establish and construct Aslan's godlike status by demonstrating that submission and obedience to his word and will are the most important virtues.

By the end, Aslan even rescripts people's conscious intentions: in *The Last Battle*, Emeth, the sole Calormene who ends up in Aslan's country after the end of the Narnian world, is told by Aslan that in spite of his conscious allegiance, his honest search for the good and the true overrides his incorrect belief in Tash. He recounts Aslan's saying to him, "all the service thou hast done to Tash, I account as service done to me.... [B]ecause we are opposites, I take to me the services which thou hast done to him" (2000a, 188–89). Here Emeth's elegant narrative with its semi-biblical cadence underscores the sublime message of the oneness of the good and the impossibility of avoiding or escaping Aslan's powerful definitions of who is in, and who is outside, the kingdom of heaven.

The Chronicles of Narnia are not carefully thought-out fantasy; Lewis meant to go back and reedit them but died before he had the opportunity. Tolkien had reservations about their imaginative coherence, and gaffes are noticeable from minor issues such as inconsistency in the spelling of names (Kalormene/Calormene) to larger issues. Why would a 100-year-winter not have more impact on animals' access to foods such as bread or marmalade (where were these things purchased/traded for?)? How did the grown-up kings and queens of Narnia somehow return to England as children wearing their old clothing? (This transition is managed better in later books.) How, if (as we are told repeatedly) Narnian and earthly time run differently, can the Pevensie children conclude that they must have been summoned by Susan's horn in *Prince Caspian* because it was sounded at nine in the morning in Narnia, the same time they were sitting at the railway station in England waiting to be taken to their several schools?

Even the most obviously allegorical elements break down if examined too closely. To take the core instance, Aslan's sacrifice at the Stone Table: it is questionable whether Aslan "dies for" Narnians' sins in the same way that Jesus is said to have done for our world, as his original bargain was to save the life of an otherworldly person, Edmund, a "son of Adam." The entire Narnian world is informed by and dependent upon connections with our own world—as we learn in *Prince Caspian* from no less a person than Aslan himself, Caspian "could be no true King of Narnia unless, like the Kings of old, [he was] a son of Adam and came from the world of Adam's sons" (2000d, 217). And Aslan tells Lucy and Edmund in *The Voyage of the Dawn Treader* that they were brought to Narnia so that they might learn his name in their own world. Even though Narnia was not initially created for our world's sake (as we discover in *The Magician's Nephew*), that seems to be its function in the series. Such logical inconsistencies undercut imaginative authority or moral persuasiveness, quite aside from the difficulties analogues to doctrines in this world present. In this, the series enacts the demands Aslan makes of his followers: to believe and obey beyond reason.

Effects of Lewis' Narrator

Lewis is conceived by some as a species of Protestant saint, his writings as only slightly less authoritative than Scripture. Lewis' biographer and hagiographer Walter Hooper asserts that Lewis' description of Aslan's Last Judgment has "a terrible beauty that makes the heart ache, and which is perhaps only matched by Dante's *Paradiso*" (1979, 228) and that "we"—readers—desire Narnia because of Aslan and what he represents, "because the desire is one of the things he has implanted in us" (222). Hooper's impersonal pronoun ("he") conflates divine and authorial power much to the advantage of Lewis. For Thomas Howard, Narnia "is the very homeland which lies at the back of every man's imagination, which we all yearn for (even if we are wholly unaware of such a yearning)" (1980, 21). Such responses come from Christian readers who respond positively to Narnia's iconographic and allegorical elements and who believe that these elements can plant the seed of the Christian faith in readers.

Not everyone, however, experiences these responses, despite the claims of Lewis' promoters. Professional critics and reviewers of children's literature as frequently condemn as praise The Chronicles: acclaimed children's author Penelope Lively writes that Lewis' "underlying savagery...makes the books so sinister" that she was "disturbed, even...sickened" by them, and Peter Hollindale asserts that "the Narnia books reveal a startlingly immature and vindictive sensibility" (1968, 129, 126; 1977, 21). More recently, agnostic Philip Pullman has expressed his disgust with the series' racism and sexism, while Christian John Goldthwaite objects to the books' designation of the beautiful people as the only true heirs of the kingdom of heaven, as well as the petty and violent retributive acts legitimized by the narrative (1998, 6; 1996, 228ff).[3]

The voice of the narrator in the Narnia books evokes such a distinctive picture of God so as to elicit some anxiety even from the conscientious Christian. Responding to the letter of a woman whose son was afraid that he loved Aslan more than Jesus, Lewis wrote:

> Laurence can't *really* love Aslan more than Jesus, even if he feels that's what he is doing. For the things he loves Aslan for doing or saying are simply the things Jesus really did and said. So that when Laurence thinks he is loving Aslan, he is really loving Jesus: and perhaps loving Him more than he ever did before. Of course there is one thing Aslan has that Jesus has not—I mean, the body of a lion.... Now if Laurence is bothered because he finds the lion-body seems nicer to him than the man-body, I don't think he *need* be bothered at all. God knows all about the way a little boy's imagination works (He made it, after all) and knows that at a certain age the idea of talking and friendly animals is very attractive. (1985, 52–53)

---

[3] British critics tend to be more aware of and more sensitive to Lewis' representation of class hierarchy and find it more objectionable than do many American readers. The Narnian chronicles are informed by a Tory sensibility which sounds much more glamorous from a distance. One effect of the Narnian chronicles has been to create Anglophiles of an England that never existed and which, even if it did, would not welcome most of its admirers. Lewis is probably responsible for more English majors proposing to study medieval and Renaissance literature and for more people dressing up in armor than anyone except possibly Lewis' friend and colleague J. R. R. Tolkien.

Now while this letter may have been comforting to its recipients, it does not really solve the problem the boy raised; that is, that Jesus of Nazareth is a different sort of person represented in a radically different text than is Aslan in the books about Narnia. The consolations of most Christian philosophies are by no means as hearty as wine-saturated romps in the moonlight with Bacchus, Silenus and Aslan; as thrilling as a voyage to the edge of the world; as magical as a land in which multiple mythologies coexist in relative harmony. Not surprisingly, some readers embrace Narnia's pagan flavor in preference to its muscular Christianity.

For me, Lewis' books offered a larger world than the one I inhabited as a child; accordingly I dreamed of studying medieval and Renaissance literature at Oxford and becoming an English professor and a female C. S. Lewis. Along the way to adulthood, I became disenchanted: I realized that being a medievalist meant I should have learned Latin and Greek in childhood; that Lewis' vision of medieval wonder was ahistorical and highly idiosyncratic; that Lewis' world didn't include women as thinkers. But as a child, I took from the stories that alcohol was not sinful (after I'd looked "teetotalism" up in the dictionary and wrapped my mind around it being criticized by my idol); Lewis made fried mushrooms and tea sound so good that I made extra efforts to try them and to make them part of my regular diet. On the other hand, I've never tried Turkish Delight, and I've developed into a liberal who loathes the militaristic and chauvinistic values of Narnian rulers and who has deep skepticism about the possibility of "true kingship" by appointment from any god. Though I'm still exhilarated by tales of valiant combat, I have learned enough of war to be skeptical. Even now, many years later, the reassuring, commonsensical and humorous stance of Lewis' narrator draws me in even as his smug and retrograde pronouncements slight my politics, my ethics and my values.

Perhaps Lewis trod a more precarious tightrope than he admitted here; by acknowledging that orthodox depictions of God leave many cold and by offering imaginative alternatives that preempt and even surpass those depictions in imaginative effect, Lewis created a situation in which individuals may well be led to search for truth in less approved avenues, opening up the sluices of imagination to include not only Christianity but also other spiritual traditions. If the God in the details repels a careful reader, alternatives may be sought. Ultimately, the imaginative satisfactions of Narnia potentially subvert any easy correlation of Narnia with Christian life and may even subvert belief in Christianity itself.

> *Naomi Wood was born and raised in Congo (formerly Zaire). After years of feeling apologetic about her taste in books, she suddenly has been caught up in the popular-culture vanguard, which astonishes her. She teaches children's and adolescent literature and Victorian studies at Kansas State University, where she is an associate professor of English. She has published articles on a range of fantasy and magic realist authors including George MacDonald, Lucy Lane Clifford, Charles Kingsley, C. S. Lewis, Philip Pullman, Virginia Hamilton and others.*

References

Cameron, Eleanor. 1969. *The Green and Burning Tree: On the Writing and Enjoyment of Children's Books.* Boston: Atlantic-Little, Brown.

Goldthwaite, John. 1996. *The Natural History of Make-Believe: A Guide to the Principal Works of Britain, Europe and America.* New York and Oxford: Oxford Univ. Press.

Hollindale, Peter. 1977. "The Image of the Beast: C. S. Lewis's Chronicles of Narnia." *The Use of English* 28.2: 16–21.

Hooper, Walter. 1979. *Past Watchful Dragons: The Narnian Chronicles of C. S. Lewis.* New York: Collier Books.

Howard, Thomas. 1980. *The Achievement of C. S. Lewis.* Wheaton, IL: Harold Shaw Publishers.

Lewis, C. S. 1982. *Of This and Other Worlds.* Ed. Walter Hooper. New York: Collins.

———. 1985. *C. S. Lewis: Letters to Children.* Ed. Lyle Dorsett and Marjorie Lamp Mead. London: Macmillan.

———. 2000a. *The Last Battle.* New York: HarperTrophy.

———. 2000b. *The Lion, the Witch and the Wardrobe.* New York: HarperTrophy.

———. 2000c. *The Magician's Nephew.* New York: HarperTrophy.

———. 2000d. *Prince Caspian.* New York: HarperTrophy.

———. 2000e. *The Silver Chair.* New York: HarperTrophy.

———. 2000f. *The Voyage of the Dawn Treader.* New York: HarperTrophy.

Lively, Penelope. 1968. "The Wrath of God: An Opinion of the 'Narnia Books.'" *The Use of English* 20.1: 126–29.

Pullman, Philip. 1998. "The Dark Side of Narnia." *The Guardian* (1 Oct): 6.

Schakel, Peter J. 2002. *Imagination and the Arts in C. S. Lewis: Journeying to Narnia and Other Worlds*. Columbia: Univ. of Missouri Press.

Tolkien, J. R. R. 1947. "On Fairy-Stories." *The Monsters and the Critics and Other Essays*. Ed. Christopher Tolkien. London: George Allen & Unwin.

SAM MCBRIDE

Coming of Age in Narnia

C. S. LEWIS' NARNIAN ADVENTURES apply a convenient science fiction conceit: no matter how long one spends in Narnia, hardly any time at all has passed back on Earth. As a result, Narnian decades pass by in just a few Earth seconds. This concept is a mind-bender, as Peter and Edmund discuss in *Prince Caspian* at Aslan's How. As the two pass ancient-looking cave drawings, Edmund notes that, technically speaking, he and his siblings are still older (in Narnian time), since the drawings appeared after the Penvensie children's first visit to Narnia. "Yes," Peter responds, "That makes one think" (1951, 156).

Thinking is certainly something Lewis wants his readers to do, even readers of his children's books. Thus the Narnia stories are filled with things worth thinking about: virtues, values, emotions and an underlying Christian theology. One of the issues Lewis wants his young readers to consider is what it means to grow up, to experience the process of maturing, which itself is a central theme of nearly all children's literature.

Such growth affected even the publication of these works. The dedication page of *The Lion, the Witch and the Wardrobe* implies Lewis had in mind a specific audience while writing the book, along with the general audience of children and adults who enjoy fantasy. That specific audience was his goddaughter, Lucy Barfield, who very likely inspired the name of the story's younger heroine. Lewis' dedication implies, however, that by the time of the book's publication, Lucy Barfield had matured to a stage when she would not appreciate fantasy literature; Lewis expresses hope that after yet more growth she will come to appreciate fantasy once again.

The conjunction of the theme of growing toward maturity and Lewis' science fiction conceit gives his characters a unique experience not directly available to readers such as Lucy Barfield: while remaining children (back at home), his characters can grow and mature toward adulthood (in Narnia). Thus the process of growing toward maturity is a key to understanding the characters. In fact, the Narnia books reveal Lewis himself maturing as a writer in his ability to depict realistically admirable characters.

Lewis provides several types of maturation experience for the characters. The first of these is the most mundane: while in Narnia the children mature physically as well as emotionally. By the end of *The Lion, the Witch and the Wardrobe*, for example, the four children have grown to be adult kings and queens. Peter is tall and large-chested, while Susan is tall, beautiful and gentle; Edmund is grave, quiet and wise, while Lucy is gay, golden-haired and valiant. All four speak Elizabethan prose. On their return to Earth, they resume their childhood state, but they recall their feelings and experiences as Narnian adults; in *Prince Caspian* Susan refers to her earlier Narnian maturity as having been "sort of grown-up" (27).

The most important means of Narnian growth toward maturity is the intensely painful or frightening life-changing event. Such events produce emotional, intellectual and spiritual growth, occasionally accompanied with at least temporary physical transformation. Examples are Peter's first battle with a wolf, Edmund's rescue from the White Queen and Eustace's awakening as a dragon. For Peter, slaying the wolf is a rite of passage, symbolic of becoming a man. Edmund and Eustace's life-changing transformations are comparable to (and in fact allegorically parallel to) conversion to Christianity. For both Edmund and Eustace, however, the transformation includes putting aside childish attitudes.

Edmund's transformation is fully detailed in *The Lion, the Witch and the Wardrobe*. Edmund is the "difficult" sibling, making unpleasant company because of his childish behavior. On the children's first full day in the Professor's house, Edmund is the one grumbling because of the rain. On Lucy's return from her first visit to Narnia, he is the one questioning her sanity ("Batty," he rudely says in Lucy's presence, "Quite batty" [1950, 21]). Over the next several chapters we learn that Edmund is spiteful, self-centered, lacking in self-awareness and mean to smaller children. Much later in the book the cause of these negative character traits is revealed: the influence of Edmund's boarding school. In his autobiographical *Surprised by Joy* Lewis compares the boarding school he attended with a concentration camp. Even in his fiction he paints consistently negative pictures of life at English boarding schools.

One primary effect of Lewis' experience in boarding school can be summed up by the word "priggery." The oppressively hierarchic nature of a school, Lewis concludes, either breaks a child's spirit or produces within him arrogance, contempt for his superiors and a tendency to transfer the negative treatment one has received from superiors, or "bloods," into equally poor treatment of inferiors. Edmund seems drawn from Lewis' own experiences at the school he identifies as "Malvern" in *Surprised by Joy*. Edmund assumes he possesses a maturity level that he does not, a fundamental element of priggery. Remember that Lewis distinguishes between the two older and the two younger children, implying different stages of development for them. Peter and Susan are the two who talk among themselves and with the Professor in regard to Lucy's initial claim that she visited a country through the wardrobe. On their return visit in *Prince Caspian* Peter and Susan are the two capable of swimming, an ability Lewis connects with maturity, or at least age. Yet Edmund seeks to present himself to all three of his siblings as part of the older group. To Lucy he asserts that "everyone" knows fauns are not reliable (1951, 38), implying by this, "everyone knows except you, because you are too young to know." To Peter and Susan he says, about Lucy, "That's the worst of young kids, they always—," implying that he does not consider himself one of those "young kids" (41).

Edmund remains in this preoccupied, self-important state until he visits the castle of the White Witch. The next few hours of his life produce a remarkable transformation. While traveling in the Queen's sleigh he realizes he has deluded himself: the Queen is not good and kind; she does not have his best interests at heart; he has no right to wish himself superior to his siblings and he does not really wish for revenge against them. When he witnesses the Queen turning a celebratory group of animals into stone statutes, he begins to feel pity for someone other than himself.

By the time Edmund rejoins his siblings, he has advanced to a more mature state. The exact moment of arrival at this state is not clear, as is probably true in real life, too. While we see in Edmund a definite "before" and "after," there is no one single moment in between, but rather an extended period of experience, realization and growth. Edmund displays his newfound maturity, both through a decrease of immature behaviors and the presence of more positive character traits. The new Edmund is brave, self-sacrificing and deferent to his siblings, especially his elders.

Eustace's life-changing experience parallels Edmund's, but is more extreme. At the beginning of *The Voyage of the Dawn Treader* Eustace possesses all of Edmund's faults, along with the irritating (and un-Lewis-like) traits of pacifism, teetotaling and vegetarianism. The irony is that while Eustace does not eat meat, he acts like an animal ("I've been pretty beastly," he apologizes later [1952, 91]), and in Narnia he becomes one: a dragon. Again like Edmund, this event brings about self-revelation and transformation. Lewis takes Eustace one step further, however, when he acknowledges that his transformation, though dramatic, is not 100% effective; as Lewis says, Eustace "had relapses" (93). The maturity that results from a life-changing event includes leaving behind well-entrenched negative habits and struggling to implement new habits; in other words, it requires still more growth to achieve its full effect.

When the Pevensie children pursue the White Stag to the lamppost at the end of *The Lion, the Witch and the Wardrobe*, they "de-mature" physically (and judging by their language, intellectually as well) in an instant. This fact allows for a third method of maturing when they revisit Narnia in later books. The four Pevensies reenter Narnia in *Prince Caspian* at the physical maturity level they possessed when they left Earth. Yet a few hours in Narnia returns to their minds and bodies some of the maturity they had achieved in their earlier visits. When the children discover the gifts given them by Father Christmas during their first Narnian adventure, Peter is subtly transformed by unsheathing his sword and Susan by testing her bow. They soon feel and act differently, more like their old Narnian selves; before long Edmund beats the dwarf Trumpkin in a sword fight and Susan bests him at archery. Rather than suggesting the children had carefully maintained their skills through practice back on Earth, Lewis implies their presence in Narnia is enough to bring to their minds and bodies attitudes and skills from their previous visit. For Edmund (and later for Eustace in *The Silver Chair*), simply breathing the Narnian air causes "his arms and fingers [to remember] their old skill" (1951, 100). By her second day back in Narnia, Lucy is only one-third an English school girl and two-thirds a Narnian queen (128). When Aslan reveals himself to the children in *Prince Caspian*, after only a few days in Narnia, Lucy notes that Peter and Edmund appear "more like men than boys" (150).

The children notice the change themselves: Peter says to Susan, "It's no good behaving like kids now that we are back in Narnia. You're a queen here" (21). The Narnian context, in other words, requires a different maturity level than does the earthly context. This gives special relevance to the phrase "Once a King (or Queen) in Narnia, always a King IN Narnia"; the Earth children need only return to Narnia to resume that state, including some of the physical and mental maturity they had achieved in their earlier visit.

Some, but not all. Because the children return to Narnia as children, even though they had previously grown to adulthood there, they will experience some of the same physical and emotional growth on their later visit that they had already accomplished on their earlier visit. When the children save the life of Trumpkin the dwarf, he comments that they should hide the boat so that soldiers from Miraz's army won't see it; Peter, High King with years of military experience behind him, reproaches himself for not thinking of that himself (32). Some knowledge and skill he possessed before has been lost and must be relearned. Readers can imagine more intriguing examples of repeat growth; for example, during her journey in *The Voyage of the Dawn Treader* Lucy might lose a tooth that she had already lost once before during her earlier visits through the wardrobe. Admittedly, Lewis makes little use of this déjà vu growth, but the science fiction implications are intriguing.

At the same time, while returning to Narnia produces some rapid regrowth, it also draws to the characters' minds a disconcerting awareness of the process of maturing. When Edmund and Lucy return to Narnia in *The Voyage of the Dawn Treader*, only one Earth year has passed since their previous visits, yet Prince Caspian has experienced three Narnian years of growth. Both Pevensies recognize Caspian, but the two years' difference in age positions him as somewhat more mature and augments the occasional conflicts that arise between him and the other children (as on Deathwater Island). Even more extreme is Eustace's second visit when Caspian is no longer a teen king but an old man approaching death.

The children's return visits to Narnia are different from previous visits in part because they are reentering Narnia at a more mature state of development, in earthly terms, than when they left it. When the Pevensies arrive at Cair Paravel in *Prince Caspian*, a full Earth year after their first Narnian adventure, they are forced to survive on their own, in contrast with their first visit when they relied on the Beavers' aid. In *Surprised by Joy*, Lewis associates travel habits with maturity; the more mature an adolescent becomes, the more liberties and luxuries he will give himself on the train journey to and from boarding school (1955, 56). The Pevensies' experience suggests the opposite is equally true: the more mature they become, the greater travel-related hardships they can endure.

Maturing on Earth impacts the children's Narnian adventures in one other important way: when characters become too old (in Earth years) they are prohibited from returning to Narnia (not, at least, until their deaths). Fortunately, as Peter makes clear at the end of *Prince Caspian*, the combination of Earth and Narnian maturity makes the prohibition bearable. What, precisely, makes children "too old" to come back to Narnia remains unspoken in the novels. Since Peter would be fourteen and Susan thirteen (in Earth years) when they assist Caspian to the throne, the children are heading into their adolescence. Perhaps this is a time when children become less open to the world of the imagination and focus more on the social reality of peers, schoolwork and looming adulthood (as Lewis worried concerning Lucy Barfield). Of course, contributing to these changes is the onset of puberty, and thus sexual development is coincident with, if not the cause of, the prohibition on returning to Narnia.

Sexual development and the corresponding development of gendered self-identity is an important part of maturing. Lewis' Narnia books do not directly address sexuality, yet the books do support the development of a proper self-concept based on the fact of one's gender. Gender difference is especially pronounced for the Pevensie children while they are in Narnia. At the Beavers' home Peter goes outside with Mr. Beaver to engage in a traditional hunter-gatherer activity: fishing through a hole in the ice. Meanwhile, the girls stay indoors with Mrs. Beaver to aid her in domesticity: filling the tea kettle, setting the table, warming the plates and drawing Mr. Beaver's beer. What precisely Edmund is doing during this interval is not stated; one can presume he is doing nothing, or at least nothing helpful. Frankly, Lewis doesn't indicate Peter actually helps Mr. Beaver in any practical way while fishing, but only that he accompanies him. While girls are expected to stay busy in the domestic sphere, boys apparently are not.

Gender difference is reinforced, even taught, to three of the children during Father Christmas' visit. Father Christmas, of course, bestows gifts. The experience is a moment of realization for the children, since the gifts are individually suited to each child's temperament, and because the gifts are "adult" in nature, rather than trinkets or toys. Peter is "silent and solemn" (1951, 104) on receiving his sword and shield. Lewis notes the weapons are "just the right size" for Peter, implying they are scaled-down versions of adult weapons; yet they are indeed real weapons (not the plastic imitations that will likely be sold in conjunction with the films based on Lewis' books).

Susan's bow, arrows and horn, and Lucy's dagger are also "tools not toys," as Father Christmas puts it (104). Though not a weapon, Lucy's bottle of cordial is a serious, purposeful gift. These items bring to the children's minds a deeper realization of their position within the (fantasy) world of Narnia and a sense of personal responsibility being laid upon them. Thus the gifts themselves function to aid the children in maturing.

At the same time, the gifts, and Father Christmas' words about them, communicate a truth about the children's gendered identity. A sword is obviously a weapon for close offensive combat (we'll ignore the potential phallic associations out of deference to Lewis' distaste for Freudianism); a bow and arrow are most effective at a distance, while a dagger is at best defensive. In case the girls don't perceive this difference, Father Christmas tells them overtly that they are not to fight in the battle. In fact, they should only consider using their weapons "in great need" (104–5). When Lucy asserts she could find herself brave enough to engage in combat, Father Christmas makes clear that bravery is not the issue; rather, gender is.

This leads to one of the most deceptively clear statements in Lewis' oeuvre: "Battles are ugly when women fight." The statement begs many questions. As a statement by Father Christmas, does it also reflect the views of C. S. Lewis? What makes women's battles any uglier than men's? What does "ugly" mean, since Lewis' experience of combat during World War I taught him firsthand the ugliness of men's battles? Did Lewis learn of the ugliness of women fighting by witnessing it firsthand? If not, did he learn of its ugliness through examples of female combat in the annals of European literature? Regrettably, neither Father Christmas nor Lewis addresses such questions; instead, Father Christmas turns to the practical concerns of food and drink.

The children's activities later in the novel live out Father Christmas' injunction against women in combat. Aslan shares battle strategies with Peter, who then leads the Narnian army against that of the White Witch, aided by the valor and wisdom of Edmund. The girls, on the other hand, do not engage in the battle, but rather are given an opportunity to display feminine characteristics. As they lie in camp during the night just before Aslan's sacrifice, they intuitively perceive that something is wrong. Before, during and after Aslan's killing, they express their emotional reactions to the point of tears and engage in intimate touch with the Great Lion by burying their hands in his mane and covering him with kisses (for Peter it was only a handshake). Their experience of the great battle is restricted to the role of observer, and then only during the battle's last few minutes. Then, of course, Lucy is given the feminine role of healer, with her bottle of magic liquid.

Battle affects the age-based hierarchy of the Pevensie children. Elsewhere in the novels Lewis implies a hierarchical chain of authority for the Pevensies, with Peter at the top as High King. The second position in this hierarchy varies, depending on context. Most often Susan, as second eldest, holds this position. Yet when it comes to combat, Edmund ranks second only to Peter. Either way Lucy comes up last, unless given a leadership role by an elder (as when Peter invites her to lead the way when all four first arrive in Narnia). Central to the children's maturation, however, is a realization and acceptance of their relative positions. Edmund must learn that he should not be the most favored prince to the disadvantage of his sibling; by the time of *Prince Caspian*, he willingly submits to his older brother's authority as High King (98). So too must Lucy learn that battle is no place for a woman, despite any innate or learned willingness or ability.

Of course, *not* participating in battle can be seen as an advantage for the female gender. Yet from the perspective of maturity, it is an opportunity lost. On her reunion with her brothers after the battle, Lucy notes a transformation in her elder brother; Peter's face appears "stern and...so much older" (175). Clearly the battle has been one of those life-threatening, transforming events for Peter, for which his defeat of the wolf was only a preparatory foretaste.

The gender distinction as it relates to combat is equally apparent elsewhere in the Narnia series. When Aslan sends Eustace and Jill back to Experiment House at the end of *The Silver Chair*, he uses battle dress as an opportunity to put the fear of God into those prigs who had been persecuting Eustace and Jill just before the two had been pulled into Narnia. Yet while Eustace, along with Caspian, are allowed to display (though not use) their swords, Jill is provided with only a riding crop; while no doubt this can be a serious weapon, it is not in the same category as a broadsword.

Yet interestingly enough, Lewis gives his girls an opportunity to play a greater combat role in the later Narnia novels. In *The Horse and His Boy* Susan stays home at Cair Paravel during the wars, but Lucy accompanies the men into battle. Lewis is vague as to Lucy's exact role, but an observer describes a female, most likely Lucy, among the Narnian archers, a role which would place her in danger but distance her from direct hand-to-hand combat. In *The Last Battle* Jill plays a sturdy role as a resistance fighter waging guerrilla warfare against the enemy.

This change suggests Father Christmas' dictum may not have been a permanent injunction against all female martial involvement (though Aslan himself keeps Susan and Lucy out of combat in *Prince Caspian*). It also implies a reconsideration of the phrase "battles are ugly when women fight," or an increased willingness to allow for this particular ugliness. It may simply be that Lewis' view in this regard changed or softened over time.

For Lewis himself exemplifies the attitudes toward maturity exhibited by his Narnian characters. As a youngster he exhibited some of the priggish pseudo-maturity he depicted within Edmund and Eustace. He also suffered a phase in which he devalued the literature (and values and attitudes) of his childhood, only to embrace it once again as an adult.

Furthermore, he exhibited a need to grow and mature even into his last years. As the film *Shadowlands* makes clear, Lewis was "surprised by Joy" in more ways than one; his autobiographical *A Grief Observed* shows that his interaction with his wife, Joy, led him to further growth and maturity as a man, as a Christian and as a writer.

But studying the Narnia novels in the context of Lewis' fiction and poetry shows him maturing as a writer even before the influence of Joy Davidman. Prior to Narnia, Lewis' depictions of female characters show an extremely limited and unrealistic range. *The Pilgrim's Regress*, for example, includes just two categories of women: highly physicalized sluts or disembodied spirits. His early narrative poems are equally shallow in depicting women. The second and third volumes of his science fiction trilogy offer somewhat more complex depictions. Tinidril of *Perelandra*, however, is a pre-fall Eve, and thus hardly realistic in terms of Earth women; in addition, Lewis glosses over the fact that she is entirely naked through most of the book. Jane Studdock of *That Hideous Strength* seems to some readers a flat character, created solely to learn her rightful (i.e., limited) role as a woman. Lewis shows little affection for her.

Thus the female characters of the Narnia novels are Lewis' first realistic depictions for which he exhibits affection. In addition, Lewis obviously revels in the strengths and weaknesses of Lucy, Susan and Jill. These characters show true progress, a maturing, in Lewis' thinking and writing. Of course, given that the novels' heroes are prepubescent, they give little indication of Lewis' ability to depict an engaging adult female character. But with the benefit of hindsight, the Narnia books are a wonderful transition to Lewis' finest, most mature work, *Till We Have Faces*, in which he offers his best, most realistic and most engaging depiction of a woman.

Maturity is most often a value, in life and in fiction, something positive, desirable and beneficial. Lewis' life and writings, however, illustrate its trade-offs, negatives that accompany the positives. Lewis emphasizes that Lucy must understand her hierarchical position in the chain of authority where Aslan has placed her; she is under Aslan, under Peter the High King and (at least while they are children) under Susan and Edmund as the youngest child. Yet Lewis gives Lucy the privilege of first entering into Narnia, and a special awareness of Aslan. Why? Her lack of maturity means she lacks the barriers of experience, rational thought and common sense that prevent the others from showing faith in her visions and experiences. In *The Lion, the Witch and the Wardrobe* the older children analyze Lucy's apparently irrational statements about a magic wardrobe leading to an alternate reality, while Lucy merely trusts her experience. By *Prince Caspian*, when Lucy is a year older, the situation is more complicated. Lucy is again the first to see Aslan, and again her immediate faith in her experience is rationalized away by her siblings. Yet Lucy, having learned her hierarchical position under the High King and her other siblings, chooses to follow the other children rather than follow Aslan. When Lucy finally meets Aslan face-to-face in this volume, he mildly reprimands her, saying that she should have followed him no matter what, even if it meant going alone. This is, of course, a growth experience for Lucy, moving her toward maturity; at the same time, might she have simply and impulsively followed Aslan on his first appearance to her had she not already matured at least a simple distance away from her initial childish faith?

The final Narnia volume, *The Last Battle*, further illustrates the negative side of maturity as the earthling adventurers return to Narnia and ultimately travel to Aslan's country: all, that is, except for one. Lewis chooses not to provide a completely satisfying storybook ending, but instead leaves Susan back on Earth. The reasons for her absence connect to theological concerns as well as a further lesson about growing up.

By the end of *The Lion, the Witch and the Wardrobe*, Susan is depicted as lacking an essential character strength that would make her ideally suited for Narnia. When the four adult Kings and Queens approach the lamppost while pursuing the White Stag, Susan alone is hesitant, wishing to break off the chase and return to the castle. She is equally timid in *Prince Caspian* when the children, on their first evening in Narnia, wish to explore the treasure chamber of their now-ruined castle. Later, when Edmund engages the dwarf Trumpkin in a test of combat skills, Susan alone of the children does not enjoy it. On their journey to join Caspian's army, Edmund describes Susan as "always...a wet blanket" (114). When Lucy attempts to wake up Susan, at Aslan's command, Susan is cross and rebuffs Lucy "in her most annoying grown-up voice" (139); here she exhibits a pseudo-maturity, not as extreme as Edmund's in *The Lion, the Witch and the Wardrobe*, but perhaps equally a sign of assertive self-importance.

These are indeed the characteristics referred to by the Narnian adventurers in *The Last Battle* when asked why Susan is not in their company.

Jill points out that Susan is preoccupied with fashion, physical appearance and giving the impression of maturity. Eustace reveals that she believes her Narnia experiences were only childish games. Polly suggests that Susan's is a case of arrested development; during childhood she longed to be older, and now that she is, she will spend the rest of her life attempting to remain that same age, rather than continue the process of growth toward true maturity. Peter sums up his sister's position by saying tersely though seriously (and to American ears somewhat coldly), "My sister Susan is no longer a friend of Narnia" (1956a, 134).

In short, she is no longer a believer. Given that Aslan's country is heaven, and that Narnia is a glimpse of heaven, she has given up belief in a metaphysical reality beyond her earthly experience. From a Christian perspective, she is at best an agnostic, or at worst an atheist. This turn of affairs in Susan's life produces a brief moment of surprised discomfort for readers, who long to see all four Pevensies entering Aslan's country. Lewis has a variety of motivations for doing this to Susan. For one thing, it allows the number of earthlings entering Aslan's country to total seven, a perfect Biblical number. In addition, according to Robert Houston Smith, it allows the other three Pevensies to represent the Platonic tripartite soul: rational soul (Lucy), appetite (Edmund) and middle element (Peter) (1981, 176); in this configuration, nothing would be left for Susan except personality disorder. Susan's absence also teaches an important Christian truth; not everyone who has exhibited Christian behavior ultimately finds entrance into paradise. Yet Susan may not yet be condemned to spend eternity away from her siblings. Paul Ford argues that she may yet have hope within God's/Aslan's plan for her; the train wreck that killed her siblings may be the frightening life-changing event that pushes her to further maturity. It might be the wake-up call that returns her to faith.

Susan's situation makes clear that maturity and adulthood are not the same thing. While one might reach adulthood, maturity is a lifelong process. As a result, partial maturity, existing at a given stage in the process, may be a necessary evil, but certainly not desirable as a permanent state. Lewis' last years exhibit a willingness to grow beyond a state of arrested development. He was a self-avowed, lifelong bachelor, whose primary adult female relationship was with a highly demanding and difficult older woman. Though Lewis had a number of female friends, it is fair to say he held a negatively biased view of women. As *A Grief Observed* displays, however, Lewis abandoned some of his "mature" assumptions about the nature of women and the impossibility of deep, passionate friendship with them after falling in love with Joy Davidman, who was then instrumental in encouraging Lewis' depiction of Orual in *Till We Have Faces*. Not only did Lewis grow in his ability to depict female characters, he grew in his ability to appreciate real females as well.

A final observation: the character most like C. S. Lewis in the Narnia novels is the Professor, who also exhibits the trade-offs of growing toward maturity. Early in *The Lion, the Witch and the Wardrobe*, Peter and Susan rationalize that Lucy cannot be telling the truth and may, therefore, be mad; they display a degree of maturity and responsibility beyond that of Lucy and Edmund. Yet the Professor, with greater insight, wisdom and experience, makes clear the error of their thinking while showing great sympathy for Lucy's childish simplicity. The lesson for both the Pevensies and Lewis' readers is that true maturity involves unlearning some of the things learned while growing toward maturity. Judging by the life and work of C. S. Lewis, one is never too old to both learn and unlearn.

Sam McBride is a senior professor with DeVry University (Pomona), teaching communications courses along with twentieth-century literature and science fiction. He is coauthor, with Candice Fredrick, of Women Among the Inklings: Gender, C. S. Lewis, J. R. R. Tolkien, and Charles Williams. *He has also published on Lewis'* A Preface to Paradise Lost.

References

Ford, Paul F. 1980. *Companion to Narnia*. San Francisco: Harper and Row.
Lewis, C. S. 1944. *Perelandra*. New York: Macmillan.
———. 1946. *That Hideous Strength*. New York: Macmillan.
———. 1950. *The Lion, the Witch and the Wardrobe*. New York: Collier.
———. 1951. *Prince Caspian*. New York: Collier.
———. 1952. *The Voyage of the Dawn Treader*. New York: Collier.
———. 1953. *The Silver Chair*. New York: Collier.
———. 1954. *The Horse and His Boy*. New York: Collier.
———. 1955. *Surprised by Joy*. New York: Harcourt Brace Jovanovich.
———. 1956a. *The Last Battle*. New York: Collier.
———. 1956b. *Till We Have Faces*. San Diego: Harcourt Brace Jovanovich.
Smith, Robert Houston. 1981. *Patches of Godlight: The Pattern of Thought of C. S. Lewis*. Athens: Univ. of Georgia Press.

MARTHA C. SAMMONS

The Chronicles of Narnia: For Adults Only?

THE CHRONICLES OF NARNIA have become Lewis' most widely read and bestselling books. Estimates are that over 200 million of Lewis' books and 100 million of his Narnia chronicles have been sold. They are shelved in the children's books section of libraries and bookstores. Now Disney will release *The Chronicles of Narnia: The Lion, the Witch and the Wardrobe*, and more movies from the series are planned. Thus, the stories are associated with children. But why would a bachelor professor of medieval and Renaissance literature at Cambridge University write seven children's stories when he was in his fifties? These "fairy tales" are not just for children. In fact, it may be argued that adults "need" them more. This essay explains why.

Lewis "turned to fairy tales because that seemed the form which certain ideas and images in my mind seemed to demand." In both his letters and in his essays collected in *On Stories and Other Essays on Literature*, Lewis presents some of his views on fairy tales and writing for children. He also refers to Tolkien's essay "On Fairy-Stories," which he calls one of the most significant contributions on the subject. According to Lewis, the fairy tale form has several distinct advantages. He argues that children are not deceived by fairy tales. Rather, it is realistic stories that are confusing and improbable because they may give the reader false expectations about real life.

A theme running throughout the Narnia books is thus the importance of reading the right kinds of books, such as those that feed the imagination and contain adventure. Many of the adults in Narnia are dull, narrow-minded and unimaginative. While adults are often portrayed negatively, the heroes are children. Again, Lewis believed a "never-never land" was appropriate for making a serious comment about the real life of humans. Lewis advises that the more "unusual" the scenes and events, the more "ordinary" and "typical" the characters should be. This element not only conveys a positive view of man but also shows that the most insignificant person can be a hero. The quest is typically symbolic of an inner journey—usually one's search for God or one's identity. One of the most important results of the spiritual journey is an inner change in the characters and, in turn, the reader. Humans are responsible for bringing evil into Narnia. The tales are filled with conflict against evil forces that attempt to dominate individuals' wills and lives.

However, Lewis claims that in writing his tales he never consciously started with the moral or didactic purpose of conveying Christian principles. Lewis' goal was to strip the Christian message of its "stained-glass and Sunday school associations" and give it new form and meaning by putting all these things into an imaginary world. By stealing past inhibitions and traditional religious concepts and terminology, he could make them, for the first time, "appear in their real potency." In fact, Lewis believed that "looking for a point" may keep a reader from "getting the real effect of the story itself." Lewis claims the Christian elements welled up unconsciously into the narrative as he wrote it.

Because of the portrayal of battles and wicked characters, some people argue that fairy tales frighten children. Lewis is opposed to the idea that we must protect a child from the knowledge that he is "born into a world of death, violence, wounds, adventure, heroism and cowardice, good and evil." Fairy tales not only contain terrible figures but also comforters and protectors. Lewis believed that the presence of beings other than humans, who behave humanly, is a central element in all fairy tales. Tolkien writes that fairy tales fulfill our desires, such as our wish to communicate with living beings other than humans.

For Lewis, marvelous literature also evoked and satisfied his intense desire for the "other." As described in *Surprised by Joy*, Lewis all his life experienced this longing for a beauty that lies "on the other side" of existence, as do many of his characters. The Chronicles have the fairy-tale ending Tolkien describes in his essay "On Fairy-Stories." Tolkien says that fairy tales satisfy our "oldest and deepest desire": Escape from Death. In addition, the Consolation of the Happy Ending, or Eucatastrophe, is "a sudden glimpse of the underlying reality or truth."

Are fairy stories merely escapism or wish fulfillment, then? No, says Lewis. Lewis says fairy land gives the actual world "a new dimension of depth" and sends us back to the real world with renewed pleasure, awe and satisfaction. Lewis says the value of the myth is that it takes things we know and removes the "veil of familiarity." Lewis agrees with Tolkien that fantasy can give us "recovery"—a cleansing of our vision of the world, thereby strengthening our relish for real life. According to G. K. Chesterton, it is really adults who need fairy tales, not children, for children still have a sense of awe and wonder at the world simply as it is. Most of the adults in the Narnia books are practical and close-minded and have uninteresting explanations for things.

Lewis explains that when his imagination led him to write the Narnia tales, he did not begin by first asking what children want and then trying to dish it out to them or by treating them like a distant and inferior race. Only bad stories are enjoyed just by children. The only reason most fairy tales unfortunately "gravitated" to the nursery is because their elders ceased to like them. The association of fairy tales with children is thus an accident. Tolkien and Lewis argue that fairy tales are not necessarily for children. If a fairy story is worth reading at all it is worthy to be written for and read by adults. In the dedication to Lucy Barfield in *The Lion, the Witch and the Wardrobe*, Lewis writes, "Some day you will be old enough to start reading fairy tales again." The Chronicles should therefore be read at various stages in life. In fact, it is adults without a childlike vision who may need them more than children.

Martha C. Sammons is professor of English at Wright State University in Dayton, Ohio. Her books include A Guide Through Narnia: Revised and Expanded Edition, "A Far-Off Country": A Guide to C. S. Lewis' Fantasy Fiction, "A Better Country": The Worlds of Religious Fantasy and Science Fiction, *and* The Internet Writer's Handbook 2/e. *She has worked as a contract technical writer and consultant in several area industries.*

References

Sammons, Martha C. 1979. *A Guide Through Narnia*. Wheaton: Harold Shaw Publishers.

———. 1980. *A Guide Through C. S. Lewis' Space Trilogy*. Westchester, IL: Cornerstone Books.

———. 1988. *"A Better Country": The Worlds of Religious Fantasy and Science Fiction*. Westport, CT: Greenwood Press.

———. 1995. *A Guide Through Narnia*. London: Hodder & Stoughton.

———. 2000. *"A Far-Off Country": A Guide to C. S. Lewis' Fantasy Fiction*. Lanham, MD: Rowman & Littlefield/Univ. Press of America.

———. 2004. *A Guide Through Narnia: Revised and Expanded Edition*. Vancouver: Regent College Publishing.

———. 2005. *Living Pictures: The Fantasy Worlds of C. S. Lewis*. Vancouver: Regent College Publishing.

Believing Narnia

"It is as absurd to argue men, as to torture them, into believing."

—Cardinal Newman

THERE ONCE WAS A LITTLE BOY who believed that most animals could speak but chose not to—and that hovering above him was a cozy world presided over by a panda-like king whose favorite toy was the moon and whose greatest joy was to share it, especially with the boy as he lay abed in the dark. He could not explain these beliefs and didn't care to. His imagination had spoken. On the other hand he was not irrational. For example, his father, in response to the son's unrelenting pleas, told the story of Jack and the beanstalk over and over. Finally the boy asked what had happened to Jack and his mother after the giant fell. "Well," said the father, "that giant made a very big hole. So after they dug him out, the mother and Jack made the hole into a swimming pool and built a motel around it. They lived happily ever after." The boy spent long hours trying to figure out where that motel might be and also planning a visit once he had. After all, he had already been to a motel or two and so his imagination, not entirely untethered to reality, had been informed by both reason and experience. In short, though he was persistent in his beliefs he was not unduly credulous. Even his Russian grandmother learned this. Truly she seemed on too-intimate terms with enchanted forests, children both hungry and lost, and witches who prey upon such children; she was convincing. But he did not for a nanosecond buy a gingerbread house large enough to live in—he had never seen or known of one and it made no sense. He loved his grandmother's telling of "Hansel and Gretel" (there would be none better) only slightly less than he loved his grandmother, which was boundlessly, but he did not for an instant believe it. Moreover, just as his doubt did not swoon at personal persuasiveness, neither did it wither at authority as such. Even though his high school geometry teacher had told the class that no proof for the trisection of an angle did, or could, exist, he worked hard and long to devise just such a proof: the impossibility seemed both unimaginative and unreasonable. Finally, when he satisfied himself that she was right, he told her so—but to this day he remains vexed by that impossibility, and wonders. . . .

Then, as a young graduate student, he read The Chronicles of Narnia. Needless to say he has believed them (nearly forty years later) ever since.

The question is how—as an adult—could I? Given the nature of the believer in question, there are some likely explanations: prolonged juvenilism (a kind of fixed sentimental affection coupled with a too-lively imagination), a not unrelated stubbornness (the Trisection Syndrome), rationality-cum-rationalizing (i.e., wish fulfillment), and an anarchic streak (fairy tales by their nature are subversive). As motives for belief none of these is entirely false. Yet even in combination they do not come close to accounting for my actual assent, as opposed to a predisposition to assent. Rather, I believe The Chronicles because I regard them as *true*, the only reason (as C. S. Lewis has said) to believe anything. Of course, a claim like this is not geometrically demonstrable and only imperfectly defensible, especially to the skeptic; but, in light of an opportunity to do so, the time has come to try. So after a pass at the preliminaries of What? and How? I will sketch a Why, which, though personal ("Rhetoric may be defined as the faculty of observing in any given case the available means of persuasion."—Aristotle) and private, is not essentially uncommon.

I

What sort of thing are The Chronicles? Does this type—do these examples of type—invite belief? As fairy tales their features are typical. Among them: 1) right and wrong (and often Good and Evil) are concrete (though perhaps not explicit); events show the world to be neither a pinball machine, nor even a plant, even less a tic of Tourette's, but the issuance of a Moral Intelligence; 2) spatial (and less often temporal) dimensions are small; for example, a kingdom might be walkable in two or three days; 3) marvels (talking animals, visual spectacles) abound, although these may *not* be wondrous within the tale and they are never random; 4) prohibitions, usually one very pronounced, are prominent; 5) very often the wonderworld is marked by order and hierarchy; i.e., they are *medieval*; 6) aspects of everyday life are comfortably, even cozily, rendered; 7) the protagonists (and perhaps others) often undergo some transformation of social station, marriage or family; 8) a character's identity, either stolen, mistaken or forgotten, is often at issue; 9) portentous signs, often subtle, are central to the plot; 10) a sense of "remote proximity" is common: long ago perhaps, and maybe far away, but certainly not inaccessible to visitors from beyond the wonderworld.

There are other traits, although among scholars there is no unanimity respecting even these ten. But aren't they enough to invite—skepticism? Where is the plausibility, the quotidian recognizability, that would invite belief here and now? Nearly absent, that's where, though not entirely—in The Chronicles, at least, there is a sibling dynamic, the enervating dread of looming maternal death, Mrs. Beaver being sure to take along her sewing machine on her flight from the White Witch, and other recognizably this-worldly elements. Still: they are not nearly enough for general plausibility and common recognizability. So then what might give us a foot (if not a whole leg) up toward belief? In "Education in Fairy Tales," the great Chesterton as usual sees the big picture and suggests a big answer:

> Civilization changes; but fairy-tales never change. Some of the details of the fairy-tale may seem odd to us; but its spirit is the spirit of folk-lore; and folk-lore is, in the strict translation, the German for common-sense.... Fairy-tales are the oldest and gravest and most universal kind of human literature.... A seven-headed dragon is perhaps a very terrifying monster. But a child who has never heard about him is a much

more terrifying monster than he is. The maddest griffin or chimera is not so wild a supposition as a school without fairy-tales.... The human race that we see walking about anywhere is a race mentally fed on fairy-tales as certainly as it is a race physically fed on milk.

Common sense and milk are hard to resist: but surely figures of speech alone won't satisfy our skeptic, at least not initially? On the other hand—*initially*—The Chronicles do make belief *appetizing* (if not exactly *thinkable*, not yet) even for the skeptic, in an artistic way, by way of literary features.

Most good tales can overcome bad tellings, until one signature telling (like my grandmother's of "Hansel and Gretel") prevails. In *A Dish of Orts*, George MacDonald writes that the meaning of a fairy tale, unlike that of an allegory, may be different for each reader, but that it "cannot help having some meaning; if it have proportion and harmony it has vitality, and vitality is truth." In the case of The Chronicles there are no prior bad tellings: they *are* the signature telling, and it invites belief—or at least the initial stage of belief, precisely because of its proportion and harmony, its vitality. In this mere sketch there is no room for acute, extended literary criticism. Instead, I invite the reader to do his own analysis in light of his reading of The Chronicles along with the following, which amplifies MacDonald's two constituents of vitality.

In his seminal *The Rhetoric of Fiction* Wayne Booth identifies three narrative features that draw us through a story: *intellectual* fulfillment, cognitive recreation marked by curiosity; *qualitative* allure, the desire for a completion of a pattern; and *practical* concern, our need to witness success or failure with respect to a difficulty encountered by the protagonist. A postulate from Lewis' own neglected *An Experiment in Criticism* sums up the three:

> The exercise of our faculties is in itself a pleasure. Successful obedience to what seems worth obeying and is not quite easily obeyed is a pleasure. And if the... exercises or the dance is devised by a master, the rest and movements, the quickenings and slowing, the easier and more arduous passages, will come exactly as we need them.... [L]ooking back on the whole performance, we shall feel that we have been led through a pattern or arrangement of activities which our nature cried out for.

Now, the appeal of design, the pleasure of purposeful variety and the promise of resolution, along with "realism of presentation" (not of content, a distinction which Lewis also amplifies upon in *An Experiment in Criticism*), are all palpable in The Chronicles. They *engage*, and engagement *is* that initial stage of belief. Common sense, milk *and a willing participation by the reader* in the heavy-lifting of persuasion are hard to resist, even for the skeptic.

Among the ingredients in this recipe, however, there is one that is more salient than any other, perhaps more so than all the others combined, and that one is the element of design. *Meaning is connectedness*: that's it. Maybe it's deep, long-lasting, happy, consequential; meaning might be "meaningful." But even if it isn't, it's still meaning. And we are meaning machines. We live for it and off of it. Virtually all we do is a way of seeking it: patterns in find-a-word, clues in a crossword puzzle or *Law and Order* episodes, a cloud that isn't cumulous but is the spitting image of Aunt Mabel. It's the Word, the great switchboard Logos, *the ground of all connectedness*, there at the beginning, at work in us and through us. Sometimes, when human nature has its way with our teleology, we seek to maximize meaning, and we ask, "What's it all about?" That's why Ultimate Meaning is connectedness to some Ultimate. Near the beginning of his wonderful autobiography, *The Golden String*, Dom Bede Griffiths (first Lewis' pupil, then friend and finally a co-convert, though, unlike Lewis, to Roman Catholicism) writes that people "will not be converted by words or arguments, for God...is the very ground of existence. We have to encounter him as a fact of our existence before we can really be persuaded to believe in him. To discover God," he continues, "is not to discover an idea but to discover oneself. It is to awake to that part of one's existence which has been hidden from sight and which one has refused to recognize....It is the one thing that makes life worth living." Of course, we may not know this, or be aware of it as it happens—to all of us, whether we know it or not. For anyone over the age of sixteen must agree with the poet Keats: "A man's life of any worth is a continual allegory," he writes, "and very few eyes can see the mystery of his life—a life like the Scriptures, figurative—which...people can no more make out than they can the Hebrew Bible."

In short, virtually any design, any design that compels reader participation, any design that compels reader participation and promises an Answer as its resolution—*that* design goes beyond mere engagement and becomes a set of Signs, road signs for any pilgrim making this quizzical journey. As Walker Percy has put it, we either possess a clear problem or we participate in a rich mystery. Thus do The Chronicles compel: they leave no choice, placing the engaged reader in the midst of Mystery.

II

Here is piece of common reader's sense that picks up where MacDonald leaves off. It is from Kenneth Grahame, the author of one of Lewis' favorites, *The Wind in the Willows*, and a writer who ought to know:

> Vitality, that is the test; and whatever its components mere fact is not necessary. A dragon, for instance, is a more enduring animal than a pterodactyl. I have never yet met anyone who really believed in a pterodactyl; but every honest person believes in dragons—down in the back kitchen of his consciousness.

This idea of belief *in*, not belief *that*, makes all the difference—the difference between the What and How I've mentioned earlier. I am not being coy. If there were space enough I would eagerly undertake a gleeful butchering of the sacred cow of empirically verifiable fact as the *sine qua non* of belief, a genuinely childish premise if there ever was one. Instead, stenographically, I ask the materialist skeptic: if you think your five senses are the only conduits of reality, then wherefore your own *belief in* the inerrant supremacy of feeble sensation?

Like so many other readers I do *believe that*, if Narnia exists, then it and its history are as Lewis says. Masterfully has he pulled off his literary supposal—the What of a fairy tale of a certain kind. And like so many other readers I have been both engaged and compelled by his How. More to the point, even before I make it through some wardrobe of my own, my *belief in* Narnia will persist, rather like the reformed Eustace's. In *The Voyage of the Dawn Treader* Eustace believed *that* stars are balls of flaming gas, but he did not believe *in* them—until he met Ramandu, a retired star. What have I met? Do I posses any *believing that* at all? And, when I *believe in* the tales, what am I believing? In other words, is there a deeper How and a deeper What than I've sketched so far? Briefly and directly, I believe 1) *that* Lewis' particular How of a "mediating illusion"—nothing less than an analogous gospel—is vastly instructive and cogent; and I believe 2) *in* the sacramentalism that The Chronicles thereby impute to the world.

Lewis wrote fairy tales because, as he put it, sometimes they "say best what's to be said." They deal with a spiritual universe. This is why Lewis, who believed that "a book no longer worth reading by an adult was never worth reading in the first place," wrote with children in mind; fairy stories do what's best to be done, which is to lead forth all—every one of us—who would flee as little children. For those who would not may Susan serve as a warning. At Aslan's rising from the Stone Table she asks "How?" *She* would be grown up and understand. Finally, like some of the dwarfs at the end of *The Last Battle*, she remembers her Self, only herself, and elects not to be fooled, not to "play silly games." From within Narnia, however, where he belongs, a reader sees things differently from Susan. He stands slightly above the children as they encounter the Narnian creator face-to-face and discovers along with them many of the supernatural workings of that world. From this point of view he reads *theogony*, how the gods begin. Now, if that reader shifts his perspective to that of many of the Narnian creatures, yet another form emerges: the appearance of gods and of God in the everyday world and their participation in that world is the stuff of *theophany*. What else—for a Narnian, that is—do these stories chronicle? This combination of elements—wonder tale, theogony, theophany—add up to a sacred scripture, the analogue of Judeo-Christian scriptures that I mentioned above.

I use the word "wonder" advisedly. As Lewis puts it, ". . . the *plot*, as we call it, is only really a net whereby to catch something else. The real theme may be...something that has no sequence in it, something other than a process and much more like a state or quality," something ineffable—really a *mode of perception*. "Man loves as he sees," wrote Angela of Foligno, a mystic; and "the vision of this world," continues Carolly Erickson in *The Medieval Vision*, is "linked to the vision of the next," ours being a "graphic model of the continuous act of creation" and "conceived as embracing the geographical locus of unseen truths." The difference between Narnia and our world, and between the historical medieval vision and our own, is in precisely this view of the here-and-now. We have forgotten that it points to, compels us toward and derives from then-and-elsewhere that this world *figures* the next. The function of The Chronicles—their highest merit—is to figure that very process of figuring. The Chronicles compel us to see and to know by way of mediation. Such is the "state or quality" of Narnia, and as such should we too believe *in* it. One of the ends of The Chronicles, then, is to fix our attention on a *means* of surpassing importance: the symbolical principle that invites us to see the next world in this.

The worthy tale casts a spell. In *The Allegory of Love* Lewis suggests the right sort of spell, drawing a persevering distinction. Allegory results when we invent *visibilia* to represent immaterial facts, such as passions. "But," Lewis continues,

> there is another way of using the equivalence, which is almost the opposite of allegory, and which I would call sacramentalism or symbolism. If our passions, being immaterial, can be copied by material inventions, then it is possible that our material world in its turn is the copy of an invisible world.... The allegorist leaves the given—his own passions—to talk of that which is confessedly less real, which is a fiction. The symbolist leaves the given to find that which is more real. To put the difference in another way, for the symbolist it is we who are the allegory.

Sacramentalism carries the real power. Lewis concludes, "it is for most poets and in most poems by far the best method of writing poetry which is religious without being devotional." In "Is Theology Poetry?" he suggests how sacramentalism works for us here and now:

> The waking world is judged more real because it can thus contain the dreaming worlds: the dreaming world is judged less real because it cannot contain the waking one. For the same reason I am certain that in passing from the scientific point of view [*savoir*?] to the theological, I have passed from dream to waking.... I believe in Christianity as I believe the sun has risen not only because I see it but because by it I see everything else.

The children in *Prince Caspian* perfectly exemplify the sacramental importance of the fantasy surrogate protagonist. Upon arriving in Narnia they are confused, even lost. Before remembering who and what they are, they must know where they are; this knowledge, though, is preceded by a dawning consciousness, a recognition of an altered state of being. Even their stature and physical prowess are enhanced. They are gods, or angels, who once again know themselves as such. The children, and we by way of them, see "theogonically," as gods newly arrived. If Narnia may be so visited, may we not be as well? There opens before us a suggestion that there is indeed nothing arbitrary about our world. The Chronicles figure forth a world on the brink, a theatrical set (to paraphrase Lewis and Chesterton) about to become the real thing—a transposition in which our children-surrogates (that is, we) might have a hand.

This linking of worlds, and our ability to discern the next one in this, is at the heart of the Narnian drama, from the ringing of the bell in Charn to the triumphant gallop following the last battle. As some of the voyagers from the ship *Dawn Treader* move through "drinkable light" they realize that they are approaching the end of the world and the beginning of another. It requires Lucy—who else could it be?—to know that such an end is an end of obliqueness only. The hieroglyphs, signs, symbols and sacraments are a means by which The Chronicles direct us. "'It isn't Narnia, you know,' sobbed Lucy. 'It's you. We shan't meet you'" back in our world. "'And how can we live, never meeting you?'" Aslan reassures Lucy, and then sends us all back, out of the world figured forth by C. S. Lewis and into a world—our very own quotidian mediating illusion—figured forth by our Creator: "'This was the very reason why you were brought to Narnia, that by knowing me here for a little, you may know me better there.'" This (with no apology to Alexander Pope) seems to me to be "a thing whose truth convinc'd at sight we find, / That gives us back the image of our mind." Dom Bede would not be surprised.

Very well: so much for preliminaries.

III

Rudolf Otto's *The Idea of the Holy* comes to the point of this affirmation. What do we come to know, however obliquely? What is it that works the wonder of baptism upon the imagination? Lewis' answer is holiness, or (as Otto puts it) the *mysterium tremendum*, the *mysterium fascinosum* and the *numinous*: the fathomless mystery attaching to the sacred being, the deep enchantment of the worshipper as he contemplates that being and his accompanying awe and fear before the sacred, respectively. The imagination, when kindled by a beam of sacramental longing, encounters holiness. That is its baptism. Then the result is a feeling, an authoritative response that Lewis called Joy. But there is a catch. "Only when your whole attention and desire are fixed on something else," continues Lewis, "whether a distant mountain, or the past, or the gods of Asgard"—or the creatures and events of Narnia—"does the 'thrill' arise. It"—Joy, of course—"is a by-product." The phenomenon is central to Lewis' experience, thought and belief, and he has described it amply, not least in his spiritual autobiography *Surprised by Joy*. Joy is Desire, and it is brings us—finally—to the Why. Why do I believe The Chronicles? At its simplest: *I believe them because they reaffirm my desire*. This is certainly not wish fulfillment; I do *not* desire to believe. Rather, I desire something far beyond a state of my own mind. I desire that Ultimate Connection; I desire Reality; I desire holiness Himself.

The idea is older than Lewis. Here is how Samuel Alexander puts it in *Space, Time and Deity* (a book which greatly influenced Lewis): "The religious emotion is as unique and self-sufficient as hungry appetite or love.... There is in fact no duty to be religious any more than there is a duty to be hungry.... It is in our constitution." St. Thomas Aquinas, in the *Summa Contra Gentiles* (XLVIII) made the point generally:

> Man's last end is the term of his natural appetite, so that when he has obtained it, he desires nothing more.... Natural desire cannot be empty, since "nature does nothing in vain." Therefore man's natural desire can be fulfilled. But not in this life, as we have shown. Therefore it must be fulfilled after this life. Therefore man's ultimate happiness is after this life.

The actor (and Catholic convert) Alec Guinness, in *My Name Escapes Me*, makes it more particularly—and most elegantly:

> I think most...human beings have the grace [of desire] once in their lives.... And of course it is...God giving each man and woman, according to their capacity, a glimpse of His promise to them, an impression of what eternity could mean, a glimpse of their *adoption* as Sons of God.... We are all left with a feeling of exhilaration, and yet at the same time, hand in hand with its happiness, a sadness that we are unlikely to encounter it again in this life.

And Socrates, as coy as ever in Plato's *The Symposium,* takes it one step further, and that without having heard Aslan's reassurance of Lucy: "Now such a person, and every other person who feels longing, long for what is not at hand, for what . . . he lacks, and [this] is the [sort] of thing that desire is of, and Love?"

Well, yes. What else? *Who* else, but Love? St. Augustine *begins* his *Confessions* with that Final Cause: "You have made us for yourself, O God, and our hearts cannot find rest until they rest in you."

I had promised a reason both personal and private but not therefore uncommon. Like uncounted billions of people, I have always desired—without realizing it, of course. Realization came only after learning, from Lewis and Plato and Newman, from Sts. Augustine and Thomas, that what I've felt is Joy, and that how it has come to me has been primarily through my imagination, with my own wonderings (those animals who could speak but wouldn't, that panda-like king) and the wonderings of others, above all The Chronicles, which never fail to break my heart.

But uncounted *billions*? Yes. If you are tempted to deny the feeling, remember Keats; he means you. If you are, or know anyone, like the materialist skeptic I've mentioned above, then ponder the atheist I recently debated. We had both appeared (separately) in the PBS documentary *The Question of God*, which compared the worldviews of Sigmund Freud and Lewis. At one point he described his conversion to "the scientific point of view," which occurred as he watched Carl Sagan's *Cosmos*; specifically, he remembers the "awe and wonder" that cosmic images aroused in him. At that moment he knew: understanding the cosmos, seeing into it, seeing through it, is what he desired most. Online the next day I asked him why he had felt "awe and wonder" in the first place. After all, if we are talking about molecules randomly arranged, then what is the achievement that merits such a response—such a fundamentally religious response, as though he had beheld the . . . *numinous*? He answered by reporting having felt similarly when he gazed upon Michelangelo's Sistine Chapel. "Sure," I responded, "that Michelangelo was quite an artist, his Chapel quite a design." And then, "but surely neither measures up to the cosmos and its designer?" He protested, but I drove my point home. You've had feelings. Instead of devoting your life to understanding only their Efficient Cause, why not inquire into their Final Cause? In other words, "awe and wonder" *mean* something; they are not quite Joy, but they are certainly road signs on the way. And billions have known awe and wonder. As Chesterton might have said, it's only common sense.

Some five thousand words ago I (like my hero Socrates) was being coy. By the time I read The Chronicles I already believed that being in the presence of the Blessed Sacrament is as real as being at the foot of the Cross during the Crucifixion; and predisposition to assent certainly makes a difference to the assent itself. I trust, however, that my preliminaries of Whats and Hows have helped distinguish legitimate predisposition from wish fulfillment. Insofar that desire is a predisposition to belief, then I confess that what I claimed at the start to be irrelevant to belief turns out to be its linchpin. Cardinal Newman, in his *An Essay in Aid of a Grammar of Assent*, explains:

> We arrive at our most important conclusions not by scientific necessity independent of our own selves, but by the action of our own minds, by our own individual perception of the truth in question under a sense of duty to those conclusions and with an intellectual consciousness.

While discussing the features of the fairy tale I posed as a skeptic, challenging their plausibility and recognizability (especially recognition of a certain similitude), what philosophers call "truth models" of *coherence* and of *correspondence*. But as the submissive reader I am invited by the mediation of The Chronicles to think, "So that's how the Old Testament and, more importantly, the Gospels work," and I read them afresh, as the greatest wonder tales ever written; and I think further, "So that's how the world and I are made, respectively, to point to and to be called by the next, where, like Lucy, I belong."

The dynamic is straightforward; Desire summons the cardinal virtue of Hope. Like Lewis' own conversion, The Chronicles and so much else that he wrote is, more than anything else, about Hope—*the exalted and continual conveyance of which* (not its inspiration; that is from the Holy Spirit) *is C. S. Lewis' greatest achievement*. Yet he is no sentimentalist. With severe honesty (Lewis is a severe thinker and writer), and along with Plato and the others, Lewis reports the results of his own "dialectic of desire," his hunt for the object of his desire. Finally, what he reports is that we can never have that object here and now. In *The Problem of Pain* he puts it this way:

All the things that have ever deeply possessed your soul have been but hints of it—tantalising glimpses, promises never quite fulfilled, echoes that died away just as they caught your ear. But if it should really become manifest—if there ever came an echo that did not die away but swelled into the sound itself—you would know it. Beyond all possibility of doubt you would say "Here at last is the thing I was made for."

And *when*, we ask (our time-bound language betrays us), shall that be? "There is no need here to speak in detail of each of these seven 'days,'" writes St. Augustine near the very end of *The City of God*.

Suffice it to say that his "seventh day" will be our Sabbath and that it will end in no evening, but only in the Lord's day—that eighth and eternal day which dawned when Christ's resurrection heralded an eternal rest both for the spirit and the body. On that day we shall rest and see, see and love, love and praise—for this is to be the end without the end of all our living, that Kingdom without end, the real goal of our present life.

James Como is a professor of rhetoric and public communication at York College of the City University of New York and a founding member (1969) of the New York C. S. Lewis Society, the oldest and still the largest of such societies. He has published Remembering C. S. Lewis: Recollections of Those Who Knew Him *(3ʳᵈ ed. Ignatius Press) and* Branches to Heaven: The Geniuses of C. S. Lewis *(Spence). Parts of this essay have appeared in the latter and in* CSL: The Bulletin of the New York C. S. Lewis Society.

PETER J. SCHAKEL

The "Correct" Order for Reading The Chronicles of Narnia?

A NEW BOOK, *The Lion, the Witch and the Wardrobe,* appeared on booksellers' shelves on October 16, 1950, in Britain and about three weeks later in the United States. It turned out to be the first book in a series of seven written over the next few years, which came to be referred to as The Chronicles of Narnia. The book was well received and read widely because of its intriguing title and effectively told story, and because its author, C. S. Lewis, was well known as a writer and radio broadcaster. Fifty years later the book continues to be widely read—or should one say that a similar book of the same title is widely read? For, half a century later, the book has become the second, not the first, of The Chronicles of Narnia. Does that make it a different book? In physical terms, no: the words of the text and Pauline Baynes' drawings remain the same. But the experience of engaging with the text—the book received by the reader—is very different indeed. Significant though this change is, it has been hidden, editorially, so readers first encountering the series now may never know about the renumbering of the series and the difference the rearrangement makes in the imaginative experiencing of the stories.

For those who were reading The Chronicles in the 1950s as each book appeared, one per year from 1950 to 1956, there was only one order in which to read and experience them, the order of publication. Most reprintings of the books in the 1960s, 1970s and 1980s numbered them in that order:

1. *The Lion, the Witch and the Wardrobe: A Story for Children*
2. *Prince Caspian: The Return to Narnia*
3. *The Voyage of the Dawn Treader*
4. *The Silver Chair*
5. *The Horse and His Boy*
6. *The Magician's Nephew*
7. *The Last Battle: A Story for Children*

So they were listed in the Geoffrey Bles and Bodley Head editions in Britain and the Macmillan editions in the United States once *The Last Battle* was completed, as well as in the later Collins clothbound reprints in Britain, the Puffin paperback edition in Britain from the time they were issued in the early 1960s until the mid-1970s, and the Collier paperback edition in the United States from its publication in 1965 until the mid-1980s.

At the same time, quiet but persistent voices began urging that they be renumbered in the order in which events occur in the stories (or nearly so: the events of *The Horse and His Boy* actually occur during, not after, those of *The Lion, the Witch and the Wardrobe*):

1. *The Magician's Nephew*
2. *The Lion, the Witch and the Wardrobe*
3. *The Horse and His Boy*
4. *Prince Caspian*
5. *The Voyage of the Dawn Treader*
6. *The Silver Chair*
7. *The Last Battle*

These voices have won out, at least to the extent that the uniform, worldwide edition of The Chronicles issued in 1994 is arranged in this order.

The first time the stories were published with the new numbering was in the set of "Fontana Lions" issued by Collins in 1980. Walter Hooper comments that in this edition "for the first time the books were given the order Lewis said they should be read in" (1996, 408). They were listed in that order several years earlier, opposite the title page of the Puffin paperback edition of *Prince Caspian*. The earliest copy with such a list that I have seen is a 1974 reprint, with this intriguing heading: "All seven stories of Narnia are published in Puffins, and the correct reading order is...." Other Puffin reprints of *Prince Caspian*, from the mid-1970s on, give this ordering, though without the explanatory statement. But what does "correct" mean here? Correct by what criteria? The 1994 uniform edition includes this statement on the copyright page: "The HarperCollins editions of The Chronicles of Narnia have been renumbered in compliance with the original wishes of the author, C. S. Lewis." Again the wording is puzzling. Why "original wishes"? Does original mean from the time at which *The Magician's Nephew* was completed? If so, why did Lewis not request that the Bodley Head include this renumbering in the new book, or in *The Last Battle* the following year, or have Geoffrey Bles change the order in later reprints of the other books? If it had been a matter of importance to Lewis, surely his publishers would have complied with his wishes, or included the renumbering in the paperback editions that appeared a few years later. Thus the strongest evidence that these were deeply held wishes of the author is missing.

The renumbering presumably has grown out of a sincere respect for Lewis and desire to follow his wishes. But the attempt to dictate a "correct" way to read The Chronicles reflects an inadequate understanding of the reading process and a regrettable reliance on "authorial intention," an approach questioned by many literary scholars today. That approach assumes that the "correct" way to interpret a literary work is to find and follow what the author intended, the way the author said it should be read. Walter Hooper, in *C. S. Lewis: A Companion and Guide*, follows that approach when he calls the new ordering "the sequence in which Lewis meant for them to be read" (408). Literary scholars challenge authorial intent on two grounds. The first points out the difficulty of determining what an author intended. Often an author does not tell us what he or she intended; authorial intent in such cases is read into the work by the circular argument that the author must have intended this or that because of the structure or effect of the work. Even when authors do tell us what they intended, the question arises of whether they actually achieved what they intended, or really understood themselves what they achieved. The second asks if what the author intended makes any difference. What really matters is the effect of the work, which could fall short of or go far beyond what the author expected or sought to achieve. The unconscious dynamic of the writing process can lead a writer to achieve more than, or something different from, what he or she consciously set out to do.

Lewis gave qualified approval to the chronological arrangement in a letter to a young boy, Laurence Krieg, dated April 23, 1957. Laurence believed, after publication of *The Magician's Nephew*, that it should be read first, but his mother thought the books should continue to be read in order of publication. Laurence wrote to Lewis asking whether he or his mother was right. Lewis replied, "I think I agree with your order for reading the books more than with your mother's.... [But] perhaps it does not matter very much in which order anyone reads them" (1985, 68). Walter Hooper reports that Lewis had him take out his notebook and he dictated to Hooper "the order in which the stories should be read [beginning with *The Magician's Nephew*]" (2002, 320). Even if this letter and the dictation to Hooper are serious expressions of Lewis' intent, it is not wise to use them as a basis for limiting readers to one way of reading. Lewis himself said that an author "is not necessarily the best, and is never a perfect, judge" of a book's meaning or effect. [1] (1966, 56–57). Note that Lewis, despite expressing agreement with Laurence, does not say this is the *correct* order for reading them. When he says, "perhaps it does not matter very much," it seems clear that he means more than one order, or perhaps any order, is acceptable to him for reading The Chronicles. If, however, he is suggesting that the order makes no difference to the reading experience, then he is simply mistaken. The order of reading in that sense matters a great deal. Viewed in terms of the imaginative reading experience, the "new" arrangement may well be less desirable than the original one.

The only reason for putting *The Magician's Nephew* first is to have the reader encounter events in chronological order, the order in which they happened, and that, as every storyteller knows, is quite unimportant as a reason. Often the early events in a sequence have a greater impact or effect as a flashback, told after later events which provide background and establish perspective. Beginning a story *in medias res* ("in the middle of

---

[1] Similarly, "You must not believe all that authors tell you about how they wrote their books. This is because a man writing a story is too excited about the story itself to sit back and notice how he is doing it....And afterwards, when the story is finished, he has forgotten a good deal of what writing it was like" (Lewis 1966, 42).

things") is one of the oldest and most basic of narrative strategies, going back at least to *The Iliad* and *The Odyssey*, two of the earliest stories in the Western literary tradition. Lewis had used it before in *Perelandra* and would use it later in *Till We Have Faces*. In The Chronicles, the effect of *Prince Caspian* depends upon it. In chapter 1, the four Pevensie children are whisked away from a train platform in our world to another world. They wonder if it might be Narnia, but everything looks unfamiliar. The children discover in chapter 2 that they are not only in Narnia but in the ruins of the castle Cair Paravel, where they had lived at the end of *The Lion, the Witch and the Wardrobe* (the castle is in ruins because a thousand years have passed in Narnian time since they returned to our world). In chapter 3 they capture a Dwarf, who agrees to tell them what they need to know about events during those thousand years. Chapters 4–7 are a flashback containing the Dwarf's story. Lewis carefully arranged the first three chapters so that the reader would share imaginatively what the children experienced: the feelings of fear and uncertainty, the slowly growing awareness of where they are, the perplexity over why things have changed so much. He could have started the book with chapter 4, relating it from Caspian's point of view, the way he did with Tirian in *The Last Battle*. Doing that, however, would have sacrificed the strategies through which he led readers into the story and got them involved in the action.

So it is with The Chronicles as a whole. To read one of the other books before *The Lion, the Witch and the Wardrobe* sacrifices strategies that Lewis used to lead readers into the world of Narnia and to help them share imaginatively in the experiences of Lucy, and later the other children, as they discover what that world is like. Consider, for example, the careful use of details as Lucy enters Narnia for the first time. In an ordinary-seeming house in the country, Lucy steps into an ordinary-seeming wardrobe, to smell and feel the long fur coats in it. The vivid details enable the reader to share Lucy's experience as she reaches ahead into the darkness of the wardrobe, hears a crunching underfoot, feels the cold wetness of the snow and the prickliness of the trees, and glimpses the light of the lamppost ahead of her. The reader shares her bewilderment and uncertainty about where she is and what she has gotten into, and her surprise as she hears footsteps and comes face-to-face with, not another human, but a creature which, though having the body of a man from the waist upward, has legs shaped like a goat's, with black hair, goat's hooves, reddish skin, a short pointed beard and curly hair, two horns, and a tail.

A key strategy in the book is use of what reader-response critics call "gaps." All stories depend on gaps (details that need later to be clarified, questions that a reader wants answered, and immediately begins trying to answer by anticipating later events). *The Lion, the Witch and the Wardrobe* uses them very effectively. Its opening leads readers to ask, "Who are these four children and the Old Professor? What are they like? What is the 'something' that happened to them in the very large house far out in the country?" The story, immediately or slowly as needed, begins filling those gaps. Notice that the story creates a gap by a reference to three servants, then quickly signals the reader that this is not an important gap: "(Their names were Ivy, Margaret and Betty, but they do not come into the story much)"[2] (1950).

The first mention of the name "Narnia" creates such a gap. Tumnus the Faun asks Lucy how she came into Narnia, and Lucy asks what the reader also wants to know: "Narnia? What's that?" Tumnus replies, "This is the land of Narnia...where we are now; all that lies between the lamp-post and the great castle of Cair Paravel on the eastern sea" (9). The reader will want and need to know more, of course, but for now he or she has been supplied the necessary basic information and given adequate orientation.

The most important example of a gap in *The Lion, the Witch and the Wardrobe*, when it is read first, is the buildup to the introduction of Aslan. The first reference to Aslan is by Mr. Beaver, when he meets the children in the woods: "They say Aslan is on the move—perhaps has already landed" (54). These words create a gap for the Pevensie children and—presumably—for the reader: "None of the children knew who Aslan was any more than you do; but the moment the Beaver had spoken these words everyone felt quite different" (54). In the long paragraph that follows, Lewis seeks directly and intentionally to help readers share imaginatively what the children experienced:

> Perhaps it has happened to you in a dream that someone says some-
> thing which you don't understand but in the dream it feels as if it

---

[2] Quotations of The Chronicles in this essay are from the Macmillan edition, which includes changes made by Lewis in several of the books after their British counterparts had gone to press. This edition seems preferable for a scholarly article because it is a later text than the British edition, incorporating the author's latest revisions. The 1994 worldwide edition reproduces the first British edition and regrettably does not indicate that revisions were made in a later version. For details and discussion of the alterations, see Paul F. Ford's *A Companion to Narnia* (1994. xli–xlii (Variants) and Appendix 4) and Peter J. Schakel's *Imagination and the Arts in C. S. Lewis* (2002, 32–39).

had some enormous meaning—either a terrifying one which turns the whole dream into a nightmare or else a lovely meaning too lovely to put into words, which makes the dream so beautiful that you remember it all your life and are always wishing you could get into that dream again. It was like that now. At the name of Aslan each one of the children felt something jump in his inside. (54)

For the reader fully to participate imaginatively with this paragraph, to feel something mysterious jump in his or her inside, requires that it be the first book in the series to be read. The reader experiences the power of Aslan's name but—like the Pevensie children—is left to wonder who and what this person is. The anticipation and eventual filling of that gap is one of the great pleasures of reading the story. The fact that other books were written later, including a book describing events prior to these, does not change the artistic strategy of this passage.[3]

The gap is partially filled, and the mysteriousness heightened, in the next chapter, when the children ask Mr. Beaver to tell them more about Aslan and he replies: "Aslan?... Why, don't you know? He's the King. He's the Lord of the whole wood, but not often here, you understand. Never in my time or my father's time" (63). The gap is filled still further, and Aslan made even more exciting and mysterious, when Lucy asks if Aslan is a man and Mr. Beaver replies: "Certainly not. I tell you he is the King of the wood and the son of the great Emperor-beyond-the-Sea. Don't you know who is the King of Beasts? Aslan is a lion—the Lion, the great Lion" (64). The excitement builds as the Beavers tell the children that Aslan is good but not safe, that everyone's knees knock when they appear before him, and that the children will meet him tomorrow. For readers who have read The Magician's Nephew before encountering these passages, there are fewer, and smaller, gaps to fill, and as a result the story is less mysterious and less exciting.

The imaginative experience of the opening sentences of The Magician's Nephew is very different from that of The Lion, the Witch and the Wardrobe

---

[3] Similarly, as Doris Myers has shown, the chronological order dampens the "leap of faith—the decision to trust beyond the evidence" which the books, in order of publication, require of readers as well as of the Pevensie children. "From a position of superior knowledge, the reader watches, but does not share, the children's doubts and risks" ("Spenser's Faerie Land as a Key to Narnia," lecture delivered at Wheaton College, 24 September 1998). It "flattens" the stories, imposing a single reading on them, "whereas The Chronicles are in fact polysemic, having many layers of meaning." Myers concludes, "As far as I know, there is no evidence that Lewis ever went back and read the books in chronological order to see if they held together that way as fiction."

and has a different effect, depending on which book is read first: "This is a story about something that happened long ago when your grandfather was a child. It is a very important story because it shows how all the comings and goings between our own world and the land of Narnia first began" (1955). For someone who has previously read *The Lion, the Witch and the Wardrobe*, this invokes recognition and memory: "Narnia" immediately connects the reader with earlier imaginative experiences and awakens a flood of memories. The word will not be used again in *The Magician's Nephew* until the title of chapter 9, but that doesn't matter: knowing that this story will connect with the earlier ones engages the reader imaginatively and emotionally and enables him or her to proceed in eager and watchful anticipation.

For those who read *The Magician's Nephew* before other books in the series, the opening sentence creates not the kind of skillful, satisfying gaps found in *The Lion, the Witch and the Wardrobe*, but vague and unsettling ones. The words "all the comings and goings" create the first gap in *The Magician's Nephew*. The reader who reads this story first is left asking, "What comings and goings?" The question is never answered in this book, though the next to the last paragraph of the final chapter repeats the phrase and adds "which you can read of in other books." It does not yield the imaginative satisfaction of a skillfully filled gap (like the Aslan gap in *The Lion, the Witch and the Wardrobe*); it feels instead like the "bait" authors use to sell other books. The second gap is "the land of Narnia." The reader has the clue that it must be separate from "our own world" and is left to wonder what and where this land is. But it too is not a satisfying gap (understandably, since Lewis was crafting this as a flashback, not a first book). The second paragraph shifts abruptly to a different story, about Polly, Digory, Uncle Andrew, London and Charn, which is set up and told very effectively, with skillful creating and filling of gaps. Indications of what Narnia is do not appear until the final lines of chapter 9: "Narnia, Narnia, Narnia, awake. Love. Think. Speak. Be walking trees. Be talking beasts. Be divine waters" (103).

Consider the difference in the imaginative experiencing of these words for those who read *The Magician's Nephew* first, and those who have previously read one or more of the other Chronicles. If one reads this book first, the account of the creation of Narnia is a beautiful, powerful story, told in vivid detail. It draws the reader into the events and enables him or her to experience the excitement, emotions, mystery and magic of what is occurring. For a lion to bring a new world into being and breathe life into it is something a reader will never forget. The imaginative experience of reading it as a reader's first encounter with the world of Narnia is exciting and wonderful. However, it will be even more meaningful and powerful when the reader returns to it and rereads it after reading the other books and learning more about that mysterious lion; the memories, emotions and associations from other stories make the creation of Narnia much more significant to the reader than it can be on first reading.

For those who read other books before reading *The Magician's Nephew*, the delightful elements of surprise and recognition are added to that of deeper meaningfulness. Readers who had shared with Lucy the mysterious experience of encountering a lamppost unaccountably placed in the middle of a forest have the pleasure, upon seeing the lamppost grow in *The Magician's Nephew*, of recognition: "Oh! That's how the lamppost got there!" (For those who watch the birth of the lamppost before reading *The Lion, the Witch and the Wardrobe*, there is no mystery when they encounter it with Lucy.) Likewise, readers who have already encountered the White Witch in *The Lion, the Witch and the Wardrobe* experience surprise and recognition in *The Magician's Nephew* as they gradually figure out who Jadis is and realize the long-term significance of the events in Charn. Readers who first were introduced to Aslan in *The Lion, the Witch and the Wardrobe* experience the thrill of recognition as the lion comes into view, and perhaps the pleasure of accurate anticipation if they guess that the voice is Aslan's before he appears or before his name is mentioned. The fullest imaginative experiencing of *The Magician's Nephew* comes through reading the book as a flashback, for that is the way Lewis thought of it as he wrote it, and those are the artistic strategies he consciously or unconsciously built into it. Thus, there is no introduction to Aslan in *The Magician's Nephew*, no explanation that he is the king of the wood or the son of the great Emperor-beyond-the-Sea; there was no need to explain—readers already know all that from earlier books.

Imaginative experience extends also to the religious dimension of The Chronicles, and here too the arrangement of the books makes a difference in their effect and meaning. The religious motifs are embedded in image and story, which the reader experiences imaginatively, not (as in *Mere Christianity* or *Miracles*) in concept and logical argument. The full religious significance of The Chronicles depends on viewing them as a unified series and on reading them in order of publication. I have demonstrated elsewhere that The Chronicles, intentionally or unconsciously, echo and parallel *Mere Christianity*, which Lewis was revising for republication at the time he was writing the early Chronicles (1979). The Chronicles, read in order of publication, develop a sequential presentation of Christian ideas similar to that in *Mere Christianity*. Book 1 of *Mere Christianity* demonstrates the need for salvation; Book 2 explains the plan of salvation; Book 3 deals with morality, explaining how Christians should live as individuals and as a church, a company of the faithful, in light of their salvation; and Book 4 clarifies theological issues that cause difficulties for Christians. The arrangement of the four books is deliberate. Their full effect depends on the order in which they are read: "It is after you have realised that there is a real Moral Law, and a Power behind the law, and that you have broken that law and put yourself wrong with that Power—it is after all this, and not a moment sooner, that Christianity begins to talk" (1952, Book 1, chapter 5). The discussion in Book 3 ("Christian Behavior"), if read first, will not have the same meaning as it does when read after the sections on "Right and Wrong as a Clue to the Meaning of the Universe" and "What Christians Believe," which emphasize that the moral teachings in Book 3 grow out of the premises about law, grace and faith laid out in the earlier parts.

The Lion, the Witch and the Wardrobe lays imaginatively a theological foundation for the succeeding books, much as Book 1 of *Mere Christianity* lays a foundation for the other three parts. *The Lion, the Witch and the Wardrobe* begins, as *Mere Christianity* does, by establishing the existence of moral law, or "Deep Magic from the Dawn of Time" (108), and the fact that Edmund has broken that law and thus that his life is forfeit and he needs help if he is to be rescued. As Aslan dies in Edmund's place, the story images Book 2 of *Mere Christianity*: "Deeper Magic from *before* the Dawn of Time" (127) represents the love and grace that saves Edmund from the penalty of the law. Other themes from *Mere Christianity* are reflected in succeeding Chronicles, including the theme of Christian morality in *The Magician's Nephew*. When *The Magician's Nephew* is read in the order of publication, the earlier books create a context for the theme of morality, just as Books 1 and 2 of *Mere Christianity* establish a context for Book 3. Earlier stories imaging law, faith, spiritual growth and divine guidance and care provide a Christian basis for the moral instruction. Morality grows out of faith, not just out of a desire to "do better." Christian meanings can come through the chronological arrangement, too, but in a less unified, less imaginatively and intellectually satisfying way than the sequence that flowed out of Lewis' imagination as he wrote the stories.

In one sense, then, as Lewis said, the order in which The Chronicles are read doesn't really matter, but it unquestionably does make a difference—which he didn't acknowledge, and perhaps didn't recognize fully. The decision to renumber and rearrange The Chronicles in current editions may or may not be considered unfortunate. But it is definitely unfortunate the publishers did not indicate that a different arrangement existed in earlier versions, remains an alternative order for reading the books and is preferred by a number of Lewis scholars (Ford 1994, xix–xx, xxxiv–xxxvi; Gibson 1980, 133; Manlove 1987, 124–25; 1993, 111–15; Myers 1994, 227; Schakel 1979, 143–45). Principles of textual editing, past and present, call for signaling textual changes so the reader can evaluate the difference the variants make and perhaps choose between the alternative versions. Failure to indicate in the books what the original numbering was has the regrettable effect of wiping out the past and imposing a single, "authoritative" reading upon The Chronicles. It is a decision that detracts from, not enhances, recognition and appreciation of the artistry and meaning of Lewis' best-known books.

Peter J. Schakel has taught at Hope College since 1969 and for the past twenty years has been the Peter C. and Emajean Cook Professor of English. He has written or edited five books on C. S. Lewis, as well as three on British literature of the eighteenth century and three textbooks. His most recent books are Approaching Literature in the 21st Century: Fiction, Poetry, Drama *(Bedford/St. Martin's, 2005), co-authored with Jack Ridl, and* The Way into Narnia: A Reader's Guide *(Eerdmans 2005).*

References

Ford, Paul F. 1994. *A Companion to Narnia.* San Francisco: Harper & Row.

Gibson, Evan K. 1980. *C. S. Lewis, Spinner of Tales: A Guide to His Fiction.* Washington, D.C.: Christian Univ. Press.

Green, Roger Lancelyn, and Walter Hooper. 2002. *C. S. Lewis: A Biography.* London: HarperCollins.

Hooper, Walter. 1996. *C. S. Lewis: A Companion and Guide.* London: Harper-Collins.

Lewis, C. S. 1950. *The Lion, the Witch and the Wardrobe.* New York: Macmillan.

———. 1952. *Mere Christianity.* London: Geoffrey Bles.

———. 1955. *The Magician's Nephew.* New York: Macmillan.

———. 1966. *Of Other Worlds: Essays and Stories.* Ed. Walter Hooper. London: Geoffrey Bles.

———. 1985. *C. S. Lewis: Letters to Children.* Ed. Lyle Dorsett and Marjorie Lamp Mead. New York: Macmillan.

Manlove, Colin. 1987. *C. S. Lewis: His Literary Achievement.* New York: St. Martin's Press.

———. 1993. The Chronicles of Narnia: *The Patterning of a Fantastic World.* New York: Twayne.

Myers, Doris T. 1994. *C. S. Lewis in Context.* Kent, OH: Kent State Univ. Press.

Schakel, Peter J. 1979. *Reading with the Heart: The Way into Narnia.* Grand Rapids, MI: Wm. B. Eerdmans.

———. 2002. *Imagination and the Arts in C. S. Lewis: Journeying to Narnia and Other Worlds.* Columbia: Univ. of Missouri Press.

WESLEY A. KORT

The Chronicles of Narnia: Where to Start

I T'S A BIT OF A JOLT for some of my students to find, when they buy the boxed set of The Chronicles of Narnia for my course, that not *The Lion, The Witch and the Wardrobe* but *The Magician's Nephew* comes first. When their parents read the books to them, the order was the other way around. First was *The Lion, The Witch and the Wardrobe*, and *The Magician's Nephew* did not come until later, much later. This switch, while having precedents, became final when HarperCollins took on the publishing rights in 1994. After over a decade of the changed order, only those who encountered the series earlier notice the difference. The question is whether it matters, whether it makes a difference where in the series you begin. Lewis, in a letter and in some comments, seemed not to give the question great weight. However, I think that it does matter, and I ask students in my class to read The Chronicles in their original order. While I am not alone in my preference, the reasons for my preference may not be the same as those of others.[1]

---

[1] For an excellent review of the history and of some of the discussion concerning the order of the Narnian chronicles, including Lewis' comments, see Peter J. Schakel's *Imagination and the Arts in C. S. Lewis* (2002, 40–52). Schakel also prefers the original order, although he does so for reasons different from mine.

I

The most obvious reason for the change is that *The Magician's Nephew* depicts the creation of Narnia. By reading it first, readers can encounter Narnia from its origins to its destruction in *The Last Battle*. This gives The Chronicles a chronological order, and that seems to make good sense; "chronicles" and "chronological" seems a logical match. However, knowing as we do that Lewis valued logical thinking highly and that he was himself, by profession, a historian, it also seems strange that he didn't write them that way and, instead, left them for publishers to straighten out.

I don't think that in Lewis we have a writer whose creative impulses outstripped his capacity to put things in order. We have, rather, a deliberate and thoughtful person who cared about his readers. In this case, his readers or hearers would be children, and Lewis cared a great deal for children, not, as he admitted, because he was naturally inclined to do so but, rather, because he was not.[2] It took effort, and we can assume that rather than trying to confuse his young readers by starting them off *in medias res*, as he might have said, he was trying to meet them where they were. I would like to suggest how.

Children, it has been argued, have a more spatial than chronological imagination, and they relate more immediately and fully to spatial than to chronological arrangements. Gaston Bachelard, in his *Poetics of Space*, points out that our earliest memories are spatially and not chronologically ordered, and a principal structure for the ordering of early memories is the house of our early upbringing (1964). Lewis recognized this attachment to places in his own childhood. In *Surprised by Joy* he says that houses are almost characters in his life story, and he records his experience of the house into which his family moved when he was seven. He was excited by the house, its size, its configuration and, especially, its attics. Indeed, he associates many of his early imaginative exercises and creations with the attics of the house. Given this experience, it is helpful to see that Bachelard gives special attention to the attics of the houses in which children are reared. He argues that children go up to the attic with expectations of discovery and possibility. Attics contain interesting artifacts, and, by virtue of the geometrical

---

[2] "I myself do not enjoy the society of small children: because I speak from within the *Tao* I recognize this as a defect in myself...." (Lewis 1944, 19).

alignment of the beams of the roof, they grant a certain edifying and also protective effect.

Bachelard also points out that children are drawn to the houses of animals, to their nests and dens. They feel a common bond with animals in terms of the feelings of protection and attachment that children have to their own beds and secure places, feelings they assume animals share.

Finally, houses are so important for children, according to Bachelard, because the house provides a special place to which the child retreats when wanting to be alone or, even more, when feeling unfairly treated. Furthermore, children also think of their own place in the house as a location for personal treasures. So, a drawer or a box will contain items that, while in the eyes of others have little value, are of great significance to the child. Bachelard argues that this box and these treasures serve as warrants of the child's value in the home and, more importantly, in and for the child's move out into the wider world.

Given all of this, it is not surprising that the children who enter Narnia in *The Lion, The Witch and the Wardrobe* do so through a wardrobe in the upper part of the large house that they are visiting. Nor is it surprising that they take such an interest in the houses of the creatures, such as the beavers, whom they meet there. Nor is it surprising that in *The Magician's Nephew* movement from this to another world initiates from the attics of the London house. And it is not surprising that Polly keeps a cashbox in the attic containing "various treasures," a story she was writing and usually a few apples. Houses are important for the Narnia chronicles, and they are so important because Lewis seems to have known what Bachelard makes clear—namely, that children relate more easily and even more eagerly to spatial than to chronological order.

Indeed, the language of place and space is prominent in Lewis' narratives. His characters are arrivals to or inhabitants of places that they explore or represent. His plots, while marked by action and change, are usually also journeys to and within places that are both threatening and intriguing. For Lewis, exercising the imagination is very closely tied to the act of placement, of imagining an alternative world and imagining it as a whole. What he most liked about fictional narratives was that they allowed him to live in a different world. He was intrigued as a boy by stories about pirates or Native Americans, for example, not so much because of the action and characters as because of the intriguing world in which they were set and of which they were a part (Lewis 1982, 27).

The moral imagination is also, for Lewis, more spatial than temporal. Indeed, he distinguishes the baptized and the un-baptized imaginations from one another in moral and spatial terms (64–65). Is the world that I imagine a world that enhances my importance, my interests and my advancement? Or is it a world that intrigues me because it is morally more desirable than what presently pertains, as Malachandra and Perelandra form attractive alternatives to the "silent planet" from which, in the space trilogy, Ransom comes? Lewis had primarily a spatial imagination, and he seemed to understand that the imagination of young readers would be primarily spatial, too. This is, I think, why he began The Chronicles of Narnia where he did.

II

There is also a theological issue at stake. It concerns the relation of the doctrine of Creation to the doctrine of Redemption. By altering the sequence a question arises about which of the two doctrines is primary. In The Lion, The Witch and the Wardrobe, Aslan, as all readers graphically remember, gives himself over to the power of the White Witch and is bound, shaved, mocked, muzzled and killed. Aslan's sacrifice and his subsequent resurrection are certainly Narnian counterparts to the acts of redemption in Christian faith and doctrine. In The Magician's Nephew we read of the creation of Narnia. It is not so clearly a Narnian counterpart to the Christian doctrine of Creation as based on the opening chapters of Genesis, since so much of it depends on music. But that characteristic simply implies a textual shift, so that the account of Creation in Job 38:4–11, where music is an ingredient, becomes more important. In the original order, then, Narnian Redemption is given first attention and Narnian Creation second. Were the editors aware, when they altered the sequence, that their action had theological implications? Should the original order be restored in order to restore the primacy of Redemption?

While the question of what comes first may strike some as minor, Christian theologies can be distinguished from one another according to their answer to the question of which of these two doctrines is primary, is the more important. When the doctrine of Creation forms the basis for a theology, human beings are viewed morally and spiritually in a more positive way, and history is viewed as inherently quite trustworthy. The stronger your doctrine of Creation the less strong your doctrine of Redemption needs to be. However, if the doctrine of Redemption is primary, things are reversed. Then it is assumed that a great deal of damage has been done by evil and human sin so that people in themselves are in need of radical reconstitution. Indeed, some Christians think that the damage done by sin is so severe that there is nothing in human beings and history that the work of God in the events central to Redemption can use or to which the results of that work can be attached. The question, then, of which doctrine is the more important one for Lewis is not trivial.

Let me say first that I am uneasy about raising this question because it tends to separate Christians into liberal and conservative camps, and Lewis worked in the opposite direction. He tried very hard to be inclusive of differing Christians, and I think that it is difficult to put him with one group or with the other in terms of this divide. I also am uneasy about raising this question because many of Lewis' devotees, especially in this country, are Christians of the kind who have a doctrine of Redemption that overshadows their doctrine of Creation. They will likely prefer the original order because their doctrine of Creation is secondary to, if not occluded by, their doctrine of Redemption.[3]

Readers who think that *The Lion, The Witch and the Wardrobe* should come first in the series because the doctrine of Redemption is stronger in Lewis than his doctrine of Creation can appeal to several aspects of Lewis' work for support. For example, he is harshly critical of modern culture, a culture that was successful in marginalizing, and almost in ostracizing, Christianity. It is also clear that Lewis blamed the marginalization of Christianity in the twentieth century, especially in academic culture, in good part on the failure of Christians to counter that culture effectively and forcefully in terms that included a strong sense of human evil and the need for Redemption. This dual critique —that modern culture marginalized and disparaged faith and that Christians allowed their

---

[3] Peter J. Schakel seems to prefer the old order for this reason. He takes, as support, the fact that Lewis at the time of beginning to write The Chronicles was also giving shape to *Mere Christianity*, and there Lewis starts off with human sin and moves from sin to the doctrine of Redemption. However, I'm not convinced by this appeal. First, *Mere Christianity* is a project so very different from the Narnia project that appeals to the one for support of points regarding the other can easily be stretches. Second, there are other reasons for the order of *Mere Christianity*, primarily because of the standard models for introducing Christian faith provided, for example, by the epistle to the Romans and by catechisms. *Mere Christianity* is an epitome of Christian principles, and it understandably would follow such textual models. The Chronicles of Narnia are not, I think, determined by such models.

theologies to be shaped by that culture—was effective and powerful. It still is. The question is how far to take it. Should we settle the question of which of the two Chronicles to read first by concluding that Aslan's sacrifice, as a counterpart to the doctrine of Redemption in Christianity, should be placed in a position of primacy?

While I think that the original order should be restored, I do not think it should because the doctrine of Redemption is more important for Lewis than the doctrine of Creation. I think that Lewis, as with many contraries within Christian doctrine and life, tried to give the two doctrines equal weight. While I do not minimize the sharpness and weight of Lewis' critique both of modernity and of a Christianity that defers to it, it was not human culture itself that Lewis attacked but aspects of modern culture. There are formative ideas in modern culture that, as he points out in *The Screwtape Letters*, come, so to speak, straight from hell. However, while this philosophy from hell has had large effects on modern culture, not everything has been taken over by it. Lewis had a stout theological view of humanity, of history, of the so-called natural world and of culture. I do not think, then, that Lewis put *The Lion, The Witch and the Wardrobe* ahead of *The Magician's Nephew* because he thought that the doctrine of Redemption was the more important of the two. If he did not put it first for that reason, why then did he?

I think that he did so because of the effects of the White Witch's spell. Those effects created a condition in Narnia of constant winter without any Christmas. In other words, the White Witch turned Narnia into a homogeneous, colorless and joyless place. We can see this in several ways. While she dispenses Turkish Delight, she does so only to seduce. Those that come into her orbit are struck with stasis. She has in every way a deadening effect.

This homogenizing and deadening effect, this joyless world, is not unlike the world of contemporary Western culture that Lewis recognized around him. The principal effect of modern culture has been to disenchant and to homogenize the world. It has tried to limit the world we live in to a world that we understand and control. This means that we have little sense of wonder, of the unexpected and the possible. And anyone who lacks a sense of such things cannot begin to talk about or to understand religion, especially Christianity. People who think of themselves as Christians but cover the world, like the snow that covers Narnia, with answers and the mastery that answers give are not living in a Christian world or in the world as Christians. They are living in a world determined by their own sense of power and importance, a sense that they have wrongly Christianized. So, it is important, for understanding Lewis, to have the effects of mastery and control thawed so that the unexpected, the truly delightful and the miraculous can again have a hearing, a hearing they can only have if the curse of certainty and control is lifted. So, it is not so much the doctrine of Redemption that needs to be in place in order for the doctrine of Creation to emerge; rather, a re-enchanted world must emerge before either of the doctrines can begin to have a place. One of the two doctrines does not set the terms for the other; the two are mutually clarifying, and both require a re-enchanted world.

III

One more matter needs to be taken up—namely, warfare. There is a lot of fighting in The Chronicles of Narnia, including *The Lion, The Witch and the Wardrobe*. Perhaps *The Magician's Nephew* should be first because there is less fighting in it. Perhaps those who changed the order thought that children should be eased into warfare slowly and not thrust into it so quickly.

Why is there so much fighting and talk of fighting in The Chronicles of Narnia? The obvious answer would be that Lewis thought of the life of the Christian in the world as basically oppositional, that the world is dominated by evil and that the life of the Christian is one that can most fully be described in terms of battle and conflict. Did Lewis arrange The Chronicles in order to make conflict primary? I don't think so.

Lewis thought that it was a typically modern and especially unfortunate view of the world to consider conflict as basic and defining. The view that society is constituted by people who are primarily in competition and even at war with one another finds its origins in the early seventeenth century and takes a new and vital twist toward the end of the nineteenth century in social Darwinism. In *The Screwtape Letters* Lewis sees the assumption that life is basically conflicted as part of the philosophy of hell. He certainly did not want to import such a philosophy into Christianity.

Rather, for Lewis conflict is called for when something has to be removed, something that has covered or denies what is truly basic—

namely, celebration. This is what has to happen with the reign of the White Witch. When the obstacles to celebration have been removed, things are restored and made sound. Conflict, for Lewis, is temporary and strategic. It does not provide the basic mode of our being in the world. This is because, for Lewis, evil is not ultimate but derivative. Indeed, evil does not have a being of its own but feeds on the good. It is at times difficult to discern lies and other forms of evil, for Lewis, because they attach themselves to good things, as do the lies perpetrated by the false Aslan in *The Last Battle*. Evil and falsehood are ugly and devouring parasites, and they threaten to absorb all that is true and good, along with what is particular, and to homogenize and devour them. Delivering things from evil often takes not only hard work but also courageous and risky deeds. At times, it even takes doing battle. But conflict is not permanent and not basic for Lewis. I think that Lewis did not try to shield young readers from conflicts because he thought conflicts were not only temporary and strategic but also housed within a narrative of the more positive and enduring realities of relationships and celebration. Thanks to Aslan, the obstacles to celebration can be removed, and the potential for celebration and joy built into the Creation can be released.

IV

I wish that we could reinstate the order of The Chronicles as Lewis set it out. It gives rightful place to the spatial imagination. It restores the potential for understanding such Christian doctrines as Creation and Redemption that resides in the human capacity for wonder and for delight in the possible. And it shows that battle and conflict are not the basic terms of the Christian life but occasions and actions for removing the obstacles to that celebrative potential that Creation and Redemption contain and ensure.

Wesley A. Kort is professor in and chair of the Department of Religion and a member of the Graduate Faculty of Religion at Duke University. He has his Ph.D. degree from the University of Chicago, and, before joining the faculty at Duke, he taught in the Department of Religion at Princeton University. He was born in Hoboken, NJ, and he did his undergraduate work at Calvin College in Grand Rapids, Michigan. He is the author of many articles and of nine books, the most recent of them being Place and

Space in Modern Fiction (*University of Florida Press, 2004*) *and* C. S. Lewis Then and Now (*Oxford University Press, 2001*). *At the present time he is working on a book that will address the question of religious identity and its relation to autobiography. Professor Kort has given lectures at many universities; within the last year he presented papers at Claremont University, at the University of Calgary and at Trinity College, Oxford. He is the recipient of a distinguished teaching award at Duke University.*

References

Bachelard, Gaston. 1964. *The Poetics of Space*. New York: The Orion Press.

Lewis, C. S. 1982. *Of This and Other Worlds*. Ed. Walter Hooper. London: Collins.

———. 2001. *The Abolition of Man*. San Francisco: HarperCollins.

Schakel, Peter J. 2002. *Imagination and the Arts in C. S. Lewis: Journeying to Narnia and Other Worlds*. Columbia: Univ. of Missouri Press.

JOSEPH PEARCE

Narnia and Middle-earth: When Two Worlds Collude

BACK IN 1997 several major opinion polls in the United Kingdom confirmed the place of The Lord of the Rings by J. R. R. Tolkien as the most popular book series of the twentieth century.[1] A few years later, from the release of *The Fellowship of the Ring* in December 2001 until the release of *The Return of the King* two years later, Peter Jackson's three-part film version of Tolkien's epic became the movie phenomenon of the new century. Now, and no doubt inspired by the success of Jackson's blockbuster, Walt Disney Studios and Walden Media are releasing a movie entitled *The Chronicles of Narnia: The Lion, the Witch and the Wardrobe* in the hope that the children's classic by C. S. Lewis can emulate the success of Tolkien.

It is indeed singularly appropriate that Lewis should be following in the footsteps of his great friend, Tolkien, not least because, as we shall see, he was following in Tolkien's footsteps when he wrote The Chronicles of Narnia. It would in fact not be an exaggeration to describe Lewis as a follower of Tolkien, at least in the area of what might be termed

---

[1] For full details of these polls see Joseph Pearce's *Tolkien: Man and Myth* (1998, 1–10).

their shared philosophy of myth. A look at the history of their friendship will illustrate how Lewis was greatly influenced by his friend and how Tolkien, for his part, benefited greatly from the encouragement he received from Lewis during his writing of The Lord of the Rings.

In his autobiography, *Surprised by Joy*, C. S. Lewis describes how his first meeting with Tolkien forced him to confront his own prejudices: "At my first coming into the world I had been (implicitly) warned never to trust a Papist, and at my first coming into the English Faculty (explicitly) never to trust a philologist. Tolkien was both" (1998, 168). Lewis' upbringing in the sectarian atmosphere of Belfast had colored the way in which he perceived "Papists" (Catholics), and the prejudice persisted long after his Protestant faith had dissolved. Having lost the lukewarm Christian faith of his childhood, Lewis was a somewhat reluctant atheist at the time that he and Tolkien first met in Oxford in May 1926. Lewis' first impressions of Tolkien as "a smooth, pale, fluent little chap" (Lewis 1991, 392) gave no indication that he saw in Tolkien someone with whom he was destined to form a long and enduring friendship. The touchstone of their friendship, and the touchwood that ignited it, was their shared love for mythology.

Shortly before their first meeting, Tolkien had formed the Coalbiters, a club of Tolkien's fellow academics dedicated to the reading of the Icelandic sagas and myths. Its name derived from the Icelandic *Kolbitar*, a lighthearted term for those who lounge so close to the fire in winter that they bite the coal. Membership was restricted initially to those with a reasonable knowledge of Icelandic, but exceptions were made for enthusiastic beginners such as Lewis. By January 1927, Lewis was a regular frequenter of meetings of the Coalbiters, finding the company of Tolkien and other like-minded scholars invigorating.

Friendship with Tolkien and membership of the Coalbiters rekindled Lewis' passion for the "northernness" that had inspired the imagination of his youth. It was a reigniting of old and yet young passions. Tolkien, six years Lewis' senior, soon became not merely a friend but a mentor. In December 1929, Lewis wrote to a friend that he had been up until the early hours of the morning "talking to the Anglo-Saxon professor Tolkien...discoursing of the gods and giants of Asgard for three hours," adding that "the fire was bright and the talk was good" (Carpenter 1978, 28). If Lewis had found in Tolkien a kindred spirit who shared his love for the Norse myths, it seems that Tolkien also detected in Lewis a soul with whom he could share his own creative endeavours at myth-making. Taking Lewis into his confidence, he lent him his poem on Beren and Luthien, two heroic characters who would be alluded to in The Lord of the Rings and who would finally emerge as central figures in *The Silmarillion* following its eventual publication almost half a century later. On December 7, Lewis wrote to Tolkien expressing his enthusiasm:

> I can quite honestly say that it is ages since I have had an evening of such delight: and the personal interest of reading a friend's work had very little to do with it—I should have enjoyed it just as well if I'd picked it up in a bookshop, by an unknown author. The two things that come out clearly are the sense of reality in the background and the mythical value: the essence of a myth being that it should have no taint of allegory to the maker and yet should *suggest* incipient allegories to the reader. (30)

The last sentence has a particular resonance with regard to the work of both writers because it touches upon aspects of the philosophy of myth which inspired their creative vision and underpinned their respective literary works. Take, for instance, Lewis' denial, in the following letter to schoolchildren written in 1954, that The Chronicles of Narnia were "allegorical" in any crudely formal or clumsily intentional way:

> You are mistaken when you think that everything in the books "represents" something in this world. Things do that in *The Pilgrim's Progress* but I'm not writing in that way. I did not say to myself "Let us represent Jesus as He really is in our world by a Lion in Narnia": I said "Let us *suppose* that there were a land like Narnia and that the Son of God, as He became a Man in our world, became a Lion there, and then imagine what would have happened." If you think about it, you will see that it is quite a different thing. (Hooper 1996, 425)

Clearly, Lewis was at pains to distance the Narnian stories from the sort of formal or crude allegory of which *The Pilgrim's Progress* is perhaps the most obvious exemplar (although it is noteworthy that Lewis succumbed to the genre of formal allegory himself with great success in the semiautobiographical *The Pilgrim's Regress*). It is also evident from his discussion of the issue in *The Allegory of Love* that Lewis understood that there is a crucial distinction between formal allegory and what could be called informal allegory, the latter being the allegory of applicable significance which is almost universally present, to one degree or another, in literature and beyond:

> Allegory, in some sense, belongs not to medieval man but to man, or even to mind, in general. It is of the very nature of thought and language to represent what is immaterial in picturable terms. What is good or happy has always been high like the heavens and bright like the sun. (424)

In essence, Lewis is asserting that the human mind works allegorically at its most fundamental level. In this sense, allegory is almost universally present in all our thoughts. It is ubiquitous and inescapable. We cannot think without succumbing, at some level, to the making of allegorical connections. Lewis distinguished this broad definition of allegory from formal allegory, which he defined thus:

> [Y]ou can start with an immaterial fact, such as the passions which you actually experience, and can then invent *visibilia* [visible things] to express them. If you are hesitating between an angry retort and a soft answer, you can express your state of mind by inventing a person called *Ira* [Anger] with a torch and letting her contend with another invented person called *Patientia* [Patience]. This is allegory. (424)

In fact, *pace* Lewis, and in view of the earlier broader definition, this is not an instance of allegory *per se* but of *formal* allegory.

Perhaps at this juncture it might be helpful to look at the whole question of allegory, formal and informal, in more detail.

St. Augustine writes about the most basic level of allegory with unexcelled eloquence in *De Doctrina Christiana* (*On Christian Doctrine*), in which he distinguishes between natural and conventional signs. Natural signs signify something beyond themselves without any intention of so doing. Examples of natural signs given by Augustine include smoke signifying fire and animal tracks signifying the animal that made them (St. Augustine 1997, 34). Conventional signs signify something beyond themselves with the intention of those employing them. In human usage the most common conventional signs are words, either spoken or written. In the case of all signs, natural or conventional, the thing signified can only be ascertained through a process of quasi-allegorical applicability. One must know that a three-letter word, dog, signifies a certain type of four-legged mammal, or that the same three letters, when arranged in reverse order, signify the supreme being and creator of the universe (if the g is in upper case) or some lesser being of supernatural power (if the g is in lower case). In each case a leap of imaginative applicability needs to be made from the "dead" letter of the literal thing or things being used as *signs* to the "living" meaning *signified*, i.e., the individual letters (*signs*) arranged to make a word (another *sign*) to bring to our mind the *picture* of the thing signified, e.g., dog, or God. This involves allegory, at least in the broadest and most basic sense in which the word is used.

Moving from the most basic understanding of allegory to what could be seen as the strictest and most elaborate, St. Thomas Aquinas asserted that there were four levels of meaning in Scripture, namely the literal, the allegorical, the moral and the anagogical. It is of course arguable that this four-fold exegesis is not applicable to literature as a whole and is only applicable to, and appropriate for, a theological reading of the Bible. Such a view was not shared by the author of arguably the greatest work of literature ever written. Dante insisted that his magnificent poem, *The Divine Comedy*, should be read according to St. Thomas' four-fold method.[2] This is interesting within the context of our understanding of Narnia and Middle-earth because Dante's magnum opus is not a *formal* allegory. Dante, Virgil, Beatrice and the various individuals they meet on their travels are principally themselves. They are not mere personified abstractions even though they have an allegorical dimension. Similarly, Dante does not meet seven deadly monsters named Pride, Envy, Lust, etc., representing the seven deadly sins, as he would have done had his work been a formal allegory; he meets real historical people who were guilty of these sins. Incidentally, it should be noted that Dante's influence on Lewis was considerable, so much so that he ranks alongside Tolkien, G. K. Chesterton and George MacDonald as one of Lewis' major mentors.[3]

[2] Dante, in a letter to his patron, Can Grande della Scala, cited in Dorothy L. Sayers' *Dante: The Divine Comedy: Hell* (1949, 14–15).

[3] For an appraisal of Dante's influence on Lewis, see Joseph Pearce's *C. S. Lewis and the Catholic Church* (2003).

Amongst the best-known examples of formal allegory, i.e., allegories that follow the formula given by Lewis regarding the invention of *visibilia* to represent abstract ideas (or what Lewis calls "immaterial facts"), are Dryden's *The Hind and the Panther* and, of course, Bunyan's *The Pilgrim's Progress*. We can, however, see examples of formal allegory in Lewis' own work. In *The Pilgrim's Regress*, "Reason" is a beautiful woman, clad in armor and mounted on a horse. She has two younger sisters, "Philosophy" and "Theology," and she successfully defeats a giant called the "Spirit of the Age." In presenting characters such as these, who are mere personified abstractions, Lewis gives us a perfect example of the formal or crude allegory that he spurns elsewhere in his work. In contrast, Lewis wrote that Reepicheep, in *The Voyage of the Dawn Treader*, can be seen as a figurative representation of the spiritual life (Hooper 1996, 426). Unlike Reason, however, Reepicheep is, first and foremost, a talking mouse!

The difference between Reepicheep and Reason is crucial. Reepicheep is *himself*, i.e., not a personified abstraction, and he only reminds us of the spiritual life *incidentally* in the sense that we see *instances* of the "spiritual life" in certain *incidents* in the story in which Reepicheep is involved and in which he behaves in a certain way or says certain things. At other times he is simply a talking mouse with an inimitable and indomitable charm who does not remind us allegorically of anything in particular. Reason, on the other hand, is always what she represents. Reason is always "reason." She is never anything else. She has no personality; she has no identity beyond, or separate from, the thing she represents.

In order to visualize the difference between *formal* or crude allegory (Reason) and *informal* or subtle allegory (Reepicheep), it might be helpful to see a formal allegory as a hook or point on which the author hangs the plot and the characters of his story. The point (and the plot and the characters) only exist to make the point that the author wishes to make. The point points to the point! In formal allegory there is no escaping the purpose for which the author wrote the story or the point he is trying to make. This domination by the author over the freedom of the reader's imagination was at the root of Lewis' and Tolkien's disdain for formal allegory. In contrast, an informal allegory, or more correctly a story containing an informal allegorical dimension, can be likened to a piece of string. The string is the story line. It has a beginning, a middle and an end. At certain moments the string is tied into knots (whether consciously or unconsciously by the author) and it is only at these particular "knots" in the story that moments of allegorical applicability can be discerned. A good example of this type of allegory is *Beowulf*, a work that was greatly admired by, and hugely influential on, both Lewis and Tolkien. In this story Beowulf is a Christ figure at certain moments, particularly at the moments of his combat with the monsters, but for the rest of the time he is simply the prince (and later king) of the Geats. Needless to say, The Chronicles of Narnia and The Lord of the Rings are examples of informal or subtle allegory.

This discussion of the meaning and nature of allegory is not merely academic in the esoteric or *obscurum per obscurius* sense of the word but is essential to a true and deeper understanding of the work of both Lewis and Tolkien. Generally though not exclusively speaking, Lewis and Tolkien tended to use the word "allegory" in its formal sense. Thus Lewis, in his letter to the schoolchildren, could deny that Aslan is allegorical, and Tolkien could say that he "despised" allegory and that The Lord of the Rings "is neither allegorical nor topical."[4] On the other hand, and on other occasions, Lewis could write that the "whole Narnian story is about Christ" (Hooper 1996, 426), and Tolkien could write that "The Lord of the Rings is of course a fundamentally religious and Catholic work" (Carpenter 1981, 172). Since Christ is never mentioned by name in either Narnia or Middle-earth, the Christian significance in both works is only discernible through leaps of imaginative applicability that is certainly allegorical in the looser and broader sense of the word. How else does one discern Christ in Narnia except through making allegorical connections? How else does one unravel the "fundamentally religious and Catholic" dimension in Middle-earth without seeking and discovering the levels of Christian allegory with which the works of Tolkien are awash?

In order to understand more fully these allegorical connections in the works of Lewis and Tolkien it is necessary to return to the philosophy of myth that they shared. It is necessary, in fact, to return to the letter from Lewis to Tolkien which spoke of "the essence of a myth being that it should have no taint of allegory to the maker and yet should *suggest* incipient allegories to the reader." In the light of what we know about

---

[4] J. R. R. Tolkien, Foreword to the second edition of The Lord of the Rings.

the relationship between Tolkien and Lewis, particularly with regard to Tolkien's exposition of his philosophy of myth in a famous conversation with Lewis in September 1931, it is reasonable to assume that Lewis' words in this particular letter display the younger man in disciple mode, echoing the line of reasoning that Tolkien had already expounded to him, perhaps during the discourse on "the gods and giants of Asgard" in early December 1929 when "the fire was bright and the talk was good." Certainly it is known that Tolkien despised formal allegory precisely because it involved the author's desire to dominate the reader's imagination, forcing it into the straitjacket of personified abstraction. Myth, on the other hand, freed the writer and reader from all such straitjackets in that the purpose of myth-making, first and foremost, was to tell a story which would be allowed to grow in the telling and to develop a life of its own. This "life" would of its own creative nature convey allegorical significance beyond the intention of the author.

Tolkien's philosophy of myth, destined to have such a profound influence on Lewis, is conveyed implicitly in the Ainulindalë, the elvish Creation myth in *The Silmarillion*, and more explicitly in his two critical essays "On Fairy-Stories" (1984) and on *Beowulf*.[5] It is also expounded through the medium of unabashed allegory in his short story "Leaf by Niggle" and, most memorably, in his poem "Mythopoeia."

"Mythopoeia" was written "[t]o one who said that myths were lies and therefore worthless, even though 'breathed through silver.'" The "one" to whom this dedication referred was Lewis himself, who had claimed that myths were merely beautiful lies during a conversation on mythology in Oxford in September 1931, a conversation that has now been enshrined as being pivotal to Lewis' final embrace of Christianity. *"No,"* Tolkien had replied emphatically. *"They are not"* (Carpenter 1977, 151). He followed this blunt rebuttal with a lucid exposition of the nature and supernature of mythology which can be summarized as follows[6]:

Since we are made in the image of God and since we know that God is the Creator, it follows that our creativity is the expression of the *ima-*

---

[5] "Beowulf: The Monsters and the Critics" was the Sir Israel Gollancz Memorial Lecture to the British Academy, read on 25 November 1936.

[6] This summary is a paraphrased composite of Tolkien's exposition of the nature of myth from a variety of sources, including his essay "On Fairy-Stories," his short allegory "Leaf by Niggle," his poem "Mythopoeia," his published letters, his creation myth in *The Silmarillion* and the accounts given in a number of biographical studies.

geness of God in us. As such, all myths, as the product of human creativity, contain splintered fragments of the one true light that comes from God. Far from being lies, they are a means of gaining an inkling of the deep truths of metaphysical reality. God is the Creator, the only being able to make things from nothing, whereas we are sub-creators, beings made in God's creative image who are able to partake of His Creative Gift by making new things from other things that already exist. Put simply, we tell our stories with words, God tells His Story with History. The fact that Facts serve the Truth is another way of saying that Providence prevails. In essence, Tolkien believed that Christianity is the True Myth, the myth that really happened. It is the archetypal myth that makes sense of all the others. It is the Myth to which all other myths are in some way a reflection, a myth that works in the same way as all the others except that it exists in the realm of Fact as well as in the realm of Truth.

For Tolkien the pagan myths, far from being lies, were, in fact, God expressing Himself through the minds of poets, using the images of their "mythopoeia" to reveal fragments of His eternal truth. Most astonishing of all, Tolkien maintained that Christianity was exactly the same except for the enormous difference that the poet who invented it was God Himself, and the images He used were real men and actual history.

Tolkien's arguments had an indelible effect on Lewis. Twelve days later, Lewis wrote to his friend, Arthur Greeves, that he had "just passed on from believing in God to definitely believing in Christ," adding that his "long night talk with ... Tolkien had a good deal to do with it" (Carpenter 1978, 45). The full extent of Tolkien's influence can be gauged from another of Lewis' letters to Greeves, written only a month after the "long night talk":

> Now the story of Christ is simply a true myth: a myth working on us in the same way as the others, but with this important difference that *it really happened*: and one must be content to accept it in the same way, remembering that it is God's myth where the others are men's myths: i.e. the Pagan stories are God expressing Himself through the minds of poets, using such images as He found there, while Christianity is God expressing Himself through what we call "real things."
> (Hooper 1979, 427–28)

Lewis would expand upon this core thesis in his exposition of the "pictures" of the pagans during Father History's discourse on the difference
between the pagans and the Jews in *The Pilgrim's Regress*. It is, however,
clear that he owed his initial inspiration to Tolkien's philosophy of myth.
It is also clear that the conception of (sub)creativity which underpins
this philosophy would have a profound and pronounced effect upon
the approach of Lewis and Tolkien toward their own work. It was their
shared belief in the *gift* of creativity that led to their dislike of formal
allegory. For Tolkien and Lewis, formal allegory constituted an abuse of
the gift. The logic that led them to this conclusion runs as follows:

The product of human creativity is the fruit of the relationship between the gift and the one who receives it. At the heart of this relationship is freedom. The gift is freely given and the one who receives it is
free to use or abuse it. In the same way that God as the Giver does not
remove the gift of life the moment that it is abused through acts of sin,
so He doesn't remove the gift of creativity the moment that it is abused
through the sub-creation of immoral works. Even immoral works contain splintered fragments of the one true light insofar as they serve as
a mirror of the soul of their sub-creator and insofar as they reflect the
true ugliness of evil. It is, however, the duty of good artists to cooperate with the gift of creativity by seeking to cooperate with the Giver of
the gift. This cooperation involves faith in the gift itself to transcend
and enrich the powers of the one who receives it. Put simply, if one has
faith in the powers of the gift, derived from the power of the Giver, one
will allow the gift the freedom it needs to breathe life into the creative
work. In allowing a story to take on a life of its own a writer allows the
gift itself—or, more correctly, the Giver of the gift—to add dimensions
of truth beyond the conscious designs of the storyteller. By contrast,
in seeking in his pedagogy and didacticism to dominate the reader, the
writer of a formal allegory dominates the gift, thereby enslaving it and
depriving it of much of its power.

It is in the light of this logic that one should view Tolkien's statement
that "The Lord of the Rings is of course a fundamentally religious and
Catholic work; unconsciously so at first, but consciously in the revi-
sion" (Carpenter 1981, 172). From this one statement we can deduce
Tolkien's *modus operandi* when he was writing his *magnum opus*. He
began with no agenda aforethought and had no particular allegory in
mind. His desire was purely and simply to cooperate with the creative

gift, his *modus operandi* accepting its *modus vivendi* with the gift-giver. The story was allowed to emerge "unconsciously" and was only revised "consciously." The end result is a text of such transcendental texture that it appears to be alive, breathing life into itself so that its multilayered mythological meanings appear to multiply with successive readings. It is larger than its readers and, mystery of mysteries, is larger than its author. This is true of The Lord of the Rings as it is true of all great literature. The greater the literature, the greater the gap between the author and the work. Nonetheless, and this is crucial, there is still and is always a connection between the author and the work. Tolkien could not have written *The Lord of the Flies* any more than William Golding could have written The Lord of the Rings, both of which were published in the same year, 1954. This connection is what might be termed the incarnational aspect of the creative act. The Lord of the Rings is a reflection of the personhood of Tolkien, even though its mystical coauthor, the *gift* of creative talent, may magnify that personhood and transform and transcend it. This connection between an author and his work was discussed by Tolkien explicitly in a letter written in October 1958 in which he insisted that "only one's guardian Angel, or indeed God Himself, could unravel the real relationship between personal facts and an author's works" (288).

Having ascertained the philosophy of myth that united Lewis and Tolkien, the extent to which it influenced The Chronicles of Narnia is discernible. "The whole Narnian story is about Christ," Lewis declared, adding that it was based on the following "supposal":

> "Supposing that there really was a world like Narnia and supposing it had (like our world) gone wrong and supposing Christ wanted to go into that world and save it (as He did ours) what might have happened?" The stories are my answers. Since Narnia is a world of Talking Beasts, I thought He would become a Talking Beast there, as He became a man here. (Hooper 1996, 426)

Lewis "pictured" Aslan becoming a lion because of the lion's status as king of the beasts and because Christ is called the "Lion of Judah" in the Bible. He had also been having "strange dreams about lions" when he began writing the work.

According to Lewis' own estimation the "whole series" of Narnian stories works itself out as follows: *The Magician's Nephew* "tells the Creation and how evil entered Narnia," i.e., the Narnia Creation Myth; *The Lion, the Witch and the Wardrobe* re-presents "the Crucifixion and Resurrection"; *Prince Caspian* tells of the "restoration of the true religion after a corruption"; *The Horse and His Boy* centers on "the calling and conversion of a heathen"; *The Voyage of the Dawn Treader* reflects "the spiritual life (especially in Reepicheep)"; *The Silver Chair* exemplifies "the continued war against the powers of darkness"; and *The Last Battle* relates "the coming of the Antichrist (the Ape)" and the "end of the world and the Last Judgement" (426). In short, and in accordance with Lewis' own description of the series, The Chronicles of Narnia begin with the Narnian "Genesis" and end with the Narnian "Apocalypse," reflecting Biblical chronology at least in the alpha and omega of its beginning and end.

Although, *"in the beginning,"* Aslan's wild and glorious song of Creation in Narnia echoes the Great Music of Ilúvatar in the Creation of Middle-earth, the consummation of Narnia at the climax of *The Last Battle* has little in common with the concluding lines of The Lord of the Rings. Lewis presents us with a heavenly scenario in which "we can most truly say that they all lived happily ever after" (2001, 767). Tolkien leaves us with Samwise Gamgee stranded in "the Long Defeat" clutching "occasional glimmers of Final Victory."[7] Lewis ties up all the loose ends and leaves us with a conclusion (in both senses of the word); Tolkien leaves us at a loose end still awaiting a conclusion that remains elusive. Lewis ends with all our hopes fulfilled; Tolkien ends with our hopes awaiting fulfillment.

In spite of such important differences and all that they imply about the literary approach of both men, the influence of The Lord of the Rings on The Chronicles of Narnia remains inestimable. Tolkien read each chapter of The Lord of the Rings to Lewis at the weekly meetings of the Inklings as it was being written, and one can only wonder at the wonderful and wonder-filled hours that Tolkien spent in Lewis' company explaining the work during the catalytic process of its creation. Certainly he found in Lewis one of its greatest admirers and advocates both before and after its publication. "The unpayable debt that I owe to

---

[7] Tolkien refers to history as the "long defeat with only occasional glimmers of final victory" in one of his letters, a view that is reflected by Galadriel in The Lord of the Rings when she says that she and Celeborn "through ages of the world...have fought the long defeat."

him," Tolkien wrote of Lewis, "was not 'influence' as it is ordinarily understood, but sheer encouragement. He was for long my only audience. Only from him did I ever get the idea that my 'stuff' could be more than a private hobby" (Carpenter 1978, 32). This view of Lewis' importance as an "encourager" was reiterated by Tolkien in a letter to Professor Clyde Kilby in December 1965: "But for the encouragement of C. S. L. I do not think that I should ever have completed or offered for publication The Lord of the Rings" (Pearce 2003, 36). Lewis' own estimation of the work was expressed in a letter to Tolkien shortly after Lewis had read through the completed typescript of The Lord of the Rings in the autumn of 1949. It was, he asserted, "almost unequalled in the whole range of narrative art known to me" (Carpenter 1977, 207).

Tolkien's "unpayable debt" to Lewis was repaid more than adequately by Tolkien's positive influence on Lewis' own intellectual, spiritual and creative development. It is, however, a little surprising that Tolkien failed to sympathize with most of Lewis' work. If Lewis had been a great "encourager" to Tolkien he must have been greatly discouraged by Tolkien's lack of enthusiasm for his own efforts at fiction. In 1949, the same year that Lewis was enthusing about the finished typescript of The Lord of the Rings, Lewis began to read the first of his Narnia stories to the Inklings. This was The Lion, the Witch and the Wardrobe, destined to become one of the most popular children's books ever written. Tolkien was unimpressed. "It really won't do!" he exclaimed to Roger Lancelyn Green, a mutual friend who would later become Lewis' biographer. "I mean to say: 'Nymphs and their Ways, The Love Life of a Faun'!" (204). Later, Tolkien would write that it was "sad that 'Narnia' and all that part of C. S. L.'s work should remain outside the range of my sympathy" (Carpenter 1981, 352). Why, one wonders, should this be so?

Tolkien's almost obsessive perfectionism led to the expectation of very high standards and an intolerance of the efforts of those who failed to attain such heights. Tolkien must have been aware of his influence on Lewis and must have been aware also that Lewis' creation of Narnia was all too obviously a reflection, albeit a pale reflection in shallower creative waters, of his own creation of Middle-earth. The wistful gravitas of The Lord of the Rings grated with the whimsical gaiety of The Lion, the Witch and the Wardrobe; hence Tolkien's scoffing at the juxtaposition of mythical creatures worthy of respect, such as nymphs or fauns, with the descent into the vulgar vernacular, "and their Ways" and "Love Life."

Similarly, Tolkien would probably have been decidedly uncomfortable with the insertion of inconsistent and incompatible objects into a mythical world, such as lampposts and umbrellas. As a cultural Luddite who despised most manifestations of technological "progress," he would have looked upon the gate-crashing of these objects of modernity into the purity of a mythological world as pollutants of the world itself and of the imagination of the reader. Finally, Lewis' work, based upon what he termed "supposals," lacked the subtlety of applicability for which Tolkien strived. For all Lewis' assertions that The Chronicles of Narnia were not an "allegory," it is clear that Aslan is *always* a figure of Christ, albeit a Narnian manifestation of Christ, in all the stories and at each and every moment. Compare this with the subtlety with which Frodo, Gandalf and Aragorn *remind* us of Christ while always remaining themselves and while always being distinct from Christ, even at the moments when they most remind us of Him. Although, strictly speaking, Lewis is right to assert that the Narnia stories are not formal allegories, they can be seen to be closer to formal allegories than are the stories of Middle-earth. Put bluntly, one suspects that Tolkien's subtle sensibilities considered Narnia too close to "crude" or "formal" allegory for his liking. One suspects also that Lewis not only understood Tolkien's objections but agreed with them, at least in part. This was probably why Lewis considered his late work, *Till We Have Faces*, to be his "best book" and his "favourite of all my books" (Hooper 1996, 243). In this book, subtitled *A Myth Retold*, Lewis resists his natural inclination to didacticism and controls his desire to teach his readers a lesson. In consequence, he succeeds for the first time in submerging the allegory within the story with the subtlety that had hitherto eluded him.

In the final analysis, and in spite of Tolkien's criticism of Lewis' work, it would be wrong to suggest that Tolkien had not benefited as greatly as Lewis from their friendship, though in a different way. Tolkien's daughter Priscilla believed that her father owed an "enormous debt" to Lewis (Pearce 1998, 80), and his son, Christopher, was even more emphatic in his insistence that his father's friendship with Lewis was crucial to his creative achievement. "The profound attachment and imaginative intimacy between him and Lewis were in some ways the core to it," he said, adding that their friendship was of "profound importance...to both of them" (80). To put the matter in a nutshell, Lewis' debt to Tolkien is that if he had not known Tolkien, he would not have written

The Chronicles of Narnia; Tolkien's debt to Lewis is that if he had not known Lewis, he would never have finished The Lord of the Rings. Paradoxically, we have Tolkien to thank for Narnia, and Lewis to thank for Middle-earth. Such are the benefits, the power and the glory when two worlds collude.

Joseph Pearce, writer in residence and associate professor of literature at Ave Maria University in Naples, Florida, is the author of Tolkien: Man and Myth *and* C. S. Lewis and the Catholic Church, *both published by Ignatius Press. He is editor of the* Saint Austin Review.

References

Carpenter, Humphrey. 1977. *J. R. R. Tolkien: A Biography.* London: George Allen and Unwin.

———. 1978. *The Inklings.* London: George Allen and Unwin.

———. ed. 1981. *The Letters of J. R. R. Tolkien.* London: George Allen and Unwin.

Hooper, Walter, ed. 1979. *They Stand Together: The Letters of C. S. Lewis to Arthur Greeves (1914–1963).* New York: Macmillan.

———. 1996. *C. S. Lewis: A Companion and Guide.* London: HarperCollins.

Lewis, C. S. 1991. *All My Roads Before Me: The Diary of C. S. Lewis, 1922–1927.* New York: Harcourt Brace.

———. 1998. *Surprised by Joy.* London: HarperCollins.

———. 2001. The Chronicles of Narnia. New York: HarperCollins.

Pearce, Joseph. 1998. *Tolkien: Man and Myth.* San Francisco: Ignatius Press/London: HarperCollins.

———. 2003. *C. S. Lewis and the Catholic Church.* San Francisco: Ignatius Press.

Sayers, Dorothy L. 1949. *Dante: The Divine Comedy: Hell.* London: Penguin.

St. Augustine. 1997. *On Christian Doctrine.* Upper Saddle River, NJ: Prentice Hall.

Tolkien, J. R. R. 1984. *The Monsters and the Critics, and Other Essays.* New York: Houghton Mifflin.

RUSSELL W. DALTON

Aslan Is On the Move: Images of Providence in The Chronicles of Narnia

I S GOD A STERN AND TERRIBLE LION who is constantly acting behind the scenes to direct every aspect of our lives by scaring us and even slashing at our backs with sharp claws in order to direct us where we should go? Or is God a cuddly cat who may not intervene in our lives directly but will bring us comfort and subtle guidance? Through the character of Aslan, Lewis presents images of Christ and Christ's divine intervention in the world that reflect his own particular theological viewpoints. Lewis' picture of a sometimes gentle but often stern Lion who stands behind all events in the world may be ultimately unsatisfying and unconvincing for many readers, but it provides a rich narrative context for exploring one's own view of divine providence.

Providence and the Theology of C. S. Lewis

In theological studies, the doctrine of providence concerns a number of questions related to the manner in which God creates, sustains and directs the world. How does God work in the world today? Did God merely set the world in motion, or has God orchestrated and micromanaged every event in human history? Do accidents happen? Is there any such thing as luck? Does God work indirectly through humans and nature (Secondary Providence) or intervene directly (Primary Providence)? If God is in complete control, then do humans really have any free will or moral responsibility? Who is ultimately responsible for the good and evil that happens in the world, God or humankind? Does God cause suffering? How does God respond to us in the midst of our suffering? The questions raised by the problem of evil and suffering in the world are some of the most perplexing in the study of providence, and Christian theologians and laypeople arrive at a wide variety of answers to them. As theologian Tyron L. Inbody suggests:

> The conceptual problem in theology is called theodicy. Can I hold together without contradiction the ideas that God is omnibenevolent, that God is omnipotent, and that evil is real. Technically formulated: If God is omnipotent, God could prevent all evil. If God is all-loving, God would want to prevent all evil. But there is evil in the world. Therefore, we must question whether an omnipotent, perfectly good God exists. More broadly conceived, however, the problem is how to understand our experience of suffering and evil within the framework of what we believe God to be like. (Inbody 2005, 139-140)

Perhaps the most difficult problem facing the faithful when considering their belief about the providence of God is the image of God that it creates in their minds when they are faced with times of pain and suffering.

C. S. Lewis was one of the most well-known spokespeople and apologists for the Christian faith in his day. He dealt with issues of providence in his theological writings such as *The Problem of Pain* and *Miracles*. Perhaps part of the reason for his popularity was that he, alongside many Christian laypeople of various denominations, tried to hold together two popular strands of Christian thought that were thought to be contradictory by many of the theologians of his day. On the one hand, on matters of providence and theodicy, Lewis was a classical theist. Colin Duriez notes that Lewis was a proponent of "supernaturalism, the theistic view that the universe is a dependant creation of God. Time, space, and geometry are all God's creation, and only exist now because he chose to make them out of nothing" (Duriez 1990, 130). In classical theism, God is sovereign, in control and beyond human understanding. On the other hand, on matters of Christology, salvation and human freedom, Lewis stood more in the tradition of Western Trinitarian Orthodoxy. This approach incorporates belief in the incarnate Christ who lived as we live and was vulnerable and suffered on the cross. It holds out a greater place for human freedom and responsibility in the world. Lewis' wit, wisdom and considerable literary gifts made his work very popular, but he still faced many critiques from theologians.

C. S. Lewis' Imaginative "Supposal"

At the height of his popularity as a lay theologian, there is some indication that Lewis was growing frustrated with the difficulties he faced in making his points through rational discourse. A debate with Elizabeth Anscombe in particular, in which she successfully countered some of his arguments in *Miracles*, seemed to make him question his approach to Christian apologetics (Coren 1994, 65–67). Lewis surprised many of his readers when he abandoned writing theological essays for a time and began to write a series of fairy stories. In his essay, "Sometimes Fairy Stories May Say Best What's to be Said," Lewis explains that he thought that fairy stories could "steal past a certain inhibition which had paralyzed much of my own religion in childhood" by taking the stories of Christ and "stripping them of their stained-glass and Sunday school associations" (1982, 47).

The Chronicles of Narnia contain in Aslan an extended metaphor for Jesus Christ that Lewis hoped would teach children about Christ. Lewis was adamant, however, that The Chronicles of Narnia were not allegories of Christianity such as one would find in John Bunyan's novel *The Pilgrim's Progress*, in which every single person, place or thing represents something else (Hooper 1996, 424–25). Instead, he preferred to talk about his series as a "supposal."

> I did not say to myself "Let us represent Jesus as He really is in our world by a Lion in Narnia": I said "Let us *suppose* that there were a land like Narnia and that the Son of God, as He became a Man in our world, became a Lion there, and then imagine what would have happened." (425)

As he put it, "Supposing there was a world like Narnia, and supposing, like ours, it needed redemption, let us imagine what sort of Incarnation and Passion and Resurrection Christ would have there" (425).

A scene at the end of *The Voyage of the Dawn Treader* suggests one of Lewis' goals in writing The Chronicles. When Aslan informs Lucy and Edmund that they will not be returning to Narnia, he assures them that they will meet him again in our world:

> "Are—are you there too, Sir?" said Edmund.
>
> "I am," said Aslan. "But there I have another name. You must learn to know me by that name—this was the very reason why you were brought to Narnia, that by knowing me here for a little, you may know me better there." (2001b, 541)

What did Lewis want children to understand about Christ through Aslan? What sort of character can be both the all-powerful God of classical theism who is in complete control of creation and yet is still a crucified, merciful God who allows for and even demands human agency in the world? What sort of Christ figure intervenes at some times but not at others? In Aslan, Lewis attempted to present an image of Christ that holds together these seemingly contradictory sets of characteristics.

Aslan is Behind All Stories: Divine Sovereignty and Human Responsibility in Narnia

Lewis provides us with some intriguing images related to these issues in his Chronicles of Narnia. Who is the protagonist of the events of these books, Aslan or the children? Who is responsible for resolving the conflicts? Are Aslan's purposes accomplished through human or natural causes, or does Aslan intervene directly?

In *The Lion, the Witch and the Wardrobe*, Lewis' tale of passion and salvation, Aslan is present in the world much as Christ is in the biblical gospels. So readers might expect to see Aslan's repeated, direct and miraculous intervention to solve problems. Yet, we find that even here there is a restraint of divine, miraculous intervention. When Susan blows her magic horn, both Aslan and Peter come running to help. But Aslan does not simply defeat the enemy. Instead, he falls back and calls on Peter to win the fight, telling the others, "Back! Let the Prince win his spurs"

(170). Perhaps one reason for this type of human agency in The Chronicles is simply for the sake of dramatic effect. If every problem in the stories were solved by Aslan's all-powerful intervention, a *deus ex machina*, there would not be much drama to the stories. But it also demonstrates that Aslan wanted humans to play some role in the events of the world. Still, there are some things that only Aslan can do. When Peter wants to save Mr. Tumnus, Mr. Beaver explains that he cannot. Mr. Beaver tells Peter that "Aslan is on the move," and, "It is he, not you, who will save Mr. Tumnus" (146). In embodying Christ's role as the savior, it is only Aslan who can die and pay the price for Edmund's betrayal, and it is Aslan who miraculously breathes upon and resurrects the statues, including Mr. Tumnus. And though Aslan makes it clear that Peter cannot count on his help during the great climactic battle at Aslan's How, it is Aslan who ultimately defeats the Evil One, the White Witch.

Still, *The Lion, the Witch and the Wardrobe* introduces a limitation to Aslan's power. He cannot go against the Deep Magic that calls for blood in response to betrayal. When Lucy suggests that he do so, and simply overpower the White Witch, Aslan is stern in his reply.

> "Work against the Emperor's magic?" said Aslan, turning to her with something like a frown on his face. And nobody ever made that suggestion to him again. (176)

At first glance, then, Aslan is using humans to accomplish his plans, what is sometimes referred to in theological circles as Secondary Providence. But that is not the only way Aslan intervenes. There are clearly moments where Aslan intervenes directly, referred to as Primary Providence, in the events that follow.

The events of *Prince Caspian* take place over one thousand years after the events in *The Lion, the Witch and the Wardrobe* in Narnian years, but only one year later in the lives of the Pevensie children when they are brought back to Narnia. As the story begins Narnia is "an unhappy country" (341). The stories of Aslan's presence in Narnia are far in the past and few believe in them anymore. As the dwarf Nikabrik says about Aslan, "he was in Narnia only once that I ever heard of, and he didn't stay long" (393).

When Aslan first appears in this story he is visible only to Lucy, silently urging her to follow him. Peter balks at this. As Peter would later say, rather reasonably, "And why should Aslan be invisible to us? He never used to be. It's not like him" (383). When Lucy cannot convince her brothers and sister to follow her vision of Aslan, she gives up and goes with them. Later, Aslan chastises her for not leaving them to follow this mysterious vision of him on her own.

Even when Aslan does finally appear in physical form and talks with Lucy, it is clear that the rules are not the same as they were during the events of *The Lion, the Witch and the Wardrobe*. Lucy complains,

> "And I thought you'd come roaring in and frighten all the enemies away—like last time. And now everything is going to be horrid."
>
> "It is hard for you, little one," said Aslan. "But things never happen the same way twice. It has been hard for all of us in Narnia before now." (381)

In the end, while Aslan gives King Peter and Prince Caspian a great deal of responsibility in the battle, Aslan again takes a significant role in the battle and performs several miracles.

In the epics of the series, *The Voyage of the Dawn Treader* and *The Silver Chair*, Lewis more closely follows the mythic pattern of the heroes' quest. In ancient myths heroes often endure a trail of trials on their way to learning their true identity and their place in the world. The role of providence is present in these tales, but it is often a mysterious force that remains deep in the background of the stories (Dalton 2003, 21–26).

In *The Voyage of the Dawn Treader*, Lucy, Edmund and Eustace Scrubb are sent on a quest and endure many trials. Aslan's intervention is less apparent in these adventures. At one point, he appears as an albatross soaring high in the sky above the ship. Only Lucy recognizes this as an epiphany of Aslan, and while he does not save them from their troubles, his presence up above does grant Lucy some hope and courage.[1] In a motif that continues throughout the rest of The Chronicles, Aslan appears to them in dreamlike epiphanies in which he provides them with redemption, chastisement, moral conscience and comfort. It is a sign of their faith, virtue and good sense that they realize that they have indeed met Aslan. It is only at the end of the quest that Aslan appears in the flesh to the whole company.

In *The Silver Chair*, Aslan gives guidance to Jill Pole for her quest by

---

[1] Lewis, *The Voyage of the Dawn Treader*, 511.

providing her with "four signs" to memorize and follow. In their quest to find Prince Rilian and bring him home, Jill and her companions endure trolls, giants, a snowstorm, a terrible witch, a cave-in and many other dangers with only the signs to guide them. When a miracle does occur, it is seemingly a small one. The figure of the Lion has magically appeared on Prince Rilian's shield. They recognize this as a sign that Aslan is their Lord, and this encourages them to go on. Indeed, it is their faithfulness to Aslan's four signs, and not the direct intervention of Aslan himself, that saves them from the Underworld.

But although the children and their companions may have felt that their lives and their quest were in constant jeopardy, when they return to King Caspian's castle they discover that the happy conclusion to their quest was never in doubt. Aslan has already appeared to Caspian and told him to turn back his ship back home, for there he would find his long-lost son Prince Rilian waiting for him (Lewis 2001b, 657). So, Aslan had foreknowledge that the children would succeed in their quest, and in the end it is up to Aslan to blow the children back home and set everything right.

If Lewis' epics inched toward granting more human responsibility, his next novel would strongly reassert the primacy of divine sovereignty. In *The Horse and His Boy* Lewis ventured back into the earlier days of Narnian history just after the events of *The Lion, the Witch and the Wardrobe*. In this tale Aslan intervenes in many ways, in many forms and for many purposes. It is as if Lewis was afraid that he got carried away telling heroic tales of humans and talking animals and reasserts Aslan as the focus and the protagonist of his Chronicles.

In *The Horse and His Boy*, Aslan is everywhere, working in the shadows (unbeknownst to the main characters) in order to guide the action and orchestrate events. At one point Aslan appears as a small cat and lends comfort to the boy Shasta in the ancient tombs at night. But for much of the story Aslan is directing the action as a frightening, unseen lion who growls, snarls and terrifies. He frightens Shasta, Bree, Aravis and Hwin into coming together, scares them into going in the right direction, frightens others away from them and even terrorizes them by chasing behind them and nipping at their heels so that they will reach their destination in time to avert tragedy.

In his most shocking intervention, while chasing the children, Aslan tears at Aravis' shoulders with his claws to the point that "her back was covered with blood" (272). In *The Problem of Pain*, Lewis famously says, "God whispers to us in our pleasures, speaks in our conscience, but shouts in our pains: It is His megaphone to rouse a deaf world" (1962, 93). Lewis suggests, "[T]he proper good of a creature is to surrender itself to its Creator" (90), and pain can therefore bring about a good, for it shocks us out of our complacency and turns us toward God. But in *The Horse and His Boy*, Aslan scratches Aravis in order to teach her a lesson. In her efforts to escape her home, Aravis framed a slave to take the blame. "The scratches on your back, tear for tear, throb for throb, blood for blood, were equal to the stripes laid on the back of your stepmother's slave because of the drugged sleep you cast upon her. You needed to know what it felt like" (2001b, 299). In the story, Aravis humbly accepts this explanation and only asks if the slave girl is all right. Aslan abruptly denies her request for that information. The images in *The Horse and His Boy* suggest that it is Aslan's prerogative to intervene in the lives of people in many ways, including even inflicting pain on children, in order to direct their paths or teach them a lesson.[2]

In his book *The Four Loves*, Lewis wrote that we do not even meet our friends by chance, but rather a "secret Master of Ceremonies has been at work," bringing us together (1960, 126; Ford 1983, 334–35). Aslan is this Master of Ceremonies in *The Horse and His Boy*. When Shasta tells a still unseen Aslan that he has been unfortunate to meet so many lions, Aslan tells him that he was not unfortunate, but that it was Aslan all along directing his paths (2001b, 281). When Aravis tells the Hermit that she is lucky that the lion's scratches did not harm her more: "Daughter," said the Hermit, "I have now lived a hundred and nine winters in this world and have never yet met any such thing as Luck" (274). When Shasta discovers that he has stumbled into the country of Narnia at night, he says, "What luck that I hit it!—at least it wasn't luck at all really, it was *Him*, and now I'm in Narnia" (283). Shasta confirms this point and later when, ennobled as Prince Cor, he sagely tells the others that Aslan "seems to be at the back of all the stories" (302). So, according to *The Horse and His Boy* there is really no such thing as luck, just Aslan's unrecognized providential intervention.

In Narnia, then, Aslan can and occasionally does intervene to restore

---

[2] It is significant that Eustace Scrubb's wayward parents did not believe in spanking, and Experiment House, an example of all that is wrong in education, did not believe in strict discipline. See Lewis 2001, 549.

justice, defeat evil or test the faith of his subjects. And while humans may be given tasks to complete, Aslan is ultimately in control and orchestrating events in Narnia.

Aslan Is Not Tame: The Randomness of God's Intervention

If God can and does intervene, as Lewis seems to suggest, then why does God not always intervene for the cause of what is merciful, good and just? Some of the faithful have what appears to be a very inconsistent position on these matters. They believe that God answers their prayer for a convenient parking place when they are running late for an appointment, but have no problem accepting that God does not intervene to save the life of a child injured in a traffic accident. They thank God for providing good weather for a church picnic, but do not question why God did not turn away a tsunami that killed hundreds of thousands of people. In these situations, the seeming arbitrary nature of divine intervention can seem cruel and therefore inconsistent with the image of an all-loving and all-caring God.

If Aslan is caring and if Aslan is directing all that happens, then why does evil and suffering still occur in Narnia? If Aslan *can* intervene, and occasionally does intervene, then why does he not always bound in to prevent injustice and suffering? Why, for example, does Aslan intervene to spare Prince Caspian from death, but does not intervene earlier to prevent his father, the king, from being murdered?

The Chronicles of Narnia do not shy away from the arbitrary nature of divine intervention, but embrace it as a central characteristic of Aslan. Aslan, we are repeatedly told, is not tame. At the end of *The Lion, the Witch and the Wardrobe*, Mr. Beaver explains as much when Aslan slips away.

> "He'll be coming and going," he had said. "One day you'll see him and another you won't. He doesn't like being tied down—and of course he has other countries to attend to. It's quite all right. He'll often drop in. Only you mustn't press him. He's wild you know. Not like a *tame* lion." (194)

In *The Voyage of the Dawn Treader*, a friendly Magician tells Lucy, who's crestfallen Aslan is gone, "It's always like that, you can't keep him; it's not as if he were a *tame* lion" (500). By the time of *The Last Battle*, it appears that the phrase "He is not a Tame Lion" has become a litany and doctrine of the faithful (677).

Claiming that the Aslan is unpredictable because it is in his character to be so is not a convincing logical argument. It simply begs the question as to why God is not consistent in intervening on behalf of humankind. But by positing or supposing the character of a wild, untamed, unpredictable divinity in his narrative world, Lewis can present such actions as simply consistent with Aslan's character. Perhaps this was one area in which Lewis hoped to break down the resistance of readers, leading them simply to accept the notion that God is not consistent, rather than ask the more troubling theological questions that this inconsistency raises.

It's Digory's Fault: The Problem of Evil in Narnia

Creation is the ultimate act of providence, but one of the more problematic questions in theology concerns the origins of sin and evil. Who created evil? In Christian theology Satan is not a creator, but a fallen creation. God is the creator of all that is. This raises the question of whether God is the ultimate creator of evil. Even if one suggests that God merely created the *potential* for evil, this still makes God ultimately the creator of that potentiality. But why would and how could a wholly good God create evil?

Lewis' creation story, *The Magician's Nephew*, presents readers with a beautiful image of Aslan singing Narnia into existence. It is the classical theistic image of creation *ex nihilo*, creation out of nothing. It demonstrates creation's dependence on the Creator for its very existence. So if the wholly good Aslan created all of Narnia, how did evil enter into it?

In The Chronicles of Narnia the answer is quite simple. It is Digory Kirke's fault. In *The Magician's Nephew*, Digory has for the most part tried to be very good, but has had a very bad day. Because he nobly and quite heroically wants to rescue his friend Polly, he allows his evil uncle to send him on a dangerous journey into another world. He locates Polly, and eventually they find themselves in the dying world of Charn. There, Digory sees the sleeping members of a royal court and an intriguing bell with an inscription that calls for it to be rung. His curiosity gets the best of him and, in a momentary lapse of virtue and good judgment, he physically prevents Polly from leaving Charn and rings the bell. The bell awakens the evil witch Jadis, the queen of Charn, and her court. Through much scheming, and much to the children's pain and chagrin, Jadis is able to follow them as they travel to the crossroads of worlds. Digory and Polly are willing to sacrifice themselves in order to take Jadis out of their world, and eventually find themselves present at the creation of Narnia with Jadis in tow.

When Digory sees Aslan's power, he humbly and bravely asks the Lion if he can have some magic fruit to cure his mother. Aslan responds by shaming Digory in front of the Talking Animals and charging him with bringing evil into Narnia, in the form of the evil witch. "'You see, friends,' he said, 'that before the new, clean world I gave you is seven hours old, a force of evil has already entered it; waked and brought hither by this son of Adam'" (80).

In this way, Aslan appears to abdicate any responsibility for evil as coming into Narnia. It is not his doing, nor is there any mention of his father, the Emperor–over-the-Sea, creating Charn and its evil, or even that Jadis herself is the ultimate cause of evil. "Adam's race has done the harm" (80), he says.

While *The Magician's Nephew* clearly puts the responsibility for evil in Narnia on the shoulders of "Adam's race," it does not bother to address the stickier theological questions surrounding the origins of evil. Once again the narrative raises more questions than it answers. How, for example, did Jadis and evil get created in the first place? Who created the world of Charn where she came from?

In Lewis' story of the end of Narnia, *The Last Battle*, Aslan has once again not been seen in Narnia for a long time, and is absent for much of this story. When Aslan finally does appear, his providence and ultimate control over his creation is made perfectly clear. Aslan has the power to create the stars (677) and to blot them out (750). He created Narnia, and when its time comes, he is the one with the power to destroy it. Evil and suffering, however, are entirely the responsibility of the human race. Lewis' narrative does not offer an explanation for this seeming contradiction but again simply presents a narrative in which that is the case.

Submission to the Unknown Will of Aslan: Our Response to Providence

For those who have a classical theistic view of God's providence, the most practical question is, "How then should one live?" If God is ultimately directing the course of our lives, what is our moral responsibility in life?

In Narnia, it appears that children are to recognize that Aslan is ultimately in charge of all that happens to them. The ultimate virtue in Narnia, it seems, is to submit completely to the will of Aslan even if it does not appear to follow reason or be to one's own benefit.

In *Prince Caspian* the Pevensie children should have followed Lucy's vision of Aslan, even though that path defied all that reason would suggest that they do. In *The Silver Chair*, when Jill Pole meets the large Lion for the first time, Aslan is standing between her and a stream of water. Aslan affirms Jill Pole's fear that he might "eat girls" but he still expects her to walk up to him and take a drink (558). Later in *The Silver Chair*, a seemingly mad and violent knight cries out for the children to release him from his bonds in Aslan's name. Since invoking Aslan's name is the final of the four signs, they release him, despite the fact that they believe it may lead to their deaths. Later, when the prince sees the figure of a lion appear on his shield, he recognizes it as a "sign has that Aslan will be our good Lord, whether he means us to live or die" (673). Faith in Aslan offers no assurance that you will not die, then. Just that Aslan will be your Lord.

In *The Horse and His Boy*, the faithful talking horse Hwin takes this devotion to Aslan to a disturbing extreme. "Please," she said, "you're so beautiful. You may eat me if you like. I'd sooner be eaten by you than fed by anyone else" (299).

In *The Magician's Nephew*, Digory learns that Aslan's ultimate control is a good thing. Digory wants to negotiate a deal with Aslan to help heal his mother, but quickly realizes that "the Lion was not at all the sort of person one could try to make bargains with" (83). So he considers stealing a magic apple from Aslan's garden to heal her. But as Aslan explains, "Understand, then, that it would have healed her; but not to your joy or hers. The day would have come when both you and she would have looked back and said that it would have been better to die in that illness" (100). Aslan knows best, and the human perspective is insufficient to recognize the mercy in Aslan's work in the world.

In *The Last Battle*, King Tirian agrees that "they could come with him and take their chance, or, as he much more sensibly called it, 'the adventure that Aslan would send them'" (719). Although in grave danger, Jill Pole does not regret being brought back into Narnia, for, she says, "Even if we *are* killed. I'd rather be fighting for Narnia than grow old and stupid at home" (720).

Virtue in Narnia, then, is to recognize and submit to the will of Aslan. That is the greatest joy in life, even if it leads to trials and even death. People and Talking Animals can call upon Aslan for help, but they should not presume that they have been able to cause him to lend aid. They are called upon to be good and faithful, but they should not presume that they can really accomplish any good. As M. A. Manzalaoui writes:

> With this point, we are at the heart of the theology of the Narnia books. Human beings, forced by their good natures into vocations they never expected to adopt, conquer fear, persevere, grow in ability, determination and courage, but they often fail—yet there is virtue in such failure for it brings about the intervention of grace. Aslan, as Lewis says, comes bounding in. In fact, the virtuous actions were really the actions of Aslan." (1998, 214)

Certainly Aslan is in control. The efforts of the faithful often lead to failure and humble submission to the providence of Aslan.

In *The Last Battle* there is an acknowledgement that such unquestioning devotion to an unpredictable deity could go wrong. Even the good King Trilian is subject to error. He comes to believe that Aslan is commanding murder and destruction in Narnia. The unicorn Jewel questions his King.

> "But Sire, how *could* Aslan be commanding such dreadful things?"
> "He is not a *tame* lion," said Tirian. "How should we know what he would do?" (2001b, 682)

In this story, Lewis seems to be recognizing the potential misuse of a doctrine of the unpredictability of God. But in the end he affirms it, and The Chronicles do not seem to offer any practical defense against its misuse other than recognizing the true Aslan over all pretenders.

Aslan the Good and Terrible: A Helpful Image of Christ?

In Aslan, Lewis tries to develop an appealing character that holds together the classical theistic view of a God who is all powerful and in
control, who chooses when and where to intervene, and at the same
time resonates with the Western Orthodox view of the incarnate, crucified Christ. While Lewis' Aslan incorporates all of the necessary characteristics, the result may not be the most appealing character for many
contemporary readers or theologians. In The Chronicles of Narnia our
introduction to Aslan shows us someone who is "good and terrible at
the same time" (168). Lewis' Aslan is at times comforting and compas-
sionate, but to be consistent with classical theistic views, he must demonstrate that he is in control of every situation. He repeatedly asserts his
power and sovereignty and he brooks no questions or complaints from
people for the way things are. When children in Narnia face hardship
or evil, Aslan often comes across as a regal figure who claims authority
but accepts no blame. He gives gentle kisses and at times is even huggable,[3] but more often has a stern face (558) and is quite put out with
children who dare to question his purposes or ask the reasons for their
suffering or trials. At times he chastises them for not figuring out what
they should do given the subtle clues he has provided. He does not shy
away from bringing shame or even physical punishment to those who
misuse the moral agency he allows them, and he calls for unquestioning
submission even when it defies reason or self-interest.

The children who are featured in these stories have parents who are
either absent, ill or unengaged.[4] They are in need of a strong authority
figure. Aslan provides them with adventures to undertake, but also assures them that he is in complete control of a world that seems out of
control. To the most faithful, he rewards their loyalty with his kindness
and solemn praise. There are some people in our lives who are very difficult to please and, since their approval can be hard-won, gaining their
acceptance may cause us a special, if not entirely healthy, joy. Perhaps
there is a measure of pleasure in gaining the approval of a stern, regal
character like Aslan for some, but for others this image of providence
will not suffice.

---

[3] Besides being a huggable lion, Aslan also appears briefly as a lamb and a small cat.

[4] In this way their childhoods parallel Lewis' own. He lost his mother when he was nine, his father
was unengaged with the children, and he was sent off to a strict boarding school.

The beginning of this essay suggested that times of pain and suffering are most challenging to one's concept of what God is like. This was certainly the case for Lewis himself. Near the end of his life, Lewis suffered the loss of his wife Joy and experienced the deep grief that comes with such a profound loss. He wrote and later anonymously published *A Grief Observed*, a very personal journal of his mourning and grief. In the journal Lewis lashes out at the God who took his wife, or at least did not prevent her from dying, and provided no acceptable reason for it. Lewis wonders, "[W]here is God?" (2001a, 5). He questions God and complains about God's lack of answers. At one point he even ponders whether God is "The Cosmic Sadist, the spiteful imbecile" (30). In the journal Lewis does not worry about losing faith that there is a God. The real danger, he says, was "of coming to believe such dreadful things about him" (6). He continues, "The conclusion I dread is not 'So there's no God after all,' but 'So this is what God is like. Deceive yourself no longer" (6–7). If it was God's plan for his wife to die, and He is simply to submit to that plan, then what does that say about God?

> The word *good*, applied to Him, becomes meaningless: like abracadabra. We have no motive for obeying Him. Not even fear. It is true we have His threats and promises. But why should we believe them? If cruelty is from His point of view "good," telling lies may be "good" too. (32)

Lewis quickly dismisses these thoughts as "filth and nonsense" (33) and in the end he affirms his faith in God and many of his previous beliefs about the nature of God's providence. Still, Lewis' views on God's providential role in evil and suffering led to great distress in his time of grief.

One wonders what images of Aslan Lewis might have offered if he had written a volume of The Chronicles after experiencing such a loss. In *The Magician's Nephew* Shasta notes that "Aslan was bigger and more beautiful and more brightly golden and more terrible than he had thought. He dared not look into the great eyes" (2001b, 79). Perhaps, in the midst of our times of grief or suffering, we may prefer a Christ figure more like the titular character in Walter Wangerin Jr.'s fantasy novel *The Book of the Dun Cow*. The Dun Cow is not a confident, all-knowing lion who may chide others for not understanding the divine purposes behind struggles or sorrows, but a vulnerable figure whose eyes "melt for grief" as she stands present and mourns with those who mourn and brings healing to those who look into her eyes (Wangerin 1978, 227).

This is the sort of suffering and transforming God that Inbody and other theologians allude to when they seek a revisionary theism shaped by a radical doctrine of incarnation, cross and resurrection. As Inbody suggests, "God does not look on our suffering from the outside but from within, from the brow and hands of Jesus hanging on the cross" (2005, 160). This move away from classical theism and toward a God acquainted with our sufferings may lead us to a more empathetic Aslan, a more fully incarnate Christ, who does not feel the need to assert his authority and control in the midst of our suffering.

An Opportunity for Theological Reflection

In the midst of this analysis, it is helpful to remember that The Chronicles of Narnia are children's stories, "supposals" that imagine an alternative world, and not intended to be exact allegories. In these books, Lewis provides not so much an apologetic as an imaginative narrative with images of his version of Christian theology and piety. He presents us with images of Aslan, and they are allowed to resonate or not resonate with the reader.

In the Chronicles of Narnia, Lewis offers many images of divine intervention in many forms. Some theologians and popular readers may not embrace some of these images, but in any case, the imaginative world of Narnia can allow its visitors a rich opportunity for creative theological reflection. After reflecting on their own understanding of providence, readers can envision their own images of Aslan. In these alternative versions, how and when would Aslan intervene in Narnia? What would happen if someone were in trouble and blew Susan's horn? What sorts of quests would Aslan give his followers, and what sort of aid would he grant them on the way? How would he respond to those who are enduring hardships or those who question the reasons behind their suffering? C. S. Lewis created an intriguing fantasy world, and many more adventures await us there.

Russell W. Dalton is the associate professor of Christian education at Brite Divinity School of Texas Christian University in Fort Worth, Texas. He is the author of Faith Journey through Fantasy Lands: A Christian Dialogue with Harry Potter, Star Wars and The Lord of the Rings *and* Video, Kids, and Christian Education. *He is a popular conference speaker on issues of religious education and faith and popular culture.*

References

Coren, Michael. 1994. *The Man Who Created Narnia: The Story of C. S. Lewis.* Grand Rapids, MI: Wm. B. Eerdmans.

Dalton, Russell W. 2003. *Faith Journey through Fantasy Lands: A Christian Dialogue with Harry Potter, Star Wars and the Lord of the Rings.* Minneapolis: Augsburg Fortress.

Duriez, Colin. 1990. *The C. S. Lewis Handbook.* Grand Rapids, MI: Baker Book House.

———. 2004. *A Field Guide to Narnia.* Downers Grove, IL: InterVarsity Press.

Ford, Paul F., and Lorinda Bryan Cauley. 1983. "Providence." *Companion to Narnia.* San Francisco: Harper & Row.

Hooper, Walter. 1996. *C. S. Lewis: A Companion and Guide.* San Francisco: HarperSanFrancisco

Inbody, Tyron. 1997. *The Transforming God: An Interpretation of Suffering and Evil.* Louisville, KY: Westminster John Knox Press.

———. 2005. *The Faith of the Christian Church: An Introduction to Theology.* Grand Rapids, MI: Wm. B. Eerdmans.

Lewis, C. S. 1947. *Miracles: A Preliminary Study.* New York: Macmillan.

———. 1960. *The Four Loves.* New York: Harcourt.

———. 1962. *The Problem of Pain.* New York: Macmillan.

———. 1982. "Sometimes Fairy Stories May Say Best What's to Be Said." *On Stories and Other Essays on Literature.* Ed. Walter Hooper. New York: Harcourt Brace Jovanovich.

———. 2001. *A Grief Observed.* San Francisco: HarperSanFrancisco.

———. 2001. The Chronicles of Narnia. New York: HarperCollins.

Lindskoog, Kathryn Ann. 1998. *Journey into Narnia.* Pasadena: Hope Publishing House.

Manzalaoui, M. A. 1998. "Narnia: The Domain of Lewis's Beliefs." *Journey into Narnia.* Ed. Kathryn Ann Lindskoog. Pasadena: Hope Pub House.

Wangerin, Walter. 1978. *The Book of the Dun Cow.* New York: Harper & Row.

JAMES V. SCHALL, S. J.

The Beginning of the Real Story

"And for us, this is the end of all the stories, and we can most truly say that they all lived happily ever after. But for them, it was only *the beginning of the real story*. All their life in this world and all their adventures in Narnia had only been the cover and the title page...."

—C. S. Lewis, *The Last Battle* (1956, 184)

"The ungentle laws and customs touched upon in this tale are historical, and the episodes which are used to illustrate them are also historical. It is not pretended that these laws and customs existed in England in the sixth century, no, it is only pretended that inasmuch as they existed in the English and other civilizations in far later times, it is safe to consider that it is no libel upon the sixth century to suppose them to have been in practice in that day also. One is quite justified in inferring that whatever one of these laws or customs was lacking in that remote time, its place was competently filled by a worse one."

—Mark Twain, *A Connecticut Yankee in King Arthur's Court* (1889, Preface)

I

Narnia, too, like our own fallen world from which it differs in many ways, was not intended to last forever. This truth does not mean that there is no everlastingness, only that it is not ultimately found in Narnia or in this world. Yet, intimations of forever are found both in Narnia and in this world in which our own dramas are played out. Our own existence, as Chesterton put it in "The Ethics of Elfland," reveals "a hairbreadth escape: everything has been saved from a wreck. Every man has had one horrible adventure: as a hidden, untimely birth he had not been, as infants that had never seen the light" (1959, 64). The fairy tale makes us aware that we need not be—the "might-not-have-beens" include our own "hidden, untimely births." Our, to us, unexpected existences teach us both a gratefulness that we are at all and a deep awareness of the risks of our being what we are, of our freedom. Living "happily ever after" is not a sure thing because, as all good fairy tales teach us, it depends on how we ourselves choose to live.

Mark Twain was aware of what we do with our freedom, of the abiding disorders of our world, present, past and, no doubt, future, a world full, as it is, of "ungentle laws and customs." Indeed, Twain suspected, like Augustine, that, as this world grows older, it will manifest, in human terms, mostly things that are worse than the world our ancestors knew. Not a few ancient tales pictured the world as a continual declination from an aboriginal good. Later thinkers of liberal or Marxist persuasions maintained, on the contrary and in spite of considerable evidence, that history is a progress to an inner-worldly good not yet achieved, one achieved solely by our own efforts. The Garden of Eden and what happened there, however, was a "beginning" that did not cause itself. We all still have, as Chesterton said, some sense of a primordial "wreck" in which we participate.

Yet, the story of our achievements and joys, of our sins and disorders is a "real story" into which we are caught up by the very fact that we are born into this world as human, rational beings, not something else. How do we live with these signs of disorder found everywhere around us? Can we escape them? On what terms? In The Last Battle, the last of the Narnian tales, C. S. Lewis suggests that the story which we are living out in our lives is not the one we would describe ourselves to be experiencing. We omit so much from our autobiographies, most often the part that urgently needs repentance. We find it odd that the first thing that the Gospels tell us to do is precisely to "repent." Still, we long to see and know this "real story," *our own story*. We wonder, in the light of this dire record, why we have this unsettling idea of happiness in the first place. And why do we think that somehow this record of how, in practice, we define our happiness by our choices relates to our personal destiny? Still we wonder if the picture that we make for ourselves is the one that is really best for us, the one that is seen by what sees the order of things.

Readers of *The Republic* by Plato are aware of the "shadows" on the wall of the cave, shadows which imply that the ordinary opinions and lives of normal citizens in any real city, however vivid, obscure something more fundamental about their lives. Knowing our Plato and *The Republic*, the most fundamental book of our philosophic tradition, we again read (I presume everyone has read it before) in the last book of The Chronicles of Narnia: "'There *was* a real railway accident,' said Aslan softly. 'Your father and mother and all of you are—as you used to call it in the Shadowlands—dead. The term is over: the holidays have begun. The dream is ended: this is the morning'" (1956, 183). Here are Plato's "shadows" again. Here is again the same image of light that the philosopher who turned around in the cave beheld in the Sun, the Good.

This tradition of intense searching through the shadows, through the "Shadowlands," goes on, looking for the reality that such shadows seem to obscure yet imply. However, in Narnia, this desire for clarity and sight, the end of the Shadowlands, is presented not so much as light but as sacrifice. "The light came into the world, and the world comprehended it not." The heart of the first book of The Chronicles of Narnia, and that which runs through all the other six tales, shows the evil White Witch killing Aslan on the Stone Table. Did she succeed? Is evil stronger than good? Aslan dies, but He really cannot be permanently killed by creatures.

On initially discovering the truth and reality of Aslan, Susan wants to know what it means. Aslan replies:

It means that though the Witch knew the Deep Magic, there is a magic deeper still which she did not know. Her knowledge goes back only to the dawn of Time. But if she could have looked a little further back, into the stillness and the darkness before Time dawned, she would have read there a different incantation. She would have known that when a willing victim who had committed no treachery was killed in a traitor's stead, the Table would crack and Death itself would start working backward.... (1950, 159–60)

Here, we are already beyond philosophy without leaving it unnoticed. Socrates, in *The Apology*, did not fear death because he did not know if it was evil or not. All he knew was that to do evil was wrong, even more wrong than death, a death he, as the philosopher, suffered rather than do evil. Philosophy takes us this far.

Without philosophy, moreover, we do not know that it does not itself answer the questions. Attempted answers, though not always true, are preparatory for true answers. They reveal our puzzlement. Sophocles had said that "man learns by suffering," perhaps only by suffering. Thought alone, as Aristotle said, moves nothing. The Innocent Victim is connected with what is before Time and likewise with the beginning of the elimination of death, through death. The Innocent Victim is betrayed and put to death, not unlike what Glaucon, in the second book of *The Republic*, intimates to be the fate of any just man appearing in any actual city. The Innocent Victim is "willing," obedient. What is the command He follows? We know it leads to death. Yet, as Dylan Thomas said, following St. Paul, "death has no dominion." After the killing of Aslan at the Stone Table, "Death itself would start working backward." What is "backward" from death must be life, must be the "title page," a new adventure just begun.

II

We are used to fairy stories. We are fortunate if someone reads them to us in our youth, even more so if we read them, reread them ourselves as adults. "You have not read a great book at all if you have only read it once," Lewis himself once said. Fairy tales—themselves often truly great books—take place in "never-never land," however it be called, even in Narnia, even on Earth. We are startled when, on reading such far-fetched, presumably "childish" narratives, they tell us more about ourselves and our world than do our latest conversations in the city in which we live, or in the universities in which we study, or in the media that we watch. This *reality-in-fairy-tales* seems peculiar to us, unsettling even. The world of fantasy is a world full of truth, often of truth that we are not aware of, or even allowed to speak of in existing cities (Schall 1999, 67–72). It is also full of truths that we often choose not to know if we do not want to learn our real stories.

"People who have not been to Narnia sometimes think that a thing cannot be good and terrible at the same time" (1950, 123). We read these words in the first of the Narnia chronicles. The good can be terrible both because it can freely be rejected and because we did not ourselves constitute its validity. When we reject it, we must defend ourselves and make as if what we rejected was not good, even if it is. In the fairy tales themselves, the rejection of the good is never so easily resolved. Free decisions have consequences both for good and for ill, both to ourselves and to others, consequences that the tales trace out for us. Good deeds, paradoxically, can cause hatred; evil ones can incite remorse. We somehow suspect that this inevitable result of free decisions is also true in our own personal world, though we are not often told this. Indeed, every effort is made to obscure this realization from our active attention. Choices have consequences. We are loath to be held responsible. Yet without responsibility for our deeds, we cannot be what we are.

In tales, we notice, things always work their way to a happy or tragic ending, even worse than "tragic" for those who willfully oppose what is good. The evil figures in fairy tales, who are often directly involved in the cause of the ongoing plot, the White Witch in Narnia, for instance, are not, in the end, "saved." And we are not somehow disappointed that they are not. Though there are happy endings, not everyone ends happily. Fairy tales do not pretend that no one is lost, though they do intimate that no one is lost except through his own volition, a truth seen in the lives of the rulers of Mordor in The Lord of the Rings. Or as it is said in the Lion, the Witch and the Wardrobe, in the land of the White Witch, "it is always winter and never Christmas" (56).

The order of the universe includes places where there is no Christmas, not because Christmas was not offered, but because it was rejected by at least some of our kind and not a few those of other free species beyond our limited powers. Plato said the same thing at the end of The Republic. The world would not be complete if what was not just was not exactly identified and punished, if what was good was not specifically rewarded.

This overall sense of what is "just" is often why those who want to prevent children from reading, say, Grimm's fairy tales, with their many frightening figures, on the ground that they are too scary, really work to prevent children from understanding what the world is really like. Chesterton put the theoretical consideration behind such objections well. The first time children realize the disorder in the world is not from tales they read.

> Fairy tales, then, are not responsible for producing in children fear, or any of the shapes of fear; fairy tales do not give the child the idea of the evil or the ugly; that is in the child already, because it is in the world already. Fairy tales do not give a child his first idea of bogey. What fairy tales give is the first clear idea of the possible defeat of bogey. The baby has known the dragon intimately ever since he had an imagination. What the fairy tale provides for him is a St. George to kill the dragon. (1910, 129–30)

A human being cannot avoid knowing that something is wrong with himself and his world, even if he knows that both himself and the world are created to be good. What any person needs to wonder about is whether this is all there is. This wondering is where fairy tales provide us with a suspicion that, even if we cannot save ourselves, it does not follow that there is nothing that will save us. Both the dragon and St. George exist.

III

In *Prince Caspian*, Lucy wants Aslan to perform deeds he had previously done. She also wants to know how things might have turned out "all right." "'To know what *would* have happened, child?' said Aslan. 'No, Nobody is ever told that'" (1951, 137). In the order in which they are made, our choices are always final, irreversible. As the logic textbooks say, "once Socrates has sat down, it is eternally true that he sat down, even though he need not have sat down when he did." The world now includes made choices. This does not mean that what could have been otherwise was not a real possibility. It was, for good or ill. We are judged on what we do, including our not doing what we ought to do. We are not judged on what we might have done. Yet, what might have been is part of our choices, though we are, no doubt, mercifully at times, spared from knowing what might have been. We cannot forget that the Angel of Light, perhaps the brightest of the angels, need not have chosen as he did. The mystery of evil is directly related to the mystery of free choice, to the mystery of why there is something rather than nothing. The drama of Aslan at the Stone Table is a consequence of what need not have been, but was.

The Narnian chronicles are a fairy story within the story of young English students in a common English town. The Chronicles constantly suggest that the disorder in the actual English school world of the young heroes, and *a fortiori* of England itself, is more of a problem than the Narnia that confronts the heroes and heroines of the adventure. The great fairy tale question is asked, "How did the adventure begin?" (1950, 4). It began like all stories, even like all knowledge, with curiosity and wonder, with what is behind a door. But before the children discovered the door, there was their school.

At the beginning of *The Silver Chair*, Jill Pole is crying behind the gym. Why? Other students have been "bullying her." We are merely told that we shall "say as little as possible about Jill's school" (1953, 1). What kind of a school is it?

> It was "Co-educational," a school for both boys and girls, what used to be called a "mixed" school. Some said it is not nearly so mixed as the minds of the people who ran it. These people had the idea that boys and girls should be allowed to do what they liked. And unfortunately what ten or fifteen of the biggest boys and girls liked best was bullying the others. All sorts of things, horrid things, went on which at an ordinary school would have been found out and stopped in half a term, but at this school they weren't. Or even if they were, the people who did them were not expelled or punished. The Head said they were interesting psychological cases and sent for them and talked to them for hours. And if you knew the right sort of things to say to the Head, the main result was that you became rather a favourite than otherwise. (1–2)

Condensed in this brief description is already found a blunt critique of the modern world and its principles and language—the Rousseauian notion that we should let the young do what they want, the substitution of psychology for common sense, the belief that punishment has no purpose.

Narnia exists, as it were, over and against a world that is unable to see its own disorders. *The Silver Chair* has to do with the reeducation of Eustace, a cousin who typifies the student who at first believes in the education given at Experiment House. In the end, Prince Caspian, who has died, still wants to see something of the world in which Jill and Eustace came from "if that would not be wrong." Aslan tells him, "You cannot want wrong things any more, now that you have died, my son" (214). So Aslan explains about the school, Experiment House, to Caspian. But Aslan sends Caspian, Jill and Eustace back to it, where they immediately get rid of the bullies.

And what happens to the Head? Eventually, after Caspian goes back to his land and Aslan repairs the damage, the Head is fired but her friends made her the Education Inspector, a kick upstairs. "And when they found she wasn't much good even at that, they got her into Parliament where she lived happily ever after" (216). With this amusing comment, we see that Lewis hints that the disorder of our world reaches its very topmost ranks and constantly recurs.

IV

All of the central real-world figures in the Narnian tales have about them a sense of longing, an awareness that something is not right or complete with what they know. This feeling is true of Shasta in *The Horse and His Boy*. "But he was very interested in everything that lay to the north because no-one ever went that way and he was never allowed to go there himself. When he was sitting out of doors mending the nets, and all alone, he would often look eagerly to the north" (1954, 2). Again we have a sense of adventure, of concern why something is forbidden to us, of a sense that something lies beyond our ken, something that concerns us.

In fairy tales is there found this sense of an adventure not yet begun. We find also a need to retell, appreciate what was once done. We need to retell and relive a tale that is now completed, as if we need to comprehend again and again what has happened to us. We love to know our part of the adventure in which all men are engaged. We know that our part was real and yet only a part.

And the wine flowed and tales were told and jokes were cracked, and then silence was made and the King's poet with two fiddles stepped out into the middle of the circle. Aravis and Cor prepared themselves to be bored, for the only poetry they knew was the Calormene kind, and you know now what that was like. But at the very first scrape of the fiddles a rocket seemed to go up inside their heads, and the poet sang the great old lay of Fair Olvin and how he fought the Giant Pire...and won the Lady Liln for his bride; and when it was over they wished it was going to begin again....And Lucy told again...the tale of the Wardrobe and how she and King Edmund and Queen Susan and Peter the High King had first come into Narnia. (2)

The retelling of the beginning is necessary to retell the end of the adventure. But all retelling of the past is in the present, as if to say, as fairy tales do say, that it is the ending that counts.

We likewise find a great sense of longing in Reepicheep, the gallant mouse in *The Voyage of the Dawn Treader:*

"I will gladly tell you that, my son," said the Old Man. "To break this enchantment you must sail to the World's End, or as near as you can come to it, and you must come back having left at least one of your companions behind." "And what is to happen to that one?" asked Reepicheep. "He must go on into the utter east and never return into the world." (1952, 179)

This "going on" is precisely what Reepicheep does. He is the one who is left behind. He is the one who has the courage and the faith to go on eastward to "never return into the world." But this never returning, we are aware, would not be possible if the voyage of Reepicheep was not to a better world, the "World's End."

The reading of fairy tales, the reading and rereading of Narnia, as I have suggested, reveals to us truths that we do not otherwise see in our daily living. Why is this? We read in *The Magician's Nephew:* "For what you see and hear depends a good deal on where you are standing: it also depends on what sort of person you are" (1955, 125). It depends on where we are standing, but also on "what sort of person" we are. That we are human persons is not under our control. That is what is given to us by our birth. We do not make ourselves to be what we are.

But what we do with what we are is indeed ours to fashion. We can not see the light because of where we are standing. But we can also reject it because we do not want to see by it. Fairy tales are full of the blind who will not see what is there to be seen. "You see," says Aslan in *The Last Battle*, "they will not let us help them. They have chosen cunning instead of belief. Their prison is only in their own minds, yet they are in that prison; and so afraid of being taken in that they cannot be taken out" (1956, 148). In fairy tales, the ultimate prison is self-made.

Time ends. Indeed, Father Time does wake up "on the day the world ended" (150). One would expect the opposite expression—that time would end when the world ended. Instead, that is only when time wakes up. Yet, as I recalled in the beginning, Narnia itself ends.

> "So," said Peter, "Night falls on Narnia.! You're not *crying*? With Aslan ahead, and all of us here?"
>
> "Don't try to stop me, Peter," said Lucy, "I am sure Aslan would not. I am sure it is not wrong to mourn for Narnia. Think of all that lies dead and frozen behind that door."
>
> "Yes and I *did* hope," said Jill, "that it might go on forever. I knew *our* world couldn't. I did think Narnia might."
>
> "I saw it begin," said the Lord Digory. "I did not think I would live to see it die."
>
> "Sirs," said Tirian. "The ladies do well to weep. What world but Narnia have I ever known? It were no virtue, but great discourtesy, if we did not mourn." (158)

Shadowlands—how are these things to be explained? In their trying to figure out the reality of the Narnia they knew, the Unicorn remarks, "The reason why we loved the old Narnia is that it sometimes looked a little like this," that is, our "real country" (171). Lord Digory has just said to Peter,

> "Listen, Peter. When Aslan said you could never go back to Narnia, he meant the Narnia you were thinking of. But that was not the real Narnia. That had a beginning and an end. It was only a shadow or a copy of the real Narnia, which has always been here and always will be here, just as our own world, England and all, is only a shadow or copy of something in Aslan's real world." (169)

So there is the imaginary Narnia, the real Narnia that ended, and another more "real" Narnia that all the others imitated.

This is all familiar, or should be. But Digory, who had a reputation of being a bit pedantic, adds, "under his breath," still loud enough for the others to hear, "It's all in Plato, all in Plato: bless me, what *do* they teach them at these schools!" (170). Everyone about him laughs at Digory's classical reference. He laughs himself. But he becomes "grave again." He recalls that "there is a kind of happiness and wonder that makes you serious." It is not merely a "joke." In *The Republic* by Plato we are told that our human affairs are not "serious." And in *The Laws*, we are told that only one thing is "serious," against which all things will seem insignificant, and that is God. This is what Aslan is all about.

We are to love those things we know, and mourn for them when they cease, because they are loveable in their own order. But the reading of the tales of Narnia brings us to the "beginning of the real story," to the living happily ever after. Perhaps it is in fairy tales, which he himself so severely criticized, that we first encounter what Plato was talking about. But the Stone Table we do not find in Plato, though there are intimations of it. We do find it in Narnia, and indeed in our own world, if we, with grace, but will to see it.

"One is quite justified in inferring that whatever one of these laws or customs was lacking in that remote time, its place was competently filled by a worse one."

"The baby has known the dragon intimately ever since he had an imagination. What the fairy tale provides for him is a St. George to kill the dragon."

"But for them, it was only *the beginning of the real story*. All their life in this world and all their adventures in Narnia had only been the cover and the title page...."

James V. Schall, S. J., is a professor in the Department of Government at Georgetown University. His books include, among others, The Unseriousness of Human Affairs, At the Limits of Political Philosophy, The Sum Total of Human Happiness *and* Another Sort of Learning. *He writes a monthly column, "Sense and Nonsense" in* Crisis *Magazine and "Schall on Chesterton," in* Gilbert *Magazine.*

References

Chesterton, G. K. 1910. "The Red Angel." *Tremendous Trifles*. New York: Dodd, Mead.

———. 1959. *Orthodoxy*. Garden City, NY: Doubleday Image.

Lewis, C. S. 1950. *The Lion, the Witch and the Wardrobe*. New York: Collins.

———. 1951. *Prince Caspian*. New York: Collier.

———. 1952. *The Voyage of the Dawn Treader*. New York: Collier.

———. 1953. *The Silver Chair*. New York: Collier.

———. 1954. *The Horse and His Boy*. New York: Collier.

———. 1955. *The Magician's Nephew*. New York: Collier.

———. 1956. *The Last Battle*. New York: Collier.

Schall, James V. 1999. "On the Reality of Fantasy." *Tolkien: A Celebration*. Ed. Joseph Pearce. London: Fount/HarperCollins.

JACQUELINE CAREY

Heathen Eye
for the Christian Guy

WHEN MY MOTHER WAS A YOUNG GIRL, she had the same thing for breakfast every day: a glass of chocolate milk with a raw egg in it.

Except she didn't know about the egg.

She's one of those people who get queasy at the thought of solid food before noon. At a certain age, she simply began refusing to eat breakfast. Concerned about her growing daughter's lack of proper nutrition, my grandmother devised a cunning compromise. Chocolate milk? No problem. Every morning, my grandmother waited at the foot of the stairs to hand my mother a glass of chocolate milk as she hurried to school. And every morning, my mother downed it without a qualm, having no idea that my grandmother had surreptitiously whipped a raw egg into the milk.

Years later, she found out. To this day, she still blanches in disgust at the thought of all of those dozens upon dozens of raw eggs she drank so willingly. I know, because her children enjoy reminding her of it. The entire incident remains a monstrous betrayal of her sensibilities.

Listening to a panel discussion on how our perception of books changes from childhood to adulthood, I discovered that many non-Christian and agnostic readers feel much the same way about C. S. Lewis' The Chronicles of Narnia. As children, they read the books without recognizing the element of allegorical Christianity within them. As adults, they know better. They feel tricked and betrayed, conned into devouring it all unwitting. A sense of resentment lingers. Narnia is tainted. They can never revisit its wonders with unalloyed pleasure. They will never share Narnia with their own children, nieces or nephews with wholehearted joy.

It's a viewpoint I can understand. I was raised in an agnostic household. When I first read the The Chronicles of Narnia, I was seven years old; a happily unbaptized little heathen ignorant of Christian symbolism. It wasn't until the umpteenth rereading, when I was an older and more well-informed heathen, that the realization struck me with dawning shock. The lion, the lamb...*Aslan* is a metaphor for *Jesus*!

I felt duped. C. S. Lewis had slipped a yucky egg of Christianity into the paganish goodness of my Narnia, with all its fauns and dryads and river gods. Aslan, my wonderful, glorious Aslan, was a Trojan Lion. I'd been bamboozled.

But I got over it.

Change is inevitable. Books we loved as children are altered in our eyes as we grow older and change and the world changes with us. I am not a Christian, nor am I likely to become one, but I live in a world— and most certainly, a nation—where a great many people are. As a writer and a human being, it is my business to attempt to understand humankind in all its faiths and foibles.

When it comes to grasping the mind-set of the driver with the "In Case of the Rapture, this Vehicle Will Be Unmanned!" bumper sticker, I fall short. However, through the allegorical elements in The Chronicles of Narnia, I can begin to perceive the glory and majesty of the Christian mythos, and why it inspires devotion and awe in its adherents.

In the heart of religious faith, there is always a kernel of story. That's how religions perpetuate. And the best stories, the most effective stories, engage us emotionally. Lewis elucidated the emotional appeal of Christianity with devastating brilliance. Out here in the noisy, complicated, real world, one (a heathenish one, at any rate) can take issue with the notion of Christ's sacrifice, with Original Sin, with the need for redemption and the entire issue of sin altogether. One might say, as Patti Smith sang, "Jesus died for somebody's sins, but not mine" (Smith 1975).

Not in Narnia. In Narnia, the matter is stark and clear, and the rules were carved in stone since Time began. Edmund is a traitor and his life is forfeit. Aslan takes his place, and Narnia is redeemed by his sacrifice thanks to the workings of a magic even older and deeper than the Deep Magic.

Out here in the bustling, pragmatic real world, one might read the books of the Apocrypha and the Pseudepigrapha, consider conflicting accounts and debate whether or not a Jewish prophet was truly the Son of God. One might speculate on his motives, on the politics of the time, on the myriad translations of the Scripture that exist and the multitude of writings that just didn't make the cut and the role of the Council of Nicea in shaping our vision of Christianity. One might note, coolly, that while crucifixion is surely an awful fate, it was a common method of execution at the time. One might measure it against the tales of horrible victimhood that crop up regularly in tabloids and *People* magazine and CNN's news coverage, and fail to be moved by *The Passion of the Christ* in all its visceral voyeurism.

But one cannot argue with a lion's dignity.

One cannot—one *should* not—fail to be moved by the notion of a being of tremendous power and might submitting himself, willingly, to humiliation and degradation. To the spittle and jeers, to the muzzle and shears. Because that is the essence, the true heart, of the story. That is why it endures, that is why it perpetuates itself. It behooves us all to seek to understand.

And I, a heathen all grown up, am grateful to C. S. Lewis for couching it in terms I can comprehend. It is a story of terrible beauty. I appreciate that, now. It brings me a step closer to understanding my fellows who embrace the salvation they find in it. Through Narnia-tinted lenses, I catch a glimpse of the world as seen through their eyes.

One might suppose that this would bring joy to all manner of Christians. After all, it brings the strayed sheep within shouting distance of the fold. One would be very much mistaken. Surely, there are churches which would hear the news gladly; churches such as the United Church of Christ, whose president issued a statement assuring the world that the UCC would extend an unequivocal welcome to Sponge-Bob SquarePants, despite recent allegations that the cartoon character was insidiously promoting the infamous homosexual agenda by holding hands with Patrick Starfish. And there are always the Unitarians, of course. Doubtless they would welcome Narnia's maenads and centaurs and Mr. and Mrs. Beaver with open arms.

Indeed, there is reverence for The Chronicles of Narnia in much of mainstream Christianity. When a false rumor went about in 2001 that HarperCollins intended to release a "de-Christianized" version of the books, there were editorials on the pages of many major newspapers decrying the move.

However, there is also the Rapture Ready crowd. I had the good fortune to find a Web site called "C. S. Lewis: The Devil's Wisest Fool," which dissects The Chronicles in excruciating detail and explains why "Clive Staples Lewis has been perhaps the single most useful tool of Satan since his appearance in the Christian community sometime around World War II" (Van Nattan).

The reasons cited range from the obvious, such as the indubitably pagan Bacchus and his maenads taking part in the revels in *Prince Caspian*, to the slightly absurd, such as Digory's uncle's use of profanity in referring to Jadis as a "dem fine woman" in *The Magician's Nephew*, to a valid theological dispute.

Lewis is accused of Universalism, the belief that all people throughout history will be reconciled with God, regardless of whether or not they accepted Jesus Christ as their personal savior within their lifetimes. Well, yes. That's quite evident in *The Last Battle*, wherein the young Calormene warrior relates his encounter with Aslan. In a portion of his longest single passage of dialogue in all seven of the books—although perhaps that may be attributed to the Calormene style of storytelling—Aslan tells the young man, "Therefore, if any man swear by Tash and keep his oath for the oath's sake, it is by me that he has truly sworn, though he knows it not, and it is I who reward him. And if any man do a cruelty in my name, then though he says the name Aslan, it is Tash whom he serves and by Tash his deed is accepted." When the Calormene reluctantly protests that he has spent his life seeking Tash, Aslan says, "Beloved, unless thy desire had been for me thou would not have sought so long and so truly. For all find what they truly seek" (1973, 165).

Now, there's a heresy I can live with.

Another charge with some resonance is the suggestion that Lewis rejects belief in a literal hell in which the damned suffer eternal punishment in favor of the view that hell is a construct of our own making.

Indeed, John Milton ascribed a similar sentiment to Satan, who says in *Paradise Lost*, "The mind is its own place and in itself, can make a Heaven of Hell, a Hell of Heaven" (1952, 99). In *The Last Battle*, when the bad Dwarfs who have passed through the Stable Door can neither see nor smell nor taste the bounty around them, Aslan says, "Their prison is only in their own minds, yet they are in that prison; and so afraid of being taken in that they can not be taken out" (1973, 148).

Of course, Tash also makes an appearance to snatch up the Tarkaan and departs with his lawful prey, so one can't claim Lewis was all that soft on sinners. But certainly, one can interpret the Stable passage to suggest that we all contain the power to effect our own damnation and redemption.

I'm okay with that, too.

And then there's the matter of spirits. Booze! Narnia's practically dripping with it. There are a couple of occasions where it's viewed in a unfavorable light—Digory's uncle relies on the proverbial Dutch courage, and Puddleglum makes a drunken fool of himself at the giant's castle—but for the most part, wine and beer are perfectly acceptable beverages consumed at regular intervals and flowing freely during revels. And sailors, naturally, drink rum.

Works for me!

In fact, I can think of another book that's fairly oozing with wine, from Noah's drunkenness to the Wedding at Cana. It seems fairly clear throughout the Bible that wine is a blessing from the Lord. It's best consumed in moderation, but it ought to be served in abundance during times of celebration. That's the way they do it in Narnia.

Not every aspect of The Chronicles holds up to the changing perceptions of maturity. As an adult, I resent the implication that a fondness for invitations and lipstick can render one no longer a friend of Narnia. Poor Susan got shafted! And the characterization of the Calormenes—except for a couple "good apples"—could provide fodder for a whole other essay.

But I have come to terms with the Christian allegory within its pages. It is a beautiful expression of the faith that C. S. Lewis espoused, and it is a great, good thing to be able to see the beauty in another's faith. The vision of Christianity that The Chronicles of Narnia offers celebrates goodness, kindness and courage. It repudiates cruelty, selfishness and greed.

And it's filled with magic.

For my agnostic and non-Christian fellows, I would hope that they might find it in themselves to forgive the sense of being tricked by the egg in the chocolate milk and reclaim Narnia's wonder. For my Christian fellows who tread a narrow path, I would wish that they might be willing, some day, to consider the possibility that like the world beyond the Stable Door, that which we call the divine is infinitely more vast than we can comprehend, and the further up and further in you go, the bigger it gets.

Jacqueline Carey is the bestselling author of the critically acclaimed Kushiel's Legacy trilogy of historical fantasy novels and The Sundering epic fantasy duology. Jacqueline enjoys doing research on a wide variety of arcane topics, and an affinity for travel has taken her from Finland to Egypt to date. She currently lives in west Michigan, where she is a member of the oldest Mardi Gras krewe in the state. Although often asked by inquiring fans, she does not, in fact, have any tattoos.

References

Lewis, C. S. 1973. *The Last Battle.* New York: Collier.

Milton, John. 1952. "Paradise Lost." *Great Books of the Western World: John Milton.* Ed.

Mortimer J. Adler. Encyclopedia Britannica, Inc.

Smith, Patti. 1975. "Gloria." *Horses.* Arista.

Van Nattan, Mary. "C. S. Lewis: The Devil's Wisest Fool," http://www.balaams-ass.com/journal/homemake/cslewis.htm.

INGRID NEWKIRK

Would the Modern-Day
C. S. Lewis Be a PETA Protester?

W HEN I WAS A LITTLE GIRL, of about the same age as Susan and the other children who entered C. S. Lewis' Narnia through the professor's wardrobe, I was sent away to an English boarding school in the everlasting snows of the Himalayas. There, the nuns told the children stories that they hoped would convince us that there was a God. Not a god with eight arms or the god with an elephant face that we saw in the marketplace or set on the stone altars in Hindu houses and shops, but their God, the God of Christianity: C. S. Lewis' God.

The lesson of the stories was always the same. In one, a little boy abandoned as a child through some quirk of fate would be found by a search party many years later, on his knees worshipping God in a sun-drenched clearing. Another involved a doubting Catholic who secreted the Holy Eucharist—the wafer believed to be made of Christ's body—in his sleeve when the priest performed Holy Communion. Upon reaching his private room, the doubter bit into the Eucharist to see what it was actually made of, only to be drowned in the outpouring of Christ's blood.

Divine revelation delivered, blind faith required, order restored a familiar theme for those of us who read Lewis' books.

Animals, the nuns told us, had no souls (something disputed by modern theologians and others who see the spark of creation in their eyes). But rather than indict the animals or grant us a license to treat them poorly, the nuns taught us to treat them well, because unlike us, theirs would be the only life they would ever enjoy.

That outlook shines from Lewis' writing, particularly in his outrage when animals (like humans) are deprived of this life, either by being turned to stone by an evil force or as the subject of nasty experiments, such as those performed on guinea pigs by Uncle Andrew in Lewis' *The Magician's Nephew*. In *The Problem of Pain*, Lewis writes, "Vivisection can only be defended by showing it to be right that one species should suffer in order that another species be happier....If we cut up beasts simply because they cannot prevent us, and because we are backing our own side in the struggle for existence, it is only logical to cut up imbeciles, criminals, enemies or capitalists for the same reasons."

Lewis not only imbues in his child heroes his own empathy and fondness for the animals he understands (in keeping with the values of his time, which I will get to later on), but he also strives to elevate animals, to make them more than the limited creatures he thinks they are. A thinker ahead of his time, Lewis sought to blur the species barrier (such as when he created his *faun,* a creature with goat horns and hooves but with a human face and torso), a barrier that would later be blurred with knowledge of shared DNA.

The belief in a higher power that has specifically created you (and a few million others like you) and deems you to be special is a comforting one, and it is a theme that runs through Lewis' work. There are those who find their way (through the wardrobe) and those who don't (the danger of choosing the wrong door), those who are blessed with powers (talking animals in *The Silver Chair*) and those who aren't. The theme of good versus evil is, of course, central to Christianity—to Catholicism certainly—and it is the central theme in Lewis' The Chronicles of Narnia.

As much as Lewis feels for animals, however, his religion and his era fail him. In the *Journal of the American Scientific Affiliation* 35, you find this comment:

The existence of animal pain was a challenge to [Lewis'] philosophy. He himself was not satisfied with his chapter on animal suffering in

The Problem of Pain. He did not wish to see animals suffer and found it difficult to reconcile accidental injury, disease, and predation in animals with his concept of a supremely good creator. (LeBar 1983)

And reading The Chronicles brings these lines by M. Frida Hartley into my head:

From beasts we scorn as soulless,
In the forest, field and den,
The cry goes up to witness
The soullessness of men.

Lewis, a man who sought solace and acceptance through his devotion to the faith he embraced, was the absolute reflection of his time, and had his chosen faith had a more open attitude toward animals, he might have been among the first animal rights advocates. However, although Christians were taught to be kind, and although Lewis' kindness is apparent, it was a practical, narrow kindness meted out within the context of exploitation, strictly according to the mores and ignorance of the times.

Christianity, in particular, was at the slow end of the morals train, especially with regard to the Holy Roman Empire, missionary zeal, women's struggle for equality, human slavery and, certainly, animals "put here by God for our use." Lewis' religious-based values, therefore, while informing him within the unenlightened social context of his time, provided him with no depth of understanding of who animals are. Accordingly, he failed to achieve all he could in his goal of helping to shape moral values in his young readers. Instead, he reinforced the status quo of animals and the "fairer sex" as inferior life-forms with intellectual and behavioral limitations.

Perhaps he would have been even more open to the idea of expanding his ethical horizons if he had studied Buddhism. Buddhists were, at least in theory, doing better than Christians in the animal-protection arena, believing, as the Dalai Lama does today, that "kindness is the ultimate religion."

Lewis was hindered, too, by being eager to conform and be accepted in then-snobbish Britain, where he lived, studied and taught. He was also a traditionalist, which meant that he felt it proper and right to view animals, women and, most likely, the poor as subspecies to be treated with magnanimity, within bounds.

Lewis wrote at a time when major breakthroughs were happening in consciousness about animals. Unfortunately, though he was clearly drawn to animals, no body of knowledge existed to help him on his journey. Had he lived today, his views would have been made mince-meat of by "progressive" religious ethicists like the Reverend Andrew Linzey, Lewis' compatriot and a professor at Oxford University. "Why," Linzey might have asked Lewis, "do you not extend the constituency deserving of the magnanimity and mercy you convey beyond the golden retriever at your hearthside?"

Lewis grew up during World War I, and he served in World War II, so he was understandably sympathetic to the plight of children who were taken from their homes during the 1940 London Blitz and who at other times saw their brothers, fathers and uncles marching off to war. He was also sympathetic to the dogs and horses that were very much a part of British life and commerce, although he saw them not as individuals or self-aware "others," but as accoutrements to the lifestyle and whims of English (or Irish) gentlemen or the "proper" English (or Irish) family.

These prejudices led Lewis to make keen distinctions in the hierar-chy of beings, between girls and boys and humans and animals—even when seeking to protect them from harm. Girls, for instance, were to be shielded from nastiness and physical labor (the boys in *The Lion, the Witch and the Wardrobe*, Edmund and Peter, often whisper to spare Lucy and Susan the harsh details or scary bits), and they were expected to en-dure masculine ribbing for their sensitivities. A grown woman's place, Lewis believed, was in the home, tidying and packing sandwiches. Boys and men were the sole strategists, and they were definitely in charge. They hunted, fought for justice and otherwise organized the universe on a diet of animal flesh and goods stolen from animals, lavishly buttered ham sandwiches, "fresh" fish, extra-creamy milk with golden honey, and roasted chickens. (Vegetarianism was associated with the occult, mysticism and cranks in Lewis' time.)

The comparison that springs to mind in reading Lewis' The Chron-icles of Narnia is that Lewis was basically a well-meaning bigot, much like the respectable, stereotypical British bwana, the great white hunter one sees in old tintype photographs. Imagine this scene: He's stand-ing in the jungle, all done up in his khakis and topi. He's flanked by a bevy of grinning black porters (who have carried his trunks on their heads and are now obeying the command "Big smile!"), and he rests his leg triumphantly on the shoulder of a dead tiger. Such men were not thought to be racist, sexist or speciesist. Kindness was distributed according to the rules of the age. Men conducted themselves according to how they understood their place and the place of others. Nature was to be conquered and domesticated; savages and beasts were welcome to play peripheral roles as long as they behaved themselves.

In Lewis' time (he was born just twenty years after Stanley and Livingstone penetrated what Lewis would have described as "deepest, darkest Africa"), new species of animals were still being discovered in far-flung outposts of the British empire. Millions of "specimens" found themselves in crates, dead or alive, aboard ships bound for Britain, where each was carefully dissected, labeled and displayed under glass or filed away in trunks and chests. The exotic animal kingdom had revealed itself as a vast King Solomon's mine, a treasure trove of living baubles for society to gawk at. Hats of bird-of-paradise feathers adorned heads, ostrich boas and colobus monkey-skin shawls covered society ladies' shoulders, tortoise shell was fashioned into brooches, and tiger-skin rugs and elephant-foot umbrella stands "enriched" country club and country home décor. Crowds gathered at London's Regents Park Zoo to watch crates of young giraffes, chimpanzees, gazelles and gorillas unloaded and placed into cement cells, their families having been shot and left to die as they had tried to defend their young or flee.

The idea of preserving habitat or the thought that animals actually have feelings and can enjoy, love, be devoted to and grieve for their fellows, had not yet been born. Lewis might well have marveled at how close other animals' DNA is to our own, but no such findings had appeared in scientific periodicals, and the *Times* of London published no letters debating animals' behavioral needs and innate intelligence. The father of ethology, Konrad Lorenz, was Lewis' contemporary, but his groundbreaking observations of the emotional lives of animals, including his beloved geese, were published a couple of decades later.

As we see, Lewis' portrayal of animals falls into three distinct categories that reflect his lack of enlightenment: 1) as symbols of upper middle-class values and stability, such as the well-bred family dog and the well-groomed horse; 2) as objects, such as fur coats that the children wear to keep out the cold, as food and as sport, such as fishing and riding; and 3) as larger-than-life, mythological figures such as Aslan, the oversized talking lion. (For Lewis, women, like animals, could be powerful only if they were fantasy figures. The White Witch is so powerfully cruel that she can deprive us even of Christmas! And, even when girls become queens, they are still subordinate to boys, and they must deliver their obeisance to the kings.)

It was not until the 1990s, a good thirty years after Lewis' death, that behaviorists discovered something that might have shaken his outlook. Using sophisticated recording equipment and keen observation, researchers discovered that elephants and mice communicate subsonically at frequencies inaudible to the human ear. More recent evidence backs up that discovery: Minutes after the Indonesian earthquake of 2005, villagers far away in Thailand were baffled as to why the elephants they used to log the forests started trumpeting wildly and pulling at their chains. The animals had heard seismic activity and knew that something large and ugly was heading their way. Since Lewis' time, we have also learned that rhinoceroses "speak" to each other via breathing patterns, that gulls sing lullabies to their chicks in the nest, that squid send messages via dermal patterns of light and color, that fish use "words" and even "phrases" to pass on messages and that prairie dogs, like vervet monkeys, utter different sounds to announce the presence of friend, foe or stranger.

In 1998, scholars gathered in Cambridge and Oxford, England, to honor Lewis. Among the tributes was the reminder that Lewis had abhorred vivisection and that he had warned in *The Screwtape Letters* that worldliness can gradually corrupt a person's soul, something worth remembering when, today, experimenters seem to dream up new "research" tortures simply in order to pay their mortgages.

In university laboratories in Maryland, Oregon, North Carolina and California, men and women in white coats have rotated kittens' eyeballs, then made them jump from a high platform onto a plank in a pan of water; sewn rabbits' eyelids closed, chained them in stocks, shocked them and given them LSD; shocked squirrel monkeys in fear-conditioning chambers; shocked rats' feet until the animals reached a pathetic state of "learned helplessness" and scalded their tails with hot water; harnessed cats fitted with "cranial implants" to treadmills and subjected them to tail and paw shocks, producing loud cries and "excessive struggling"—and worse.

I think Lewis would be pleased that scholars pay attention to his view of animals and experimentation. I think he would be pleased if we all did. It would go a long way toward renewing the soul of humankind, for Lewis was a kind man. We can excuse him for having thought that it is only in fairy tales that animals talk and for not realizing that there was no need to pretend: by now, he would have realized that when it comes to the rest of the animal kingdom, reality itself is astonishing and fascinating enough.

Ingrid E. Newkirk, fifty-six, author of the book Making Kind Choices *(St. Martin's, January 2005), is founder and president of People for the Ethical Treatment of Animals, the largest animal rights organization in the world. Her campaigns to promote cruelty-free living have made the front pages of the* Washington Post *and other national newspapers.*

References

LaBar, Martin. 1983. "A World Is Not Made to Last Forever: The Bioethics of C. S. Lewis." *Journal of the American Scientific Affiliation* 35: 104–107.

Lewis, C. S. 1994. The Chronicles of Narnia Boxed Set. New York: HarperTrophy.

———. 2001a. *The Problem of Pain.* San Francisco: Harper.

———. 2001b. *The Screwtape Letters.* San Francisco: Harper.

Greek Delight:
What If C. S. Lewis
Had Been Eastern Orthodox?

WHAT I REMEMBER MOST from my initial encounter with *The Lion, the Witch and the Wardrobe* as a child is the Turkish Delight. My little friends were all curious about the treat, it being virtually unheard of in Bensonhurst, Brooklyn, the land where Pop Rocks and cannoli held sway. But I was Greek, not Italian, and thus I knew the horrible secret of Turkish Delight. Greeks call the candy *loukoumia*, and it is among the most foul of foodstuffs in existence. It comes in many gross flavors, but if you'd like to eat something roughly equivalent, just go into your bathroom, find a well-worn sliver of fragrant soap, dip it in confectioner's sugar, and eat it.

Needless to say, I was not impressed with Edmund's desire-unto-treason for the sweets.

I was also not impressed with the story of the book itself. In it, Edmund betrays the other Pevensies to the White Witch, mainly because he's a brat who desires to be prince. Having sinned, the White Witch claims the right to kill him, saying to Aslan, "You at least know the Magic which the Emperor put into Narnia at the very beginning. You know that every traitor belongs to me as my lawful prey and that for every treachery I have a right to a kill.... [T]hat human creature is mine. His life is forfeit to me. His blood is my property."

Aslan, as a proper Christ figure, offers himself in Edmund's stead, and he is killed to appease the Deep Magic, only to have an even deeper magic resurrect him. It helps that Aslan's father, the Emperor-beyond-the-Sea, wrote the rules in the first place. This is a tale of Lewis' own Christianity; the redemptive text is a nearly moment-by-moment reenactment of Christ's death and resurrection, stage-managed by God, in order pay the price for humanity's sins against God's law. This form of soteriology is called substitutionary atonement, and can be boiled down to the shouted street-corner aphorism, "Jesus died for your sins! Take him into your heart and be forgiven!"

And I'd never heard of it. Not because I wasn't a fresh-faced Christian who was occasionally crammed into scratchy suits by my parents and plopped onto a pew; I sure was. But like the secret knowledge of Turkish Delight, I knew that Christ didn't die for my sins at all. The notion is virtually unknown in Greek Orthodoxy, the religion of my youth.

To be Greek in America is to be in an odd position. Greeks were targeted by racist groups like the Ku Klux Klan in Nebraska and Utah in the 1920s; today in Tarpon Springs, Florida—a Hellenic neighborhood/tourist trap—Klan members slink into local establishments and try to recruit Greek members. Today, as "whiteness" is a moveable feast, Greeks look white, except to one another. Not a week goes by where some other Greek person doesn't come up to me on the street or a restaurant and introduce him or herself (often with a Greek-language test). While writing this essay in the spring of 2005, I'm planning, on March 28, to buy half-priced Easter candy from the local store. I'm going to put the chocolate bunnies in my freezer and take them out on May 1, Orthodox Easter. In those years when Orthodox Easter happens to fall on the same date as Western Easter, I actually find myself a little annoyed. And I'm not even religious.

I wasn't religious as a kid either, the machinations of my mother and great-aunts notwithstanding, but *The Lion, the Witch and the Wardrobe* never sat well with me. Between the tale of redemption that struck me as alien as Easter in May would strike Catholics and those damned Turkish Delights, I just didn't like the book. I read a ton of juvenile fantasy, most of it utterly forgettable, over the other Narnia books. Twenty-five years later, Edmund's nasty little betrayals, and his solemn frown after an off-page lecture by the newly resurrected Aslan, still turn me off. And it suggests a thought experiment. What if Clive Staples Lewis had been named Constantine Soulis Louverdis, and what if he had written his works from an Orthodox perspective?

First, we must understand the Orthodox perspective of soteriology. Frederica Mathewes-Green explains:

> For most Western Christians, sin is a matter of doing bad things, which create a debt to God, and which somebody has to pay off. They believe that Jesus paid the debt for our sins on the Cross—paid the Father, that is, so we would not longer bear the penalty.... Orthodox, of course, have a completely different understanding of Christ's saving work. We hold to the view of the early church, that "God was in Christ, reconciling the world to himself." Our sins made us captives of Death, and God in Christ went into Hades to set us free. The penalty of sin is not a debt we owe the Father; it is the soul-death that is the immediate and inevitable consequence of sin. We need healing and rescue, not someone to step in and square the bill.

Subtitutionary atonement did not emerge as a central doctrine for Christianity until after the Great Schism between East and West. First systematized by Anselm of Canterbury, substitutionary atonement sees sin as an infraction that needs to be repaid. In his *Cur Deus Homo*, Anselm wrote "nothing is less tolerable...than that the creature should take away from the Creator the honor due to Him, and not repay what he takes away." Sin is so horrible that we can't pay the debt; only God has the power to do it, but it must be man that does the paying. Thus God became man and was tortured and killed on the Cross in order to pay the debt owed to God.

Instead of this, the Orthodox have a different view. The crucifixion and suffering isn't the point, as it even is in *The Lion, the Witch and the Wardrobe* (Aslan's mane is shaved, ogres and hags brutalize him, and only then does the White Witch take up the knife, with Lucy and Susan watching every moment), and is generally considered secondary. Mathewes-Green notes: "Athanasius, writing about 318, addresses the question of why, then, Jesus had to be crucified at all; couldn't he have died of old age? Athanasius offers a number of reasons—the Creator of life could not have grown ill, that Crucifixion gave public proof of death—but he does not entertain any concept that suffering itself was the point."

Nor is a God upset and feeling dishonored over humanity's sin the point. Eastern Orthodoxy doesn't have the same conception of Original Sin as Western Christianity. We're not carrying around the burden of a purloined apple. Adam and Eve were removed from the Garden of Eden not as a punishment, but to keep them from eating from the Tree of Life and thus perpetuating their sins indefinitely. This brought mortality to Adam's and Eve's descendents, and the debased world in which we live, tainted by death, makes us sin. God has no wrath toward sin, nor does He create the evil in the world. Christ's incarnation, death and resurrection were designed to defeat death. As the Easter hymn says, "Christ is risen from the dead, trampling down death by death, And upon those in the tombs bestowing life."

These differing stances on sin and Christ's crucifixion have both theological and cultural implications. The common phenomenon of "Catholic guilt" is virtually unknown among Orthodox believers. Indeed, while Orthodoxy has the sacrament of Confession, just like Catholicism, even the most devout Greek Orthodox believers tend to skip it. I didn't grow up worrying about going to hell, or being terrorized by priests, even though I spent a few years in a Greek Orthodox parochial school. (I was, however, terrorized by the maroon bow tie that was part of the uniform.) Some even say—well, Olympia Dukakis said it on the PBS documentary *The Greek Americans*—that egoism and arrogance are the defining traits of Greek Americans. I'd apologize for that being true, but really, who cares what *you* think. Anyway, this does become important later.

Lewis himself wasn't necessarily married to the idea of substitutionary atonement. In his attempt to "reunify" the religion in *Mere Christianity*, he leaves the concept out. Lewis also makes references to other conceptions of redemption throughout his nonfiction work, as part of his interest in ecclesiastical unity. The Narnia books certainly adopt substitutionary atonement, but given *Mere Christianity*, I doubt Lewis would mind if I move the story a bit to the East to see what would happen.

So, what would have happened to poor Edmund and Aslan if C. S. Louverdis wrote the book? Well, the Turkish Delight would have been called *loukoumia*, of course, and it wouldn't have needed to be enchanted in order to beguile Edmund. (My own antipathy toward the treat is definitely a minority taste.) Louverdis may have decided to keep the enchantment, though, as the enchantment places the impetus for sin in the debased world, rather than in some inherent guilt that Edmund was born with. Indeed, some observers feel that Lewis made the Turkish Delight magical in order to "blunt" the impact of Edmund's sin for the book's juvenile audience, but in the Eastern mode the idea of sin being a result of the environment fits well anyway. And yes, Edmund would have betrayed his siblings and would have wanted to be prince all by himself, though his motivation would have been, in part, to protect himself from the cold of Narnia's eternal winter. Sin isn't an infraction in Eastern theology, but is rather an infection, something that we commit due to the reality of death in this world.

However, the White Witch, when she decided to kill Edmund, would not have had any Stone Table full of cosmic rules, written by the Emperor-beyond-the-Sea, to justify her trickery and murder. The Emperor, God the Father, has no interest in punishing people for sin, or demanding death as the penalty for sinning. Aslan would take to the slab, but not due to legal wrangling over the particulars of Deep Magic. Instead, he'd do so to get close to the White Witch, who is our Satanic analogue. And then, after his death, which would not be depicted with such abject relish, he would reappear and defeat the Witch, and then celebrate the victory with the children.

But the most important thing is what would happen to Edmund. In *The Lion, the Witch and the Wardrobe*, Aslan and Edmund move off-page for a discussion, one where, presumably, Aslan does most of the talking. Lewis skimps on the details:

> There is no need to tell you (and no one ever heard) what Aslan was saying, but it was a conversation which Edmund never forgot. As the others drew nearer Aslan turned to meet them bringing Edmund with him. "Here is your brother," he said, "and—there is no need to talk to him about what is past." Then Edmund turned to the others and said "I'm sorry," and everyone said "That's all right."

And then, after his somber reunion with the other children, "Edmund [became] a graver and quieter man than Peter, and great in council and judgment. He was called Edmund the Just."

Aslan's a bully, ultimately, and a guilt-mongering prig who doesn't fail to let Edmund know that the only reason that Edmund is alive is due to Aslan's sacrifice—a sacrifice that was stage-managed by the Emperor and lasted all of one day anyway. Edmund, young and with an under-developed personality, has little choice but to go through life crippled with guilt and humble remorse, and becomes a rather humorless prig himself. Ah, what a message of faith and redemption!

What would Louverdis have done? We would have gotten a glimpse of the discussion between Aslan and Edmund, and it wouldn't have been a tongue-lashing. Instead, the pair would have exchanged heartfelt declarations of love. And Edmund wouldn't have simply had his personality altered and transformed into a fantasy version of a middle-class British bureaucrat, but would have experienced something much more profound.

The Greeks call it *theosis*, and it, not redemption from sin, is the reason for the Gospel, the Church and the whole mess. John Meyendorff, in *Byzantine Theology*, explains:

> Communion in the risen body of Christ; participation in divine life; sanctification through the energy of God, which penetrates the humanity and restores it to its "natural" state, rather than justification, or remission of inherited guilt—these are at the center of Byzantine understanding of the Christian Gospel.

Theosis is the process by which one becomes more Godlike. As humanity is made in God's image (an image distorted by the world of matter, in which death exists) there is the potential within us all to come ever closer to God's image. Human beings can and do cooperate with God (this cooperation is called *synergy*) in their own salvation, which is a process, not an event. Like most everything in Orthodoxy, the idea of theosis quickly gets mystical. Various theologians have made a distinction between God's essence (the core of His being) and His "energies" (His characteristics, which humanity experiences); theosis is all about union with the energies. Our individual personalities are not subsumed into God, nor do we become our very own little Gods of the diner and the real estate agency. How this all works is intentionally left vague, even though it has been discussed and commented upon for upwards of 1900 years; Orthodoxy rejects logic, scholasticism and pragmatism.

But clearly, theosis wouldn't turn a kid into a "grave" and "quiet" being ruled by logic and remorse.

Instead, Edmund would be rather more like Aslan. Aslan is seen as a fearsome king, but he is also playful, joyful and personable. He is "terrible and good." Edmund, however, remains one-dimensional: the brat becomes the steward with the stiff upper lip. Salvation in *The Lion, the Witch and the Wardrobe* is seemingly a minimalist program—the least one has to do to be saved is what one does. A few apologies, a bit of solemnity and that's it.

If the book were written from an Eastern standpoint, there would be little solemnity, no lecture from Aslan and no remorse and guilt. Edmund the Just might even be as interesting a character as he was back when he was Edmund the Insufferable Little Twat. Remember the peculiar egoism of the Greeks mentioned above? It's not necessarily a negative trait, and certainly not something to be avoided as thoroughly as Lewis and the rest of postwar Britain would have us believe. God does not weigh us down, He communes with us, and we take on His characteristics. God is not riven by guilt or wrath, after all, so why should we be? Why should Edmund be? Heck, why should I be, and I'm sitting here rewriting a classic piece of fantasy literature to fit religious conceptions I don't even believe in? There is no reason for us to feel guilty, or to believe ourselves depraved and worthless beings living in the shadow of an angry God. There is, in the East, a hope for something much, much better. C. S. Lewis himself makes the point in *Mere Christianity*:

> He will make the feeblest and filthiest of us into a god or goddess, dazzling, radiant, immortal creature, pulsating all through with such energy and joy and wisdom and love as we cannot now imagine, a bright stainless mirror which reflects back to God perfectly (though, of course, on a smaller scale) His own boundless power and delight and goodness. The process will be long and in parts very painful; but that is what we are in for.

Sounds pretty exciting, doesn't it? Then why is Aslan so supercilious and Edmund so incredibly boring? I blame Western guilt.

Nick Mamatas is the author of the Lovecraftian Beat road novel Move Under Ground *(Night Shade Books, 2004) and the Marxist Civil War ghost story* Northern Gothic *(Soft Skull Press, 2001), both of which were nominated for the Bram Stoker Award for dark fiction. He's pub-lished over 200 articles and essays in the* Village Voice, *the men's maga-zine* Razor, In These Times, Clamor, Poets & Writers, Silicon Alley Reporter, Artbytes, *the* UK Guardian, *five Disinformation Books an-thologies and many other venues, and over forty short stories and comic strips in magazines including* Razor, Strange Horizons, ChiZine, Po-lyphony *and others. Some of his short pieces were collected in* 3000MPH In Every Direction At Once: Stories and Essays *(Prime Books, 2003). A native New Yorker, Nick now splits his time between New York City and Vermont.*

SARAH ZETTEL

Why I Love Narnia: A Liberal, Feminist Agnostic Tells All

GOOD EVENING. Permit me to introduce myself. I am Sarah, and I am a non-Christian, progressive, feminist liberal. I am so much a liberal, in fact, that I don't mind being *called* a liberal.

Because of all of the above, the Narnia books remain some of my all-time favorite children's books ever, and this essay is my explanation for it. And yes, I said "because" up there, not despite. Because.

There are a lot of ways to explain this, but I've decided to focus on the lessons of the books for the sake of this discussion. People determined to be critical of a piece of children's literature seldom criticize plot, characters or quality of writing. They do, however, go on endlessly about the "lessons" of the story. What lessons, they ask, are these books teaching our children?

Normally, this question annoys me. I never once as a kid read a novel in order to get a lesson out of it. The only time, outside school, I ever read a novel for the lesson was the time I was given *Starring Sally J. Freedman as Herself* to try to teach me that my habit of telling myself stories was childish. As I eventually became a professional author, I can't say that lesson took really well.

However, fiction can strongly engage the emotion. It can leave an impression on the mind and it can make you think about things in a new light. Good novels, and bad ones, can affect outlook. Because of this, I'm prepared to examine the following questions: what lessons did the Narnia books teach me as a child, and what do they teach me again as an adult?

First, let's be clear on a few things. I am fully aware that C. S. Lewis was a devout Christian. The Christian symbolism and metaphor in the Narnia books is so thinly veiled you could read a newspaper through it. I am also fully aware that Prof. Lewis also spent much of his life in an all but monastic setting, which was not conducive to creating a good opinion of the abilities and attributes of women. It is known, for example, that Lewis had a very poor opinion of the wife of one of his academic colleagues. This shocking woman wrote professionally, and ran a school. In fact, it's her school he's taking potshots at in *The Silver Chair*. Lewis certainly didn't have any use for feminism, as we can see by Eustace's overbearing attempts to explain why Lucy shouldn't get the nice cabin in *The Voyage of the Dawn Treader*. The books are also very clear on the importance of obeying the divinely appointed king.

But are these the main lessons of Narnia? I don't think so.

Why not? Well, I'll start with the three things that most attracted me to the Narnia books. Lucy, Jill and Aravis.

Lucy Pevensie, the first to enter the wardrobe, was not, on the face of it, the most likely candidate for me to adopt as a hero. She is, most of the time, just too darned sweet to be believed. In real life, to this day, I've never met a little girl so well-behaved and kind. There were, however, things about Lucy that drew me in as a child, and kept me as an adult, and I don't mean her ability to find magic countries in cupboards, which is, of course, just cool on the face of it.

Lucy always has the courage of her convictions. When her older siblings try to talk her out of her initial story she sticks to it, even when pretending would be easier. Having myself had a contentious relationship with an older sibling, I was completely in Lucy's corner when Peter and Susan (reasonably), and Edmund (nastily), tried to get her to stop believing in what she knew to be true. As an adult, I understand the metaphor about the necessity of being true to one's faith. At the time I was first reading it, however, I saw only a girl who was being unfairly picked on by her siblings. After that, the story could have been just about anything else, and I was going to root for Lucy. Universal themes of man, nature and the divine, nothing. Lewis, the childless Cambridge professor, had hit on two of the universal themes of childhood right off the bat—not being believed, and being teased.

We see this again in *Prince Caspian*. Once more, Lucy must stand up for what she knows is the truth in the face of her older sister's belittling of her. This time, she almost fails and has to reclaim her faith, but this aspect of the scene only served to reinforce the emotional impact for me both as a child and an adult. There are very few people of any age who can honestly say they do not fear the scorn of their peers or family. Ridicule is as much the weapon of the adult bully on the job as it is of the child bully on the playground. Standing strong in the face of ridicule is an act of bravery to be understood and admired by anyone, no matter what his or her age.

There was something else about sweet, little Lucy. It came later, but it was something I had never seen before. Queen Lucy went to war.

She was back with the archers, and, admittedly, her participation is qualified with the statement, "she's as good as a man, or, at least a boy." But there she was, in the ranks, facing death and hazard and dealing her own blows to the enemy. Lucy was a physical fighter, not just a moral one. She took up arms.

Now, that it was Lucy who was my first girl fighter may be a function of age. You see, I grew up in the seventies, and the literary landscape for children, especially for girls, was very different then. First off, fantasy was very thin on the ground. In our public library (which was easier to get to than the 'burb's one bookstore (no, the Internet didn't exist, Borders wasn't a chain yet, and yes, I did walk a mile to school, in the snow)), I managed to find every girl-and-her-brother-find-a-magical-something-or-the-other-and-have-a-series-of-adventures they had. I read those hungrily. E. Nesbit was a major favorite, of course. I learned to read out of the Oz books and was addicted to the adventures of Dorothy, Trot and Betsy Bobbin. But it was this conservative, fusty old man author who showed me a girl could be a warrior.

If anything, I like Jill Pole even better than Lucy. Jill complains. Jill gets uncomfortable, and angry, and argues. Jill is stubborn and claustrophobic, and gets things wrong. More than once, Jill makes a stupid move that almost ruins everything. Despite all this, the narrative treats Jill as a hero, and, like Lucy, she is not just a passive, supportive hero.

Jill also fights. She fights in *The Last Battle* standing right beside Eustace and King Tirian. Jill may die in a railway accident, but Jill also dies bravely in battle right beside the men and boys. Jill also saves Eustace and Puddleglum from being eaten for dinner by giants, holds off the witch's spell in the underworld, rescues poor Puzzle the donkey from captivity and gets to give the school bullies a good beating (okay, maybe beating on the bully girls with a riding crop is not the best lesson in the world, but it sure was emotionally satisfying when I was twelve).

It is true that during the climactic battle in *The Silver Chair*, Jill sits in the corner and does nothing.

Or does she?

Here's what she *doesn't* do. She doesn't get into the fight at that point, but, she also doesn't scream, faint or run. She certainly doesn't get in the way. She doesn't do any of the hundred clichéd things we see poorly armed and untrained women do in a hundred bad comedies and fantasies which either hinder the fight or result in their needing a rescue. Jill, understanding she is poorly armed for this particular fight, does keep her head, her nerve and her dignity, and gets out of the way, allowing the fight to be quickly resolved. This is no small thing. It is, in fact, a sort of bravery not frequently portrayed in fantasy novels, and it is a moment I have always enjoyed.

You'll notice something else about this scene. It's not Jill who's got to be rescued. It's the prince who's in immediate danger and has to be saved. Lewis' girls are never abducted, never bound and gagged where the men and boys are free. They are never snatched up and held with swords or knives to their throats. Not once in any of the Narnia books does Lewis give in to such scenarios which are shown repeatedly in our more modern, egalitarian fantasy novels. He never renders his girls more helpless than his boys.

The last girl hero on the list is Aravis, whom we meet only once, in *The Horse and His Boy*. Aravis is a heroine of epic. About to be forced into a terrible marriage, she disguises herself and escapes. Aravis comes out of an old, grand tradition, but it is one separate from Lucy and Jill's. That's one more thing I know now but did not know when I first met her. I'd only read the most common of *The Arabian Nights*. Sagas such as *Orlando Furioso* and *The Song of Roland* were well in the future. What I saw then was that Aravis is brave, loyal, quick-thinking and, at times, thoughtless. She is the one genuine tomboy of the girl heroes, preferring the rough life she finds on the road with Shasta and the horses to a life in a palace.

For all her separate traditional background, Aravis does have the one common trait shared by all of Lewis' girl heroines. She is straightforward. Lewis never made his girls foolish or coy, or had them say what they did not mean to try to get their way. He did not let their courage, or their brains, fail them in a crisis, not even to showcase the courage of his boys. Even Susan, the older sister who ultimately falls from the faith and doesn't climb back, helps save herself from the wolf in *The Lion, the Witch and the Wardrobe.* Yes, Peter has to kill the beast, but Susan is strong enough to stay alive and summon help so Peter can finish the task.

I will freely admit that adult women, what few there are, do not come off well in these books. There are only two mothers in the seven books. One dies from an enchanted snakebite; the other is an invalid who must be healed by her son. The women with actual power are two witches and a headmistress, and they are irredeemably bad. There is not even a cursory examination of character. The witches simply want to usurp power in Narnia, which must be wrong because power in Narnia is divinely appointed. It is also, except for the queens Susan and Lucy, male. What lesson is this giving the reader? What answer can the feminist make to that?

None. It's there, and is as real as the Christian tradition behind the stories.

But, what does this mean, and what does it do to the stories? Does reading the Narnia books make children believe that grown women should not have power, or that when they do it's bad?

Ummmm...no.

It didn't even make me believe grown female witches are bad, and believe you me, if there were pagans in my 'burb when I was growing up, they were way, way back in the broom closet. You see, I had counter examples to work with. Remember I said I learned to read out of the Oz books? Trust me, in those books Glinda the Good does more than float around in a pink bubble. She commands an army and rules a kingdom of her own, and it's happy and it's prosperous. I also repeatedly read the work of the prestigious and very Christian Madeleine L'Engle, whose "witches" are messengers of God.

Am I making excuses? Perhaps. But this is what I believe: no single story has to be positive and laudable in all aspects in order to be a good story. There are very few flawless stories, and this is perhaps Narnia's biggest flaw, at least from a feminist standpoint.

However, one does not even have to leave the world of Narnia to find the counter lesson to the unexamined evil in the female witches, and that is, of course, the steady heroism of the girls. The girls are consistently strong, respected and wholly themselves. The presence of kings, princes and older brothers never reduces the girls in any way. Their personal flaws are individual to them, not the result of their sex or their age. Even the inability to keep the points of a compass in one's head is not held by the narrator to be universal female fault. And never do their flaws diminish the girls as humans. It is part of their heroism that they meet these internal demons and vanquish them, with the help of Aslan, of course, but then, *everyone* needs Aslan's help in these books, and even a king can, and does, require a stern lecture from the Great Lion.

But what of the progressive in Narnia? Surely, you say, if these books teach any social lessons, they're reactionary in the extreme. The books are relentlessly hierarchical, patriarchal and static. Narnia exists for hundreds of generations, and yet it does not change, except when the Telmarines invade, and that's a bad change. Advanced technology never makes an appearance (except in the disguised form of the Deplorable Word); there are certainly no social revolutions in Narnia proper.

But they are not completely devoid of their progressive elements. The notion of girls and women going to war beside men and boys is still a radical one, at least in the U.S. And there is something else. It may appear small, but it is not insignificant.

It is the choice of the first ruler of Narnia. To start the line of kings in Narnia, Aslan chooses a London cabby, a member of the working class. Every English writer must at some point and in some way deal with the class system. Issues of class are as endemic in English society as racial issues are in the U.S., and they can be as damaging. An English writer can choose not to discuss implications of class differences in their work, but class is going to be part of the story all the same.

So, here Lewis is writing about Christ appointing the first of a line of kings. Who is this king? Is he a priest or saint? A great warrior? Does this guy give anybody so much as a punch in the nose? No. He's a nice, hardworking guy who refuses to panic in an exceptionally strange situation. He likes animals and has an overworked wife whom he loves, and who, incidentally, also refuses to panic in the face of an exceptionally strange situation. As I've grown older, and become an overworked wife myself, I can really get behind the notion that this is the sort of person you want to make into royalty (Aslan summons her to queenship on laundry day too—bonus!).

Many English (and U.S.) writers portray the working-class man as the salt of the earth, but, especially in the mid-fifties, the salt of the earth is seldom elevated above his allotted station. Indeed, in some stories, attempting to leave one's class is a recipe for disaster. To take just one example, the only reason working-class Samwise Gamgee in The Lord of the Rings is able to resist the call of the One Ring is that he knows his social place and he will not leave it. Violation of the class structure in Tolkien's fantasy is the call for evil to come in and wreak havoc. Lewis takes his working-class hero, makes him a king and has him blessed directly by the divinity.

It's a short-lived incident in the books but, given the cultural context, it is not insignificant, and it is one more layer of complexity to add to the story.

Which leaves us with the Christianity. I was raised as a Unitarian Universalist, which teaches that the search for truth is personal and ongoing and that to be a good person, I must respect the dignity and worth of every human being. If you stop and think about it, this is a tough road to truly follow, and I stumble a lot (it's hard to respect the worth of the guy on the cell phone who just ran the stop sign when I've got my son in the car with me), but do I try. Personal reflection has led me to become an agnostic. I in fact describe myself as a militant agnostic. I firmly believe there is absolutely no way anybody can truly know what happens beyond this life, and that includes whether or not there is one or more gods out there who have plans or views about humanity. This means we all have to do our best with the tools we have, and use our heads as well as our hearts, because all we've got for certain is ourselves.

So, what am I to do when faced with such rock-hard Christian certainty as is taught in the Narnia books?

First, I admire it. Yes, I said admire. Lewis used Christianity as the basis for some very good, very consistent world-building. In a conversation I once had with Jacqueline Carey (whose essay is in this book, and you should read it as soon as you're done with mine), Ms. Carey remarked that fantasy was full of religion and yet there was almost no faith. Fantasy authors create reams of gods and goddesses and a plethora of churches to go with them. Seldom, however, do the inhabitants of those worlds conduct themselves as if they truly believed in the assorted divinities, even if those divine beings show up from time to time.

In Narnia, from the get-go, people proceed in the utter certainty of their divinity's reality. It is faith in Aslan that leads Lucy over a cliff and allows Puddleglum to overcome evil magic. It is faith in Tash that causes a young Calormene to walk into darkness. The reality of Aslan is the root and wellspring of the books, and the characters all act accordingly, even when they are in denial of that reality, like the dwarves in *The Last Battle*. That is good, internally sound world-building, and it helps make for a good fantasy read.

But a contribution to good world-building or not, the faith underlying Narnia is still Christianity, and as an agnostic, you might expect I'm not happy with Christian lessons being taught in my children's literature. Actually, as an agnostic, and as a questioning human being, I welcome a reasoned and eloquent discussion of the nature of faith, religion and the world. That is what Lewis provides in the Narnia books.

An examination of the type of Christianity preached shows up some very interesting details. First of all, although Aslan is clearly Jesus Christ in lion form, there are other gods in Narnia. Bacchus is there on special occasions. The dryads, hamadryads, are referred to as gods. Even the Beruna River is personified as a god. In fact, it is Aslan's absence from Narnia that silences these other powers, and his arrival in Narnia that reawakens them. Lewis is acknowledging that the natural world is a layered one, with many powers present. Christ may be over all, but these others exist, and they are part of the greater picture, and they may be honored and celebrated without the celebrator being evil.

Lewis does not even condemn the existence of other faiths. He asserts the basic will and ability for good in all people, whatever shape that divinity may take for them. The statement that tells all is in *The Last Battle*. When the Narnians meet Emeth, the Calormene warrior, in heaven, he recounts his encounter with Aslan, where he admits to having worshipped Tash. Here is a part of his exchange with Aslan:

"...Lord, is it true then, as the Ape said, that thou and Tash are one?...It is false. Not because he and I are one, but because we are opposites. I take to me the services which thou hast done for him. For I and he are of such different kinds that no service which is vile can be done to me and none which is not vile can be done to him. Therefore, if any man swear by Tash and keep his oath for the oath's sake, it is by me he has truly sworn, though he know it not, and it is I who reward him. And if any man do a cruelty in my name, then, though he says the name Aslan, it is Tash whom he serves and by Tash the deed is accepted."

I'm good with this. In fact, I go around quoting it at people. It asserts the universality of good, and that the divine cares nothing for name and shape. It is very close to the Hindu idea that the path of a good man leads to heaven. It doesn't matter to whom you pray; what matters is that you do right in this world. Do your best, hold to a good path, be honest, seek the truth, and you are on the side of the angels, or the Lion.

Come to that, it's very close to the Unitarian idea that the search for truth is personal and ongoing.

The unforgivable in Narnia is not worship of alternate gods, but false worship. The deliberate corruption of faith for personal gain precedes the end of the world. The evil of this is not a lesson I'm going to argue with. The deliberate corruption and manipulation of faith is a wrong that has led to some of the most horrific acts of human cruelty in history. It might even yet bring us down so far we believe we are at the end of the world.

One more point I'd like to make. Lewis writes a great deal about faith in Narnia, but it is not a blind faith he portrays. Doubt in what you cannot see, mistaken belief about what you have never seen, is forgivable, if you are honest in your mistake and solid in your character. Trumpkin the dwarf is forgiven for doubting Aslan's existence, if tossed around a bit, because he has acted selflessly and for the best. Bree, another flawed hero of the books, is forgiven for getting his ideas on Aslan's true nature wrong, because he too has suffered bravely and acted for the best. Shift the ape is not forgiven, nor is Nikabrik the dwarf, less because they worshipped falsely than because they acted duplicitously and selfishly.

The path of a good man leads to heaven. Questions are not only allowable, they can lead to a stronger faith and a truer heart. Kindness is worth raising to kingship. A girl can be as brave and as smart as a boy, and can find magic countries in the cupboard if she bothers to look. These are the lessons of Narnia, and it is well worth a walk back through the wardrobe to remember them.

Sarah Zettel was born in Sacramento, California. Since then she has lived in ten cities, four states, two countries and become an author of a dozen science fiction and fantasy books, a host of short stories and novellas as well as a handful of essays about the pop culture she finds herself immersed in. She lives in Michigan with her husband Tim, son Alexander and cat, Buffy the Vermin Slayer. When not writing, she drinks tea, gardens, practices tai chi and plays the fiddle, but not all at once.

CATHY MCSPORRAN

Daughters of Lilith: Witches and Wicked Women in The Chronicles of Narnia

IN C. S. LEWIS' FANTASY of the great Christian struggle, the image of Lilith looms larger than that of Satan. She lives in her female descendants: the Witches. According to Ancient Hebraic legend, Lilith was Adam's first wife, who rebelled against her husband and became a "demon of the night" (Hefner 1997b); similarly, we are told that the White Witch is a descendant of "Adam's first wife, her they called Lilith. And she was one of the Jinn" (Lewis 1998, 147). Therefore, although the Witch claims to be human, there is not "a drop of real human blood" in her. She has been disqualified from the human race, thanks to her wicked ancestor, Lilith.

A Witch, then, is not simply—as in J. K. Rowling's Harry Potter books—a female version of a Wizard. Wizards, or magicians, are human men; they attempt to use illicit magical powers but, we are told, they are "working with things they do not really understand" (30). Uncle Andrew, the titular magician from *The Magician's Nephew*, has no real magic of his own; he simply possesses the magic rings of his Witchlike fairy godmother, "old Mrs. Lefay" (who is clearly a relative of another magical *femme fatale*, Morgan le Fay). When the rings are confiscated, he is powerless; and, having "learned his lesson," is pardoned and becomes "a nicer and less selfish old man than he had ever been before" (106).

A Witch, however, is a different proposition. She is not human: she is a "daughter of Lilith," and will never "learn her lesson." Nor can she be pardoned, or offered pity: as the usually placid Mr. Beaver explains, when it comes to "things that look like humans and aren't," the only response is to "keep your eyes on it and feel for your hatchet" (147). A Witch is a "thing," not a person. Although she is by definition female, she is not to be spoken of as *she*, but as *it*. So what, then, is a "Witch," to have deserved such violent loathing?

In this essay, I will examine the two Witches—Jadis the White Witch, and the unnamed "Lady of the Green Kirtle"—who appear in The Chronicles of Narnia. I will show how Lewis uses the Hebrew legend of Lilith to define their characters and to portray them as evil and inhuman; I will demonstrate how, in the Witches, wickedness is conflated with rebellion against the principle of "natural" authority, particularly masculine authority. I will argue that while villainous males in The Chronicles are shown as human (and therefore capable of redemption and worthy of mercy), villainous females tend to be depicted as monstrous and unnatural, and as such are to be killed as swiftly as possible. I will argue that when human women—"Daughters of Eve"—become corrupt, they take on attributes of Lilith and her witch-descendants, and so are much less likely to be redeemed than transgressive males.

Lilith

The Ancient Hebrew legend of Lilith, first wife of Adam, is related in *The Alphabet of Ben Sira*. Adam, who *has* "tried coupling" with each female animal in Eden but "found no satisfaction in the act" (Graves and Patai 1964, 65–69), asks for a mate of his own:

[God] then created a woman for Adam, from the earth, as He had created Adam himself, and called her Lilith. Adam and Lilith began to fight. She said, "I will not lie below," and he said, "I will not lie beneath you, but only on top. For you are fit only to be in the bottom position, while I am to be in the superior one." Lilith responded, "We are equal to each other inasmuch as we were both created from the earth." But they would not listen to one another. When Lilith saw this, she pronounced the Ineffable Name and flew away into the air. (Humm 2001)

Lilith never returns to Adam, even when she is cursed with the loss of "one hundred of her children every day." She becomes the mother of demons, and will jealously slay human infants whenever possible; her rebellion against "proper" masculine authority has made her monstrous.

Lewis demonizes her even further by making her a jinn: Lilith gave birth to the jinn ("demons" or "fiery spirits" (Hefner 1997a)) but was herself created human. For Lewis, however, her rejection of her husband's authority was an unnatural and destructive act; indeed, her rejection of the principle of authority itself was unnatural and destructive. In *Mere Christianity*, Lewis lays out the belief that, in marriage, absolute equality is impossible; one partner must have authority over the other, one must be the "head" and have the "casting vote," or the marriage will fail. He goes on to add that this casting vote must rightly belong to the husband, since "there must be something unnatural about the rule of wives over husbands, because the wives themselves are half ashamed of it and despise the husbands whom they rule" (1997, 93).

Throughout The Chronicles, Lewis expands this highly dubious conclusion from husbandly authority alone to masculine authority in general: particularly Divine authority, in the shape of Narnia's god, the lion Aslan. The lion-shape is aptly chosen: out of all the animals Lewis could have selected to represent his deity, the lion is the one whose gender is immediately obvious (in the possession—or lack of—a mane). It is significant that at the moment of Aslan's martyrdom, when he is at his weakest, his mane is cut off; when he returns, Samson-like in his strength and glory, his mane has miraculously regrown. Lewis did not toss a coin to determine his God's gender; he makes Aslan deliberately and thoroughly male.

Female revolt against Aslan, therefore, is doubly threatening, and so the Witches are his most powerful and terrifying enemies. Lewis, always supporting the principle of rightful authority, makes them out-Lilith Lilith: they demand not "equality," as she did, but cruel and tyrannical domination. Like another Lilith, the eponymous Witch-princess of George MacDonald's *Lilith*, she insists on being "queen of Hell, and mistress of the worlds" (1994, 215).

A Witch (the word is always capitalized) then is not just an evildoer;

unlike MacDonald's Lilith, who ultimately is another sinner to be redeemed, a Witch is evil itself. Descendants of Adam can do harm, but "Adam's race" can sometimes "help to heal it" (Lewis 1998, 80). Uncle Andrew and Digory are responsible for having "waked and brought hither...an evil" into Narnia: but neither the magician nor his nephew constitute the evil itself. That is the "evil Witch in this world": the Empress Jadis, commonly known as the White Witch.

The White Witch

The White Witch is one of fantasy's greatest villains, and the major opponent of Aslan. She tries to usurp Aslan's authority as sovereign of Narnia, and therefore represents not just her foremother Lilith (rebel against male authority) but Satan (rebel against God's authority). The White Witch, therefore, as both Lilith and Satan, has a double dose of what Lewis has described as the "Great Sin": Pride, through which "the devil became the devil...the complete anti-God state of mind" (1997, 100). Lilith demands equality; the White Witch demands, like Milton's Satan, to "reign in Hell," even if she must turn Narnia into hell to achieve her aim.

To show his abhorrence of such pride, Lewis makes the White Witch not only doubly unsympathetic but doubly unnatural. The White Witch is not just dressed in white; she is defined by whiteness: a specific kind of whiteness, the chilly pallor of ice and snow. Her skin is white, "deadly white, white as salt" (Lewis 1998, 93); Lewis is quick to stress that this does not imply "fair-skinned" (the "lovely" and natural people of Narnia are "fair-skinned"), but a stark and unnatural white, "not merely pale, but white like snow or paper or icing-sugar" (123). Like MacDonald's Lilith, she exists in the state of "Life in Death—life dead, yet existent" (MacDonald 1994, 215); her undead pallor, together with her "very red mouth," makes her appearance vampiric. The White Witch produces whiteness, the snow of eternal winter; she turns her enemies into stone, freezing them into her own state of un-death. Icy whiteness also defines her heart: she destroyed her own people with a single word, not the "Ineffable Name" of God, but the destructive "Deplorable Word." Lilith agrees to others sacrificing her "one hundred children" every day; the Witch goes further, deliberately slaughtering her own so that no one else may rule them.

A Witch's powers, however, are not always so combative. She is at her most formidable when being seductive. Lilith, of course, is the *femme fatale* to end all *femmes fatales*; she is "the sweetness of sin and the evil tongue...she fornicates with men who sleep below in the impurity of spontaneous emission, and from them are born demons and spirits" (Patai 1981). The female "demons and spirits" are succubi, "lusty she-demons" who, like their mother, "copulate with men in all their dreams" (Hefner 1997b). These nocturnal couplings do not, of course, take place in The Chronicles; but Lilith's Witch-daughters are still capable of corrupting men. They embody the "infernal Venus" of Lewis' *The Screwtape Letters*, the female "type" most effective in leading a man to his perdition:

> You will find, if you look carefully into any human's heart, that he is haunted by at least two imaginary women—a terrestrial and an infernal Venus, and that his desire differs qualitatively according to its object.
>
> There is one type for which his desire is such as to be...readily mixed with charity, readily obedient to marriage, coloured all through with [the] golden light of reverence and naturalness...there is another type which he desires brutally, and desires to desire brutally...which, even within marriage, he would tend to treat as a slave, an idol, or an accomplice. (1978, 104)

The Witches are, quite obviously, highly desirable. While most women are routinely described as beautiful in Narnia, the Witches are the *most* beautiful: the Green Witch is "the most beautiful lady" Drinian has ever seen (1998, 576), while Digory reflects in later life that he has "never known a woman so beautiful" as the White Witch (34). In The Chronicles, male desire for the infernal Venus is not just "qualitatively" different: it is *quantitatively* different, more powerful and more extreme. The terrestrial Venus, "golden light" notwithstanding, never possesses *supreme* beauty; that distinction belongs to the seductresses, the daughters of Lilith.

Accordingly, the White Witch plays two great tempters, both the Serpent and Eve; she offers Digory the forbidden apple of "knowledge that would have made you happy all your life," promising "sweetly" that she and he will "live for ever and be king and queen of this whole world" (93). Why the Witch is so keen for the company of Digory, a "common child" whom she dislikes, is never explained: nor is it relevant. It is merely her idiom: she is a Daughter of Lilith, and therefore she tries to seduce, even if the male she targets is still young enough to refuse her because "mother herself...wouldn't like it" (94). Faced with a child's asexual innocence, the Witch can only lose.

Ultimately, too, the White Witch loses her battle for possession of the child-world of Narnia. As a Daughter of Lilith, she can hope for no mercy from the vengeful Aslan:

> [Aslan] flung himself upon the White Witch....Then the Lion and the Witch had rolled over together but with the Witch underneath. (191)

And so, at the moment of her death, Lilith is returned to her "place": underneath a male. Divine masculine authority is restored; terrifying female rebellion has been crushed, at least for today.

The Lady of the Green Kirtle

Evil female rebellion soon rears its head again. (How can it not, since an adventure story needs an effective villain, and male evil here is so ineffectual?) It does so in the more plausible (and therefore more dangerous) shape of the Witch-Queen of the Underland, given no name other than "The Lady of the Green Kirtle."

This Lady (commonly titled the Green Witch) is of unknown origin; we are not informed of how "human" or otherwise she is. We have every reason, however, to regard her as an honorary Daughter of Lilith, if not a literal one. Constant parallels are drawn between her and the White Witch; she is "one of the same crew" (577), one of the "Witches of the North." She is a shape-shifter, a Lamia-like creature; Lamia, as Lewis notes in *The Discarded Image*, was sometimes equated with Lilith (2004, 124–25). The Green Witch can transform into a giant snake "so quickly that there was only just time to see it" (Lewis 1998, 633); such powers are not likely to belong to human magicians who "don't know what they're doing."

Like the White Witch, the Green Witch is defined by her appearance: or more specifically, by her greenness. As we have seen with the White Witch, a Witch's color is crucial. Narnia-oriented Internet chat rooms often focus on the Witches' coloring—are they blonde? brunette? red-haired?[1]—and appearance; at first glance this may seem trivial, but in fact has touched upon a central point. The Green Witch is defined by her color, or rather by that color's negative associations: her "green" is not the shade of grass and living things, but the color of poison. Poison is what she is and what she does. In human form she wears "dazzling" green, attractive and deluding—but the serpent she turns into is "green as poison" (633), and it is in serpent form that she kills Rilian's mother with her venom; "green with envy," perhaps, of this rival for Rilian's affection. Her green "fire-herbs" poison the mind; her silver chair poisons Rilian's memory and personality. She is, literally, poison. In this she is a true child of Lilith, whose lover was said to be the demon Samael, "Poison of God" (Hefner 1997b).

She is also, like Lilith, a seductress. Like the White Witch, she is "the most beautiful lady" someone has ever seen (in this case, Drinian); like Lilith, she has a penchant for stealing children, and, again like the White Witch, she prefers boys and young men. Her attempt to abduct Rilian is more successful than Jadis' attempt to win over Digory; the Green Witch, a much craftier "infernal Venus," waits until her target is older than Digory, "a very young knight" (and therefore presumably at least adolescent), and so ripe to be seduced.

Also, the Green Witch has taken the precaution of dispatching Rilian's mother. As we have seen, a saintly mother is a boy's best defense against the infernal Venus: maternal instructions have a good influence on Digory, and presumably the Green Witch wishes to avoid the same pitfall. Also, Rilian's mother is by nature an opponent of any Witch. She is the daughter of Ramandu the star, and thereby a celestial being; she is also the keeper of the "Knife of Stone" used in Aslan's martyrdom, and therefore reminiscent of the "Grail Maiden" who keeps the Holy Grail and the spear used to pierce Christ's side. She is the only woman whose beauty surpasses that of the Witches: we are told that when the *Dawn Treader*'s passengers saw her, they "thought they had never before known what beauty meant" (1998, 517). If such a thing as a "celestial Venus" can exist, Ramandu's daughter fits the bill; thus she is the natural opponent of the Green Witch, whose realm is the "infernal" Under-

---

[1] For example, NarniaWeb Discussion Forum: "[The Green Witch] needs something of a Latin beauty...." "While I think blonde is what I envisage, I wouldn't mind a red-head at all. Or even a reddish blonde...." www.narniaweb.com/forum/forum_posts.asp?TID=1348&TPN=7 (accessed February 18, 2005).

land. What is more, Ramandu's daughter can instinctively see through a Witch's disguises; she dies "trying hard to tell" Rilian that the "great serpent" was truly the Green Witch.

Small wonder, then, that the Witch must get her out of the way; one of them must die so the other can exist in Rilian's world. The Witch therefore wishes not just to destroy Rilian's mother, but to replace her. Beside "that same fountain where the Queen got her death," the Green Witch appears "wrapped in a thin garment as green as poison"; in an instant Rilian has "almost forgotten the worm" that killed his mother, as he stares at the Witch "like a man out of his wits" (576). And well he might be. Aside from the Oedipal complications of the situation—the death of a mother in the same space as the newfound object of desire—Rilian is confronted by one of the very few openly erotic figures in the whole sequence. It is left to our imagination just how "thin" the green garment is, and how insecurely it is "wrapped" (rather than securely "worn"). Later, even after her spell has been broken, Rilian "shivers" when she speaks to him; it is, we are informed, "not easy to throw off in half an hour an enchantment which has made one a slave for ten years" (628).

The Green Witch is, in many ways, more of a threat than her White counterpart; and her heresies against Aslan are more extreme. Jadis dismisses Aslan as a mere "wild animal" (94); the Queen of Underland casts doubt upon his very existence. Using hypnotic music and green fire-herbs, she persuades her prisoners to doubt the existence of Narnia, the sun and Aslan himself:

> "You've seen cats, and now you want a bigger and better cat, and it's to be called a *lion*.... Well, 'tis a pretty make-believe, though, to say truth, it would suit you all better if you were younger." (632)

This is worse than rebellion against God; this is atheism. (It is significant too that heretical unbelief is associated with being "grown up"; those who are too "grown up" do not thrive in Narnia, as we shall see.) The Green Witch cannot be permitted to survive such blasphemy; she cannot even keep her human shape. She transforms into a giant snake, attacks and has her head "hacked off" (633–34). Rilian is glad that she "took to her serpent form at the last," since "it would not have suited well either with my heart or with my honour to have slain a woman." Thus Lewis can pass smoothly over the piece of doublethink essential to accepting his portrait of Witches: Witches are the most powerfully dangerous beings in Narnia, and must be destroyed; but Witches are female, and females are weaker and therefore cannot honorably be attacked. But the snake has neither humanity nor gender, and is quickly reduced to something that does not even have organic life: a "horrible thing" that keeps moving after death, creating a "nasty mess." A Witch's inhumanity negates her femininity, and justifies any form of violence against her.

So much then for the Witches, the outright Daughters of Lilith. What about the Daughters of Eve? What happens when they go "wrong"? Can Eve ever turn into Lilith?

Susan

"My sister Susan," answered Peter shortly and gravely, "is no longer a friend of Narnia."

"Yes," said Eustace, "and whenever you've tried to get her to come and talk about Narnia, she says 'What wonderful memories you have! Fancy your still thinking about all those funny games we used to play when we were children.'"

"Oh, Susan!" said Jill. "She's interested in nothing nowadays except nylons and lipstick and invitations. She always was a jolly sight too keen on being grown-up."

"Grown-up, indeed," said the Lady Polly. "I wish she *would* grow up. She wasted all her school time wanting to be the age she is now, and she'll waste all the rest of her life trying to stay that age. Her whole idea is to race on to the silliest time of one's life as quick as she can and then stop there as long as she can." (741)

It is too reductive to suggest that Susan is shut out of paradise because of her fondness for "nylons and lipstick and invitations." She is excluded for her loss of faith; she has fallen into the Green Witch's heresy, regarding Aslan as a childish tale to be outgrown. She may not be irretrievably damned; even if she has lost her chance of Narnia, she may have turned her attentions to the grown-up-friendly Aslan of her own world—that is, Christ (indeed, it is to be hoped that she can find some religious consolation for the death of her entire family).

And yet, the question remains: why, out of the eight "Friends of

Narnia," should Susan be the one to fall? Is she simply, as Jill accuses her, "too keen on being grown-up"? Admittedly issues of Susan being "grown up" arise quite frequently: she is considered "very old for her age" (426). However, as Polly notes ("I wish she *would* grow up"), there are ways of becoming an adult woman that do not center around "lipstick and nylons and invitations."

And yet, Susan as an adult is always problematic. As far as we are told, Susan is the only one of the eight to consider getting married. Her brothers and sister are content with the company of one another, and the Talking Beasts and mythological creatures who make up the court of Narnia. But Susan doesn't want this childish idyll. Susan wants a man. Like Adam in the Garden, Susan wants a spouse; and as with Adam, no good can come of it. Susan further complicates matters by not restricting her choice to a near neighbor of whom her family might approve; she is prepared to consider an outsider. Even worse, she considers an outsider of a different race; she finally rejects her Prince, whom her brother insists on describing as her "dark-faced lover"(234), not because of his color but because of his conduct.

Susan, in other words, is conducting her love life rather more as real-world adults do. From what we have seen so far, marriage in Narnia is either an extension of childhood friendship (Aravis and Cor) or love at first sight, passing into marriage and happily-ever-after with no points in between (Caspian and Ramandu's daughter). Susan's affairs, however, involve the (more prosaic) trying and testing of lovers, followed by rejection if she finds them incompatible. Susan reserves the right to make mistakes; she reserves the right to change her mind.

The whole business, of course, ends in disaster. Susan ends up as a Helen-of-Troy figure, whose rejection of one man leads hundreds of others to war; she, like Helen, has not asked nor desired them to go to war, but of course this did not prevent the blame being placed on Helen. Helen-like, Susan is branded a "false jade," the subject of public distaste; Corin feels obliged to fight for her name when "a boy in the street made a beastly joke about Queen Susan" (241). This is the first time we have seen such adult terms and concepts being applied to a female Friend of Narnia. Susan has a "lover" (probably not meant here to suggest a full sexual relationship—but a strong word, used of no other couple in the series); her brother must fight for "the honour of the Queen" (237), to spare her from darkly hinted-at sexual slavery.

Blameless as Susan still is, there are already parallels here between her and the Witches. Her beauty is supreme beauty: she is "the most beautiful lady" Shasta has ever seen. For the rejected Prince Rabadash she is an "infernal Venus" to be "desired brutally," one whom he can only imagine treating as a "slave" to be "dragged by her hair" (307); although this, admittedly, has more to do with Rabadash's personality than with Susan's. Yet Susan has—once again, unwittingly—the effect that Lucy can only fantasize jealously about: great lords are fighting for her favors. (Lucy is also described as "beautiful"; but Susan is the "beauty of the family" (496). Moreover, we are told that Lucy's appearance is "merry" (287)); it is hard to imagine a seductress, an infernal Venus or Daughter of Lilith, as "merry." Also, Susan lacks the tomboy attributes of the other female Friends. Lucy and Jill both ride to war, and are, in Corin's (admittedly childish) view, "as good as a man, or at any rate as good as a boy" (290). Susan, however, stays at home "like an ordinary grown-up lady." Susan is purely female—in the rather Boy's Own world of Narnia, she is dangerous stuff.

When we consider Lucy's desire to be more beautiful than her sister, we see yet again the association of being "most beautiful" with witchcraft and wrongdoing. When Lucy looks in the Magician's Book, she is offered the chance to attain supreme beauty—but this would involve her, too, being transformed into a Witch:

> Lucy (for the girl in the picture was Lucy herself) was standing up with her mouth open and a rather terrible expression on her face, chanting or reciting something. In the third picture the beauty beyond the lot of mortals had come to her....
>
> She saw herself throned on high...and all the Kings in the world fought because of her beauty. And Susan was jealous of the dazzling beauty of Lucy, but that didn't matter a bit because no-one cared anything about Susan now. (495–96)

Once again the equation is confirmed: great beauty equals witchcraft equals wickedness. It is revealing that, when Lucy considers all of these things, her mind turns inevitably to thoughts of Susan.

It is interesting that not just men and boys are led astray by the Lilith-like beauty of a female form; Lucy, too, is almost seduced *by her own image*, beautified. In folktales of Lilith, girls are turned wanton (i.e., possessed by Lilith) not by looking at men, but by looking at themselves in the mirror:

> The girl glanced at herself in the mirror all the time, and in this way she was drawn into Lilith's web.... For that mirror had hung in the den of demons, and a daughter of Lilith had made her home there.
>
> Now the daughter of Lilith who made her home in that mirror watched every movement of the girl who posed before it. She bided her time and one day she slipped out of the mirror and took possession of the girl, entering through her eyes. In this way she took control of her, stirring her desire at will.... So it happened that this young girl, driven by the evil wishes of Lilith's daughter, ran around with young men who lived in the same neighborhood. (Schwartz 1998)

Lucy and Susan both undergo this narcissistic temptation. Lucy, however, is spared when a picture of Aslan replaces her own mirror-image, and so comes to her senses.

Susan, however, is not redeemed. She has become, like the Witches, defined by how she appears. Wearing "lipstick and nylons," after all, requires a fair amount of time before the mirror—dressing up for "invitations" requires even more. According to Polly, Susan is not merely trying to *look* a certain age; like Dorian Gray, she is trying to *be* that age, to "stop" or "stay" there. It would seem Susan wishes to alter time or to make herself immortal—forgetting the state of ghastly un-death in which the White Witch now exists—by turning her appearance into her substance. The mirror is Lilith's territory—Susan, who has forgotten the image of Aslan that might save her, can see nothing but herself.

Nor, it seems, does anyone go to great lengths to ask that Susan be pardoned. Two of the "Sons of Adam" amongst the Friends have committed sins that seem worse than Susan's: Edmund was a traitor, and Eustace was turned into a dragon for his greed. But both have been rehabilitated and redeemed. Susan, however, seems to have too much of Lilith in her—and she is most roundly denounced by the female Friends of Narnia. When condemning Susan, the males stick to stating the facts; the insulting epithets are applied by Jill and Polly: Susan is "too keen on being grown-up" (but still immature), she is "silly," she is "wasting her life." Susan cannot be more than twenty-one years old, since her elder brother Peter is "hardly full grown" (Lewis 1998, 691); yet Polly, now in her old age, shows a disturbing lack of charity toward a young woman indulging—perhaps temporarily—in the trappings of womanhood.

In the past, however, Polly has been prepared to intervene for wicked Uncle Andrew, asking Aslan to "unfrighten" him and send him home unharmed (98); similarly, Lucy asks "through her tears" that Aslan help the treacherous and murderous Dwarfs (747). But for her sister Susan, neither Lucy nor anyone else will speak. Perhaps Aslan would be unwilling or unable to help her; this goes unexplored, because no one asks. Little sense of sisterhood exists in Narnia, either in the Friends of Narnia or in native Narnians.

Affirmations of masculine supremacy are often placed in the mouths of females. Jill is the first to contest the Green Witch's magic with the name of Aslan; and, paraphrasing Lewis' unsubstantiated claim that wives "despise the husbands whom they rule," she is swift to find Rilian's obedience to the Green Witch distasteful: "Where I come from...they don't think much of men who are bossed about by their wives" (622). While Digory is admiring how "wonderfully brave" and "strong" Jadis is, Polly finds her simply a "terrible woman" (39). Women, it seems, should beware women in Narnia; Daughters of Lilith will not find allies in Daughters of Eve.

Conclusion

It is perhaps too glib to claim, as Philip Pullman does, that C. S. Lewis did not like women, and that this dislike is palpable in The Chronicles of Narnia [2] It is undeniable, however, that some aspects of female being and behavior are treated as terrifying, even demoniac. In the legends, Lilith demands only to be "equal," but in the hierarchy of Narnia this is unthinkable, and freedom from authority can only take the form of lust for absolute power.

In this insistence upon "natural" authority and hierarchy, Narnia is a quasi-medieval world created in the twentieth century; yet, in its demonization of magical women, it is perhaps more medieval than the Middle Ages itself. Lewis draws on aspects of Arthurian romance, but the benign enchantresses of Malory or des Troyes—the Ladies of the Lake, or the healers of Avalon—are conspicuous by their absence. The

---

[2] "Lewis...didn't like women in general, or sexuality at all, at least at the stage in his life when he wrote the Narnia books" (Pullman 1998).

Witches in Narnia are simply "bad"—just like their foremother, Lilith the "Jinn."

In The Chronicles of Narnia, Lilith is invoked; but the complexities and ambiguities of her story go unexplored. This is not simply because the sexual context of her rebellion may be thought unsuitable for child readers. It is also because a reader—especially a child reader—would be strongly inclined to sympathize with her desire for "equality" in the face of one who thinks she is "only fit" to be an inferior. And so Lewis must dismiss Lilith as a "Jinn," and make her seditious, seductive Witch-daughters unequivocally evil. It is sad that one of our greatest fantasy writers should have had, at least in this respect, so little imagination.

Cathy McSporran is in her third year of a Ph.D. in Creative Writing. She has published over a dozen short stories and won several awards. She has written papers and essays on C. S. Lewis, Elizabeth Hand and Philip Pullman and teaches classes on Creative Writing, Arthurian Studies and Dante's Divine Comedy. She is currently working on a novel, Cold City. Cathy lives in Glasgow, Scotland, with her husband and a large roving population of cats.

References

Graves, Robert, and Raphael Patai. 1964. *Hebrew Myths*. New York: Doubleday.

Hefner, Alan G. 1997a. "Jinn." *Encyclopedia Mythica*, www.pantheon.org/articles/j/jinn.html (accessed December 16, 2004).

———. 1997b. "Lilith." *Encyclopedia Mythica*, www.pantheon.org/articles/l/lilith.html (accessed February 21, 2005).

Humm, Alan. 2001. "The Story of Lilith," ccat.sas.upenn.edu/~humm/Topics/Lileth/alphabet.html (accessed December 15, 2004).

Lewis, C. S. 1978. *The Screwtape Letters*. Glasgow: Collins.

———. 1997. *Mere Christianity*. London: Fontana Books.

———. 1998. The Chronicles of Narnia. London: Collins.

———. 2004. *The Discarded Image*. Cambridge: Cambridge Univ. Press.

MacDonald, George. 1994. *Lilith*. Whitethorn, CA: Johannesen.

Patai, Raphael. 1981. *Gates to the Old City*. Detroit: Wayne State Univ. Press.

Pullman, Philip. 1998. "The Dark Side of Narnia." *Guardian*, October 1.

Schwartz, Howard, ed. 1998. "Lilith's Cave." *Lilith's Cave: Jewish Tales of the Supernatural*. San Francisco: Harper & Row.

PEG ALOI

The Last of the Bibliophiles: Narnia's Enduring Impact on the Pagan Community

FIRST, A REMINISCENCE…

Some years ago I spent the summer in Oxford, England, as part of a study abroad program. Ever been on one of these? There tends to be a just-about-equal mix of snotty, shallow, spoiled-rich college kids and artsy, vibrant, dirt-poor college kids—all of whom are Euro-curious but perhaps for different reasons. Guess which one I was? Since Oxford is an ancient, culturally alive city, full of old pubs, museums, bookstores, ethnic restaurants and public gardens, but also one with plenty of trendy wine bars, nightclubs, shopping malls and overpriced cream tea tourist traps, there is a bit of something for everyone. So naturally students gravitate toward one another based on similar interests, and depending on where they bump into each when they're not in class. My closest friends that summer were Tracy and Bob. Tracy was a young woman from Smith: a slender, freckle-faced photographer who seemed at first terribly shy and unassuming but later revealed herself to be a wordly, funny, clever and soulful person. Bob was a defiantly gay graduate student acquaintance from my own department who I got to know much better over Pims, who shared my penchant for raunchy humor. Thank goodness for them, or I might have had to make conversation or go drinking with one of the Laura Ashley-clad harpies from Wellesley or the chowder-headed dolts from UMass.

But one thing we also shared was our love of literature, which was, of course, why we were there: to study with English tutors amid the dreaming spires along the quixotic Thames. Bob and I were in a Gothic literature course together, and Tracy was doing a feminist novel course. On our jaunts about the city we'd look for obscure little tea shops down crooked alleys, and bookshops where the dust-motes of history twinkled in the streaming sunlight beyond the grimy windows. I remember Bob saying he wanted to find the pub where C. S. Lewis met with the Inklings, The Eagle and Child (the Inklings apparently nicknamed it the "Bird and Baby"). I asked about this, and when Bob mentioned The Chronicles of Narnia I realized I had not thought about these books in years, but pictured my battered old copy of *The Lion, the Witch and the Wardrobe* on my bookshelf. We never did find The Eagle and Child that summer (it was too easy to end up at The White Horse or The Blue Boar), although I did go there just several years ago with a friend when we were passing through. It's a large bustling place just off the High Street. Excellent lamb chops.

Another time that summer at Oxford we took a jaunt to Stourhead Gardens, a huge Victorian-era estate, thousands of acres of manicured vistas with huge trees from all over the world and the odd grotto or gazebo tucked away behind some copse. It was raining but magical that day: peacocks lolling in the mist, hydrangeas so blue we might have been tripping. Tracy and I ended up walking several miles that day (we were far keener on walking than some of the other students in the program; one day we took a group of young women shopping in Headington, which was about a two-mile walk from our dorm; they all pleaded exhaustion and took the bus on the way home while she and I relished the trudge home, stopping at a pub on the way). At Stourhead, in the rain, she and I ended up on a hill that slanted and sloped oddly, with an enormous tree on top of it. "It looks like Narnia," she said, this girl who was immersed in a course on the Brontës. Her father was a street poet, and she went on to make films, and I visited her in Little Italy where she showed me the ancient camera she liked to take to the park. Not surprising, then, her love of the magical world created by C. S. Lewis. She'd have been out there photographing fairies, a hundred years earlier.

There were many things that became clearer to me after I spent those two summers in England. I saw stone circles up close and understood why objects of antiquity fascinate us even when we know next to nothing about them. I lay on the ground looking up through the branches of huge trees at Tintern Abbey and grasped the impassioned awe between the lines of Wordsworth's orderly poems. I walked along the canal and saw people living on boats, ending up at The Trout, where Lewis also liked to drink and dine (order the fish). I told my tutor she had put salt instead of sugar on the berries and cream after first mentioning a similar scene in *Little Women*. But those summers of books and beer and goggle-eyed walks through cobbled streets under trees dripping English rain awakened my love of literature in ways I did not think possible. I felt for the first time the desire to visualize the lives of well-loved authors. Before my two summers in Oxford, during which time I also visited many other places in the countryside and nearby cities, I had always more easily pictured Eudora Welty or F. Scott Fitzgerald, or John Updike or Mark Twain working on their novels and stories, than I had Jane Austen, Elizabeth Bowen, D. H. Lawrence or Graham Swift.

Writers of little reputation love to imagine the workrooms and sidewalk cafés haunted by writers of large reputation: I do, anyway. Here in the city where many English writers were educated, I liked to think I saw and felt and smelled and touched things as they did. I was always more interested in tactile, experiential forms of knowledge than I was in abstractions: England clinched it for me, this place so rich in texture and color and scents, so full of contradictions—how could one fail to be inspired? Back among my American peers, I noted how talkative, how obvious, how devoid of wit and magic everything was. All those years ago, Lewis sat in The Eagle and Child with his friends and talked about religion and myth and war and death and love. That first summer, I sat in The Rathskeller and had conversations about Madonna. I felt sick sometimes. I started smoking and gave it up. I'd bolt into the night, into the gardens, soaking my shoes with dew, mist turning the streetlights into candles, listening for the sound of my heart. You have to go away to come home. That first summer, I also understood I was a witch. I went home and finished graduate school and waited for what came next. For the first time, I felt like my path was actually leading somewhere, and for the first time I understood that each day is full of meaning.

As with so many other things in contemporary American culture, we all seem to express ourselves in the language given us by formative texts experienced by "our generation." Books, magazines, songs, albums, TV shows, advertising, films and all of the print and celluloid ephemeral matter of our collective youth has, these days, become fodder for movie remakes, publisher reissues, thrift shop price markups and theme parties complete with new names for girl drinks made with at least three liqueurs, one flavored vodka and several fruit juices of dubious provenance (I swear, this year's Frodo Love Juice is last year's Casual but Meaningful Sex on the Beach, which is more or less identical to the Slow Slightly Uncomfortable Screw or Thompson Twins of my college days—and oddly, sloe gin always seems to be involved). We've all heard it said that the current times are rabidly recycling earlier eras, such that one can attend an "Early '90s" theme party without irony. Then again, many people do things without irony these days, but that's Another Essay, as they say.

Those of us beyond age twenty-five can probably point to any number of trendy texts or films or comics or 'zines or, increasingly these days, newsgroups or blogs, that have told us what to wear, how to talk, where to hang out, what to eat, what to drink (and how to avoid getting sick from drinking too much of it), when to lose our virginity (not to mention how), where to shop and maybe, if we had a smidgen of humanity beneath our consumerism-encrusted souls, how to make the world a better place through political or social activism. Just mention a book or film or record album (what we called them when CDs were big, black and breakable) or song or poem in a group of your friends or coworkers and watch for the telltale twitch of the eyelid or rueful half-smile that tells you they know, they understand, they were there, too. This is true even for texts that came into being well before our births, because the rediscovery of artists of bygone eras is a trendy thing that comes in waves, too. I'm not talking about bestselling self-help books or pop music here, though our absorption of them also has its impact. I'm talking arts and letters territory here. I'm talking stuff that captures our hearts and guts and imaginations and doesn't let go for years and years. In no particular order, these might include: *Terrapin Station. On the Road. Songs from the Wood. A Clockwork Orange. The Brady Bunch. Hounds of Love. Excalibur. Frampton Comes Alive! Atlas Shrugged. The White Album.* That episode of *The Twilight Zone. Howl. Repo Man. The Waste Land. Court and Spark. The Stand. Star Wars. The Second Coming.*

Say Anything. Passion. Moving Pictures. Love in the Time of Cholera. Syn-chronicity. M*A*S*H. Still Life With Woodpecker. Bless Its Little Pointed Head. In Utero. Xena: Warrior Princess. The Sandman.

Am I right?

Here's the thing: for pagans (or call us neo-pagans, if you wish, and some of us want to be called witches, Wiccans, heathens, druids, etc. Just don't call us late for the potluck feast, ha ha), these formative texts tend to be every bit as eclectic as the list above. However, there are certain classics that I have found to be common to a certain generation of us who, ahem, "came of age" prior to, say, 1996. Those years have come to be called by me "B.C." meaning "Before Craft" meaning before the film *The Craft* came out, and that same year paganism and witchcraft exploded on the Net, and a whole slew of teenagers who had previously only dabbled in the occult suddenly got the Old Religion in a Big Way. This is also the same general time during which all-night bad drumming became *de rigueur* at pagan gatherings, and the old-timers (who enjoyed bawdy sing-alongs and provocative conversation around the campfire at night) got disgusted and stopped coming (although, I believe, this second phenomenon is unconnected to the first).

The pagan canon (hey, why shouldn't we have one?) consists of wholly different texts depending upon someone's demographic digits: age, geographic area, socioeconomic status, political affiliation, etc. But the number one determining factor of a pagan's cultural literacy with regard to the entire community over the past thirty years can also be delineated along what I like to call the Crap Continuum. That is, at one end of the continuum are classics, high art, the well-written books, well-made films we can be proud to love. At the other end is crap that we are usually familiar with and which we may even have read or viewed and taken seriously at the time (like Whitley Strieber's *Cat Magic*, or the terrible film version of the excellent novel *The Witches of Eastwick*). Guilty pleasures are somewhere in between and include campy treats like *Witchblade* or *Satan's School for Girls*. It is a useful barometer for those who tend to be dismissive of others. Some people read/watch Crap, and some people read/watch the same stuff you do. Some pagans attend science fiction conventions for fun, some attend pagan gatherings, some attend fetish flea markets. Gods help us, some attend all three. Oddly enough, our social proclivities inform our tastes in literature and media—we live large, y'see. Some of us in the "Not Menopausal or Mid-Life

Crisis-y yet, but No Longer Prone to All-Night Games of Risk Fueled by Jägermeister, Either" demographic maintain a precious list of formative, epiphany-inducing texts that we believe every pagan worth his or her ritually consecrated salt should have read/viewed/listened to. Tastes differ, of course: some of us had geeky, swords-and-sorcery tastes, and some of us had dark, goth, absinthe-flavored tastes, while some of us had righteous, angry, the-world-is-my-phosphate-free-soapbox tastes. But common to many lists of the B.C. pagan generation you might find the following, some well-loved for many years, some newly on the radar but appealing to certain like-minded folks: *Stranger in a Strange Land. Kolchak: The Night Stalker. A Wizard of Earthsea. The Wicker Man. Songs from the Wood* (again). *The Golden Bough. Jitterbug Perfume. Hounds of Love* (again). *The Crow. Mythago Wood. Edward Scissorhands. Excalibur* (again). *The Mists of Avalon.* The Lord of the Rings trilogy. *The X-Files. The White Goddess. Buffy the Vampire Slayer. Ivory and Horn. Xena: Warrior Princess* (again). *The Secret History. The Sandman* (again). *American Gods. Bewitched. Practical Magic.*

And (you were waiting for this one I bet): The Chronicles of Narnia. Specifically, *The Lion, the Witch and the Wardrobe.* Yup, we read it 'cuz we knew it had a WITCH in it! And it turned out to be a damn fine story. We may have later learned it was a Christian allegory, and that was fine but it wasn't necessarily important. Even later we may have realized it contained the universal message of what happens when we interfere with the natural world in order to fulfill our selfish desires. A lovely metaphor for the rebirth of paganism and the back-to-the-earth movement that so many of us were finding in the 1970s and 1980s.What is sad is that many of the New Pagans on the Block have not read these delightful books and made these delightful discoveries for themselves! But as it often goes these days, a fine film can kindle the flame that leads someone to read its literary forbears. Look at the Lord of the Rings trilogy. I can only hope this new remake of *The Lion, the Witch and the Wardrobe,* with its wonderful cast, attracts leagues of readers, young and old, to discover Lewis' magical tomes.

I asked around to see what sort of impact and influence reading these books had on developing attitudes about paganism or spirituality in general. Some of my respondents were practicing pagans, some not. Stormcat (only online pseudonyms are used) said: "I ended up seeing (not immediately, but the books planted the concept) that different paths (Christianity and the ones tied to Nature) can have a lot in common. That led to a lifelong study of (in spare time, dribs and drabs, sort of thing) comparative world religions and seeing what they have in common." April said: "I list Wiccan (solo) amongst my varied religions/ beliefs and the Narnia stories couldn't be more in synch with that kind of belief structure. I happen to think those creatures and such do exist, they just operate at a higher vibrational level then [sic] us so most of us cannot see them physically. And Lewis was one tuned in guy." Shelby said: "If you read a lot of his writings about Narnia he talks about how he never meant them to be a direct Christian allegory. He was very spiritual, and not just an adamant Christian. And I know for a fact my dogs are Talking Animals. Unfortunately all they say is, 'I'm hungry.'" And one online respondent whose pseudonym is DawnTreader had this to say: "When I was two, my father read The Chronicles to me, as he had to all my siblings. I read them again when I was older, as the books were conversational touchstones in the family. Although certain elements of the books have stuck with me, most specifics have not. I did, however, always feel an affinity with the Dawn Treader. There was just something so compelling about a vessel ordained to carry faithful companions on a voyage that would test their mettle, draw them together, and ultimately carry them to a destination they did not know they sought. And since my name means "dawn," I tend to wander the earth (lots of travel, lots of walking, lots of wilderness), and I view life as a voyage during which I will be open to the unexpected, it made sense.... It awakened my imagination to a realm of magic that has *meaning*. In other words, I think most children have vivid imaginations, but The Chronicles of Narnia show children that the magical worlds they play in can also teach them things—that only deepen as we grow older!"

I have also found in casual conversation with some pagans who have read the books that they are quite charmed by the way that Aslan, the character who represents Christ in allegorical terms, is portrayed as a lion. Since the lion is associated in Western occultism with the sun and with solar gods, this underscores the many-faceted imagery and meaning in the books. Of course, the fact that these books might have meaning beyond Christian allegory is infuriating to some. But the idea that Narnia's denizens might actually just be a bunch of heathen gods in animal drag did not become apparent to potential detractors until, oddly enough, rather recently. It's all the fault of a young man with horn-rimmed glasses who rides around on a high-powered broomstick and, bless his lightning-bolt scarred little head, got the video-poisoned youngsters of the world back into reading. But let's backtrack a bit.

After *The Craft* Exploded in popularity (A.C.E. if you like) and every teen was a wanna-be witch, well, it would be an understatement to say that the right-wing Christian community had a field day. Faster than their kids could ask, "Would you buy me Silver Ravenwolf's Teen Witch Kit?" parents were installing software to block them from investigating Web sites with words like "witch," "craft," "magic," "wizard," "spell," "charm," "pentagram," "coven" and of course the ever-unpopular "satanism," "devil," "demon," "Lucifer" and "how to worship my dark lord and master." Then came Harry Potter, and the silly protests staged by concerned fanatical Christians that somehow these books were inundating our youth (who were reading again! We can't have them doing that now, can we?) with all manner of occult subliminals. They'd not only become interested in witchcraft, they'd want to start practicing it! And, oh me, oh my, that clever costume of the modern-day witch is just another guise for Satan. The youth of America were headed straight to hell in a handbasket. It was the libraries I felt worst for: they finally had kids coming in their doors hot on the trail of Harry, and in some cases, these kids discovered other books. Reading making a comeback? Opinions may differ on What's Wrong with Kids Today, but I think it has a great deal to do with their failure to utilize their imaginations and put themselves, if only for a few moments, into the lives of other people. Reading lets them through doors into other worlds, into the minds and problems and decisions of other people not too different from them. This teaches compassion, if nothing else. But I digress: The Decline of Reading and the Numbing of the American Mind is, of course, Another Essay.

Back to Harry: amid the many righteous (there's that word again, funny how it applies to us when we're right, and to other people when they're wrong, huh?) diatribes I read online that castigated the Harry Potter books for indoctrinating unsuspecting children into the occult or, sometimes specifically, Wicca (which is a joke—ANOTHER ESSAY!), I also found a startling tendency to equate the Harry Potter problem with that of C. S. Lewis' Narnia books. In other words, these books about talking lions, white witches and magical wardrobes were also lying in wait to snatch our children into their clutches and deliver them to Beelzebub's front door. I even found entire Web sites devoted to exposing the occult imagery and language in all of Lewis' novels. Never mind that Lewis was an avowed Christian and that the biblical themes in the Narnia series are as plain as day.

Here's an example of one Web site author's take on this issue, a guy I like to call "Salami Ass" because his URL is "balaams-ass.com." And it is such a great image, carnal and phallic and geeky all at once. Why, I can almost picture him sitting at his computer eating salami as he writes! In his honor, I have been eating salami at the computer myself while composing my thoughts. From a page entitled "Further into the Depths of Satanism in C. S. Lewis' *Chronicles of Narnia*"[1] we get the following: "Having already delved into the vile doctrines of sun worship that C. S. Lewis has hidden in his books for children, *The Chronicles of Narnia*, it would seem that it could not get much worse, but it does." The author then goes on to make some dubious connections to Jezebel, comparing Lewis to her because they are both "seducers," and Jezebel is a "graphic example of where sun worship leads a person." Hmm. He then writes: "The time is long past due to cry out against this wicked man's unspeakable Baal worship. God has a profound hate for what Lewis has done, as can be seen in the passage above. Lewis has endeavored to lead the children of Christians into the depths of Satan!" It's all about the children, folks. If we liberal-thinking heathens of letters are not busy trying to rip the unborn from their mother's wombs in untimely feminist fashion, we're despoiling their young minds by recommending books. Said Web site author goes on to say "we find what a gross pagan Lewis really was when we notice that he portrayed Dionysus (Bacchus), Silenus and the Maenads as *good* characters in his stories!" Ewww, C. S. Lewis was a gross pagan! I understand he hung out in pubs, too. Why, he even referred "jokingly" to The Eagle and Child as The Bird and Baby! Clearly this suggests a man who was well-versed in the act of human sacrifice. Perhaps he would place infants upon his stone altar in the woods and slit their throats and drink their blood and leave their remains for the local birds of prey. See, when you put your mind to it, you can sound like a lunatic, too.

It's not just human sacrifice this guy is trying to root out, oh no. Apparently these baby killers were also sodomites. He loves to offer highly

---

[1] This page can be found at www.blessedquietness.com/journal/homemake/lewisdep.htm, and subsequent quotes are taken from pages linked to this one.

conjectured interpretations of the activities of these gods of mythology, equating their vices and practices with what he sees as the worst of human behavior, as here: "Silenus in mythology was the son of Hermes or Pan (Satan). He was said to be a nymph and was the companion and nurse of Dionysus. Which gives room for speculation regarding sodomy since Hermes was associated with such." No wonder my pal Bob liked these stories so much! They were full of references to gay sex! And the "companion and nurse" thing, what's *that* about? You can extend this metaphor and conclude that Florence Nightingale was doing about a hundred soldiers a night...no wonder they called her "Lady with the Lamp"—Lady with the Red Light, more like! Strumpet!

Our esteemed Lewis scholar next quotes the passage from *Prince Caspian* where Lucy witnesses a dancing crowd around Aslan:

"The crowd and *the dance round Aslan* (for it had become a dance once more) *grew so thick and rapid that Lucy was confused.* She never saw where certain other people came from who were soon capering among the trees. One was *a youth, dressed only in a fawn-skin, with vine-leaves wreathed in his curly hair. His face* would have bee [sic] almost too pretty for a boy's, if it had not looked so *extremely wild.* You felt, as Edmund said when he saw him a few days later, 'There's a chap who might do anything—absolutely anything.' *He seemed to have a great many names—Bromios, Bassareus*, and *the Ram*, were three of them. There were *a lot of girls with him, as wild as he.* There was even, unexpectedly, *someone on a donkey.* And everybody was laughing: and *everybody was shouting out, "Euan, euan, eu-oi-oi-oi."* [Emphasis added.]

Yeah, dude, no kidding!

Salami Ass then has this to say: "Note the wild dance, the extremely wild faced youth that is Bromios (otherwise known as Dionysus or Bacchus), the wild girls (Maenads), the man on the donkey (Silenus) who is also said to cry "Refreshments!" (which in the context of Dionysus would be wine), and the cries of "Euoi!" What Lewis is describing here is nothing other than a Bacchanalian orgy!" Uh, except that there's no sex. Then, to make things absolutely crystal clear, we get a biblical quote that, apparently, sums it all up for us. "Notice also that Lucy is confused.

Lewis gives himself away on this one. I Corinthians 14:33 'For God is not *the author* of confusion, but of peace, as in all churches of the saints.'" Notice that both passages contain some version of the word "confusion." And since the original biblical quote also says "author" we may surmise that Lewis was trying to cleverly pull the goatskin over our eyes. If God is not the author of confusion, well then, C. S. Lewis must be, since he uses the word "confused" in this passage, and furthermore this must mean that Lewis is the antithesis of God, and therefore, Satan!

Another author on the site (who I like to call Merry Vanquisher of Satan, but maybe we should refer to her as a Guest Lecturer) analyzes a passage (also from *Prince Caspian*) for evidence of witchcraft and paganism, thusly:

> "Then three or four of the *Red Dwarfs* came forward with their tinder boxes and set light to the pile, which first crackled, and then blazed, and finally roared as a woodland *bonfire on midsummer night* ought to do. And *everyone sat down in a wide circle* around it. Then *Bacchus and Silenus and the Maenads began a dance, far wilder than the dance of the trees*, not merely a dance for fun and beauty (though it was that too) but *a magic dance of plenty*, and *where their hands touched, and where their feet fell, the feast came into existence*—sides of roasted meat that filled the grove with delicious smell, and *wheaten cakes and oaten cakes, honey* and many-coloured sugars and cream as think [*sic*] as porridge, and as smooth as still water, peaches, nectarines, *pomegranates*, pears, grapes, strawberries, raspberries—*pyramids* and cataracts of fruit. *Then, in great wooden cups and bowls and mazers, wreathed with ivy, came the wines*; dark, thick ones like syrups of mulberry juice, and clear red ones like red jellies liquefied, and yellow wines and green wines and yellowy-green and greenish-yellow." [Emphasis added.]

Oh really?

First off, we have Red Dwarfs lighting the fire, and that the fire is for "midsummer night." The fact that they are Red Dwarfs, meaning they have red hair, may not seem significant at a glance, but it emphasizes that nothing is lost on Lewis for symbolism. Red hair, according to Cirlot's book, symbolizes the lower regions—hell. (This is a good reason to stop the myth of the "red head's fiery temper," by the way.)

Why stop it? I get lots of satanic nookie this way, all from a $5 bag of henna!

Midsummer night is the night for the sun-god's death and temporary descent into hell, so Lewis has the Red Dwarfs light the fire.

Next, we note that it says a woodland bonfire on midsummer night. Not just A fire and not just A midsummer night. This is the real thing. The worship of the sun-god. The burning of the bones from the sacrifices in the *bonfire* (bone-fire) on the summer solstice, an [sic] high day of witchcraft.

Hmm, does she mean high holiday? Well, every day is high for us; we use drugs to get in the mood for all that sodomizin' and baby-killin'!

Everyone sits in a circle around it. Again a symbol of the sun and a powerful witchcraft symbol.

I think Target and Dunkin Donuts use this one, too.

The wild, magic dance of plenty. Another pagan/witchy thing. They are famous for their magic dances.

Yes, we are! Now if only I knew what a "magic dance" was so I could go get famous for it!

Pomegranates are a symbol of fertility, and according to the Greeks sprang from the blood of Dionysos. (Cirlot, pg. 261)

Surprised she did not mention Persephone/Proserpine here, or the Mysteries of Eleusis...and there is a pagan band called Pomegranate, too, and an academic journal devoted to pagan studies that is also called *The Pomegranate*. It is also RED (see above). And has lots of SEEDS (code for semen?). And since these fruits are also very tasty when chilled before eating, are we maybe getting into the oral appropriation of the famously cold manjuice of Lucifer, here?

The fruit is stacked in a pyramid—a powerful withcraft [sic]/Luciferian/Masonic symbol.

It is also found on the dollar bill and I am sure she will enlighten us as to Lewis' having been paid money upon the publication of these books and how this is further evidence of the stinking corruption characteristic of his occupation.

To be continued.

Well, I can hardly wait! I am dying to know what she has to say about the "wooden cups"—possible reference to sadomasochistic undergarment design here?—and the "dark, thick syrups of mulberry juice" which, I have it on reliable authority, is a euphemism for the semen of mulberry tree spirits (also known as mulbrydryads).

Anyway, you get the idea.

I especially love the part where the first author, Salami Ass, claims to know the mind of god. Isn't that a sin of some kind?

As much fun as it is to read about how these books are clearly the work of Satan, written by his minions to lure ingenuous youths to his lair, I have also found sites passionately defending the literary integrity of these books and dismissing the fundamentalist Christian paranoid rambling as, well, paranoid rambling. I have even found some sites claiming that, if read carefully, the Harry Potter novels can be seen to have a clearly *Christian* worldview, in terms of their attitudes toward evil. I have no idea if the vast majority of children, teenagers and adults who have read the Harry Potter series have considered the religious implications; I mean, these are damn fine stories in their own right, and one could, with effort, I suppose, ignore their depth and symbolism and metaphorical language and, and...well, maybe not. J. K. Rowling is no C. S. Lewis, but, well, C. S. Lewis is no J. K. Rowling. I see no way in which one author's scope of vision is any narrower than the other. The only difference seems to be the generation of audiences they have reached.

Although I wish newbie pagans would read and listen to and watch all those classics that us "old-timers" are familiar with (if for no other reason than that they'd be able to interpret our eye-rolling and hand-clenching exhibited when they react with a blank stare when we refer to Robert Graves' inventing Ogham, or the training of Avalon priestesses as a thinly veiled model of contemporary feminist coven structuring, or the references to agrarian fertility cults and seasonal festivals in Jethro Tull songs), I try not to obsess about it. They'll find their way to these well-loved canonical works eventually. Hollywood is seeing to it. And that's not a cynical pronouncement. Amid the vapidity of reality TV, Vin Diesel vehicles and digital-video *Blair Witch* imitators, there is an attempt to create art that considers the bigger picture of our lives. Think *Donnie Darko. Waking Life. Six Feet Under.* Smart television! And I can only think that intelligent film and television texts will somehow lead to more reading. Today's youth are no less intellectually curious, spiritually hungry or politically disenfranchised than any generation that has come before, or will come anon. You may disagree. But I have hope for the future. Visionary filmmakers are recasting the magical literature of our formative years into accessible, beautiful texts. Viewers seek out books they've never heard of before. A renascence of reading is afoot. Tolkien, Lewis, who's next? Ursula Le Guin? Robert Heinlein? Neil Gaiman?

Neil Gaiman, the Charles Dickens/William Blake/Christina Rossetti of our generation (he is exactly my age in fact). Neil Gaiman, the target of rabid right-wing Christians. I can't wait. The only difference is there's no allegorical pussyfooting: he calls a sun worshipper a sun worshipper.

Peg Aloi is a practicing witch and ardent bibliophile who is inordinately fond of pomegranates and youths dressed only in fawn-skins. She writes all sorts of stuff: fiction, poetry, reviews, screenplays, academic essays and rants on popular culture. She is also actively corrupting the young minds of America through her work teaching film studies and creative writing. As we speak. This very minute.

C. S. Lewis and the Problem of Religion in Science Fiction and Fantasy

I

N THE CENTER OF OXFORD, there is a brass sign indicating the proximity of The Eagle and Child, the pub in which the informal group known as the Inklings used to gather on Thursdays. Three of these men eventually became fantasy writers of some renown; one of them, J. R. R. Tolkien, stamped a conceptual image on the genre which, sixty years and three movies later, remains indelible. And yet, while the fantasy fiction the Inklings pioneered is arguably more popular than ever before, the abandonment of the moral and religious foundation of their visions has seriously crippled the literary achievements of their modern successors.

J. R. R. Tolkien, C. S. Lewis and Charles Williams were not only Oxford men—Tolkien and Lewis were dons while Williams was an editor at the university press—but were also devout Christians. Ironically, while Lewis is now considered to be the more recognizably Christian figure thanks to works of Christian apologetics such as *Mere Christianity* and *Miracles*, it was Tolkien who played a major role in the atheist Lewis' conversion to Christianity in 1931.

The Christian themes in both Lewis' fantasy and science fiction are undeniable. Even a child conversant with both The Chronicles of Narnia and the Bible will readily recognize that the lion Aslan, who voluntarily lays down his life in exchange for the life of a criminal condemned to death in The Lion, the Witch and the Wardrobe, is a barely disguised metaphor for Jesus Christ. And this diaphanous veil disappears entirely six books later when the link between Aslan's country and heaven is disclosed upon the death of the Pevensie family at a railway station in The Last Battle.

The religious themes are even more overt in Lewis' space trilogy. From the name of the protagonist—Ransom—to the replay of the Edenic temptation in Perelandra, Lewis consciously provides a fictional retelling of vignettes straight from the Bible. Indeed, the very title of the first volume, Out of the Silent Planet, refers directly to Lewis' concept of God's divine invasion[1] of nature, which he lays out explicitly in Mere Christianity.

The Christian foundation of the other famous Inkling's work is less blatant, yet almost as obvious to all but the most willfully blind. While there have been a few brave souls foolhardy enough to attempt to deny the self-evident[2], even those with no discernible Christian agenda freely acknowledge the powerful religious elements integral to The Lord of the Rings.[3] For the Secret Fire of which Gandalf is a servant, as Tolkien explained for the benefit of those too unfamiliar with the book of Acts to recognize the symbolism, is nothing less than the Holy Spirit whose flames were first seen at Pentecost, and in case things were still not perfectly clear, the author later described his landmark trilogy as "a fundamentally religious and Catholic work."

Thus, it is not the fantasy elements—which are actually not very similar in the particulars—but the Christian themes running through

---

[1] Philip K. Dick, of all people, appears to have been familiar with the concept, as it provides the title for one of his more esoteric novels, The Divine Invasion.

[2] For all that his portrayal of Gandalf was flawlessly informed by the book, the deeper aspects of his character appeared to have escaped Sir Ian McKellen when he said: "Despite being a Catholic, [Tolkien] was not trying to write a Catholic parable.... The Lord of the Rings is just part of the mythology that he wrote, and I'm not familiar with the rest of it, but I do know it isn't very helpful in this story to refer to a deity. Because there are vague higher powers who send Gandalf back to finish off the job, and there seems to be something that might be mistaken for heaven as the boat sails into the sunset. But it ain't very specific, is it?" (2004).

[3] "But again, to understand Tolkien, one must return to his Christian roots. While at Oxford, he and C. S. Lewis would discuss at great length and critique each other's writing. They were also both members of a literary group that performed the same kinds of evaluations from the same Christian foundation. So at every step of the way, Tolkien had a Christian perspective guiding his writing. This is abundantly apparent in his finished works and even comes through in the recent movie release of The Fellowship of the Ring." (Asadullah 2001).

both that tie Lewis' and Tolkien's works together in our minds. Nor are these themes the only relationship. Tolkien, Lewis and Williams were all influenced to varying degrees by the same literary and spiritual mentor, a Scottish minister and prolific author by the name of George MacDonald.[4] MacDonald is largely forgotten now, but he was a well-known author of the late nineteenth century; among other things, he corresponded regularly with a certain American writer he had befriended by the name of Samuel Clemens. In one letter, Clemens even mentioned to MacDonald how his daughter Susy had worn out her copy of MacDonald's *At the Back of the North Wind* and asked if MacDonald would be so kind as to send her a replacement.[5]

It is interesting to note that while Jules Verne and H. G. Wells are generally considered to be the fathers of science fiction, as far as the literary historians are concerned, modern fantasy is imagined to have leaped like Athena, fully accoutered, into the pulp magazines of the 1920s. And yet, George MacDonald's claim to paternity is difficult to dismiss. His first work of fantasy fiction, the aptly named *Phantastes*, was published in 1858, six years before Jules Verne published *Journey to the Centre of the Earth*, seven years before Lewis Carroll published *Alice in Wonderland* and before H. G. Wells, H. P. Lovecraft or Lord Dunsany, three men who are often mentioned as early pioneers of fantasy fiction, were even born.

This failure to recognize MacDonald's influence on the genre[6] appears to stem primarily from the radical secularization of the science fiction and fantasy genres dating from science fiction's Golden Age. While the short stories and novels of the Golden Age are fondly recalled by many, and are rightly known for many entertaining elements, one must admit that character development was seldom one of them. This is unfortunate, because the Golden Age preference for plot over personalities and

---

[4] Lewis and Williams openly acknowledged their debt to MacDonald, while Tolkien was rather less enthusiastic. Tolkien once described MacDonald's *The Golden Key* as "illwritten, incoherent, and bad, in spite of a few memorable passages." Of course, Lewis would be hard-pressed to deny it, as the first paragraphs of *The Princess and the Goblin* will be shockingly familiar to anyone who has ever read *The Lion, the Witch and the Wardrobe*.

[5] "All these things might move and interest one. But how desperately more I have been moved tonight by the thought of a little old copy in the nursery of *At the Back of the North Wind*. Oh, what happy days they were when that little book was read, and how Susy loved it!" Mark Twain, letter to William Dean Howells, 1899.

[6] There are 125 science fiction and fantasy writers listed on the SF Site's M page (see www.sfsite. com), including four MacDonalds. Despite his enormous contribution to the genre, George MacDonald is not one of them.

for ideas over individuals[7] played a significant role in the relegation of science fiction to a literary ghetto disdained by the *New York Times* Book Review and others too self-consciously erudite to take seriously what is still often dismissed as juvenile space opera and futuristic twiddle-twaddle. While character development in science fiction has improved dramatically of late, it is still only the exceptional work that manages to transcend the genre and break out of the ghetto.[8]

This disdain for character left a mark on the genre which lasts to this day. Almost to a man, the writers of the Golden Age were secular humanists, and they felt as strongly about the deleterious effects of religion on collective human development as did Sigmund Freud with regards to the individual. Their antipathy toward all forms of traditional religion in favor of a dogmatic faith in the scientific method cast science fiction into an artistic ghetto from which it has not yet even begun to escape.

Fortunately, science and religion need no longer be at war, as developments in modern physics have shown (especially those relating to the significance of the fundamental constants), which may indicate that the time for mutual hostilities may finally be over. It is interesting to note that the "multiple universes" concept which has inspired so many short stories in the past decade is a purely hypothetical theory developed without any experimental basis in an attempt to answer the "anthropic principle" which not only has a solid foundation in current scientific method, but threatens to demolish the entire notion of a random, mechanistic universe. The concept does not, of course, provide the least bit of evidence for the legitimacy of the Prophet's revelation, the infallibility of the Pope or the likelihood of the Second Coming; what it does demonstrate is that what has been long considered an inherently antagonistic dichotomy between science and religion may not turn out to exist at all.

---

[7] This is not to say that a religious writer such as Lewis lacked ideas, but the essence of religion in general and Christianity in particular requires a focus on individuals in order to demonstrate the transformative power of faith or the lack thereof. Technology, on the other hand, requires no such focus. This is why there is, as yet, no Dostoevsky of science fiction, or arguably, modern literature.

[8] And when they do, the science fiction community has a terrible tendency to disown them. Neal Stephenson is arguably the finest science fiction author writing today; I happen to have been a member of the SFWA's 2005 Nebula novel jury, and we actually engaged in a discussion as to whether *The System of the World* qualifies as science fiction or not! This may be why a sufficiently literary author of fantasy, such as Italo Calvino, ends up being known to the world as a fabulist instead of a fantasist.

Still, this distaste for all things religious has been a costly one, both in artistic and financial terms.[9] While sufficient evidence exists to reject the idea that only a true believer is capable of writing accurately about his faith, it is true that presenting a reasonable and believable image of a religious individual presents a greater challenge to one who has no experience of such strange beings and therefore lacks even the most basic information about them. One would not expect one who knows nothing of math beyond addition and subtraction to write a convincing portrayal of calculus, after all. And while one may no more believe in aliens than in Jesus Christ, a survey of the current literature suggests that far more thought typically goes into depictions of the former than into those who profess to believe in the latter.

Compare, the vast difference between the guilt-racked seducer of Hawthorne's *The Scarlet Letter* and the foam-flecked fundamentalists that haunt mediocre short stories in *Asimov's Science Fiction* magazine like clockwork cartoon bogeymen. Is it any wonder that the science fiction and fantasy writer's pretense to literary status is scoffed at by those familiar with Dostoevsky, Goethe and Tolstoy?

Lewis himself almost appears to have been on the verge of contemplating a similar question when he wrote to a gentleman by the name of Warfield Firor regarding the limits of Mark Twain as an author.

> I have been regaling myself on *Tom Sawyer* and *Huckleberry Finn*. I wonder why that man never wrote anything else on the same level. The scene in which Huck decides to be "good" by betraying Jim, and then finds he can't and concludes that he is a reprobate, is unparalleled in humour, pathos, and tenderness. And it goes down to the very depth of all moral problems. (Griffin 1986, 314)

This passage should also suffice to demonstrate that one's personal belief or disbelief in God, even in the basic concept of morality itself, is no bar to successfully creating deep and convincing moral characters, given that Twain, a self-proclaimed atheist, succeeded admirably. Like Twain, C. S. Lewis populated his fictitious land with moral characters, as

---

[9] No doubt we science fiction and fantasy authors are far too pure in art to ever allow petty pecuniary matters to enter our minds, but the fact that the Christian publishers of the 50 million-selling Left Behind series have gone out of their way to ensure that their books are not confused with either science fiction or fantasy might give pause to even the most staunchly secular SFWA writer.

diverse as the noble, but flawed Caspian, the once-traitorous Edmund, the self-absorbed Eustace and the arrogant Rabadash. His character studies are necessarily less deep, for the most part, given the broader scope of his stories, but the most significant attributes of his characters are almost always their moral qualities.

As with individuals, cultures, too, require some element of religious faith to be convincing given that the overwhelming majority of historical cultures were centered, at some level, around faith in something, from the Roman founder legends to the Judeo-Christianity of the Western tradition. In the faithless storyscapes of science fiction, the implacable Fremen of Frank Herbert's *Dune* stand out as a chillingly believable vision of a galaxy-spanning Islamic culture, while Dan Simmons' Hyperion Cantos is unique in presenting an unusual but compelling projection of the Vatican hierarchy into a dark and ominous technological future.

These varying examples prove that while it is not necessary to kowtow before the icons of any religion, for the sake of the writer's art, it is imperative to pay enough attention to the details in order to get them right! Many writers go to great lengths to "get the science right," but for those who harbor any literary pretensions at all, the same must be done with regards to the beliefs and behaviors of their fictional characters, as well as the structure of their organized religions.

While it's hardly surprising that a field dominated for decades by self-professed secular humanists should prove hostile to religion—any honest reader will admit that Asimov was for more successful with his far-reaching ideas than his character development or his infamous naming conventions—the fact that this artistic flaw transcends genres demonstrates that the problem is more widespread than one might think, to the great detriment of literature in general. It is, it seems, more a cultural defect than one easily laid at the feet of individual writers.

For example, Wendy Shalit criticized the tendency of Jewish writers she calls "outsider-insiders" to make fundamental errors about Orthodox Judaism in the Sunday *New York Times* Book Review:

> Consider, for example, Nathan Englander, a talented writer whose collection of stories, "'For the Relief of Unbearable Urges,'" brimmed with revelations of hypocrisy and self-inflicted misery: a fistfight that breaks out in synagogue over who will read from the Torah; a sect

whose members fast three days instead of one and drink a dozen glasses of wine at the Passover seders instead of four; a man whose rabbi sends him to a prostitute when his wife won't sleep with him. Of course, the Orthodox don't actually brawl over who reads the Torah, no rabbi is allowed to write a dispensation for a man to see a prostitute, and even extremely pious Jews can't invent their own traditions for fast days or seders. (2005)

These basic errors are as *a priori* ludicrous to the haredi as the low-brow Star Trek hand-waving that attempts to pass for science is to the astrophysicist. Worse, they are used to paint what are necessarily false characters, based as they are on an erroneous foundation.

Although religion in science fiction may be shallow, more often than not it is simply absent. Fantasy, for all that its early masters were usually Christian, tends to go more horribly awry. It frequently embraces a form of what on the surface appears to be religion, for what is a fat fantasy trilogy without a token cleric or priest, but nearly always warps the concept into something wholly unrecognizable. For example, there is not a single traditional religion, including Taoism, which revolves around the concept of a precarious Balance maintained between good and evil, and yet a religious structure built around some form of the Balance cliché is ubiquitous in modern fantasy. This mythical Balance-centered religion is a nonsensical concept wherein too much Evil is bad and too much Good is bad, a notion which tells the reader more about the writer's inclination toward political moderation than about morality, the problem of evil, the nature of the divine or any other question with which nearly every historical religion attempts to address in some way.

Another oddity is the fantasy genre's strange treatment of the medieval era. Most modern fantasy fiction is based in a medieval time period, often with readily identifiable historical societies, and yet the most quintessentially medieval institution, the Catholic Church, is noticeably absent for the most part. Even more bizarre: it is quite common for authors to recreate the obvious trappings of a divine right of kings without any reference to the divinity which is presumably providing that right to rule.

Although the common use of the terms "good" and "evil" make it appear as if these fictions of Balance are reasonable facsimiles of historical religions, a closer examination will quickly reveal that they are not. In every Western religious tradition, evil is a subservient shadow of good, an aspect of Creation gone wrong, not a peer. This is generally true for most Eastern traditions as well, some of which do not even recognize the concept of evil at all. For example, the Hindu concept of the Supreme is described thusly:

> There is none second to It, neither third not even fourth.
> There is none fifth to It, neither sixth not even seventh.
> There is none eighth to It, neither ninth not even tenth.
> It is the only Supreme. This is to be known. (Shaivam.org)

And yet, examples of modern fantasy's fixation with balance are easy to find. In Roger Zelazny's Amber Chronicles, the godlike beings who inhabit the two divine realms of which all other worlds are but shadows are also engaged in an endless struggle. Amber represents order, while the Courts of Chaos signify the polar opposite. In *The Courts of Chaos*, Dara, a daughter of Chaos, explains to Amber's king that a rebel prince of Amber is threatening the balance between the two realms and therefore must be stopped.

> "Brand was given what he wanted," she said, "but he was not trusted. It was feared that once he possessed the power to shape the world as he would, he would not stop with ruling over a revised Amber. He would attempt to extend his dominion over Chaos as well. A weakened Amber was what was desired, so that Chaos would be stronger than it now is—the striking of a new balance, giving to us more of the shadowlands that lie between our realms. It was realized long ago that the two kingdoms can never be merged, or one destroyed, without also disrupting all the processes that lie in flux between us. Total stasis or complete chaos would be the result." (Zelazny 1978)

Although Robert Jordan's bestselling Wheel of Time series draws heavily on traditional elements of various historical faiths, it too features a theosophy designed around an indifferent Pattern that lies in the middle between two dichotomous poles.

> The Creator is good, Perrin. The Father of Lies is evil. The Pattern of Age, the Age Lace itself, is neither. The Pattern is what is. The Wheel

of Time weaves all lives into the Pattern, all actions. A pattern that is all one color is no pattern. For the Pattern of an Age, good and ill are the warp and the woof. (Jordan 1992, 378)

Now, it is certainly no crime to envision a world that is free of religion in general or Christianity in particular, for science fiction is the art of the conceivable while fantasy is the art of the inconceivable. But one can legitimately question is why this fascination with a world without faith, with characters without souls, with what Lewis called men without chests, should so thoroughly pervade modern literature.

Lewis himself provides the answer; indeed, he predicted the likelihood of just such a result (albeit in a more general sense) when he reviewed an English textbook written for schoolboys back in the 1940s. In *The Abolition of Man*, he could be writing of either today's authors or their flawed, cardboard characters when he writes:

It is not that they are bad men. They are not men at all. Stepping outside the Tao[10], they have stepped into the void. Nor are their subjects necessarily unhappy men. They are not men at all: they are artifacts. Man's final conquest has proved to be the abolition of Man.

What is not a crime can, however, be a serious transgression in artistic terms. In abolishing faith and morality from their characters, the heirs of C. S. Lewis' literary tradition have not only failed themselves, but more importantly, they have failed their readers. For it is not that they are bad observers of the human condition, it is that they are not observers of the human condition at all, chronicling instead an imaginary inhumanity that never existed, does not exist and never will exist.

Vox Day is a nationally syndicated political columnist and fantasy author. He has published four novels with Pocket Books as well as three graphic novels and was a founder of the award-winning techno band Psykosonik. He maintains a popular blog, Vox Popoli, and is an active member of the Science Fiction and Fantasy Writers Association.

---

[10] Lewis uses "the Tao" to refer to the concept more often described by philosophers as Natural Law.

References

Asadullah, Ali. 2001. "Lord of the Rings: Christian Myth at Work." IslamOnline, December 26. www.islamonline.net/english/ArtCulture/2001/12/article12.shtml.

Griffin, William. 1986. *C. S. Lewis: A Dramatic Life*. San Francisco: Harper.

Jordan, Robert. 1992. *The Dragon Reborn*. New York: Tor.

McKellen, Ian. 2004. Interview by Hollywood Jesus, www.hollywoodjesus.com.

Shaivam.org. "Hinduism: A Perspective." www.shaivam.org/hipgodco.htm.

Shalit, Wendy. 2005. "Essay; The Observant Reader." *New York Times*, January 30.

Zelazny, Roger. 1978. *The Courts of Chaos*. New York: Doubleday.

LOUIS A. MARKOS

Redeeming Postmodernism: At Play in the Fields of Narnia

IKE THE DREADED HYDRA of Greek mythology, postmodernism is a beast with many heads. The terrified undergraduate, the beleaguered pastor, the confused lay reader: all try their best to lop off the heads of the Hydra. But, such is the nature of the beast, the moment they lop off one head, two more grow in its place. With each passing year, the varieties of postmodernism seem to expand exponentially. "Where are we to go," the critic of postmodernism cries out, "to find another Hercules to defeat this new Hydra?" We must seek him, I would argue, in that same locale where we always find our most necessary saviors: in the most unlikely of places.

Could it be that our longed-for hero was not a flashy, politicized celebrity but a humble Oxford don who lived and died before postmodernism began its long, slow climb to ascendancy? And could he have leveled his deadly (anachronistic) thrust against postmodernism not in a philosophical manifesto or a theoretical tract but in a series of fairy tales written for children? The hero of whom I speak is, of course, C. S. Lewis, the great Christian apologist, literary critic and fiction writer, and his two-headed axe goes by the name of The Chronicles of Narnia.

But before we can set Lewis loose to decapitate each of the snaky, twisting heads of the Hydra and then cauterize the necks lest they sprout new ones, we must first understand the exact nature of the beast. Though daunting, this task is far from impossible. For, despite all its complexities and permutations, postmodernism rests on a single, fairly simple concept: that there has been a breakdown of signifier and signified.

In the parlance of postmodernism (the terminology is actually much, much older), the signifier is the word (John, tree) and the signified is the concept that the word points back to (John himself, the actual tree). In the central, Platonic tradition of Western philosophy and linguistics, the relationship between the signifier (the word) and the signified (the meaning behind the word) was considered an integral and real one. Indeed, just as it was obvious to all that a real tree (signified) stood behind the word "tree" (signifier), so was it believed that behind abstract nouns (signifiers) like beauty, justice and love stood real signifieds that embodied the full essence of the word (Beauty, Justice, Love).

Plato called these capital-letter signifieds the Forms, and he believed that they not only lent authority and meaning to the words that we use but that they were, in fact, the transcendent, permanent *origins* of our limited, earthly words (signifiers). More than that, the Forms (signifieds) supplied their signifiers with a purposeful end (what the Greeks called a *telos*) toward which they (and all human language) could strive. Though there are a thousand varieties of trees, we recognize all of them as trees, argued Plato, because they all capture and reflect something of the Form of the Tree ("tree-ness"). Just so, even though our human attempts to strive for truth may not always be successful, we are emboldened in our search by the knowledge that behind the human reaching for truth lies the Form or Idea of Truth. Granted, most people rarely come close to apprehending such Forms (what postmodernists call Transcendental Signifieds) directly; nevertheless, their existence gives both an originary and final meaning to language and to those who use it.

For the postmodernist, this is all illusion. The words (signifiers) that we use are not names or markers of a greater, transcendent reality, but arbitrary sounds or images that human beings have chosen to use. No fixed concept or reality lies behind these signifiers, not only because the signifiers are arbitrary but because signifieds (at least in the Platonic sense) simply do not exist. In the world there exist only signifiers, and those signifiers are constantly at play. No Forms or supernatural essences exist to stabilize that play; meaning has no fixed center. There is no grand story (what postmodernists call a "meta-narrative" from the Greek prefix, meta, which means "beyond" or "transcending") along which and into which all the signifiers can be neatly arranged. Language is slippery, unreliable and, finally, self-destructive. This linguistic despair lies at the back of all the various forms of postmodernism, a despair that has had repercussions in every branch of the arts and humanities, and which may someday soon infect the sciences (it has already left its mark on the social sciences of psychology, anthropology and sociology).

It poses as well a threat to the doctrines, scriptures and sacred history of Christianity: one of whose central truth claims rests on the belief that "in the beginning was the Word (*Logos*) and the Word was with God and the Word was God" (John 1:1). Christians use the phrase Word of God (*Logos Theou*) to refer both to the Bible and to Christ. Indeed, for those of us who believe in the Christian revelation, the Bible is the signified toward which all of our faith statements point back, and Christ is the Transcendental Signified toward which the Bible itself points back. And *as* signifieds, Christ and the Bible provide the measure or touchstone against which all our religious signifiers can be tested, and through which many of those signifiers can be raised up to become themselves signifieds in that sacred tradition that lies alongside the Bible (at least for Catholic and Orthodox believers).

Perhaps the best example of this Christian interchange between (earthly) signifier and (divine) signified is to be found in the Catholic celebration of the Eucharist. During the Mass, the priest calls upon the Holy Spirit to transform ("metamorphose" in Greek) the signifiers of bread and wine into the signifieds of Body and Blood. Though, physically and chemically speaking, the signifiers remain signifiers (they are still bread and wine), they are believed now to contain and embody the signifieds (the Body and Blood of Christ) that lie behind them and give them their full meaning and purpose. And behind those signifieds (the historic Body and Blood of Christ that was broken and poured out on the Cross) lies the Transcendent Signified (the Second Person of the Trinity, the Incarnate Son, the Eternal Lamb that, according to Revelation 13:8, was slain from the foundation of the world). In Catholicism, the Mass is considered one of seven sacraments, all of which convey a divine, spiritual grace (signified) through the medium of a physical, earthly rite (signifier).

Given both the logocentric ("word-centered") and sacramental nature of Christianity, it is not hard to see that if a true breakdown ever *were* to occur either between the creeds and the Bible or the Bible and Christ, the claims of Christianity would be seriously compromised. The postmodernists, of course, are well aware of this and take considerable pride in trying to demolish the truth claims of Christianity by demonstrating how slippery language really is. With a deft sleight of hand, they unpack the densely woven imagery of the Scriptures in such a way that the symbols and metaphors clash with and deconstruct each other. Rather than lining up like Jacob's Ladder to build a bridge between heaven and earth, the symbols detach themselves from any fixed signified to participate in a dance without pattern or resolution: one signifier pointing back to another and another and another in an endless circle of futility.

It is no coincidence that the postmodern academy (and even seminary) has embraced so enthusiastically the gnostic gospels. In these only-recently discovered texts (all of which are several hundred years later than the canonical Gospels), Christ is portrayed as a sort of mystical guru spouting words of wisdom meant to enlighten his devotees. Such texts as the Gospel of Thomas and the Gospel of Philip (anthologized in the Nag Hammadi Library) are perfect tools to begin the deconstruction of the Bible, for they are profoundly ahistorical (if not antihistorical) texts: the speakers of these two "gospels" could be changed from Christ to Buddha without finally changing anything. Although Matthew, Mark, Luke and John are presented as fully historical documents centered around the life, death and resurrection of a real, flesh-and-blood human being, those who come to them from the postmodern perspective of the gnostic gospels tend to strip away their historical underpinnings and leave them stranded in a limbo of words with no fixed referents (signifieds). In the work of such writers as Bishop Spong, Elaine Pagels and John Dominic Crossan, biblical metaphors meant to locate Christ as both the Jewish Messiah and the Only Begotten Son of God (lamb, shepherd, light, Son of Man, Son of God, etc.) are used against themselves. The metaphorical is set against the historical, the figurative against the literal, the vaguely spiritual against the concretely miraculous, with none of them pointing back to any Transcendent Biblical-

Christological Meaning. To do so, the postmodernist argues, would be to freeze and reduce the play of images. Whether or not the Incarnation or Resurrection is historical is inconsequential to the postmodernist: the metaphors of the Bible are just too slippery to be fixed in any type of sacred doctrine or credal statement.

Ironically, by uncovering the slippery nature of biblical imagery, the postmodernists have not weakened the central mysteries of Christianity but strengthened them. For true (Trinitarian) Christianity, as opposed to mere Deism or Unitarianism, is *itself* slippery and relies precisely on the slippery nature of metaphorical language to express its metaphysical paradoxes (that God can be both three and one, that Christ can be fully human and fully divine, etc.). Yes, Christianity rejects the linguistic despair of postmodernism, but it also rejects the scientific, Enlightenment mindset that wants to find a simple, concrete one-to-one correspondence between statements (signifiers) and the meaning of those statements (signifieds). Christians worship a God whose greatest act in human history (the Incarnation) affected a breakdown in signifier and signified that was not deconstructive but redemptive: a breakdown, that is, whose slipperiness leads us not away from Meaning but toward it. In the Incarnation (if I may be allowed to express it in linguistic terms) the Transcendental Signified (God) entered into the life of (indeed, became) a lowly signifier (a carpenter from Nazareth) without ceasing to be the Transcendental Signified. In the person of Christ (the Word made Flesh), God and man, spiritual and physical, signified and signifier, met and joined hands across a divide that is at once metaphysical and linguistic. The eternal "invaded" the temporal, splitting history into two halves (B.C./A.D.) and providing a final reference point for all the prophecies (metaphorical or otherwise) of the Old Testament.

Signified became signifier without sacrificing its "signified-ness," and, by so doing, it effected (metaphysically, historically and linguistically) the reconciliation of signifier and signified. And it did so permanently, for, according to the Scriptures, three days after Christ died, he rose again in a perfected Resurrection Body that will forever be fully physical (signifier) and fully divine (signified). The promise held out by the historical events of Christmas and Easter is that the signified could not only reach down and inhabit the signifier, but that the signifier could be taken up out of the playhouse of signifiers into the realm of the signified. According to the Orthodox doctrine of theosis (best expressed by Athanasius in his fourth-century treatise, *On the Incarnation of the Word*), God (the Signified) became like us (the signifier) so that we could someday become like him. Just as the Word came down and became flesh two thousand years ago, so all those who put their faith in him will find their own flesh taken up to share in the glory of the Triune Transcendental Signified. Indeed, each time a Catholic believer celebrates the Mass (or any of the other sacraments) he catches a glimpse, a foretaste of that final, crowning moment when the lowly bread and wine of our fallen earth will be metamorphosed into the exalted Body and Blood of the Eternal Lamb.

In the Christian meta-narrative, even the lowliest of signifiers can be redeemed.

The great Christian poets and writers from Augustine to Dante to Milton to Donne to Herbert to Dostoevsky have all been well aware of the incarnational nature of Christianity and have sounded the fullness of that mystery in their poetry and prose. They understood not only the historical and metaphysical but the linguistic repercussions of the Nativity, and they trusted that though language (like mankind) was fallen, it could be redeemed and used as a fit receptacle for Meaning. C. S. Lewis, as a Christian whose faith was centered on the Incarnation, shared this great trust and devoted much of his life and art to celebrating what I like to call redemptive postmodernism. What is unique about Lewis, however, is that whereas the writings of Augustine, et al. can be intimidating and obscure to the lay reader, Lewis' beloved Chronicles of Narnia are written in a language that all can understand and enjoy.

While maintaining the simplicity and directness of his beguiling tales of magic and adventure, Lewis (to use his own phrase) "smuggles" in a hefty amount of Christian theology. In that sense, the seven novels that make up The Chronicles of Narnia are like the parables of Jesus: both have a mundane, concrete surface meaning under which hides (for those who have eyes to see) a deeper meaning that points either to the nature and ministry of Jesus or to the nature and ministry of the Kingdom of God (or, more usually, both at the same time). Though The Chronicles of Narnia can be read and enjoyed solely as fairy tales without any knowledge of their Christian subtext (as I read them myself as a boy), one's reading experience is enhanced tenfold when the realization strikes that woven into the very fabric of the tales is a wealth of reflection on Christ, theology and the Christian life. And, woven into the weave itself, a celebration of how the incarnational nature of the Christian revelation can redeem us from the metaphysical and linguistic despair of postmodernism.

The secret to the success of The Chronicles is that (if I may speak a bit cryptically myself) they are allegorical without being allegorical. As most fans of The Chronicles can tell you, Lewis made it clear in several essays that he wrote (anthologized in both *On Stories* and *Of Other Worlds*) that the Narnia books are not, technically speaking, Christian allegories. That is to say, they do not follow the aesthetic/linguistic pattern of *The Pilgrim's Progress* (or Lewis' own *The Pilgrim's Regress*) in which each character and place in the work stands in for one (and only one) meaning. The Giant Despair in *The Pilgrim's Progress* does not have a biography of his own; he is simply a physical embodiment of the effect that despair has on the Christian walk. Though Lewis did not reject allegory as a form, he decided that the kind of (almost scientific) one-to-one correspondence that lurks behind allegory was not appropriate for what he wanted to say and do in his tales. To have made The Chronicles of Narnia into mere allegories would have been to schematize them too much, to have robbed Narnia and its Lion King of their integrity. Though allegories can inspire a sense of wonder in their readers, the specific kind of magic that Lewis sought to conjure in The Chronicles could not be conveyed via the genre of allegory.

As his friend and fellow Inkling (J. R. R. Tolkien) had done in The Lord of the Rings, Lewis wanted to perform an act of sub-creation (the phrase is Tolkien's) through which he would bring into being a wholly other world that ran in accordance with its own principles and laws. Though Lewis was certainly less precise and exacting in his sub-creation (a "lapse" for which Tolkien faulted him), Narnia nevertheless emerges from The Chronicles as a distinct and "real" world that one can imagine visiting, rather than a mere backdrop for working out a spiritual or intellectual proposition (in that sense, though Narnia may be slightly less real than Middle-earth, it is certainly more so than the Lilliput of *Gulliver's Travels*, the ideal city of More's *Utopia* or the El Dorado of Voltaire's *Candide*). Likewise, though Aslan is an allegory for Christ, he is also a distinct character with his own history, his own motivations and his own "personality." As such, Aslan and The Chronicles are like the events and characters in Dante's *The Divine Comedy*, which *is* technically an allegory (Dante called it so himself) but is also something far different. Dante's hell, purgatory and paradise are both representations of spiritual (and psychological) states of being and very concrete places with a real geography that can be mapped out. More vitally, Virgil and Beatrice do not simply represent human reason and divine grace; they are also fully, historically real characters in their own right. The *Comedy* would have been a different thing altogether had Dante replaced Virgil and Beatrice with two nondescript, allegorical characters named Reason and Grace.

Aslan, then, both is and is not an allegory of Christ, just as Narnia both is and is not an arena for acting out vital spiritual choices. Lewis explained it best himself when he wrote in a letter to a child named Patricia that Aslan is not so much an allegory of Christ as the Christ of Narnia: he is what the Second Person of the Trinity might have been like had he been incarnated in a magical world of talking beasts and trees. "The Passion and Resurrection of Aslan," Lewis explains in his letter (which is dated June 8, 1960), "are the Passion and Resurrection Christ might be supposed to have had in *that* world—like those in our world but not exactly alike" (1985, 92–93). Thus, at the end of *The Voyage of the Dawn Treader*, Aslan tells Lucy that he also exists in our world, but that there he goes by another name.

Or, to express this same truth in linguistic terms, Aslan and Jesus of Nazareth are two radically different signifiers that nevertheless point back to the same signified (or, better, Transcendental Signified). According to the First Epistle of John, one of the central characteristics of God (the Transcendental Signified) is love; he not only gives love, he *is* the essence of Love itself (as he is also, the Gospel of John tells us, the Way, the Truth and the Life). In our world, he expressed that Love most perfectly in the Incarnation and Crucifixion of Christ; in Narnia, that same Love takes physical form (becomes a signifier) in the ministry of Aslan and his sacrifice on the Stone Table. This is why, though Lewis did not want his readers simply to replace the name Aslan with Jesus, he *did* hope that his readers (especially children) would experience numinous emotions of awe and wonder in the presence of Aslan that they could then transfer to Christ. Aslan and Christ finally elicit (or should elicit) from us the same emotional response because they both participate in the same Transcendental Signified.

Now a purist might say that we do not need a mythical lion to teach us how to feel about the Second Person of the Trinity; but, if that is true, then we also do not need the rituals, the masses and the icons that are so central to the Christian tradition. As we saw earlier, the full sacramental life of the church consists in a number of rites that, though they are not themselves Christ, embody the same incarnational mystery. In that sense, all the sacraments are symbols that point back to Christ. (In *The Allegory of Love*, Lewis treats the words symbolism and sacramentalism as synonyms.) Of course, the Protestant Reformation took upon itself the task of ridding the Church of most of its sacramental rituals, but then this shedding of mystery and of the sacred from Christian life and art was one of the things that the Anglo-Catholic Lewis hoped to counteract.

As an advocate for the Middle Ages and its aesthetic and spiritual richness, Lewis sought to baptize our imagination (as his had been by George MacDonald's allegorically non-allegorical fairy tale, *Phantastes*). He knew that for most people living in the rational, scientific twentieth century (*whether or not* they were believers), Christ and the Gospels were things to be studied and interpreted rather than experienced and felt, things to be believed in or not rather than loved, embraced and marveled at. For the modern world, either the Christian story is *only* a myth (that is, untrue) or it is an objective propositional truth to be understood and assented to as one would to a mathematical proof. Or, to revert again to linguistic terms, either the signifiers of Christianity point back to signifieds that are finally unreal (or, at best, legendary) or the signifiers line up in a one-to-one correspondence with their fixed, frozen signifieds, leaving no room for play or mystery or imagination. Either way, the signifiers are locked in place.

In the face of this cold, dry biblical literalism and colder, dryer secular rationalism, a growing number of postmodernists (which includes not only academics but those in the New Age movement) have sought to demolish both Christian and secular modernism and set the signifier free. For deconstructionists like the late Jacques Derrida, this linguistic play is a liberating one that allows the reader to chase around the signifier in an endless game of cat-and-mouse. Certainly Pagels and Crossan have found such doctrinal liberation in the ahistorical gnostic gospels. But this playfulness is finally self-defeating. Just as games are meaningless and finally futile if they have no rules and no endpoint, so signifiers that can never be traced back to a signified are ultimately empty and hollow. Like much of pop culture today (which includes, I'm afraid, both the Jesus Seminar and the hoopla over the gnostic gospels and *The Da Vinci Code*), they are all flash and no substance, all packaging and no content.

In The Chronicles of Narnia, we find a way out of this impasse: a playfulness and a freedom that lead not away from meaning but toward it. With a high seriousness that is at once philosophically earnest and aesthetically whimsical, Lewis reaches his hand into the dusty old box of Christian signifiers and gives it a whack. What remains when the dust settles is a world that, though it is as different from our own as the characters of the Chinese language are from the letters of the English alphabet, nevertheless points back to the same essential signifieds (as the very different words that make up the two languages point back to the same basic concepts). Edmund, who betrays Aslan and his siblings to the White Witch is to be confused neither with Adam (who disobeyed God and caused the Fall of Man) or Judas (who betrayed the Christ to his enemies). He is rather a very real, very recognizable type of boy who allows his own spite and peevishness to drive him toward committing a terrible act of disobedience and treachery whose consequences are even more terrible. And yet, the nature of that treachery is such that it can be "plugged in" to the same signifieds that make up the Christian meta-narrative.

When the god Bacchus appears on the scene in *Prince Caspian* to help rescue Narnia from King Miraz and the Telmarines, he is at once the mythical Bacchus of ancient Greece and a tutelary deity who "really exists" in Narnia and who cooperates with Aslan in the restoration of Narnia. The playfulness this time is even more complex than in the case of Edmund. For the two Bacchuses (Greek and Narnian) are dual signifiers that point, simultaneously, forward and backward to the historical Jesus of Nazareth (signified) who himself participates directly in the Second Person of the Trinity (Transcendental Signified). Or, to put it another way, the Greek Bacchus and the Narnian Bacchus are mythical types (symbols) of Jesus and Aslan, both of whom are real types (incarnations) of the Second Person of the Trinity in their respective worlds.

With such unforgettable characters as Reepicheep the mouse, Puddleglum the Marsh-wiggle and Jewel the unicorn, Lewis allows his Narnian signifiers even more freedom. None of these three noble personages can be linked to any one specific person from biblical or Christian history (as Aslan can be linked to Christ or Edmund to Adam); they are free to

work out their destinies and meanings vis-à-vis signifieds that are purely Narnian. Yet, they too (by the slipperiness of the signifier) are to be
numbered in that roll call of the faithful that wends its way through the
eleventh chapter of Hebrews. Their suffering, their determination, their
sacrifice cluster finally around the same signifieds as all those crusading
knights who (like Reepicheep) stayed true to the honor of Christ, or
all those irascible missionaries who (like Puddleglum) pressed on into
the jungle even after the vision had gone cold, or all those indomitable
Russian martyrs who (like Jewel) resisted to the last the ungodly com-
munist usurpers who stole their nation and their traditions from them.

Or, to put it (once again) another way, both the characters in the Narnian story and the knights/missionaries/martyrs of the Christian story
represent diverse signifiers that participate in the same sacred narrative:
the transcendent chronicle of those who "through faith subdued kingdoms, wrought righteousness, [and] obtained promises... [who] out of
weakness were made strong, waxed valiant in fight, [and] turned to
flight the armies of the aliens" (Hebrews 11:33–34). Two chapters earlier, the anonymous author of Hebrews explains how the earthly Temple
was but a shadow of the heavenly Temple; yet another two chapters
earlier we are told that the shadowy figure of Melchizedek was a type
or foreshadowing of the True King-Priest, Jesus Christ. Hebrews, like
The Chronicles of Narnia, is a slippery book, but that is only because it
seeks, like Lewis, to express in slippery words the nature of a universe
and a salvation story fashioned after the image of a slippery, triune God
who did not deign to descend into the signifiers he had made.

As Lewis worked his way through the seven Chronicles, his "re-
demptively postmodern" vision, I believe, expanded. By the time we
reach the last three published Chronicles (The Horse and His Boy, The
Magician's Nephew and The Last Battle), Lewis has moved from sub-
creating his own world to sub-creating his own Narnian Bible. As the
Word of God, the Second Person of the Trinity (he who lies behind all
the stories: human or Narnian) reveals himself both in sacred history
and in the Scriptures. The signifiers that embody that Divine Person are
both historical and linguistic, both deed-based (Incarnation-Crucifix-
ion-Resurrection) and word-based (the books of the Bible). In his first
four Chronicles, Lewis cleverly weaves an unbroken narrative thread,
carefully uniting his four separate tales via overlapping groups of Earth
children (first the four Pevensies, then two of the Pevensies + Eustace,

then Eustace + Jill) and via the Narnian Caspian who appears in (and links together) all three of the tales that follow *The Lion, the Witch and the Wardrobe*. In these initial four Chronicles, Lewis lays out something akin to the main narrative thrust of the Bible: the history of Israel and the Church as seen through successive historical periods (the Patriarchs; the Exodus and the Conquest; the Kings and Prophets; the Exile and Return; the Birth, Ministry, Death and Resurrection of the Messiah; Pentecost and the Church). Indeed, just as The Chronicles mimic this inexorable progression from period to period, so does the character of Caspian embody all those biblical characters (Abraham, Moses, David, Peter, Paul) whom we meet at various stages in their chronological and spiritual growth. Caspian is, in fact, a signifier run riot; we cannot pin him down as a type of any single biblical figure, for he inhabits them all: he is truly the hero (both sacred and secular) with a thousand faces.

Caspian and Aslan, like Abraham-Moses-David and Christ, are the linchpins on which hang the narrative thread of The Chronicles and the Bible. But that is not the whole story. In addition to the strictly historical books (Judges, Kings, the Gospels, Acts, etc.), the Bible boasts a number of interpolated works that round out the fuller vision and that allow space for divine signifiers that are tangential to the "main story": tales of exiles and misanthropic prophets, passionate psalms and earthy proverbs, seduction poems and world-weary meditations, didactic epistles and prophetic visions. And the list goes on. Though the main signifiers may line up in linear fashion along the historical periods mapped out above, the full meaning does not emerge until all the peripheral signifiers are allowed to cluster around the Transcendental Signified. Just so, Lewis rounds off his seven Chronicles by ending the series with three stories that stand, as it were, in the gaps of the central narrative thread. In the first (as in Ruth, Esther, Daniel and Jonah), we are allowed a glimpse into the ways in which Aslan works in the countries that lie outside the "Holy Land" of Narnia. In the second and third, Lewis gives us the Genesis and Revelation of Narnia: not that we may know the beginning and end of history, but that we may be given a new perspective *on* history itself. The first eleven chapters of Genesis are more etiological than they are historical; Revelation does not mimic Kings or Chronicles but the apocryphal parts of Daniel and the other Major and Minor Prophets. It is archaeology and eschatology (rather than history per se) that drives both the biblical books and their Narnian equivalents.

The fullness of the Transcendental Signified is too wide and too rich to be contained by historical signifiers alone. That is why the Bible must not be read in simple chronological order but intertextually, paying close and subtle attention to its complex pattern of overlapping signifiers. And that is why The Chronicles of Narnia must be read in the same way. In his seven timeless novels, Lewis performs nothing less than an incarnational feat: one that encompasses the multifaceted, multivalenced, multi-genred approach of the Bible itself.

Against the Hydra of Postmodernism only a many-headed hero can hope to stand.

Louis A. Markos (http://fc.hbu.edu/~lmarkos) is a professor in English at Houston Baptist University. He is the author of Lewis Agonistes: How C. S. Lewis Can Train Us to Wrestle with the Modern and Postmodern World *(Broadman & Holman, 2003).*

References

Lewis, C. S. 1985. *C. S. Lewis: Letters to Children.* Ed. Lyle Dorsett and Marjorie Lamp Mead. New York: Macmillan.

DAVID E. BUMBAUGH

The Horse and His Boy: The Theology of Bree

Narnia.... The happy land of Narnia—Narnia of the heathery mountains and the thymy downs, Narnia of the many rivers, the plashing glens, the mossy caverns and the deep forests ringing with the hammers of the Dwarfs. Oh the sweet air of Narnia! An hour's life there is better than a thousand years in Calormen.

—*The Horse and His Boy*

The evolutionary process...does not, then, allow us to suppose there is any complete structural genetic demarcation between us and other animals. Indeed much of current biotechnological research is based on the opposite premise.... Why are we so resistant to the idea that we are "kin" to "lower" animals, and draw dividing lines between them and us?

—Anne Primavesi, *Sacred Gaia*

THE STORY OF *THE HORSE AND HIS BOY* is a tale of redemption. It is a story of the journey from slavery to freedom, from ignorance to wisdom, from confusion to enlightenment. It is, at its core, a theological statement, exploring the possibility of transformation and the conditions that must be met if that possibility is to be realized.

The story is driven by the inescapable tensions between the two polar kingdoms, Narnia and Calormen, and by the different visions of reality they represent. To understand the theological claims built into this deceptively simple story, it is necessary to explore the contrast between these realms.

Calormen, as we encounter it, is a harsh and colorless place. It is a land where people are ignorant of their origins and of their true natures. It is a land where slavery in various forms is commonplace. It is a land where truth is devalued and language is used more to conceal than reveal, a land where appearance is prized more highly than reality. Above all, it is a land of rigid hierarchy and brutal power.

Our glimpses into the structure of Calormen society serve to bear out this judgment. Shasta, Bree, Hwin and Aravis are all caught in a system that denies their fundamental natures and requires them to serve ends and purposes not their own. Shasta, bound to a brutal foster father and a life of daily drudgery, confronts the certainty that his foster father intends to sell him into slavery to an equally brutal warrior. Aravis struggles against a system that will bind her to a loveless marriage with an elderly nobleman in order to advance her family's dreams of prestige and wealth. Bree must live the pretense that he is an ordinary horse and lives to serve the needs of his warrior master, and Hwin dares not acknowledge or speak her innate wisdom, even to herself. Bound in a hierarchal system, each serves an agenda not of his or her choosing.

This pattern repeats itself throughout Calormen society, where each person exists to serve the whims of social and political betters. All citizens of Calormen are placed somewhere on a rigid hierarchical ladder. Those above on the ladder are free to abuse and mistreat those below; those below are free to accept the blows and kicks of their betters and pass them on. Thus, this fear-based system functions to transfer pain and humiliation from top to bottom of the social structure. From servant and slave to Vizier and Crown Prince, this immutable system bends all energies and all loyalties to advance and serve the corrupt and cynical schemes of the Great Tisroc.

The effect of this system is to create a culture of deception, a realm in which truth cannot be expressed, and language is used to obscure rather than to clarify. Indeed, language becomes a game of innuendo and indirection. The Vizier dare not speak plain truth to the Tisroc, lest he lose his position and perhaps his head. The Tisroc, the Vizier and the Crown Prince engage each other obliquely, hinting at a truth none is willing to speak directly. Nor is the great city of Tashbaan all it seems to be. From the outside the city is a gleaming vision of power and beauty; within its walls, filth and dirt and the rigid rules of caste and class soon become evident. In Calormen wisdom is displaced by fearful, carefully calculated dissembling, carefully designed appearances and highly embroidered language. And for this reason, Calormen is cut off from any real understanding of the natural order of things. All is seen, understood, evaluated and judged in relation to the unnatural order that has been erected by legend and custom and preserved by dissembling and circumlocution.

By contrast, Narnia is a land of mountains and meadows and woodlands and flowing streams. Narnia is a land where differences in station exist, but hierarchy is neither rigid nor immutable. In Narnia, even strangers from beyond the borders, from the world beyond the wardrobe may become leaders and rulers. In Narnia the line between ruler and ruled, between human and nonhuman is blurred and indistinct. This is a place where horses and hedgehogs and beavers and ravens and rabbits and squirrels talk the same tongue as human beings and converse, not only with each other, but with kings and queens. In Narnia, trees speak and conserve great wisdom over long generations. In Narnia, centaurs and giants and fauns coexist and cooperate to sustain the common good. In Narnia creatures are free, belonging to no one, responsible to each other. Narnia is a land of deep wisdom and abiding truth.

Narnia is the world as it exists before human beings abstract themselves from it and impose upon it rigid hierarchical distinctions. Narnia is a world in which each living thing is of worth in and of itself, containing within itself its own justification for being. Narnia is a world in which each has a unique gift, each has a contribution to make, and the welfare of all rests upon the continuing community of living things. Narnia is a world in which language unites rather than divides, reveals rather than hides, and each living thing has the ability to listen to all other living things, learning from each other the greater wisdom of the earth. Narnia is the land where "no one is told any story but their own" precisely because there is only one story to tell, a story which includes all: the great meta-narrative of a living, throbbing, grace-filled world in which each is an incarnation of holy truth and sacred wisdom.

Inevitably, of course, Narnia, by its very existence, represents a challenge and a reproach to Calormen. It offers freedom over subservience; it values truth over deception; it prizes courage over self-serving cowardice; it embraces deep wisdom rather than cynical deception. Small wonder that the rulers of Calormen should level a charge of witchcraft and barbarism against Narnia, insisting that by contrast with their own state, Narnia and her allies are "idle, disordered and unprofitable." Small wonder that Calormen should seek the destruction of Narnia and all she represents.

It goes without saying that the world in which we live is much more like Calormen than it is Narnia. Ours is a world so ensorcelled by its own highly structured and carefully constructed self-understanding that it has lost sight of the larger reality in which we are rooted and the deeper wisdom that sustains and informs our daily existence. Ours is a world deeply invested in self-deception. If the story of *The Horse and His Boy* is a story of redemption, it is also our story, and it is an invitation to all of us to make the journey from Calormen to Narnia.

The theological vision presented by this story is, in many ways, a Gaian theology—a theology rooted in the theory of Gaia, the living planet. Gaian theology understands that all life is of the earth and that the sacred is manifested in the whole community of the living earth. The theology presented by this story affirms a wisdom that is deeper and older and more profound than the wisdom produced by any human culture or civilization. The theology presented by this story warns us that we lose touch with that deeper wisdom at our own peril. The theology presented by this tale calls us to see ourselves as expressions of the living earth, as part of the life of the earth—not its master, but defined by the larger ecology out of which we have emerged, and free to the extent that we respect the limits imposed upon us by the greater community of life. The theology presented by this tale reminds us that there is no salvation for any of us that does not involve the salvation of others, indeed of the whole community of living things.

To understand more fully the nature of this theological vision and the challenge it presents to those of us who would make the journey from Calormen to Narnia, it is important to understand the origins of Gaian thought.

At a meeting of the American Astronautical Society in 1968, James Lovelock first broached an insight that would be more fully developed over the next few years and eventually come to be known as the Gaia Hypothesis. Lovelock, an independent British scientist, and a self-confessed eccentric, began this journey while working on experiments intended to discover whether Mars supported life.

While his colleagues at the Jet Propulsion Laboratory were designing and developing probes to our sister planet, and mechanisms for collecting and testing samples of the Martian soil, it occurred to Lovelock that the answer to the question of whether Mars supported life could be determined from Earth without all the expensive hardware involved in sending a probe to our sister planet. By asking what the effect of life is upon a planet's atmosphere, and then sampling the Martian atmosphere for signs of those effects, one might well discover whether the red planet supported life, or was barren.

This was not a very exciting suggestion for a scientific establishment committed to sending probes to Mars, but it began a significant train of thought in Lovelock's mind. He began to look at the Earth from the outside and from a holistic perspective, exploring the interlocking cycles and processes by which life is sustained on this third planet out from the sun. What he discovered is a profoundly complex interactive process in which the existence of life alters and ultimately adjusts planetary conditions so that they remain within a range hospitable to life. Increasingly he became convinced that life cannot be understood as simply a collection of biological forms that happen to share a water-washed rock circling the sun. Rather, life must be seen as an integrated phenomenon in which all forms, from the simplest to the most complex, relate to, depend upon, influence and shape all other forms. More than this, life is a phenomenon made possible by constantly shifting interaction with the processes of the Earth itself. The balance of atmospheric gases, the temperature of the planet in the context of a slowly warming sun, the nitrogen and carbon and oxygen cycles, even the shifting of tectonic plates influence and are influenced by the life-forms of the planet.

Working in collaboration with the biologist Lynn Margulis, Lovelock came to the conclusion that the Earth does not support life, but rather that life is a fundamental phenomenon of the Earth. Earthly processes do not simply favor the existence of living things. Rather, through a series of richly complex feedback systems, life regulates those conditions that make life on Earth possible. In Lovelock's words, "Life and its environment are so closely coupled that evolution concerns Gaia, not the organisms of the environment taken separately." In short, the Earth must be seen as a living entity, and life must be understood as an artifact of the Earth. Lovelock goes on to say, "Gaia, as a total planetary being, has properties that are not necessarily discernible by just knowing individual species or populations of organisms living together."

Margulis contributed to the emergence of this theory the insight that all of life is symbiotic—that rather than a struggle for scarce resources, life can be understood as a cooperative, or at least as a mutually supportive process in which the interaction of various biotic forms creates and sustains the conditions that make life possible and that serve to enlarge its functioning. Whether the focus is upon the macro level of the planetary systems, or the micro level of single-celled organisms, living forms are all interrelated, are mutually supporting and comprise an indivisible whole.

Many scientists greeted Lovelock's hypothesis with great skepticism, and many remain skeptical still. Probably it did not reassure the doubters when Lovelock's friend, the novelist William Golding, suggested that if the planet is alive, if it is defined by life, then it would be appropriate to name the planet for the ancient Greek goddess of the Earth, Gaia. Thus Lovelock's hypothesis became the Gaia Hypothesis.

If this reference to a Greek goddess contributed to scientific skepticism, it had the unexpected consequence of attracting a significant number of so-called "New Age" thinkers and enthusiasts. Lovelock and Margulis were quick to remind those who would listen that their theory was based in a rigorous respect for and engagement with scientific process. It was not their intent to engage religious enthusiasms.

Nonetheless, a number of theologians, particularly those working at the interface between ecology and religion, saw profoundly religious themes emerging from the work Lovelock and Margulis were doing. If Lovelock is right in his suggestion that life is not just something that inhabits the Earth, but that life is an expression of interconnected planetary cycles, this forces a reexamination of fundamental assumptions made by Western religion. If Margulis is right, that life—from the microscopic to the planetary—must be understood as symbiotic, long-cherished assumptions in Western religion are profoundly challenged. If Lovelock and Margulis are right, that all of life participates in the process by which planetary forces and cycles maintain the conditions necessary for sustaining life, then Western religion needs to rethink its teaching about the place of humanity in the eternal scheme of things.

If Gaia is more than a platform on which life exists, but is, instead, a vast symbiotic process in which all living things participate, the Earth begins to assume a sacred quality. The Earth is not just the creation of an outside agent; it is itself a creative process to which all living things, in their living and in their dying, contribute. We cannot assume that the Earth was created for us to exploit and or use as we wish, for we are no more privileged in the Gaian process that the moth or the cyprus, the adder or the asp.

If life is a joint venture in which every living thing has a stake, then our hierarchy of value and worth, placing humans above all other forms and only a little lower than the angels, is profoundly challenged. We are not some special order of creation; we are of the Earth, earthy. Our history is the history of Gaia; our destiny is Gaia's destiny. We late-coming participants in Gaia's life process cannot sustain the presumption that we are of greater ultimate significance than microbes or earthworms. Their fate and our fate are one; we are bound forever together as expressions of the life that is Gaia.

If life functions to regulate the planetary forces and cycles by which Gaia maintains the necessary conditions for sustaining life, then it must be clear that there is an inherent, inchoate wisdom in the world—a wisdom that is bodied forth in the often unconscious interaction of life with life, of life with minerals and gases, of life with climatic cycles and shifting tectonic plates, all of which interact to create a stable environment in which life continues. It is equally clear that human intelligence is an expression of this deeper wisdom and that to the degree we separate ourselves from the implicate wisdom of Gaia; to that degree we endanger our own existence.

By now it becomes obvious that the themes of redemption that drive the story of *The Horse and His Boy* and the claims of Gaian theology are mutually reinforcing. Both speak to the transformations that must happen if we are to make the journey from Calormen to Narnia successfully. It remains to tease out and make explicit some of those themes and claims.

In the story, from beginning to end, the journey from slavery to freedom is only possible when human and nonhuman cooperate and contribute equally to the venture. The brutal caste system of Calormen is founded upon an unwillingness to grant those lower on the social or biological order any voice. Escape from that system requires that this pattern be broken. Thus, at the outset, it is only when Bree breaks silence and warns Shasta that his new master will be a harsh and brutal man that Shasta is able to entertain the possibility of escape. Bree knows how to use his harness, and can instruct Shasta on the use of the harness, but only Shasta can use that instruction effectively. Only the presence of Shasta and his willingness to cooperate in the scheme offers any hope that Bree can escape and avoid recapture. Freedom is not escape from relationship; it is to be found in enlarging relationship and in embracing the necessity of symbiotic, mutually reinforcing relationship. In the voice of Gaian theology, life is defined as mutually dependent, mutually enlarging relationship.

The story is rich in its recognition that wisdom is not confined to a narrow segment of living beings. Each living thing incarnates a wisdom that is deep and rooted in the life processes—a wisdom that must be respected if the journey is to be successfully made. Shasta, Bree, Aravis and Hwin each bring to the common enterprise a peculiar kind of wisdom. Aravis understands the social structure of the world they seek to escape; Shasta has a kind of naïve courage; Bree has a vision of a world he once knew and dreams of knowing again; Hwin, beneath her self-effacing language, embodies a kind of practical willingness to embrace the possible. Each of them, at crucial moments, makes it possible for the group to avoid entrapment and to move on. More than this, at the penultimate moment, when the fate of Narnia hangs in the balance, it is the combined wisdom and courage of human and nonhuman that defeats the stratagems of Calormen. Gaian theology would urge us to understand that every living form embodies a wisdom that is uniquely its own, a wisdom rooted deep in Gaia's inescapable processes, but a wisdom that we must be able to access if we would avoid the traps and snares we have set for ourselves. It is a wisdom that includes our sharp and sometimes brittle human intellect but is larger and deeper and more pervasive—the wisdom of the grass and the grasshopper, the bee and the blossom.

The story of *The Horse and His Boy* offers a subtle redefinition of freedom. On the surface, the story appears to be about a desperate bid for escape. But over and over the story whispers that freedom only exists within boundaries. Thus, as Bree and Shasta and Hwin and Aravis flee on separate journeys, their trajectories are gently but firmly coerced until two separate paths converge. Aslan, a fearsome force beyond their ken, has driven them together, and their freedom consists in their ability to accept that necessity and embrace the opportunity it presents. Gaian theology would affirm that as part of the life process that is the Earth, our journey, too, is constrained. We cannot live and know freedom outside the limits imposed upon us by Gaia and the community of living things in which we are embedded. There is no freedom that is not grounded in an acceptance of the limits imposed by the cycles and resources of the planet. To be free is to embrace those limits and those necessary structures that make life possible—not only for us, but for all the community of living things. Freedom exists within the bounds of necessity and it consists in our ability to shape our response, to embrace the potential that exists within that which can neither be escaped nor avoided.

The story of *The Horse and His Boy* reminds us, too, of our inescapable unity with all that exists. As Aravis plans to flee from the marriage her family has planned for her, she sedates her servant so that there will be no one to raise the alarm before Aravis is well away. She knows the servant will be punished, but soothes her conscience with the thought that the servant probably deserves the punishment. Later, as they flee across the desert, Aslan, that fearsome fate beyond all ken, pursues and claws Aravis. In explaining this seeming random violence, Aslan affirms that each stripe Aravis bears is the equivalent of the stripe received by her servant as punishment for allowing her mistress to escape. Clearly, Aslan intends us to understand that the damage we inflict on others or on the world comes back as punishment to us. The painful injuries we cause others and the larger world show up, at last, as scar tissue on our own hearts. Gaian theology would endorse that claim. As part of the community of life, there cannot be something good for one that is not, ultimately, good for all. Damage caused to any part of the web of life is damage to all. Within the moral vision, all of life is one sacred reality, and no living thing can be considered dispensable or of lesser worth.

Gaian theology helps illuminate the moral vision that is expressed by the story of *The Horse and His Boy*. That vision affirms the underlying unity of all living things. It warns us of the dangerous consequences that arise when human beings seek to lift themselves out of the natural processes and to construct a world that is disconnected from the constraints of those natural processes. It makes clear the arrogance and the self-deception that result when we seek to separate ourselves from the deep wisdom of the Earth. It illustrates in a graphic manner the way we enslave ourselves to our own passions and narrow self-interest when we seek to escape our appropriate limitations and our broader responsibilities.

The Gaian theology that is expressed in this story reminds us that all the world is sacred and holy and regularly whispers profound revelations to those who have ears to hear. The world is everywhere alive with beauty and promise for those who have eyes to see. The world is filled with deep wisdom for those with minds to understand. The journey from Calormen to Narnia is a journey of redemption and self-discovery—redemption from the folly that insists that human beings constitute a special order of creation, freed from the constraints that define all other life-forms, and discovery of the deeper freedom that emerges once we see ourselves for what we truly are—expressions of the life force that incarnates itself in every living thing and in the community of living things that is Gaia, the living Earth. The journey from Calormen to Narnia is a journey we must take if the human venture is to survive and retain its place within the community of living things.

A graduate of Wilmington College in Ohio, David E. Bumbaugh is a Unitarian Universalist minister who has served congregations in the Midwest and the Northeast for forty years. He is currently professor of ministry at Meadville Lombard Theological School in Chicago since 1999. The author of two books, The Education of God *(1994) and* Unitarian Universalism: A Narrative History *(2000), he has contributed articles to various journals, chapters for several books and poems to various publications.*

References

Lovelock, James. 1995. *The Ages of Gaia: A Biography of Our Living Earth.* W.W. Norton & Company.

MARY FRANCES ZAMBRENO

A Reconstructed Image: Medieval Time and Space in The Chronicles of Narnia

C. S. LEWIS WAS ONE OF THE FOREMOST medieval scholars of his generation, and one of the most influential of any generation. That fact is often overlooked, or at least underestimated, by fans of his fiction. It is not overlooked by scholars. Kathryn Kerby-Fulton asserts Lewis' influence as basic: "The Allegory [of Love, Lewis' landmark study of medieval literature] has become so much a part of our thinking, along with a number of Lewis's other studies, that those of us who have grown up with him at our elbows find it hard to appreciate what the pre-Lewis study of medieval literature was like" (1991). As something of a medievalist myself (my degree is in medieval literature), I would tend to agree with Kerby-Fulton's assessment. However, and aside from occasional attempts to read Lewis' fiction in terms of specific medieval authors, C. S.-Lewis-the-medievalist remains a relatively shadowy figure to most people, especially when compared to Lewis-the-fantasy-writer, or even to Lewis-the-Christian-apologist.

Perhaps part of the problem is that the connection between fantasy and medieval studies has seemed too obvious to be worth discussing. As a group, medieval scholars do appear to have a strange attraction to the writing of fantasy. For example, in scholarly circles J. R. R. Tolkien has always been as well known for writing "Beowulf: The Monsters and the Critics" as for *The Hobbit* or The Lord of the Rings; while *The Book of Beasts*, T. H. White's translation of a twelfth-century Latin bestiary, is still a charming, and useful, resource for students—and so on. The affinity between medievalism and fantasy is so profound that it might almost be fair to reverse the equation and say that fantasy writers seem to have a strange attraction to medieval studies...which is what originally led me to wonder whether there might be something similar in writing fantasy and in studying the Middle Ages, something that might lead the same people to both fields.

I have decided that there is. And I think that one way to investigate that "something similar" is to consider The Chronicles of Narnia. In creating Narnia, Lewis has reflected not the modern world, but the medieval one, using medieval concepts of time and space in order to shape his fictional universe and the narrative that occurs within it. To the medieval mind, history began at a specific moment (Genesis, or *The Magician's Nephew*) and will end with an equally specific event (Armageddon, or *The Last Battle*). It was even possible, as medieval travel-narratives demonstrate, for a determined individual to accomplish the feat of journeying to the "end" of the world (*The Voyage of the Dawn Treader*). As Lewis himself repeatedly pointed out, the Middle Ages had no modern concept of infinity, or of progress—and neither does Narnia.

First, a qualification. When I say that The Chronicles "reflect" the medieval world, I do not mean to imply that Narnia is medieval England (or medieval anywhere) in disguise. It isn't. True, there are medieval elements in Narnia—quests, tournaments, knights, castles—but medieval elements are not enough to create, or even recreate, the Middle Ages. Rather, I am talking about the medieval worldview, what Lewis calls the Model of the Medieval Universe and celebrates in *The Discarded Image: An Introduction to Medieval and Renaissance Literature* and in two lectures that he gave at the Cambridge Zoological Laboratory in 1956 (later published as "Imagination and Thought in the Middle Ages"). The Model, he argues, is "a supreme medieval work of art...in a sense the central work, that in which most particular works were embedded." I believe that a reconstruction of this "discarded image" is what Lewis is using to build the world of Narnia, in much the same way that medieval authors would have used the Ptolemaic cosmos and its medieval elaborations as the backdrop and context for their works.

I would like to begin by considering Narnia and medieval time. From *The Lion, the Witch and the Wardrobe* on, time runs "differently" in Narnia. This is such an obvious convenience to Lewis-the-fantasy-writer (he can send his child protagonists on adventures, and still bring them home in time for tea) that it is easy to overlook how really peculiar Narnian time is. First of all, it is inconsistent, being sometimes faster and sometimes slower than time in the "real" world of England. In *The Lion, the Witch and the Wardrobe*, Narnian time flies; between *Lion* and *Prince Caspian*, centuries pass in Narnia while only a year goes by in England. However, between *Prince Caspian* and *The Voyage of the Dawn Treader*, the difference between Narnian time and English time seems minimal, while between *Voyage* and *The Silver Chair* a man's lifetime passes in Narnia and in England less than a school term. Finally, in *The Last Battle*, Tirian wakes from a dream of England to find that Eustace and Jill have come to Narnia to free him, while in England nearly a week has gone by. Lewis puts it succinctly in *Voyage*:

> If you spend a hundred years in Narnia, you would still come back to our world at the very same hour of the very same day on which you left. And then, if you went back to Narnia after spending a week here, you might find that a thousand Narnia years had passed, or only a day, or no time at all. You never know until you get there.

In *The Lion, The Witch and the Wardrobe*, the Professor makes this temporal inconsistency relative to the existence not just of Narnia, but of all possible "other" worlds: "If there really is a door in this house that leads to some other world," he says, "I should not be at all surprised to find that the other world had a separate time of its own." Variant time is thus implicit in the idea of variant space: another world—if it existed, and if we could reach it—would logically run according to another clock.

This multiplicity of worlds, each with its own time, is part of the medieval world. In medieval romances in particular, sojourns in Fairyland or in the Earthly Paradise often seem to take no time at all, but upon returning to their homelands travelers may crumble to dust from sheer age, or just find that so many years have passed that no one is alive who can still remember them. According to Patch (1970), the former fate is particularly common in Celtic lore, and turns up later in such places as Walter Map's story of King Herla (twelfth century), while the latter can be seen in such sources as the Italian tale of three monks visiting Paradise (fourteenth century). Patch also finds "otherworldly" time reversed in the Celtic "The Adventures of Nera," in which the hero spends three days nights and nights in a "fairy mound" and then returns to find people sitting "around the same caldron at which they were sitting when he left." Clearly, Lewis didn't have to look far to find other worlds with other times.

However, it is time within Narnia that is most significantly medieval, in my opinion. Lewis spends a great deal of both *The Discarded Image* and of "Imagination and Thought in the Middle Ages" describing medieval time as essentially limited rather than infinite, and limited to the span of human history. In the medieval sense, Time is History: "Christianity, going on from [Judaism], makes world-history in its entirety a singly, transcendentally significant story, with a well-defined plot pivoted on Creation, Fall, Redemption, and Judgment." Medieval historians sometimes disagreed about the specific age of God's universe, but they never doubted that it had an age; the *Anglo-Saxon Chronicle*, commissioned around 890 A.D. by King Alfred of Wessex, begins each entry with the word "Her" (here), which can mean both "in this year" and "in this place."[1] Year one is the Birth of Christ, while year thirty-three, the year of the Crucifixion and Resurrection, is also "about five thousand two hundred and twenty six winters from the beginning of the world." Narnian creation also has a limited span, according to Lewis' timeline. Narnia begins when Aslan sings it into being in *The Magician's Nephew*; it ends 2,555 years later, when Aslan uncreates it in *The Last Battle* (Hooper 1996). Peter J. Schakel (*Reading with the Heart: The Way into Narnia*) has pointed out the particular importance of the dying world of Charn in *Nephew*: not only do the progressively more "dreadful" expressions on the faces of Charn's kings and queens demonstrate the "devolution" of history, but the line of empty chairs after Jadis indicates that Charn has come to an end before its time. By implication, a certain amount of time, or history, is granted to each created universe; that time be can ended prematurely by the misdeeds of the world's inhabitants, but—and this is the most important point—it cannot be extended (1979).

---

[1] For a useful and easily accessible translation of the Anglo-Saxon Chronicle, edited and prepared by Douglas B. Killing, see Berkeley's *Online Medieval and Classical Library*.

World's End in the temporal sense is thus a very real presence in both Narnia and in the medieval world. Of course, biblical accounts of the Coming of Antichrist and of the Last Days are the ultimate source of this concept (see Matthew 24, Mark 13 and Luke 21, as well as the prophecies of John in the Book of Revelation). However, medieval art and literature often feature the biblical Apocalypse. For example, all four of the surviving major Corpus Christi play cycles (Bevington 1975) end with a Play of the Last Judgment, in which various devils drag damned souls off to hell (see Tash and the fate of Rishda Tarkaan in *The Last Battle*), while the Chester Corpus Christi cycle contains two plays about the coming of Antichrist—a process comically and horrifically reimagined by Lewis in the careers of Puzzle the Donkey and Shift the Ape. For another medieval example of the coming of Antichrist, we can look to *Piers Plowman*, William Langland's magnificent fourteenth-century dream vision, which climaxes when the dreamer-narrator witnesses Antichrist attacking Truth and replacing it with False.[2] Images of the Last Judgement in medieval art are also consistent, whether in medieval Books of Hours such as the *Très Riches Heures* of the Duke of Berry (illuminated by Pol de Limbourg and his brothers in the early fifteenth century, and completed by Jean Colombe around 1485; Museé Condé, Chantilly 1969), or in frescoes such as the monumental Triumph of Death and Last Judgment on the walls of the Pisa Camposanto (fourteenth century)—or in Michelangelo's vision of the Last Judgment in the Sistine Chapel, for that matter. Christ is central, judging the souls of the living and the dead as they pass before him; the saved are on his left, while the damned are on the right, and bat-winged devils carry condemned souls off to a burning hell. And Aslan stands at the stable door, his shadow streaming off to the right... strong stuff, but the most significant image is still the closing of the door—the fact of an ending. Aslan even makes it a cautionary message to Polly and Digory in their last visit to the Wood Between the Worlds: all worlds end, as all worlds once began.

As important to the medieval worldview as the finite nature of hu-

---

[2] The original version of *The Magician's Nephew* even contained an episode in which Digory revisits Charn and stays with a humble farmer named Piers (Roger Lancelyn Green referred to him as "Piers the Plowman"; see Hooper, 1996) and his wife. While I don't doubt that cutting the episode made good narrative sense, I rather regret it for thematic reasons. Not only might it make the possible medieval background of The Chronicles even clearer, it would also provide an even stronger parallel between the beginning of Narnia and its end.

man history is the lack of a concept of progress, coupled with what Lewis dubs "permanence" in "De Descriptione Temporum," his inaugural lecture as the Chair of Medieval and Renaissance Literature at Cambridge. Lewis regards the idea that "everything is provisional and soon to be superseded" as one of the great "frontiers" dividing our modern era from earlier ones. The Middle Ages saw the past "in terms of their own age," he says in *The Discarded Image*, but he adds that this "imagined past" was a "packed and gorgeous" version of the medieval present. When medieval historians looked to the past, they saw not "clumsiness, inefficiency, barbarity" (as modern historians sometimes do, per "De Descriptione Temporum"), but "the centuries... filled with shining and ordered figures, with the deeds of Hector and Roland, with the splendours of Charlemagne, Arthur, Priam, and Solomon." When Narnians look to the past, they see something very similar, as Jewel the Unicorn explains both to Jill and to the readers of *The Last Battle*:

> He said that the Sons and Daughters of Adam and Eve were brought out of their own strange world into Narnia only at times when Narnia was stirred and upset, but she mustn't think it was always like that. In between their visits there were hundreds and thousands of years when peaceful King followed peaceful King till you could hardly remember their names or count their numbers, and there was really hardly anything to put into the History books. And he went on to talk of old Queens and heroes she had never heard of. . . .

The Narnian "image" of time and the medieval world's are thus close to identical: not progress, but a splendid permanence throughout the ages of a purely human (or at least intelligently inhabited) history.

The way that medieval space informs Narnian space is even more intriguing. According to Lewis, medieval space is also finite; in "Imagination and Thought," he even calculates that medieval stars were approximately "118 million miles" away from the Earth—a large number, certainly, but nowhere near the distances of modern astronomy. The Medieval Model of the Universe consists of a set of seven transparent, rotating spheres, each ruled by a different "Intelligence": the Moon, Mercury, Venus, the Sun, Mars, Jupiter and Saturn. Beyond Saturn is the sphere of the Fixed Stars; beyond the Fixed Stars is the Primum Mobile, "the very Heaven." Earth is at the center of the Model, and Hell is within, and under, the Earth. In medieval maps such as the great Hereford World Map, Jerusalem is depicted as the center of the inhabited world—literally the world's navel on the Ebstorf World Map, which depicts the physical world as the Body of Christ (Kline 2001). Again, the parallel to Narnia is clear in that Narnia is also the center of its world. The Lone Islands and Aslan's country are to the East; the Western Wilds and the Garden are to the West. To the North is the Northern Frontier, and to the South is Calormen, which corresponds to the Islamic kingdoms of the Middle Ages, complete with deserts, Moors and exotic walled cities. Beneath the Narnian world are the Deep Lands, or Underland, while deeper is the Really Deep Land of Bism; beneath the medieval world are various Otherworlds, such as the one in the medieval romance of *Sir Orfeo*. Medieval travelers in the underworld are even occasionally granted glimpses of a fiery, deeper realm; see for example the adventures of Owen the Knight in the twelfth-century *Saint Patrick's Purgatory* (Patch 1970; LeGoff 1981)—although that lower world is, of course, hell and not the more appealing Bism.

Finally, and perhaps most significantly for comparing Narnian and medieval geography, there is the location of Aslan's country. In *The Voyage of the Dawn Treader*, it is in the ultimate East, which is where the Medieval Model locates the Earthly Paradise—and, to make the parallel more precise, it is on a mountain, also a typical medieval element in descriptions of Paradise (Patch 1970; Campbell 1988). By *The Magician's Nephew*, however, Narnian Paradise (the Walled Garden) is in the West, too, where the medieval maps and legends placed such idyllic locales as the Garden of the Hesperides and St. Brendan's Isles of the Blest (Baudet 1965; Patch 1970). Then, by *The Last Battle*, Narnia has somehow moved to the "fringe" of the universe—so that the creation becomes "anthroperipheral," as Lewis describes the Medieval Model. To the medieval mind, Earth may be the center; it is also "by cosmic standards, a point—it had no appreciable magnitude." Lewis quotes the medieval philosopher Alanus ab Insulis as placing Earth and her inhabitants "outside the city wall" of heaven, so that it becomes both center and margin. In "Imagination and Thought," he gives us Dante's *The Divine Comedy*, with space "turning inside out" and Earth as "the edge, the very point at which all being and reality finally peter out." Narnia is the center because it is where Aslan stood to create the world and because (like Jerusalem) it is where his Death and Resurrection occurred; but Narnia is also somehow "outside" of Paradise, so that we can reach Aslan's country from either the ultimate East or the remote West.

And yet, paradoxically, the world of Narnia isn't round. It should be, if Lewis were using the standard Medieval Model in its entirety (Russell 1991). Lewis is perfectly aware that the Middle Ages saw the world as a globe, that it was later scholars ("whose purpose demanded some denigration of the past") who insisted that medieval man was a flat-earther. But in choosing the shape of Narnia from the Medieval Model, Lewis hit two possible snags. First, I suspect that a round world for Narnia would be boring, too much like our own and inconsistent with Narnia's essential "otherness." Besides, the medieval mind might have no difficulty in sailing to the "ultimate East" of a round world, but the modern mind probably would. The second—and in some ways more fundamental—problem, I believe, is that the medieval globe isn't our modern globe; it is divided into five zones, only two of which are inhabitable (the Arctic and Antarctic are too cold, the equatorial Torrid Zone is too hot). The Torrid Zone is also impassible, so that "the Antipodes, the 'contrariwise-footed' people who 'plant their footsteps in the direction opposite to you'...are nothing to us." The Antipodes were actually a serious problem to medieval theology—if missionaries couldn't reach them, how could they be converted and redeemed?— and I doubt that Lewis wanted to waste narrative time trying to explain such a complicated system.[3]

But I don't believe that an ordinary flat world would have suited Lewis' reconstruction either. He does pay lip service to the popular concept when he presents sailors in Narrowhaven (in *Voyage of the Dawn Treader*) talking of sailing too far east until "you would come into the surges of a sea without lands that swirled perpetually round the rim of the world," and again when Reepicheep the Mouse eagerly anticipates reaching his goal of "the utter East":

"Yes, yes," cried Reepicheep, clapping his paws together. "That's how I've always imagined it—the World like a great round table and the waters of all the oceans endlessly pouring over the edge. The ship will

---

[3] Although the presence of a "poor kangaroo" in the White Witch's house in *The Lion, the Witch and the Wardrobe* may be a mild joke about the supposed "inaccessibility" of the Antipodes—or then again, maybe not.

tip up—stand on her head—for one moment we shall see over the edge—and then, down down, the rush, the speed—"

Lewis' ultimate solution to the shape of Narnia is more explicitly medieval than the "anti-Columbus" concept would be: he uses the image of the universe originally proposed by the sixth-century monk Cosmas Indicopleustes (the name means "Cosmas the Indian Sea Traveler" (Woodard and Harley 1987)). Cosmas saw the universe as a flat oblong vaulted by the heavens, rather like an old-fashioned humpbacked steamer trunk. Lewis knew perfectly well that Cosmas' *Christian Topography* wasn't widely known or respected in the Middle Ages proper, and says so in *The Discarded Image*, but his use of Cosmas in *Voyage* is specific, if subtle:

> And of course, as it always does in a perfectly flat place without trees, it looked as if the sky came down to meet the grass in front of them. But as they went on they got the strangest impression that here at last the sky did really come down and join the earth—a blue wall, very bright, but real and solid: more like glass than anything else. And soon they were quite sure of it. It was very near now.

And so is Aslan's country: this flat world is mysterious and strange and fascinating, and yet it is also very concrete and believable. Narratively and metaphorically, it works.

The Medieval Model's inhabitants also work in The Chronicles, providing Narnia with characters who are both distantly familiar and imaginative engaging. Many Narnians are drawn from classical mythology, but they tend to be the myths that survived in some form into the Middle Ages: Centaurs and Fauns and Dryads; Bacchus and Silenus; the Phoenix, whose home is in the abode of the sun; and Pegasus reborn as Fledge, "the father of all flying horses." There are also what Lewis calls "native" figures, such giants, unicorns, dwarfs, gnomes, werewolves and witches. From *Mandeville's Travels* and other medieval travel-narratives come the sciopods or "shadow-foots," little one-legged people who live in the East; Lewis' dufflepuds might have been taken right off of the pages of a medieval manuscript, or from medieval maps with illuminations of "strange races" (Friedman 2000). And then, of course, there are the intelligent stars, the "great lords of the upper sky," who dance in the heavens much as human beings dance on the earth.

Lewis refers to the more supernatural of these figures as "longaevi," or long-livers, "perhaps the only creatures to whom the Model does not assign, as it were, an official status." He borrows the word from Martianus Capella's *The Marriage of Philology and Mercury* (a text extremely important to medieval thought), in an effort to avoid using the word "Fairies." However, the absence of fairies or elves from Narnia is worth noting. In *The Discarded Image* Lewis argues that the word—and presumably the concept—of "Fairies" has been "tarnished by pantomime and bad children's books with worse illustrations"; that what "Fairy" meant to our ancestors was awe-inspiring and multilayered, and requires an effort of imaginative reconstruction on our part to understand. But this does not quite answer why there are no Narnian elves; the Fair Folk are native figures, and Lewis says of all such that they "are not, even now, quite so innocuous as the classical" (perhaps because they are closer to us in time and belief, he hypothesizes). Besides, he has no problem including, say, giants, dwarfs and werewolves in The Chronicles, and they might be said to have been almost equally damaged by popular culture.

I suspect the real reason that Lewis didn't want elves in Narnia is the position that he assigned to human beings. The Sons of Adam and Daughters of Eve are, after all, not "native" to Narnia; they are as strange and "otherworldly" as elves would be in our world. (In fact, the episode at the end of *The Silver Chair* when Caspian is granted his "glimpse" of England might even be roughly analogous to medieval journeys to Fairyland, in a way.) But from beginning to end of The Chronicles, human beings remain dominant in Narnia: only a Son of Adam or Daughter of Eve can rule at Cair Paravel. Elves might challenge that position: they almost always enter the everyday world from "somewhere else," and Narnia already *is* "somewhere else." In fact, Lewis consistently and carefully subordinates all of the humanlike creatures in Narnia to humans; they are either humorous (giants, dwarfs, dufflepuds and marsh-wiggles—though I have been unable to find a specific medieval analogue for Puddleglum) or purely evil (witches, hags, werewolves). The closer to human a Narnian is, the more likely that he or she will be evil—Jadis, the White Witch, is the daughter of Lilith, "Adam's first wife," which is about as close to human as half.

Dwarfs are an interesting case in point. Undeniably competent, they are either evil (bitter Nikabrik in *Prince Caspian*), pathetically foolish (the resolutely materialist dwarfs in *The Last Battle*), or trustworthy but slightly comic companions (Trumpkin in *Prince Caspian* and *The Silver Chair*). Trumpkin takes the place of the commonsensible adult faced with children who insist on believing in the impossible; unlike most adults, he is capable of learning better... but the "common sense" strain in his character makes him prone to error. He means well—he's a good dwarf to have on your side, as is Poggin in *The Last Battle*—but he has little of the imaginative power that seems to be the birthright of human beings in Narnia.

Also standing subordinate to human beings in the Narnian Chain of Being are the Talking Beasts, arguably Lewis' most endearing characters. They are probably inspired by several sources—*The Wind in the Willows* and *Gulliver's Travels*, among others. But they also owe something to the beast fables of Marie de France; to medieval stories of Reynard the Fox; and even to Chaucer's magnificent chickens, Chauntecleer and Pertelote of the "Nun's Priest's Tale." Then there is chapter 4 of *The Silver Chair*, "A Parliament of Owls," the title offering a sly reference to *The Parliament of Fowls*—although (perhaps fortunately) Glimfeather the Owl and the rest of his "tu-whooing" flock don't much resemble the three tercel-eagles who woo the ladylike formel-eagle in Chaucer's Valentine's Day poem. In other words, the Talking Beasts are obviously quite comfortable within the Medieval Model, and thus may serve as one more example of how Lewis has used the Model as context for his fictional fantasy world.

At this point, I think I have successfully made my case: the Medieval Model is reconstructed in Narnia. But that leaves me back at my original question: the reason why so many medievalists write fantasy. Aside from the sheer fun of it, what was Lewis' purpose in using this "discarded" image of the universe to create his fantasy otherworld? I don't underestimate the fun; as Evan K. Gibson has said: "*The Chronicles* are lightly told. It would be disastrous to hang weights on their wings" (1980). Lewis obviously loved the Medieval Model for its own sake; he says as much in the Epilogue to *The Discarded Image* ("I have made no serious effort to hide the fact that the old Model delights me as I believe it delighted our ancestors"). But the reason he gives for his delight is instructive: "Few constructions of the imagination seem to me to have combined splendour, sobriety, *and coherence* in the same degree" [italics mine]. Lewis' famous "experiment" in looking at the night sky with medieval eyes is even more relevant:

> You must go out on a starry night and walk about for half an hour trying to see the sky in terms of the old cosmology. Remember that you now have an absolute Up and Down. The Earth is really the centre, really the lowest place; movement to it from whatever direction is downward movement.... Again, because the medieval universe is finite, it has a shape, the perfect spherical shape, containing within itself an ordered variety.... The "space" of modern astronomy may arouse terror, or bewilderment or vague reverie; the spheres of the old present us with an object in which the mind can rest, overwhelming in its greatness but satisfying in its harmony.

What Lewis sees when he "looks" at the sky through the Medieval Model is a whole world, one like-but-not-like our own, and hence both stimulating and satisfying to the human imagination. Few eras had, or have, such a complete and varied—and fundamentally *different*—image of the universe, but it is not the Model itself that matters. Rather, it is the idea of the Model: the opportunity it offers to explore an alternate reality.

And that, of course, is what fantasy also offers both to its writers and to its readers. No wonder medievalists are drawn to fantasy, and fantasy writers to medieval studies: they are all seeking to satisfy the same impulse. Tolkien (Tolkien 1947) calls the "story-maker" a successful "sub-creator" of the universe: "He makes a Secondary World which your mind can enter. Inside it, what he relates is 'true': it accords with the laws of that world. You therefore believe it, while you are, as it were, inside." Did Lewis need the Medieval Model in order to create Narnia? Probably not, in one sense; there were other "worlds" for him to enter, after all. (For example, in "On Stories" Lewis takes a similar pleasure in books about "Red Indians," declaring that what he enjoyed in them "was not the momentary suspense but that whole world to which it belonged—the snow and the snow-shoes, beavers and canoes, war-paths and wigwams, and Hiawatha names.") In another sense, the Model is as necessary as fantasy itself. Campbell (1968) has put it succinctly: "No one has ever needed a griffin, only the idea of a griffin, or the idea of a world in which griffins are possible" (1988).

The idea of a world in which griffins are possible…that is what the Medieval Model offered C. S. Lewis, and, I contend, it is part of what has kept people returning to The Chronicles of Narnia—and to all fantasy—ever since.

Mary Frances Zambreno first became a friend of Narnia when her third grade teacher read The Lion, the Witch and the Wardrobe *out loud to the class—and then mentioned that there were six other books in the series. Since then, she has become a teacher herself, earned a doctorate in medieval literature and learned to read six languages (including English). Currently, she teaches at a college in the Chicago area. Her YA fantasy novel,* A Plague of Sorcerers, *was named to the ALA's list of Best Books for Young Adults in 1992; its sequel,* Journeyman Wizard, *was a New York Public Library Book for the Teen Age in 1994.*

References

Baudet, Henri. 1965. *Paradise on Earth: Some Thoughts on European Images of Non-European Man.* Trans. Elizabeth Wentholt. New Haven: Yale Univ. Press.

Bevington, David. 1975. *Medieval Drama.* Boston: Houghton Mifflin.

Campbell, Mary. 1988. *The Witness and the Other World: Exotic European Travel Writing, 400-1600.* Ithaca: Cornell Univ. Press.

Friedman, John. 2000. *The Monstrous Races in Medieval Art and Thought.* Syracuse: Syracuse Univ. Press.

Gibson, Evan. K. 1980. *C. S. Lewis, Spinner of Tales: A Guide to His Fiction.* Washington, D.C.: Christian Univ. Press.

Harley, J. B., and David Woodward, eds. 1987. *The History of Cartography, Volume I.* Chicago: Univ. of Chicago Press.

Hooper, Walter. 1996. *C. S. Lewis: A Companion and Guide.* New York: HarperCollins.

Kerby-Fulton, Kathryn. 1991. "'Standing on Lewis's Shoulders': C. S. Lewis as Critic of Medieval Literature." *Studies in Medievalism 3*, no. 3-4: 257-78.

Killings, Douglas B. "The Anglo-Saxon Chronicle." *Online Medieval and Classical Library.* July 1996. http://sunsite.berkeley.edu/OMACL/Anglo.

Kline, Naomi Reed. 2001. *Maps of Medieval Thought: The Hereford Paradigm.* Woodbridge: Boydell.

LeGoff, Jacques. 1981. The Birth of Purgatory. Trans. Arthur Goldhammer. Chicago: Univ. of Chicago Press.

Lewis, C. S. 1964. *The Discarded Image*. Cambridge: Cambridge Univ. Press.

————.1966. "Imagination and Thought in the Middle Ages." *Studies in Medieval and Renaissance Literature*. Cambridge: Cambridge Univ. Press.

————.1947; rpt. 1966. "On Stories." *Of Other Worlds: Essays and Stories*. New York: Harcourt.

————. 1955; rpt. 1969. "De Descriptione Temporum." *Selected Literary Essays*. Cambridge: Cambridge Univ. Press.

————. 1994a. *The Lion, the Witch and the Wardrobe*. New York: HarperCollins.

————. 1994b. *Prince Caspian*. New York: HarperCollins.

————. 1994c. *The Voyage of the Dawn Treader*. New York: HarperCollins.

————. 1994d. *The Silver Chair*. New York: HarperCollins.

————. 1994e. *The Horse and His Boy*. New York: HarperCollins.

————. 1994f. *The Magician's Nephew*. New York: HarperCollins.

————. 1994g. *The Last Battle*. New York: HarperCollins.

Musée Condé, Chantilly. 1969. *The Trés Riche Heures of Jean, Duke of Berry*. New York: George Braziller, Inc.

Patch, Howard Rollin. 1970. *The Other World, According to Descriptions in Medieval Literature*. New York: Octagon.

Russell, Jeffrey Burton. 1991. *Inventing the Flat Earth: Columbus and Modern Historians*. New York: Praeger.

Schakel, Peter J. 1979. *Reading with the Heart: The Way into Narnia*. Grand Rapids, MI: Wm. B. Eerdmans.

Tolkien, J. R. R. 1947. "On Fairy-Stories." *The Monsters and the Critics and Other Essays*. 1984. Boston: Houghton Mifflin.

MARIE-CATHERINE CAILLAVA

A Knight in the Mud

ALL BOOKS ARE TIME TRAVELERS.

Narnia was written in the fifties. We miss some points: there were ration cards; in those days, kids had never eaten chocolate. Was selling your family to the White Witch in exchange for sweets as shocking then as it is now?

We forget the book time-traveled to us.

Very few people are time travelers.

Scholar whose daily vocabulary was made of such words as *pneumatology, numen, Aristotelian* and *stellatum.*

Christian, whose books converted many a soul and won him the boundless admiration of the Pope.

Allegorist read by millions of kids.

Friend who dedicated his life to faithfulness.

Foe who wanted a fair fight and did not shun acknowledging his errors.

Subject of Her Gracious Majesty who refused a knighthood on account of higher imperatives.

Humble servant to his ideals who died famous, yet ignored by all.

Do you know anyone like that today? No, our century can't make such men anymore. Just as there is a time displacement between us and the Narnia books, there was one between Lewis and his time.

Many say that he was a "Renaissance Man," meaning a very knowledgeable person. We should take the expression far more literally. Lewis said that he suffered of *chronological snobbery*. But his life was in fact a temporal-displacement case: time had gotten out of joint on the day C. S. was born, and a typical man from the early Renaissance—Christian Knight, Teacher and Poet—was thus born in the last years of the nineteenth century, just in time to join two sickening and dishonorable world wars and the loss of innocence of the whole of mankind.

Perhaps it was all planned by Aslan. No matter your beliefs, he was a Renaissance Knight.

The first time a bullet missed him in a WWI trench, his thought was not "Oh cor blimey!" but "So this is war, this is what Homer wrote about!"

A Knight in the mud.

Our mud.

In Belfast is a statue of a man opening a wardrobe. He is officially Digory, the character from *The Magician's Nephew*, but his likeness to Lewis is so striking that it's almost touching.

Geographical as well as temporal displacements tint the way we perceive a man. Seen from the U.S., C. S. Lewis is a British scholar (translate: "a bore for schoolkids") and a Christian writer (translate: "an inspiration"). But in the U.K. he is—get your capital letters ready: The Great Man From Ulster. The rest is considered mere details on his flamboyant résumé.

Back in his days, being an Ulsterman necessarily meant being prejudiced, or as Tolkien did put it: having *Ulsterior* motives. During his studies, Lewis, like most of his peers, painstakingly got rid of his unEnglish accent, but amazingly he also erased the basic notions that had been instilled into him at birth: don't ever trust a Catholic, don't ever listen to a philologist. Lewis did just the reverse from what his culture told him to: Tolkien was both a Papist and a philologist, and yet became one of his dearest friends. Imagine a Yankee becoming best buddies with a Confederate during the Civil War. That's the best equivalent in Americana.

As for time displacement, it is almost impossible for us to picture accurately the world into which C. S. was born. Ulster was about to explode, national social changes were the talk of the day. A brand-new law said that, mind-boggling as it could be, husbands did not have the legal right to beat or rape their wives anymore. The Salvation Army had just been created, Karl Marx had published the first version of *Das Kapital*, Einstein was scratching his head thoughtfully while turning the light on and off, and Freud was back from Charcot's lab and preparing his *Interpretation of Dreams*. Religion was part of everybody's daily routine, but it was regarded absolute common sense to firmly believe that science was going to make the Golden Age a reality. No more diseases, no more wars. The wonders of the Steam Age as depicted by Jules Verne.

It was a time of total faith in science, and the firm trust that man and technology would soon totally rule nature, as God had meant it from the start.

Lewis was supposed to blend in. He tried, but not the way we'd think. Most of us imagine that young C. S. decided his name was "Jack" because "Clive" was ridiculous. No, it was a common handle then, like "Cecil," but being called Christopher meant "please bully me."

Just as those days are alien to us, C. S. was soon about to become a stranger in his own time, like a Son of Adam lost in a winter-land led by Witches and Goblins.

Young Jack's falling in love with books was at first the normal fondness for reading common to all kids in those days, until one fateful evening that would cut him forever from his time and make him brother to Virgil.

His first nine years had been the perfect childhood: tender mother, solid father, beloved brother. But at the age of nine, while in bed, crying with pain (bad health plagued him all of his life), he called out for his mother. Dad came to see him instead, and told him that the doctors were there, but not for him, for Mammy. She had a cancer. The poor woman died soon. It is little wonder that the magic object Santa gives to Susan in Narnia is a horn that gets you help, no matter where you are.

Jack, feeling betrayed by a father who was falling apart (Albert lost his wife, father and brother within a month's time) redirected all his love toward books, and found his solace there. He ran away into Anglo-Saxon texts like other boys would have run away from home to follow a traveling circus.

Poetry, adventure books, then when he had read them all, old sagas. This universe was new to him, and bottomless. The more he read, the more he found books to look for: read *Orlando Furioso* and you'll just *have* to read Homer, read Homer and a bit of Chaucer and you *have* to go into *Beowulf*. Young Jack was reliving very precisely what had happened to the European civilization at the beginning of the Renaissance, the "rebirth" that had happened at the end of the Middle Ages. Lewis was discovering the great classics, the old books that spoke of exciting adventures, written in a weird and fascinating language.

When Dante's most brilliant pupil, Boccaccio, decided to study ancient Greek in order to translate Homer into Latin, the world changed. Jack Lewis was changing too, by falling into books, just like one goes through a magical wardrobe. There was no stopping, and just like the Renaissance progressively spread from Florence to the rest of Europe, Lewis began with poetry, quickly moved on to literature and then Wagner's sagas.

C. S. wrote of the emotions he felt when visiting Grandpa at his parsonage, at the sight of the endless bookshelves. Above the door was a lion's head, a quaint sculpture of a gentlemanly animal. Was this watcher of the treasure hold the Grandpa of Aslan?

Nothing called Jack back to his century: sickness, bullying—not unlike that depicted in *The Silver Chair*—schoolmasters who were either incompetent or certifiable. His father was more a hazard than a friend, as he searched his son's pockets and would still do so decades later. His brother had to leave. Lewis' only steady friends became people like Thucydides, Plutarch and Milton. Blessed with a superior intellect, he thrived in the old masters' company.

And they would have loved him: the two Daughters of Eve in prayer while Aslan of gold and fire walked to the sacrificial Altar—a dream subject for Caravaggio!

Jack's world changed brutally at the very age when young boys became apprentices of masters like da Vinci, or Dante; or began to learn the rules of chivalry along with Greek and Latin.

Chivalry meant Knight, and Knight meant battle. Battle was coming Jack's way, as if the Deep Magic had carefully planned his lost-in-time but Knightly education.

War. It would be the last one; the old grudges that festered in Europe would be purged. People did not run away in horror when the call came. It all made sense; the Golden Age would come once Europe got rid of its ghosts.

No one saw the horror coming.

Being Irish, Jack did not legally have to join, but like many young men, he volunteered, this without taking his weak health into consideration.

It was then that he performed his first Knightly act. Not when he stepped into the mud of the trenches, but when he simply walked out of his roommate's home. Paddy Moore was being shipped that day and asked: "Jack, if anything happens to me, please take care of my mother and sister for me." Jack gave his word. Paddy was killed shortly after that. Lewis, for the rest of his life, took care of cranky Mrs. Moore and her young daughter.

By taking on the part of Mrs. Moore's son, Jack was also clearly casting her as his own dead mother. Alas, Janie Moore was a very difficult person to live with. Yet he refused discussing "her," even with his brother. How could he explain to anyone his motivation for giving that matron the proverbial best years of his life? Millions went to the butcher's shop called WWI and had a cousin swear he would take care of the kids, of Granny. It was as common as death in the trenches. But for Lewis, giving one's word had a very deep meaning. Not a Christian one, as he was not a "Lover or Our Lord" yet, as Tolkien once put it, but a meaning that found an echo in every single thing he held dear, every book, every page that had helped him survive, that had taken over his soul. How could a man read and love *Le Morte d'Arthur* and then give his word lightly to a friend leaving for war?

The "last war of all" turned out to be a massacre with millions killed in the mud in an endless stalemate, a war unlike any other before: machines killing men from afar, emotionless officers giving orders as if this were all a chess game, mutinies. And gas, the blind and faceless killer, rolling over the trenches.

C. S. Lewis always claimed that his memories of boarding school plagued him more than those of WWI. Yet his very short account of what he saw in the trenches is one of his most powerful pieces. His description of the no-man's land, burnt and scorched, echoes very disturbingly the dead country of the witch in *The Magician's Nephew*.

The first piece C. S. Lewis ever published, outside of a school magazine, was (alongside one by young Robert Graves, later of *I, Claudius* fame) a poem.

It was called "Death in Battle."

On a personal level, the war was a catastrophe. Lewis first caught Trench Fever, a disease caused by the omnipresent lice. This left him with bladder problems for the rest of his life, not a dignified ailment but a crippling one. Poor Jack then got exploded at in the back by a British shell. That ironic, if terrible, wound left him with a piece of shrapnel in his body.

And yet he never complained. He came home a physical wreck, but not mentally damaged, contrary to all of his mates.

Again, it is no surprise that another of Santa's gifts, to Lucy, was a healing essence. Lewis wanted solace for all people.

As the soldiers went home, the British Prime Minister announced reforms that would make the country "fit for our heroes to live in." The fact is the said heroes came back from the trenches to a homeland where there was no work and no social place for them.

It was there and then that the gap between Jack and his time became fully visible, even to him.

The war had orphaned and widowed millions. Far from the Thames, the Soviets were going on with some *shocking* anti-royal revolution, the Americans had arrived in the trenches with amazing equipment, and the "Brits" were wondering why their own army had not issued the same. Mutiny, a terrible offense, had proven justifiable; almighty science could produce such things as gas that kills or cripples people standing miles away. The world was tumbling; an answer had to be found, something that would give everything a meaning and bring back hope.

The time of Isms began: communism, socialism, naturalism, humanism, fascism, existentialism. In one word, ideolog-ism. On the streets of Oxford, students who often had a wooden leg, a torn-off face under a leather mask or crippled lungs lived with a voice in their head repeating the mantra: "Why did I make it and poor Johnny died?" They all frantically looked for answers outside of religion and mainstream science.

Except for Lewis, of course.

In that most unlikely of times, he suddenly experienced an *epiphany*, a.k.a. *a mystic revelation*. While sitting in a bus, it struck him as brutally obvious that God was fact! So far he had believed in *naturalism*: the steadiness of natural laws.

Lewis, who had, for years, mocked God-worshippers with his usual wit, faced this change with good grace, knelt and prayed. He conceded both defeat and victory, like a Knight.

Jack was so honest at heart that he could not, would not, deny a fact. Never mind those who would mock his being a "turncoat," never mind his ego. Years later, he would illustrate this honest and brave change of attitude through two of his characters in Narnia: traitor Edmund's open-hearted repentance, and super-brat Eustace's realizing what he was doing. Evil becomes Good when loving people are ready to welcome you back; this was what Lewis believed.

And old pious masters welcomed Lewis in their midst.

In *Le Morte d'Arthur* the Christian King says (this quote is in modern English, no need to hide under your desk):

> You should not fail in these things:
> Charity, abstinence and truth.
> Only by stainless and honourable lives
> and not by prowess and courage shall
> the final goal be reached.

Lewis had been brave in battle, but in vain. His real valor had been shown in front of this unexpected faith. And, following Arthur's rules, he had accepted Truth. C. S. had, by kneeling to his victor—God, no less—become a Knight by the standards of the Round Table.

From that day on, Jack plunged deeper each day into a countercurrent stream of ideas that befitted a Renaissance Knight but not a survivor of WWI. Much later in his life, his Oxford peers unfairly rejected him. The root of his alienation lies here.

Knight Lewis did put friendship above all else, and the brotherly love between him and Tolkien, a.k.a. Tollers, is still famous today. Myths were what Lewis thrived on; they were an expression of the real nature of things. It was therefore to be expected that Tolkien, the Papist, would talk to him about Christ from a mythical angle.

For the second time Jack conceded defeat, and recognized Christ's victory over his skepticism. His first revelation had taken place in a bus. This one took place in a motorcycle sidecar, in front of a zoo. (There was probably a lion in one of the cages. Aslan had obviously a clear-cut plan in mind for Jack, just as he had for each and every kid who visited Narnia.)

For all those extraordinary happenings, Lewis did not lose his sense of humor, and even wrote a friend to hurry if he wanted to see him, as next week he might be in a monastery!

In fact C. S. was not made for the monastery but for the battlefield of faith and words. *Christianity is a fighting religion* was his motto, and he lived by it, starting immediately after his second conversion.

In the late thirties, Jesus was not much in the newsreels shown in the cinemas before the all-singing all-dancing film. Mr. Hitler was the big star. A terrifying one. He wanted it all and wanted it now. In the U.K., the men who had seen the horrors of WWI had now only two things on their minds: their family and the word "gas." WWI had ended just as the use of gas was intensifying. Obviously, a lunatic like the mustached demon would use it to attack. People began carrying gas masks wherever they went.

Lewis, as usual, reacted differently from all other people. He was still knee-deep in books, whether kneeling to pray or standing tall to teach. Being awarded a prize for his study of Renaissance literature, *The Allegory of Love*, he would spend his daily life teaching, writing and talking with his Inkling friends.

Jack adopted toward his time much the same attitude as the ever-questioning thinkers of the Renaissance. When the nation prayed around its King, asking God to help their rightful cause, Lewis stood up and said (my words, not a quote): "Wait a minute, how dare we tell God what is right and wrong? Let's think about all this!" Of course his pondering led him to the conclusion that Hitler was indeed the devil itself (he sent him to hell in *The Screwtape Letters*). Question all, and only then can you have an opinion about things. Old master Occam would have been proud.

Perhaps Tolkien's Treebeard is not like Lewis so much because of its booming voice, but more because of this "let's not be hasty" attitude.

War again.

The army gave Lewis some service to do: guarding one of the roads. It's difficult not to smile when imagining this respected teacher, with his rugby-player frame and typically British reddish face, armed with an old rifle, waiting for Hitler's mighty army in case it showed up that night in Oxford. The idea brings to mind Don Quixote and his makeshift armor. But nothing could be further from the truth. Jack's gun was loaded. His watch did not seem useless at the time. The invasion of Europe by the

Nazis had taken place so fast that it was clear the war would be lost. The island would be invaded. Prime Minister Churchill had promised the Commons blood, sweat, tears and nothing else.

Lewis had to act—like a Christian Knight, of course. He did what he did best: teach.

Troops' morale was Britain's last weapon. Members of the clergy often talked to the "lads." Their sermons were met with yawns.

But Jack was a layman, he knew about life and pain, he was a former nonbeliever and the best speaker in the land. He began talking to the RAF troops through BBC broadcasts. It was a bit of a novelty. Today the BBC seems to be as old and permanent as Shakespeare, but Auntie, as it is called in the U.K., had only been created in 1920 with the mission of educating the nation.

His talks were a popular success. C. S. made it very easy to understand faith: good and evil exist, there is no shade of grey between them, nature and our longing for joy are the proof of God's existence, and the war against Hitler is the primordial fight between good and evil.

He would show us exactly the same in each Narnia chronicle: Aslan versus the Witch—it was the only fight that existed to Lewis.

His uplifting radio speeches were welcomed even by those who accused him of being part of a plot to crush left-wing thinking (he turned down a knighthood to avoid giving some credit to this rumor). In a nation still tired from the last war, expecting defeat, and whose soldiers were orphans from WWI, what one needed was some pep talk. If one did not agree with Lewis, then one could always talk and fight back.

And boy, did Jack love a good fight! A verbal one, of course.

The concept of Christianity as a fighting religion was one of the keys to the history of the Middle Ages, while debating was a central part to the Renaissance spirit. Quite logically, C. S. cofounded an arena called the Socratic Club.

The Socratic was a place where everybody could come and watch the show. An atheist speaker would defend his point of view, then a Christian—generally Lewis—would talk, and the debate began. The meetings often resembled a boxing match. On one occasion the heat was unbearable, and the atheist talker, just like the captivated audience, took his jacket off after asking for permission to do so (it was the time when even hooligans wore a hat and tie). But when someone suggested Lewis to do the same, he answered that he could not: he had a hole in his shirt. Considering the shortage of everything—including shortages—it's possible that Professor Lewis had a torn shirt on. But it's far more likely that he refused to remove his jacket for the same reason that he once corrected the MC who had announced "and now Professor Lewis will answer!" by saying with a smile "Begin the *debate,* you mean!"

Two sweaty men in their shirtsleeves, talking loudly for the audience's sake about their totally opposing views, accusing each other of being illogical—it could have looked like a wrestling match so easily, and Lewis was a Knight and did not want things to turn *gladiatorial,* as a witness once described it.

And when it came to debating, Jack was a killer, perfectly aware of the power of speech, and probably self-conscious about his own. He said the reason why Hitler scared him was that, while you listened to him, the horrors he said seemed to make sense, until he shut up and your brain came back online.

The art of debate had died with the Middle Ages. Lewis used to complain that most people could not have a proper discussion anymore. They had lost the training for it. He called it Bulverism after a man whose wife replied to his stating a math formula by the words: "Oh, you only say that because you're a man!"

Knight Lewis wanted honest and open speakers who would use logic, reason and counterarguments to convince the audience.

Historically the last time such a real debate had happened was in the days of Arab-occupied Spain, when Muslim, Jewish and Christian scholars discussed the Holy Texts in front of students on equal terms, with passion and yet enough open-mindedness to not just dismiss the others by saying: "Oh, you say that just because you are a heretic!"

Eventually, the U.K. did get invaded, but it was a most welcome invasion, that of the "Yankees," (Europeans had no idea what the Civil War was about, and nicknamed all Americans "Yankees"). Hope reappeared, even if, as a dock worker said when the first battalion disembarked: "Oh my! Where are we going to put all those big blokes? What a problem!"

The war was won, quite amazingly.

But the emotional roller coaster was not over. On April 19, 1945, Richard Dimbleby, reporter for the BBC, reached the camp of Belsen and had five minutes of airtime to describe hell. People were familiar with the concept of millions dying in a war, something that was, alas, part of human history. But the extermination camps were without equivalent in horror. Four months later, another shock came: the atom bomb.

Humanity was evil enough to create the horrors of Belsen, and was now technically capable of blowing itself up. Human psyche never recovered.

Once more, the British began looking for new ideologies—global ones, this time. This was the time of Maoism, cynicism, negativism.

While people argued about national identity, Lewis took, as usual, everyone by surprise, and wrote the very last thing anybody expected: a fairy tale.

Not particularly for children, not necessarily for Christians. Just a story for the young at heart, containing symbols that would make particular sense to people familiar with the Bible.

Jack, lost in time as always, had not noticed that kids did not say "crikey!" anymore. His editor was there to correct such tiny errors.

Lewis was reacting to the troubled times by doing what Homer, Dante and almost all the old masters had done before him: by creating a myth, an allegory.

It would become his all-time bestseller. C. S. always said that it began with his wondering what animal Christ would be. Jesus is often referred to as "the Lamb of God." But Knight Lewis, keeping in tune with his fighting vision of Christianity, had another answer: Jesus would be a lion! Powerful, so impressive that only a few people could watch him in the eye (ask Mrs. Beaver) but incarnating Good itself. When Aslan chooses to give his life to save a traitor, he does so all the more of his own free will, because he could, if he wanted to, tear apart the Witch and her cronies with one paw. This corresponds to the image of Jesus that you'll see in medieval Notre Dame, for example. Their vision of Jesus was not that of an ethereal being as he would be represented in later art, but that of a manly, solid man, with piercing eyes, square jaw and a posture that spoke of physical might and great will. Lewis once said: "God is a source of *facthood*." He also thought that Jesus was an all-powerful being and believed in his miracles.

Aslan performs many miracles in Narnia. But in each book the most fascinating one is always that of the birth of a Knight.

The Chronicles of Narnia are all about Knights: *The Lion, the Witch and the Wardrobe* is about Peter, a "normal" boy in short trousers, becoming a Knight. *Prince Caspian* is about young Caspian learning to be a Knight alongside his elder, Peter. *The Voyage of the Dawn Treader* is about two Knights on a classic quest—Peter is this time younger than Caspian and learns from him—and *The Silver Chair* is about a new Knight overwhelmed by his mission, saving another Knight from the delusions of sins, all in the name of Aslan.

But of course, we all know that, according to myths, Knights save widows and orphans. And Lewis lived for myths. So you say he was a Knight? Well, did he save any Lady in distress?

Oh yes.

And, according to some, God even acknowledged his deeds by performing a real miracle.

Joy—what a beautiful name—was born Jewish, but became a Marxist before converting to Christianity after reading books by a Britisher called C. S. Lewis.

From a strictly Christian point of view, he had already saved her soul.

She met him. Soon, abandoned and divorced by her husband, alone with her two sons and dying of cancer (yes, like Jack's mother) she found herself about to be kicked out of the U.K.

Lewis did the only thing he could do, being a Knight: marry the Lady in peril. A white and civil wedding, of course, not a real or religious one.

Not long after this, when Jack realized that he could not help falling in love with Joy, he married her "under God," still respecting the chivalry code.

What happened next was, to him, a clear sign sent by God. Joy had a terminal cancer. Doctors had given her a week to live. But unexpectedly, she had a remission. It was, in her doctors' own words, a miracle. To them "miracle" was just an everyday expression meaning "something wonderful that we can't explain." But to Lewis this was actually a supernatural fact, a divine intervention. He believed that Jesus, God and prayers, had a power beyond our understanding. And he had prayed for days.

When Joy eventually passed away, after they had had time to enjoy their newfound love, Lewis did not hide away or collapse. As always, wanting to share his experience and so help others, he wrote a book, a very moving one, but still a treatise in the form of Renaissance treatises of science: a manual about grief.

He had already written one about pain.

Now he had to face the cruel question: what reason have we got to believe that God is *good* in our understanding of the concept?

C. S. once wrote that Christians were heretics in this world, a provocation meant to stress the fact that most people who claimed to be Christians did not behave in a Christian way. Erasmus, in the early sixteenth century, wrote in his *Manual of a Christian Knight*: "He must be a fool in this world that will be wise in God."

A Knight? C. S. Lewis was that. Whether or not you share his beliefs or faith, his sincerity is irresistible.

He died discreetly, the day before Kennedy was shot. No one much mentioned his passing. But today, he is still read by scholars, people of faith and children all around the world.

He had done his duty and been true to his beliefs.

And all this without taking himself seriously—after all, he always and only referred to his prize-winning opus *The Allegory of Love* as *The Alligator of Love*.

Marie-Catherine Caillava lives in London. She's a writer, ghostwriter, translator and radio critic. Her hobbies are Zen calligraphy, Kyudo, hunting for old books in Oxford bookshops and investigating the contents of wardrobes.

SALLY D. STABB, PH.D.

"Most Right and Proper, I'm Sure..." Manners and Politeness in The Chronicles of Narnia

M Y GOOD LADIES AND GENTLEMEN, have you ever noticed that in the middle of all sorts of nasty goings-on, most of the main characters in Narnia are exquisitely polite? Ah yes, and it's a very British sort of politeness too. Rather! Teatime all around, even during the most trying of moments. Or perhaps because they *are* the most trying of moments. How many bleak adventures and desperate situations have been turned around by the warm hearth, spread with honest, wholesome foods, and shared by mannered guests and new friends? Quite a few, I might argue.

But beyond that, we may question, why be so polite in the first place? What good is it? Couldn't we just have our adventures without it, thank you very much? I suppose we could, but C. S. Lewis did not write it so. Perhaps we should make the best of it, then, and take a look, shall we?

Early on, Lewis establishes the children as concerned about politeness. From *The Magician's Nephew*, for example, here are two early demonstrations of such consideration. First, when Polly meets Digory, who is described as "very grubby," Polly says:

"At any rate I *do* wash my face...which is what you need to do; especially after—" and then she stopped. She had been going to say "After you've been blubbering," but she thought that wouldn't be polite. (2–3).

In a second example, Digory and Polly are arguing once back in London at Uncle Andrew's. Polly needs to go home:

"It's frightfully late. I shall catch it."
    "Hang it all, you can't leave me alone in a scrape like this."
    "And if you want me to come back, hadn't you better say you're sorry?"
    "Sorry?...What have I done?"

When Polly lists the series of unfortunate events leading to their predicament (mostly caused by Digory) he responds,

"Oh," said Digory, very surprised, "Well, all right, I'll say I'm sorry. And I really am sorry about what happened in the waxworks room...."
    "All right. We'll call it Pax...." (86–87)

The children Do the Right Thing and make up after a spat, apologizing for bad behavior. In real life, apologies serve to keep our relationships intact, and to grease the social gears so that interaction can proceed again after rupture.

In *The Lion, the Witch and the Wardrobe*, concern for propriety, delicacy and hospitality are again in evidence, as illustrated by Lucy's initial meeting with Tumnus, the faun. Lucy begins the exchange:

"Good evening."
    "Good evening, good evening...excuse me—I don't want to be inquisitive—but should I be right in thinking that you are a Daughter of Eve?"
    "My name's Lucy," said she, not quite understanding him.
    "But are you—forgive me—you are what they call a girl?"

Shortly thereafter, when introductions have been completed, Tumnus says,

"Daughter of Eve from the far land of Spare Oom where eternal summer reigns around the bright city of War Drobe, how would it be if you came and had tea with me?" (11)

These are but three of dozens of such mannerly interactions throughout the Narnia chronicles. Having set the stage with these exemplars, let's delve a bit more deeply into just what politeness is all about. It's not quite as simple as common sense would have us believe.

Politeness in Context

Well, of course you know what politeness is, don't you? Saying "please" and "thank you" and not picking your nose in public and all that lot, right? Rather self-evident, you say. But is it? Is it the way you move? Dress? The words you speak? How you speak? Truly, politeness can encompass all of these—what we say and what we do, and when we do it and with whom. Politeness is a slippery concept. Academics in the fields of sociolinguistics, social psychology, sociology, anthropology, linguistics and pragmatics have actually developed politeness theories, and argue about the details therein quite hotly; in fact, *they* do not yet have agreement on a definition!

In spite of this higher-education hair-splitting, it is possible to map out the basics of politeness theories. Spencer-Oatey suggests three themes. First is the idea of using politeness to manage one's social image with others, commonly known as "face." The second major theme is that politeness maintains cooperation as people interact and try to reach their various goals. The third concept, a bit more abstract, is that parties in conversation have some mutual expectations about how discussions will proceed, and that politeness is a part of these shared rights and obligations in speech (Spencer-Oatey 2002, 529–45). While many of these aspects of politeness are about what we say ("linguistic politeness"), Bargiela-Chiappini reminds us that politeness is also about what we do ... and what we don't do—nonverbal politeness (2003). For example, depending on both culture and the situation, it may be polite to lower your gaze, bow or hold a door open for someone carrying a heavy load. It may also be polite to refrain from talking, or to avoid interaction altogether. In the end, however, it is remarkable how closely the formal research is to our everyday wisdom about politeness, from countless parental lectures to Miss Manners to the self-help section of the bookstore.

As a case in point, outside the ivory tower, books on manners have been written for decades. In fact, I searched out such sources on etiquette, written in Britain, contemporary with C. S. Lewis' writing of the Narnia chronicles. For example, in *Modern Etiquette*, published in 1952, Agnes Miall begins:

> Etiquette is a social code, a set of rules which enables people to live more comfortably and happily together...it matters imperishably, in all ages and in all countries, for good manners are based on unselfishness and consideration for others, and these of course, are all-important....Our manners are almost the first thing strangers know about us—so they had better be good! (vii)

A more tongue-in-cheek introduction by Virginia Graham in her 1949 book *Say Please* notes:

> This is a book on Etiquette for Ladies, neither of which or whom now exists, as everybody knows; so the whole thing, both from my point of view and from yours, is the most shocking waste of time, and I really have no idea how it happened.... (i)

Graham expresses strong ambivalence throughout her book, commenting repeatedly on the societal transformations occurring in England at the time, such that, "The standard set by our parents regarding the use of words has been lowered to such a degree it can almost be said to be furled" (87). She can't seem to make up her mind whether or not to try to maintain the principles of the past or to throw them out on the winds of social change (but her book makes for hilarious reading). Regardless of her mixed emotions, C. S. Lewis very clearly valued manners, and this concern for propriety permeates the Narnia chronicles.

The point is really that both Graham and Miall have hit on key elements of politeness. Politeness can only be understood in a particular historical context. Manners vary by class and culture, and change over time. In spite of books on the topic, manners and politeness are most often unwritten rules, norms we grow up learning in our families and own social circles. Miall is quite right in noting that manners provide important social lubrication, not only within our own social sphere but when we step outside it. Our sensitivity to what is appropriate is highly dependent on situation and status.

For example, it is one thing for the children in Narnia to be both direct and occasionally rude with one another. They are social peers, making such an exchange perfectly acceptable, as in this passage from *The Voyage of the Dawn Treader*, in which Eustace is needling Lucy and Edmund:

> "Still playing your old game?" said Eustace Clarence who had been listening outside the door and now came grinning into the room....
> "You're not wanted here," said Edmund curtly. (4–5)

Yet we—and they—would be appalled to speak so to a respected elder, much less to Aslan. Contrast the first example with the conversation below, from *The Horse and His Boy*, in which the social status between the two speakers is quite different.

> "Oh impeccable Tisroc," said the Vizier. "In comparison with you, I love neither the Prince nor my own life nor bread nor water nor the light of the sun."
> "Your sentiments," said the Tisroc, "are elevated and correct." (129)

The tone here is noticeably different, as is the use of honorifics. Honorifics are the titles or names given to those in power (Nevala 2004). Miall includes a full section in *Modern Etiquette* on such modes of address, with details regarding the proper forms in which to speak or write to royal princes, dukes, marquises, earls, viscounts, barons, baronets, knights, ambassadors, archbishops, archdeacons, bishops, consuls, deans, judges, governor-generals, lords, mayors, privy councilors, secretaries of state, cardinals, the Queen, Queen Mother, princesses, duchesses, marchionesses, countesses, viscountesses, baronesses, peeresses, dowagers, dames, etc., etc. In this way, we know who is to be "Your Excellency" versus "My Lord" versus "Sir" and who is to be "My Lady" versus "Madam." It simply will not do to fail to address one deserving of respect without his or her proper honorific, and to do so may get you into all sorts of trouble, as is exactly the case for Aunt Letty in the presence of Queen Jadis in *The Magician's Nephew*:

"Get out of my house this moment, you shameless hussy, or I'll send for the police.... No strong language in this house *if* you please, young woman," said Aunt Letty.... The Queen towered up to an even greater height.... Without wasting a thought... she lunged forward, caught Aunt Letty round the neck and the knees, raised her high above her head as if she had been no heavier than a doll, and threw her across the room. (94–95).

A related idea is that of indirectness, that when making a request of someone who is above us in social rank, we must show deference and respect, and cannot be blunt or confrontational (Bargiela-Chiappini 2003; Jameson 2004). In essence, we must acknowledge in words, tone and action that we are *lower* than the other, and that the granting of our wishes is at the mercy and discretion of a superior. Such interactions are common in the Narnia chronicles. Here, Digory is speaking to Aslan in *The Magician's Nephew*:

He dared not look into the great eyes. "Please—Mr. Lion—Aslan—Sir... could you—may I—please, will you give me some magic fruit of this country to make Mother well?" (158–59).

In *The Silver Chair*, even Prince Rilian's long-trusted captain must be humble in his requests:

"Fair Prince," said Drinian, "of your courtesy, let me ride with you tomorrow...." (59)

Knowing one's place in the social order is essential in even the most egalitarian of societies. England in the 1950s was certainly deeply rooted in a hierarchical class system. The Narnia chronicles mirror the British class structure in the ways in which polite language is used, the types of language used and in terms of class-related accents (still a marker today). In *The Magician's Nephew*, the lower-class cabbie addresses the royal Queen Jadis:

"Now Missie, let me get at 'is 'ead, and just you get off. You're a Lidy, and you don't want all these roughs going for you, do you? You want to 'ome and 'ave a nice cup of tea and a lay down quiet like...." (107)

The status difference between the cabbie and the queen dictates that he must use the appropriate honorific with her, that he must make her life easier by helping her out of the cab, and his comments reflect his ideas about how the upper classes properly spend their time.

Politeness and Face

As noted briefly before, politeness is also one way of showing (or saving) face. Another elusive idea, "face" and "facework" were concepts originally presented by Goffman (1963), elaborated by Brown and Levinson (1987) and then critiqued extensively in both the Western and cross-cultural literature (Spencer-Oatey and Jiang 2003; Haugh and Hinze 2003; Spencer-Oatey 2002). What we end up with is fundamentally the idea that face/facework are strategies or ways to preserve a positive image of oneself or of one's social group in human interactions. Politeness is one way to do this—to show that you are cultured, refined or in some other way legitimate. In *Prince Caspian*, when Doctor Cornelius reveals to Caspian that he is half-Dwarf, for example, he works hard to demonstrate to "his dear Prince" that he is worthy and loyal:

> "I'm not a pure dwarf. I have human blood in me too....But never in all these years have we forgotten our own people and all the other happy creatures of Narnia, and the long-lost days of freedom." (43)

Politeness also helps us to save face when we've got ourselves in a muddle. This happens at the end of *The Silver Chair*, when Eustace mistakenly believes the Dwarfs have taken Jill, and that they are about to capture him. He initially tries to fight them off, but soon learns of his error:

> "Stop, Eustace, stop," cried Jill. "They're all friends. Can't you see? We've come up in Narnia. Everything's alright." Then Eustace did see, and apologized to the Dwarfs (and the Dwarfs said not to mention it). (235)

Knowing Politeness by Its Opposite

Current politeness theorists note that we discover what is polite as often as not by encountering its opposite—rudeness or negative reactions to a failure to be polite (Culpeper, Bousfield, and Wichmann 2003). Who is rude and impolite in the Narnia chronicles? The children occasionally are with each other, but as noted earlier, such exchanges among peers are more acceptable, and they are consistently mended with apologies. Grown-ups are only rude when they are Bad People. This sets up a fundamental dynamic seen over and over again in the Narnia chronicles: Good People are mannerly and polite, Bad People are not. Jolly obvious, you say? Yes and no. In our everyday lives, we all have learned that manners and politeness are signs of goodness, whether or not they really are. Bad people are certainly capable of being polite, and good people are guilty of the occasional lapse in manners. But in the Narnia chronicles, it tends to be more black-and-white, with bad people only being polite in the service of their evil ends. A case in point might be the White Witch in *The Lion, the Witch and the Wardrobe* as she schemes to get Edmund under her spell with Turkish Delight:

> "My poor child," she said in quite a different voice, "how cold you look! Come and sit with me here on the sledge and I will put my mantle around you and we will talk.…Perhaps something hot to drink.…Should you like that?…What would you like best to eat?" (36–88)

We also come to know badness by outright rude behavior. In *The Last Battle*, we understand Shift the Ape to be evil by the way he manipulates Puzzle the Donkey, as well as by the condescending way in which he speaks to the other animals in front of the stable:

> "You *thought*!" repeated the Ape. "As if anyone could call what goes on in your head *thinking*.…Get back! Quiet! Not so fast!…The Ape waddled to and fro, jeering at them. "Ho ho ho!" he chuckled. "I thought you were all so eager to see Tashlan face to face! Changed your mind, eh?" (119–21)

In fact, manners and politeness come to symbolize all that is civilized. In a very broad sense, these social markers then help to distinguish which cultures are seen as desirable and dominant, and which are seen as uncivilized and in need of either appropriate education or submission or both—usually "for their own good."

The Civilizing Influence of Manners and Politeness

In the time of C. S. Lewis, Britain was a major world power, coming off over 150 years of expansion of The Empire, as well as the divvying up of North Africa post-WWII (Gerner 2000) (along with the French, and to a lesser extent, the Italians and Americans). Thus, for a long period of time, the British had seen themselves as a civilizing influence on much of the rest of the world—civilized meaning all that was White, European, educated and upper-class. Reflective of a deeply ingrained and long-standing Western prejudice (Said 1978), those who were dark and to the East were clearly *not* civilized. In the Narnia chronicles, the Northern Narnia, run by fair-haired kings and queens, is held up as the ultimately desirable place to be, in contrast to the land of the dusky Calormenes to the South. This dichotomy perfectly reflects Euro-White-Western ideals of proper society, breeding, manners and politeness in contrast to the strange and heathen ways of the Black or Brown Arab-Orientals. While Lewis shows the Calormenes to have rudimentary forms of politeness among their own people, their ways of talking—for example forms of address and honorifics—are actually mocked. One such depiction is presented here from *The Horse and His Boy*, in which Aravis introduces herself:

> "My name," said the girl at once, "is Aravis Tarkheena and I am the only daughter of Kidrash Tarkaan, the son of Rishti Tarkaan, the son of Kidrash Tarkaan, the son of Ilsombreh Tisroc, the son of Ardeeb Tisroc who was descended in a right line from the god Tash. My father is the lord of the province of Calavar and is one who has the right of standing on his feet in his shoes before the face of Tisroc himself (may he live forever)...." (37)

This passage actually continues for a number of pages, written in what Bree the horse calls "grand Calormene manner" (39), and as the representative of Narnia, Bree appears basically amused by this storytelling.

The Calormenes are so clearly set up as Arabs, with tiny illustrations of turbaned men in long robes with curved swords striding across the chapter headings in all their barbaric trappings. Lewis describes their armor in *The Last Battle*:

"Aye, lad," said Tirian. "No Narnian Dwarf smithied that. 'Tis mail of Calormen, outlandish gear." (62)

Even the name Calormene suggests "Colored Men," and these people are set apart from the trustworthy and true citizens of Narnia, with no hint of contemporary concern for multiculturalism (or, some would say, political correctness) in evidence. In the Narnia chronicles, we routinely run across descriptions of the Calormenes as unsophisticated, having poor manners, having strange or laughable manners, or just being downright mean:

> "Get on, son of sloth! Pull, you lazy pig!" cried the Calormenes, cracking their whips.
>   "Work, lazy brute," shouted one of the Calormenes: and as he spoke he struck the horse savagely.... (27)

Politeness and Humor

Speaking of things laughable, while the Narnia chronicles are not a wealth of humor, some joking and ironic moments do occur. I mention irony in particular, because it is a way to communicate impolite information masked with humor. Studies analyzing irony show that two levels are communicated in ironic statements. The first level, the overt content message, is a statement that is patently *untrue*. The second level, which is implied, is that the opposite of what was said is what is really meant. This second level is often signaled by a change in voice tone (Lucariello and Mindolovich 2002; Kotthoff 2003; Pexman and Harris 2003). For example, if your boss tells you that you are going to have to commit a full eight hours of an upcoming Saturday to a special team-building exercise with the gang at the office, you might say, "Gosh! I can't wait!"—which is the exact opposite of what you are feeling. While we can't hear inflection while reading the Narnia chronicles, examples of irony do pop up, and when they do, are often ways to convey negative/impolite information. In *The Horse and His Boy*, Prince Rabadash says:

> "Oh my father and oh the delight of my eyes," began the young man, muttering the words very quickly and sulkily, and not at all as if Tisroc *were* the delight of his eyes. "May you live forever...." (117)

In the example above, which is an exchange between those who are antagonistic to each other, people tend to respond to the covert, negative message, and "get" the rude implication. Tisroc tells his son to compose himself and later threatens him. On the other hand, among good friends, ironic statements are often used in a playful way, and no rudeness is implied, as when the Dwarf in *Prince Caspian*, chatting with Lucy, Edmund and Peter, says:

> "Oh, I'm a dangerous criminal, I am.... You've no idea what an appetite it gives one, being executed!" (29)

It is also notable that no truly rude forms of humor appear in the Narnia chronicles at all (off-color jokes, dirty limericks). Heaven forbid!

Politeness and Thought Suppression

While irony has its convoluted twists, a different sort of mental acrobatics are needed when we are asked, as C. S. Lewis occasionally does, to *not* think of something. Lewis sometimes implores us, as readers, to ignore bad behavior or not to dwell on some form of impoliteness. Such a scenario is presented in *The Voyage of the Dawn Treader*, when Eustace, as the dragon, first encounters the crew of the *Dawn Treader*:

> And Eustace nodded his terrible dragon head and thumped his tail in the sea and everyone skipped back (some of the sailors with ejaculations I will not put down in writing).... (82)

Paradoxically, this is more likely to make us think about what the sailors might be saying! You can test this out for yourself: for the next three minutes, don't think of the word "hippopotamus." Not so easy! Classic studies on thought suppression, which have come to be known as "the white bear studies" show that while we can temporarily distract ourselves from certain thoughts (such as hippos, white bears and foul language), once we lose focus, they come back with greater intensity (Wegner et al. 1987).

Why C. S. Lewis chose to occasionally use thought suppression techniques in writing the Narnia chronicles is unknown. Did he really wish us to dwell on impolite actions? Probably not. It is more likely that he was merely unaware of the rebound effects of his requests.

Some Final Thoughts: Teatime

One aspect of good manners is offering food and drink, be it to friends, family, visiting royalty or the weary stranger traveling from afar. While this is likely to be true across cultures, in the Narnia chronicles it gets played out in a very British way—with tea! Tea abounds in the Narnia chronicles, a perennial source of sustenance and comfort, and a mark of hospitality. Even the rather lowly Marsh-wiggle, Puddleglum, in *The Silver Chair* offers Jill and Scrubb what he can:

> "And now," he added, "let's see how those eels are getting on." When the meal came it was delicious and the children had two large helpings each. . . . After the meal they had tea, in tins. . . . (77)

Here's another lovely description from *The Lion, the Witch and the Wardrobe*, when the children are in the Beavers' home, finishing a meal of fresh trout with onion, potatoes, cream and butter:

> And after they had finished the fish Mrs. Beaver brought unexpectedly out of the oven a great and gloriously sticky marmalade roll, steaming hot, and at the same time moved the kettle onto the fire, so that when they had finished the marmalade roll the tea was made and ready to be poured out. And when each person had got his (or her) cup of tea, each person shoved back his (or her) stool so as to be able to lean against the wall and gave a long sigh of contentment. (83)

And so it was in the time of C. S. Lewis. In Graham's 1949 book, she quotes a charming poem, contemporary with that historical period, regarding tea etiquette:

> May every tea-time be accursed,
> May honey spill and éclairs burst,
> And may those ladies die of thirst
> Who dare to put the milk in first! (87)

I daresay it remains so today, from high tea with clotted cream and finger sandwiches (sans crust) to the everyday social ritual in average homes. I can say this with good authority, living myself with a Brit and his family for over eight years now. I have been coached in the making of a proper cup of tea (I'm approaching being civilized!) and recognize the deep cultural satisfaction that goes with "coming 'round for tea." When anything goes wrong in the family, the most immediate solution is "a nice cup of tea," over which nerves may be soothed and solutions contemplated.

My Brit, Martin, keeps tea at the office to share with his Pakistani colleague late in the afternoon, whenever possible. Recently in Cairo, Martin and I often ended a grueling afternoon of sightseeing with a cup of tea (hotels are well prepared, and bring the milk appropriately warmed). The lingering influence of the British Empire is thus evident even now.

Perhaps you imagine this quintessentially British tradition, steeped in (pun intended) politeness ritual, to be antiquated, or charming in a distant sort of way, or just downright silly. But I would argue that tea-time embodies, in microcosm, a very English valuing of manners and politeness. And that deep reverence for all that such good graces represent is evident throughout the Narnia chronicles. C. S. Lewis has not given us just a series of fantasy adventure stories, nor solely religious allegory. He has also given us a window into the mores surrounding manners and politeness of his time.

Well, jolly good, then. I think I hear the kettle, so with your kindly permission, I'll take my leave....

Sally D. Stabb, Ph.D. is an associate professor of counseling psychology at Texas Woman's University, where she trains therapists, teaches and does research with a focus on diversity, gender, emotion, sexuality and other fun stuff. She is a licensed psychologist. Outside of work, her passions include travel, world dance, music, food, scuba, reading and playing Scrabble. Sally lives with her sig-o of eight plus years, his kids and one insane Jack Russell terrier (is there any other kind?).

References

Bargiela-Chiappini, Francesca. 2003. "Face and Politeness: New (Insights) for Old (Concepts)" *Journal of Pragmatics* 35, no. 10–11: 1453–69.

Brown, Penelope, and Stephen Levinson. 1987. *Politeness: Some Universals in Language Usage*. Cambridge: Cambridge Univ. Press.

Culpeper, Jonathan, Derek Bousfield, and Anne Wichmann. 2003. "Impoliteness Revisited: With Special Reference to Dynamic and Prosodic Aspects." *Journal of Pragmatics* 35, no. 10–11: 1545–79.

Gerner, Deborah, ed. 2000. *Understanding the Contemporary Middle East*. Boulder, CO: Lynne Rienner Publishers.

Goffman, Erving. 1963. *Behavior in Public Places*. New York: Free Press.

Graham, Virginia. 1949. *Say Please*. London: Harvill Press.

Haugh, Michael, and Carl Hinze. 2003. "A Metalinguistic Approach to Deconstructing the Concepts of 'Face' and 'Politeness' in Chinese, English and Japanese." *Journal of Pragmatics* 35, no. 10–11: 1581–1611.

Hobbs, Pamela. 2003. "The Medium is the Message: Politeness Strategies in Men's and Women's Voice Mail Messages." *Journal of Pragmatics* 35, no. 2: 243–62.

Jameson, Jessica Katz. 2004. "Negotiating Autonomy and Connection through Politeness: A Dialectical Approach to Organizational Conflict Management." *Western Journal of Communication* 68, no. 3: 257–77.

Kotthoff, Helga. 2003. "Responding to Irony in Different Contexts: On Cognition in Conversation." *Journal of Pragmatics* 35, no. 9: 1387–1411.

Lucariello, Joan, and Catherine Mindolovich. 2002. "The Best Laid Plans...: Beyond Scripts are Counterscripts." *Journal of Cognition and Development* 3, no. 1: 91–115.

Miall, Agnes. 1952. *Modern Etiquette*. London: C. Arthur Pearson Ltd.

Nevala, Minna. 2004. "Accessing Politeness Axes: Forms of Address and Terms of Reference in Early English Correspondence." *Journal of Pragmatics* 36, no.12: 2125–60.

Pedlow, Robert, Ann Sanson, and Roger Wales. 2004. "Children's Production and Comprehension of Politeness in Requests: Relationships to Behavioural Adjustment, Temperament and Empathy." *First Language* 24, no. 72: 347–67.

Pexman, Penny, and Melanie Harris. 2003. "Children's Perceptions of the Social Functions of Verbal Irony." *Discourse Processes* 36, no. 3: 147–65.

Said, Edward W. 1978. *Orientalism*. New York: Vintage Books.

Spencer-Oatey, Helen. 2002. "Managing Rapport in Talk: Using Rapport Sensitive Incidents to Explore the Motivational Concerns Underlying the Management of Relations." *Journal of Pragmatics* 34, no. 5: 529–45.

Spencer-Oatey, Helen, and Wenying Jiang. 2003. "Explaining Cross-cultural

Pragmatic Findings: Moving from Politeness Maxims to Sociopragmatic Interactional Principles (SIPs)." *Journal of Pragmatics* 35, no.10–11: 1633–50.

Watts, Richard J. 2003. *Politeness*. Cambridge: Cambridge Univ. Press.

Wegner, Daniel, David Schneider, Samuel Carter, and Teri White. 1987. "Paradoxical Effects of Thought Suppression." *Journal of Personality and Social Psychology* 53, no. 1: 5–13.

COLIN DURIEZ

Narnia in the Modern World: Rehabilitating a Lost Consciousness

I N THE CHRONICLES OF NARNIA, C. S. Lewis imagines wonder, and no more so than in the figure of the talking lion, Aslan. Aslan famously is not a tame lion. His wildness draws upon the wildness that Lewis portrays in nature and in God himself, in a book written just three years before *The Lion, the Witch and the Wardrobe* (the first Narnian story he made). In Lewis' *Miracles* God is the theist's Maker of Heaven and Earth, found in Judeo-Christianity and in Islam. God is also definite, as Lewis discovered when he moved from materialism to theism and then Christian faith: he is demanding of human beings, the fact behind all facts, concrete, infinitely articulated and articulate, to be found at the beginning with the Word. He is a Person of wisdom, imagination and intelligence, in a way far deeper than can be articulated in a platonic form or archetype of each of these personal qualities. His incarnation as a human being (or as a talking beast, in the case of the Narnian world) is a spell-binding and history-making disclosure of who he is.

If we ask who C. S. Lewis is, we could truly say a storyteller and scholar, one of the most brilliant teachers of his time at Oxford University and later at Cambridge. We could focus on the elusiveness of his life—the scars of the early loss of his mother, his fighting and serious wounding in the muddy and bloody trenches of World War I, his adopting of the mother of his dead war buddy, his romance and marriage late in life to the much younger American poet and novelist Joy Davidman, his Christian conversion and popular theology, his fraternity with the Oxford Inklings literary club. Or we could simply say of C. S. Lewis that he was someone who was able to create Aslan and Narnia. Lewis said of a poet he revered, John Milton: "The marvel about Milton's Paradise or Milton's Hell is simply that they are there—that the thing has at last been done—that our dream stands before us and does not melt" (1942, 58). The same could be said of Dante's heaven and hell, and, in its own way, of Aslan and all that is Narnia. They stand before us. We can enjoy The Chronicles, which did not exist a little over a half a century ago. We can talk and argue about them. We can write books about them. We can even love them.

Such a love can be discovered in *The Child that Books Built*, where Francis Spufford brilliantly evokes a childhood created by books, usually as escape from painful realities. There is, however, one memorable incident in which a sort of bridge is crossed from the story books into this world:

> I did experiment, sometimes, with bringing Narnia back over the line into this world. I imagined dryads in the woods at Keele, smoothing out their shining hair with birch-bark combs. My friend Bernard and I swapped Narnian trivia and called ourselves Narniologists. I scattered white rose petals in the bathtub, and took a Polaroid picture of the dinghy from my Airfix model of the Golden Hind floating among them, to recreate the lily sea. But I never felt I had connected to the live thing in Narnia which could send a jolt through my nerves, except once. I had the poster-map of Narnia by Pauline Baynes up on the wall on the upstairs landing at home. In the top right-hand-corner, she'd painted Aslan's golden face in a rosette of mane. Once, when no one was around, I crept onto the landing and kissed Aslan's nose in experimental adoration—and then fled, quivering with excited shame, because I had brought something into the real world from story's realm of infinite deniability. (2002)

What was Lewis doing in his Chronicles of Narnia, this "live thing"? The most obvious answers are that he was telling an excellent story for the love of it, creating a secondary world (inspired by his friend J. R. R. Tolkien's sub-creation of Middle-earth) and embodying virtues and values as desirable and indeed essential for our continued humanity. In this essay I wish to try to go behind these answers and consider (1) Lewis' rehabilitation of old and outmoded virtues and values for our contemporary world—a world he felt to be in grave moral danger; and (2) Lewis' inculcation of a change of perception and even consciousness in his readers. Lewis was concerned to present his vision as fact, not theory, full of resonances and connections with the world of reality.

Rehabilitating Old Western Values and Virtues

In *Prince Caspian* the depth of Narnia's historical past is vividly evoked for the children by the ancient ruins of Cair Paravel, the home of the four when in a previous time they were kings and queens. There they are joined by a dwarf, Trumpkin, who has been sent by the young Prince Caspian to see if help has come from another world. Caspian has called for help by blowing the horn of Queen Susan, left behind from the Golden Age long ago. Caspian is under siege from his uncle, Miraz, a Telmarine brutally suppressing any trace of Old Narnia. The children join Caspian and, with the return of Aslan in the nick of time, defeat the enemy.

The Narnia of the Golden Age has been remembered in secret under the tyranny of Miraz. The spirits of woods and streams are seldom seen, and talking animals are in hiding. The schools banish the true history of Narnia from their dreary curriculum. Caspian, taught about Old Narnia by his nurse and then his tutor, Doctor Cornelius, could talk about it for hours.

In 1954—when the writing of the Narnia books was complete—Lewis accepted the newly created Chair of Medieval and Renaissance Literature at Cambridge University, after heavy persuasion by Tolkien, who was one of the electors. In his colorful inaugural lecture, Lewis expounded a theme central to their friendship and affinity—that the rise of modernism, socially and culturally expressed in the creation of "the Age of the Machine," was an unprecedented fracture in Western civilization. Both friends sought in their work, particularly in The Lord of the Rings and The Chronicles of Narnia, to rehabilitate the "Old Western" values that Lewis spoke of in this lecture. In The Chronicles it is always the values of Old Narnia that are in danger of being lost. This is most graphically shown in *Prince Caspian*.

> "Hush!" said Doctor Cornelius.... "Not a word more. Don't you know your Nurse was sent away for telling you about Old Narnia? The King doesn't like it. If he found me telling you secrets, you'd be whipped and I should have my head cut off." (1951)

The nurse who tells stories of Old Narnia to Caspian is dismissed for her faithfulness to it. In a bizarre real-life semi-parallel, Lewis was passed over three times for a Chair at Oxford. In her obituary to C. S. Lewis for the British Academy, a later Oxford Chair holder, Dame Helen Gardner, hazards a reason for this after rehearsing his formidable achievements:

> In spite of this, when the Merton Professorship of English Literature fell vacant in 1946, the electors passed him over and recalled his own old tutor, F. P. Wilson, from London to fill the Chair. In doing so they probably had the support of many, if not a majority, of the Faculty; for by this time a suspicion had arisen that Lewis was so committed to what he himself called "hot-gospelling" that he would have had little time for the needs of what had become a very large undergraduate school and for the problems of organization and supervision presented by the rapidly growing numbers of research students in English Literature. In addition, a good many people thought that shoemakers should stick to their lasts and disliked the thought of a professor of English Literature winning fame as an amateur theologian; and, while undoubtedly there were a good many people in Oxford who disliked Christian apologetics *per se*, there were others who were uneasy at Lewis's particular kind of apologetic, disliking both its method and its manner. These last considerations were probably the strongest, and accounted for the fact that when, in the following year, a second Chair in English Literature was established his name was again not put forward. (1965, 424)

Helen Gardner also mentioned as significant Lewis' failure to gain the Oxford Professorship of Poetry in 1951, despite huge support from his faculty.

The modernizing of Uncle Miraz in *Prince Caspian* has parallels with the materialism of Lewis' day. The wizards of the Harry Potter stories would undoubtedly call Miraz a "Muggle." In the Narnian chronicles, Lewis tends to portray the attitude of naturalism as one that reduces something rich and multifaceted to a dreadfully poorer reality. Miraz displays this attitude when he finds out that Caspian's nurse has been telling tales of Old Narnia:

> "That's all nonsense, for babies," said the King sternly. "Only fit for babies, do you hear? You're getting too old for that sort of stuff. At your age you ought to be thinking of battles and adventures, not fairy tales." (1951)

What are these old, nearly forgotten values? They can be seen vividly in an important character in *The Voyage of the Dawn Treader*. Eustace Scrubb is transformed into a dragon and requires the intervention of Aslan to become a real boy again. This marks a deeper transformation from the boorish, self-centered Eustace to a boy with Old Narnian and Old Western values of courtesy, gentleness and honor (i.e., Aslanian values). In The Chronicles Lewis draws very much on a medieval articulation of such values, in which insights of the "virtuous pagans" of antiquity are seen as being completed by the teaching, life and heroic sacrifice of Christ, the dying God. A medieval view of nature had a wildness to it lost in today's "Age of the Machine," as Lewis called it (1969).

As well as thumbnailing the "Old Western" worldview in his inaugural Cambridge lecture in 1954, Lewis devoted most of his substantial literary and philosophical scholarship to it, for instance, in such important works as *The Allegory of Love: A Study in Medieval Tradition* (1936), *A Preface to Paradise Lost* (1942), *English Literature in the Sixteenth Century Excluding Drama* (1954) and *The Discarded Image* (1964). It should be added that Lewis argued for a fundamental continuity between the medieval and Renaissance periods, finding the same values and virtues promoted in the sixteenth century, in Edmund Spenser for instance, as earlier.

By drawing upon the "Old West," particularly medieval literature, in making The Chronicles of Narnia Lewis wished to open a door for his readers, entrance through which would awaken desires and allow the experience of sensations yet unknown, pointing to a reality beyond "the walls of the world." He saw this older period of the West as having a feature rejected, he observed, by many modern poets and critics—that of stock responses, a kind of decorum of the imagination. This feature, he believed, was true of literature and art from earliest antiquity until quite recently.[1] Goodness and truth are light; evil and falsehood are shadow. Deity and worship are associated with height. Virtue is linked with loveliness. Love is sweet and constant, death bitter and endurance praiseworthy. "In my opinion," Lewis writes, "such deliberate organisation is one of the first necessities of human life, and one of the main functions of art is to assist it. All that we describe as constancy in love or friendship, as loyalty in political life, or, in general, as perseverance—all solid virtue and stable pleasure—depends on organising chosen attitudes and maintaining them against the eternal flux" (1942, 55). These are the virtues that are championed in Narnia. The virtues are reflected in the titles given to the Pevensie children when kings and queens in Narnia—Peter the Magnificent, Susan the Gentle, Edmund the Just and Lucy the Valiant.

These cultivated responses, likely enough, are closely related to mental patterns deep within us—to archetypes. Archetypes are universal and primal elements of ordinary human experience. They can be images or symbols, or the motif of a narrative plot (such as the quest, or the removal of injustice) or a character type (such as the swaggering tyrant, like Rabadash, or the noble warrior, like Emeth). They are captured in the iconography of literature and art of what Lewis called the "Old West." Preeminent in Western literature in its embodiment of such primal and elemental archetypes are the Scriptural narratives, reflected in Paul's injunction, "Whatever is true, whatever is honorable, whatever is just, whatever is pure, whatever is lovely, whatever is commendable, if there is any excellence, if there is anything worthy of praise, think about these things"(Philippians 4:8).

Archetypes are either positive or negative in implication. For instance, the rendering of landscape in literature and art can indicate the ideal and its contrary. Goodness is conveyed in landscape by a garden, grove or park; the mountaintop or hill; the fertile plain or valley; pastoral settings or farms; the safe pathway or easily traveled road; and places

---

[1] In "De Descriptione Temporum" in *Selected Literary Essays* (1969), he saw the watershed of historical change as sometime in the nineteenth century.

of natural refuge or defense (such as a rock, hill or hiding place). The sinister is rendered in landscape as the dark forest; the wilderness or wasteland (which is either too hot or too cold); the dark and dangerous valley; the tomb; the labyrinth; the dangerous or evil pathway; and the cave (associated with barbarism) or pit (as a place of confinement or imprisonment) (Ryken 1979, 86–87).

Lewis deliberately used such stock symbolism in his construction of the stories and world to which Narnia belongs. Particularly the lush valley world of Narnia is an indicator of its spiritual health. In contrast, the northern and southern lands are largely barren.

Central to Lewis' rehabilitation of "Old Western" values is his appropriation of paganism, particularly focused in the figure of Aslan. Aslan (Turkish for "lion") is the unifying symbol of all the stories. Aslan is intended to represent Christ, but not as an allegorical figure. In Narnia he appears not as a human being but, appropriately, as a Narnian talking lion.[2] In his *The Problem of Pain* Lewis writes, "I think the lion, when he has ceased to be dangerous, will still be awful."[3]

The children who visit Narnia soon of course discover that Aslan is not a tame lion. In *The Problem of Pain* Lewis had put a value on the taming of animals, a point Evelyn Underhill took issue with, in an otherwise appreciative letter to him in 1941.

> Where...I do find it impossible to follow you, is in your chapter on animals. "The tame animal is in the deepest sense the only natural animal...the beasts are to be understood only in their relation to man and through man to God." This seems to me frankly an intolerable doctrine and a frightful exaggeration of what is involved in the primacy of man. Is the cow which we have turned into a milk machine or the hen we have turned into an egg machine really nearer the mind of God than its wild ancestor?...Your own example of the good-man, good-wife, and good-dog in the good homestead is a bit smug and utilitarian, don't you think, over against the wild beauty of God's creative action in the jungle and deep sea?...When my cat goes off on her own occasions I'm sure she goes with God—but I do not feel so

---

[2] The principle of personal embodiment in a material body (animal, or even vegetable)—wider than what we know of as the human being—Lewis called *hnau* in his science fiction trilogy. This concept seems to have influenced J. R. R. Tolkien in his creation of the Ents.

[3] The symbol of the lion (an ancient image of authority) perhaps owes something to Charles Williams' novel *The Place of the Lion* (1931).

sure of her theological position when she is sitting on the best chair
before the drawing-room fire. Perhaps what it all comes to is this,
that I feel your concept of God would be improved by just a touch
of wildness. But please do not take this impertinent remark too seriously. (1943, 301)

Evelyn Underhill's remarks about a quality of wildness in animals
may have caused Lewis to rethink his position somewhat, and perhaps
allowed Aslan and the talking animals of Narnia to come bounding into
the story. Aslan perhaps provided just that touch of wildness (associated with pagan insights) to Lewis' theological imagination. The wildness
of God and the nature he created are already there in his study, *Miracles,*
but Aslan proved to be a unifying and perhaps sacramental symbol of
both (like Christ, he has two complete natures, divine and creaturely).

In tying the wildness of Aslan, and the substance of Narnian values
and virtues, to nature and its source in God, Lewis makes his rehabilitation more cosmic in scope than if it were merely a plea for restoring
traditional values. His book *The Abolition of Man* identifies the same values and virtues with what he calls the *Tao*—which he argues has been
universally accepted in the past, in East and West, as defining humanity.
A "New Western" rejection of the Tao in fact puts the future of human
beings *qua* human in jeopardy.

> In the *Tao* itself, as long as we remain within it, we find the concrete
> reality in which to participate is to be truly human: the real common
> will and common reason of humanity, alive, and growing like a tree,
> and branching out, as the situation varies, into ever new beauties and
> dignities of application. While we speak from within the *Tao* we can
> speak of Man having power over himself in a sense truly analogous
> to the individual's self-control. But the moment we step outside and
> regard the *Tao* as a mere subjective product, this possibility has disap-
> peared. What is now common to all men is a mere abstract universal,
> an H.C.F., and Man's conquest of himself means simply the rule of the
> Conditioners over the conditioned human material, the world of post-
> humanity which, some knowingly and some unknowingly, nearly all
> men in all nations are at present labouring to produce. (1943, 45)

Inculcating a Change of Perception and Consciousness

Near where I live in Leicestershire is a high hill, one side of which runs down into a particularly wooded area. One day walking there I saw a mother with a boy of about five or six. I was behind the pair as they ascended a granite outcrop which gave an excellent view of the wooded slopes and the countryside for miles around. "Look, Mummy," the boy exclaimed in wonder, "it's Narnia."

What happened, of course, was that the boy was looking at what he saw through a text, one or more of the Narnian chronicles by C. S. Lewis. That text was children's fiction, but a wider principle applies here. This is that we are meant to perceive reality through the word—and also through other art, like paintings, or musical pieces. For instance, you may walk the fells and follow the lakeshores in the English Lakeland seeing them through the poetry of Wordsworth or the paintings of William Turner. Lewis acknowledges our human dependence upon a symbolic perception of reality—a culturally shaped perception.[4] The symbolic world of Narnia, even though fictional, is in some sense solidly real. For this reason it takes us back to the ordinary world which is an inevitable part of our human living and experience, deepening both the wonders and the terrors of our world. What Lewis is suggesting is that our perception is shaped by the imagination. It also has a moral dimension.

In *The Magician's Nephew*, the narrator comments upon how Uncle Andrew perceives the scene after Narnia has come into being: "What you see and hear depends a good deal on where you are standing: it also depends on the sort of person you are." Andrew is full of terror and, after some effort, cannot even hear the sounds of talking animals, including Aslan's, as speech or song. "He had never liked animals at the best of times," the narrator continues, "being usually rather afraid of them; and of course years of doing cruel experiments on animals had made him hate and fear them far more" (1955).

C. S. Lewis gives a very simple illustration of this kind of symbolic perception in his essay "On Stories" in explaining the logic of the fairy story, which "is as strict as that of a realistic novel, though different." Referring to *The Wind in the Willows*, he asks:

---

[4] This kind of perception has a metaphorical dimension, moving from the not-this to the this by a felt recognition of likeness.

Does anyone believe that Kenneth Grahame made an arbitrary choice when he gave his principal character the form of a toad, or that a stag, a pigeon, a lion, would have done as well. The choice is based on the fact that the real toad's face has a grotesque resemblance to a certain kind of human face—a rather apoplectic face with a fatuous grin on it.... Looking at the creature we thus see, isolated and fixed, an aspect of human vanity in its funniest and most pardonable form. (1982, 37)

The Encyclopedia of Fantasy points out the subversive nature of fantasy in encouraging a perceptual shift. In it John Clute and David Langford write, "It could be argued that, if fantasy (and debatably the literature of the fantastic as a whole) has a purpose other than to entertain, it is to show readers how to perceive; an extension of the argument is that fantasy may try to alter readers' perception of reality." This point is explained more, as follows: "The best fantasy introduces its readers into a playground of rethought perception, where there are no restrictions other than those of the human imagination.... Most full fantasy texts have at their core the urge to change the reader; that is, full fantasy is by definition a subversive literary form" (1997).

The Narnian chronicles bring out strikingly different perceptions of the White Witch and Aslan. In *The Lion, the Witch and the Wardrobe* there is a marked contrast between Edmund's and Lucy's perception of the White Witch. Nikabrik the dwarf quite admires the White Witch, and the Hag calls her the "White Lady." All the beings of Narnia are ultimately judged by their perception of Aslan, passing to his right or left in *The Last Battle*.

The creatures came rushing on, their eyes brighter and brighter as they drew nearer.... But as they came right up to Aslan one or other of two things happened to each of them. They all looked straight in his face; I don't think they had any choice about that. And when some looked, the expression on their faces changed terribly—it was fear and hatred.... And all the creatures who looked at Aslan in that way swerved to their right, his left, and disappeared into his huge black shadow.... But the others looked in the face of Aslan and loved him, though some of them were very frightened at the same time. (1956)

Connected to the imaginative and moral shaping of perception is recognition. In stories like the Narnian chronicles, the prime recognition is
that someone is within a story of some kind. Aristotle saw recognition
marking a fundamental shift in the movement of a story from a tangle
of ignorance to knowledge. A protagonist recognizes that "the Story has
been telling them"—a narrative structure precedes the event they are in,
and will reach a conclusion subsequent to that event. Recognition is perhaps best illustrated by the moment in *The Last Battle* when the children
and others realize that they are in a new Narnia, a Narnia that is also
linked to England transfigured, the beginning of a new chapter in the
great story. Intermittently throughout The Chronicles, there is the recognition that Aslan is behind all the stories of the individual characters;
he shapes them. In *The Horse and His Boy*, when Shasta (now known as
Prince Cor) tells Aravis the story of how he was found as a child, he recognizes that Aslan "seems to be at the back of all the stories" (1954).

An important feature of recognition is undeception, when there is a
shift in perception, a change in consciousness. Undeception in the stories echoes Lewis the author's intent to bring about a perceptual change
in his reader.

Undeception was a favorite theme of Lewis, for whom a characteristic
of the human condition is the state of being deceived by others, by sin
or by oneself. He refers to the concept of undeception in his essay "A
Note on Jane Austen," in *Selected Literary Essays*. He finds the theme in
her novels, which were favorite reading for him. Many of Lewis' fictional
characters experience undeception, usually associated with salvation. In
The Silver Chair, Prince Rilian has an hour each day when the deception
weaved about him by the Green Witch lifts. He has to be restrained in
the enchanted Silver Chair to stop him from acting on this knowledge.
Edmund, the betrayer of his brother and sisters, undergoes undeception
in *The Lion, the Witch and the Wardrobe*, seeing the witch in her true nature. Eustace in *The Voyage of the Dawn Treader* experiences undeception
through the painful experience of turning into a dragon. In *The Horse and
His Boy*, the talking horse Bree is undeceived when he perceives the true
nature of Aslan upon encountering him at the Hermit's house.

Lewis regarded the purpose of his fiction as helping to undeceive
modern people, who are, he believed, separated from the past, with its
key to our humanity. He intended to provide knowledge of perennial
human values and an acquaintance with basic Christian teaching about

the realities of sin, redemption, immortality, divine judgment and grace. He was attempting to rehabilitate human values and virtues not only through example and instruction in the Narnian tales, but also by taking his reader into an old, nearly forgotten consciousness. He hoped to capture this elusive consciousness in the net of the stories. In this way he hoped that the consciousness of his reader might be changed, so as to perceive the world in a new (or, really, a rather old) way.

The medieval world picture, from which Lewis drew so much in making The Chronicles, is an example of a different consciousness. As a historian Lewis believed that there had been many changes in human consciousness over the ages. Such changes expressed themselves in changes in language, and in changes in art and literature, as well as in the most obvious area of ideas. It was changes in language, art and culture that most affected ordinary human beings. In this view Lewis was deeply influenced by his friend Owen Barfield, even though there were important differences between them.[5] Lewis, for instance, did not believe that historical changes in consciousness marked an evolutionary (or teleological) development. He saw history rather as a battlefield between good and evil, though he did believe good will triumph.[6] Barfield ridded Lewis of his "chronological snobbery"—the idea of progress—in which what is future is perceived as superior to the past, on the model of the machine, where new machines replace inferior old ones. This allowed him to find nourishment in the lost worlds of the Middle Ages and antiquity. Entering their old consciousness allowed him a critical vantage point on contemporary consciousness, where the richness of reality, as he saw it, was reduced to the merely material, the human to the mechanical. He aimed to provide an entry into this old consciousness of humanity for the readers of his Narnian stories, so they too

---

[5] Owen Barfield believed that, corresponding to stellar and biological evolution, there has been an evolution of consciousness. This evolution is reflected precisely in changes in language and perception, from a primitive unity of consciousness to a future achievement of a greater human consciousness. In this the subject-object dichotomy is overcome in a harmonious human participation with nature. Participation is one of Barfield's central concepts, closely tied to the original state of unified perception. The concept deeply influenced Lewis and attracted Tolkien. It had many consequences for our understanding of the nature of language and metaphor. Participation, according to Barfield, is a "predominately perceptual relation between observer and observed, between man and nature…nearer to unity than dichotomy" (Barfield 1979, 26). In this relation, mind is not yet detached from its representations; the subject and the object not divorced. Barfield believed that some of this ancient participation endures in medieval art and thought, the four elements theory, the four humors, and in astrology (Barfield 1977, 18).

[6] See, for example, his essay "Learning in Wartime," in Essay Collection and Other Short Pieces (2000).

see the world today with new and undeceived eyes. A greater spell is needed, he saw, to destroy the spell of materialism.

Colin Duriez is author of a number of books on C. S. Lewis, J. R. R. Tolkien and the Inklings, including A Field Guide to Narnia, The C. S. Lewis Encyclopedia, The C. S. Lewis Chronicles, The Inklings Handbook *(with David Porter),* Tolkien and C. S. Lewis: The Gift of Friendship *and* Tolkien and The Lord of the Rings. *He has lectured on Lewis and Tolkien in many countries and has appeared as a commentator on BBC television and on extended-version DVDs of Peter Jackson's* The Lord of the Rings *and the PBS series* The Question of God, *on Lewis and Freud.*

References

Barfield, Owen. 1977. *The Rediscovery of Meaning and Other Essays.* Middletown, CT: Wesleyan Univ. Press.

———. 1979. *History, Guilt, and Habit.* Middletown: Wesleyan Univ. Press.

Clute, John, and John Grant, eds. 1997. *The Encyclopedia of Fantasy.* London: Orbit.

Duriez, Colin. 2000. *The C. S. Lewis Encyclopedia.* Wheaton, Illinois: Crossway Books.

———. 2004. *A Field Guide to Narnia.* Downers Grove, Illinois: InterVarsity Press.

Gardner, Helen. 1965. "Clive Staples Lewis 1898–1963." *Proceedings of the British Academy* 51: 417–28.

Lewis, C. S. 1942. *A Preface to Paradise Lost.* London: Oxford Univ. Press.

———. 1943. *The Abolition of Man.* London: Oxford Univ. Press.

———. 1950. *The Lion, the Witch and the Wardrobe.* London: Bles.

———. 1951. *Prince Caspian.* London: Bles.

———. 1952. *The Voyage of the Dawn Treader.* London: Bles.

———. 1953. *The Silver Chair.* London: Bles.

———. 1954. *The Horse and His Boy.* London: Bles.

———. 1955. *The Magician's Nephew.* London: Bodley Head.

———. 1956. *The Last Battle.* London: Bodley Head.

———. 1969. *Selected Literary Essays.* Cambridge: Cambridge Univ. Press.

———. 1982. *Of This and Other Worlds.* London: Collins Fount.

———. 2000. *Essay Collection and Other Short Pieces.* London: HarperCollins.

Ryken, Leland. 1979. *Triumphs of the Imagination.* Downers Grove: InterVarsity Press.

Spufford, Francis. 2002. *The Child that Books Built*. New York: Metropolitan Books.

Underhill, Evelyn. 1943. *The Letters of Evelyn Underhill*. Ed. Charles Williams. London: Longmans, Green.

Williams, Charles. 1931. *The Place of the Lion*. London: Gollancz.

This chapter draws extensively upon my book, *A Field Guide to Narnia*.